MW00655183

Allison Astorino

The Steady

Allison Astorino

To sunshine encompassed,
An iridescent kindness,
And my greatest guidance also,

You are all my steady.

"There are chords in the hearts of the most reckless
which cannot be touched without emotion.
Even by the utterly lost,
to whom life and death are equally jests,
there are matters of which no jest can be made,"

Edgar Allen Poe, The Masque of the Red Death

Allison Astorino

One.

Moon, is it my turn to fade away?

The sun was sweltering, bright as ever in the sky overhead with no real consideration for the parade beneath. It was a parade filled with dark clothes and somber faces, a silence so deafening it would have drowned out any marching band. It was a small crowd, but it felt vast in a way – the same way it feels to stand next to strangers in a close line, their space suddenly your own. But no one there was a stranger to the other; if anything, they were all too intimate, and that was something that hurt.

There was a priest; he'd been called up from the next town over. No one standing around the hole in the ground, not more than one hundred feet from the house, was religious. But, it had seemed appropriate. It had seemed like the right thing to do. None of them had buried a person before, let alone a husband, a father, a grandfather. Ramone had never seemed old, the finality of his death wildly surprising. He'd fallen asleep on the porch of the house his parents had built with their hands and their children's hands, and had simply not gotten up when the rocking chair stilled. His wife had found him, and she had simply sat across from his body on the railing and had looked at him for a long time, quietly.

It was surprising, his death, just days before his family was to arrive for the entirety of summer, like they did every year. It was always much anticipated, but shock looks different on everyone.

For Rosemary, grief looked like dark liner, dark clothes, and a puzzled expression on her face. She stood around the hole same as everyone else, watching the wooden box being lowered, both fascinated and confused. Is this what death looked like? She'd never given it much thought, and when she had, it hadn't seemed this concrete of an experience. Wasn't death supposed to be an exploration into the grand unknown? She felt left behind if it was. Never, until this point, did she realize how much her grandfather meant to her. She kept waiting for someone to walk up behind her, put a hand on her shoulder, and say something funny, contemplative, but above all, kind. No one did. She felt strikingly alone amongst her family of strangers.

No one moved much, or cried during the final prayer. It read like bad poetry. Nobody had anything they'd like to say, when the priest asked. Rosemary felt that was wrong, but the fact that a true stranger was there with their family felt like a good enough barrier from speaking candidly about their dead. And was he gone? He was right there, in that box, not six feet away from her. That didn't seem very gone to her, not yet. Her twin was watching her, trying to mirror her reaction off her sister's, but Rosemary was giving up nothing. They weren't identical, and telepathy was child's play. For once, Lucy would have to make herself available to others. *For this, she'll have to come up with something all on her own.* Rosemary breathed in deeply.

Her cousins were there, beside her. Wolfgang, the oldest of all of them, was still and stoic like his father, though absolutely nothing remotely like him. The name had been a silly suggestion during Beth's pregnancy, but it had stuck when he clawed his way to survival, nearly three months premature. No one even remembered what it could have been before, they only knew the wildness in him, and how his father had been unable to beat it out. James was the youngest of all four of them, the spitting image of his mother in every way, especially his determination to please. A dog that keeps coming back for more, same eyes, too.

Ramone's wife didn't have much to say, either. Sara was angry. She had never been the emotional one – coupled with the weight of the situation having yet to hit her – she was solemn. She'd always been a planner, a worker, and a fighter. She weathered the storm so no one had to pick up her pieces. She planted the seeds so that others could water them. Someone had to till the land. But now, looking down at the hole in the ground, the well seemed to have dried up. She'd never known how to make the water come. She looked over at her kids, all three of them. Did they know how to water anything? She had been harsh on them all their lives so that they would be weeds, not flowers. Weeds grew anywhere, in any condition. They survived. Flowers wilted too easily, demanded special circumstances to bloom. But, looking at them now, she realized how pretty flowers were to look at, after all. People usually brought bouquets of them to funerals. She might cry for that, later sometime.

The boys' father wiped sweat off his brow, throwing in the first handful of dirt that rattled hard against the wooden box his own father was encapsulated. He was the oldest; he figured he should throw in the dirt first. Lewis's handful was dry, almost sand. He was ready to walk back to the house, his wife close behind him. Then Delphine walked forward, following his lead of birth order in their little charade of a parade. Her dirt felt different than his – moist, dark, almost muddy. She worked very hard. And lastly, little Heidi came forward, though she wasn't the child they all kept alive in their heads anymore. She grabbed a fistful of dirt off the mound to toss in, enjoying the richness against her skin before letting it fall from her hand, making no noise as it hit the casket, yet somehow echoing loudest.

The priest didn't know how to proceed. Frankly, he didn't feel comfortable in the crowd. Their silence held an incredible amount of energy, and the weight of it was crushing him. The heat was also getting to him as he tugged at his tight collar under the strength of that prairie sun. He had mistaken their gathering for a funeral. He was seeing now that it was almost a trial. A trial nobody could win, nor lose. The evidence was far from solid. All of it was so far over his head that he had to walk away. And after the last bit of dirt ran from the last grandchild's hand, he said amen and left. Everyone stayed around the hole a few moments longer, looking down and feeling empty. Then they walked out of the family cemetery together, needing a new headstone for an old place. No one was sure about anything. What did they believe?

Sara, now a widow, had made sandwiches and iced tea for her family. It was ready and waiting when they all wandered up the hill, away from the big oak they'd chosen to bury Ramone under. The house stood tall at the top of the hill, seemingly calling everyone up to it with a calm sense of rationality. It was a big house, three floors and a wide swooping porch. There was a large kitchen but also a butler's pantry tucked into the side. There were several places to gather, a living room, parlor room, sitting room, sewing room. And the upstairs floors were filled with bedrooms. Enough so that each of the three couples had their own, and the kids each had to share with their sibling at the top of the house. It was a summer tradition to stay in that house. And on the eve of summer, the hottest day so far that year and the day Ramone Pennyfather passed away, they didn't know how to do any differently. As they all changed out of their funeral clothes, they unpacked their suitcases in the same motion. Everyone, back for the summer.

"It's weird, without him here," Lucy said after a long silence between them, bouncing on her bed across from Rosemary as she carefully took out jeans and laid them on her side of the dresser. She hadn't over-packed, like her sister. She looked over at her, beautiful. They were twins, but not identical. Lucy tossed her blonde hair over her shoulder, long and flowing, maybe even a little dead at the ends. It didn't matter. Rosemary shut her drawer.

"He still feels close, though. Like if I reach out, I could feel him," Rosemary replied, sticking her arm out in front of her. She didn't feel anything in that moment, but it didn't keep her from thinking she might. She had, earlier. He was allowed to wander, wasn't he? She didn't know how hauntings worked.

"Mmm, I can't say that I do," Lucy replied, laying down flat on her back on the twin mattress, staring up at the ceiling at the old plastic stars they had stuck on the drywall when they were little kids, their biggest fear the dark. Some of them still glowed at night in the dark, creating beautiful constellations that they had created from viewing the night sky out their own window. The sisters had never known if they were real ones, but even if they didn't appear in some big book, they glowed every night in their room, whether they were there to see or not.

"Are you unpacked yet?" James asked, sliding into their doorway but not actually stepping foot into their square of space. Lucy threw a pillow at him, which he initially avoided before catching and tossing back.

"I have, but Rosemary is *folding* everything," Lucy replied easily, her voice light. She didn't quite know how to be any other way. Her response to adversity was to waltz through it with no fear, no suspicions. There was nothing that could hurt her. James, on the other hand, slightly cowered at the possibility of another pillow tossed.

"It keeps things neat," he offered, attempting diplomacy. Lucy let it slide while Rosemary nodded, looking back at her cousin. His brown hair seemed golden somehow, but soft at the edges. It fell into his face often, making him look younger than he was.

"Exactly James, exactly," Rosemary replied.

"Are you done? Wolfgang?" she asked.

"Um, yeah. More or less," James replied. Just minutes earlier, he had watched as his older brother had pulled a pile of loose clothes from a garbage bag and tossed them into the bottom of the closet. He'd then grabbed a few rolled joints from his backpack, and strutted out of the room and down the hall to the small window at the end that barely opened but was still able to fit through and sit on the roof. He liked the sun, and he liked being high while he got high. James had folded his clothes, not because he particularly enjoyed his clothes orderly, but in hopes to please.

"I'll see you down there," James said after a moment, heading downstairs. He was referring to dinner, though it was still a few hours away. They always had a big family dinner the first night everyone returned home. The house championed the title home, as it was the only place all of them could agree felt like home, had served as home at some point or another. Rosemary wasn't ready to be confined to a space with all her family quite yet. She left Lucy to talk on the phone to friends from the city, and wandered down the steps and snuck out the back door, avoiding her mother and aunt in the kitchen. She couldn't peel a potato to save her life, anyway.

She walked out towards the old barn at the back of the house, having housed no animals other than herself and her cousins for a very long time now. She climbed up into the hayloft, sunlight beaming over her body through the battered slats of the barn. She was no longer sure how much time she had left being able to sit up in that hayloft. There was of course the concern of rotting wood, but there was also the all too real edge she stood on, being twenty-two. She felt like she had made it to the other side, but the side she longed for was suddenly covered in fog even though she desperately wanted to see it again. Twenty-two was different. There was a different view. And from there on out, it only got farther and farther away from sitting in an old hayloft, staring out at acres of family land, taking in the big oak tree that her grandfather had been freshly buried under. She hadn't cried at the funeral, no one had. But up there, she did. She wept. Ramone had been a kind man, a considerate one. He was soft-spoken, but his words held weight. Everyone quieted when he finally made his declaration, naturally taking on the role of the final word. Even in old age, he had always been the final word. Now, Rosemary didn't know how any conversation would find a solution. She didn't know if she'd feel as protected from everyone else as she had with Ramone around. She hadn't realized she'd felt the need for a shield until suddenly hers vanished, and she was left to stand in the kitchen and explain that while making dinner was important, she couldn't be a part of it. Other people didn't like to hear that. They took it as an insult for their own work, as condemnation for their choices. It wasn't like that at all for Rosemary, and perhaps Ramone had sensed that. He could hear the wind too, whistling outside, sending her a personal invitation. She'd always loved summers at the family's old house.

She looked down at the yard. Some of her family was outside, sitting on the porch or talking by the fence. She spotted her cousin Wolfgang still up on the roof, smoking, hiding from his father's sight. She smirked, wondering how high he'd be at dinner. It was classic, almost comical. It was how it had to be sometimes. It had always been her favorite view. Sure, the hills and sky were nice, beautiful even, euphoric to her. But, her family sprawled around the land was even more catching. From her lofted perch, she could see her mother in the kitchen, now baking those potatoes. Her father was out by his truck in the driveway and her Aunt Beth could be caught looking out the window hastily as she promptly washed each dish, twice over. Beth's husband was lounging in a hammock on the far side of the lawn, right before the grass began to stick up unruly, never mowed, never having met a harsh blade. For a moment, she didn't know where her Aunt Heidi was, but found her soon enough emerging from down by the creek with her husband, hand in hand, whispering. They were close, in ways that didn't seem protective or secretive, simply intimate. Rosemary didn't know quite how it all worked. James remained an enigma, out of sight and out of mind, exactly as he liked.

She watched everyone, fascinated by the way they all made the old farmhouse feel like a grand estate, a self-sufficient town all on a large acreage of land. There were always so many people to watch for, and Rosemary felt like she needed to be watchful. Much like a deer stands still in the woods, she kept her eyes locked on everyone, watching, not sure if there would be teeth. If you asked, her family would always say the dog's bark was worse than the bite. Rosemary thought they stung just the same.

A loud ringing came from the dinner bell, her Aunt Beth standing on the porch and hitting the metal of the triangle harder than she needed to, but having an excuse to do so. Solemnly, everyone started wandering to the dining room. It was time for family dinner. The spread was stunning, as it usually was. All kinds of meats and vegetables, cooked in every way imaginable spread out along the dining room table, probably a hundred years old. The food that lay upon it never really changed. Everyone came and sat down in their respectful spots, everyone having their place. And then Sara came to sit at the head of the table, and she stood there for a few moments longer than she ever had before, because the person she was waiting for to sit down wasn't there. His chair sat empty; no plate before it, no longer a person to feed. Everyone stayed solemn. And then, before everyone began passing the dishes around, Sara sat and said something small that perhaps amounted to a prayer about Ramone.

At first it was quiet, the sound of chewing and swallowing echoing through the dining room, no one sure what to say or if they were to speak, where to start. They realized another vital role, and perhaps an act of service Ramone always performed was starting off the conversation, giving some kind of a welcoming speech, making the room seem alive. His absence was haunting enough.

"I'm glad you're all here, for this time together," Sara finally said, unable to be quiet any longer. She wasn't one for a lot of words, but she knew it was her role to fill now. Never could she be the beating heart of their gatherings, but she would at least formally acknowledge it. And she did mean it, in some way. It wasn't the most conventional, her love. It certainly wasn't unconditional, but it didn't seem to matter. No one was bitter about it, a little give and take was to be expected in the world.

"We are too, mom," Delphine was quick to say.

"None of us would miss this," Heidi replied. Lewis stayed quiet. Sometimes he had a hard time focusing on their family gatherings, a perpetual ringing in his ears when he was back at home. It was a calling of some kind, though he had never interpreted it correctly.

"Well, I am happy you're all here to stay, and I know it would make your father happy too," Sara replied, her words short and tone downcast. She'd never felt such emptiness in her chest before. It almost felt like she couldn't breathe. But of course she kept quiet about that, her eyes dry, her voice even. It was her way.

"Are you still passing on the meat?" Lewis asked his niece, knowing the answer and handing her the plate of cooked steaks anyway. He'd decided to take on the task of shifting everyone's minds from death to something less final, more of a challenge. Lucy nodded her head, passing the plate over almost too quickly.

"It's been eight years now, still staying steady in that," she replied, a sharp note to her words. Beth watched, envious. Lewis chuckled as he passed her the salad bowl, as if it had been a little joke between them. Rosemary chewed a piece of chicken in her mouth longer than she needed to before swallowing it dry, almost choking.

"Factory farming is one of the highest forms of unethical and unsustainable food production the world is partaking in right now, and if we all would just…" Lucy started, but her mother cut her off with a stern shake of the head. It was unexpected.

"Lucy, is now really the time for all that?" Delphine asked wanting her daughter to give into her easily, just this once. Perhaps too mighty an ask. She didn't often silence her daughters, but that particular dinner felt different in ways too heavy to push against. Her head ached. Someone who had always held her up was missing.

"When is a more convenient time to start caring?"

"Now or never, they say," Heidi was quick to add, giving her niece a little wink from across the table. Her mother swatted at her hand almost instinctually

"Why do you always encourage things?" Sara asked, her brows narrowed. She was tired from digging that six-foot hole practically herself. And, she liked order and manners, saving distemperment for her own discretion.

"I'm a good coach, ma," Heidi replied, ripping a large chunk from a bread roll with her teeth and chewing it loudly. Sara rolled her eyes at her youngest daughter, while her husband Seth looked down into his lap to keep from showcasing a smile.

"Can I have the rolls?" James's small voice asked from down the long table. Wolfgang reached into the basket, pulling one out and tossing it to his brother, barely catching it and scraping the floor with the chair, making a loud noise. Lewis glared at his oldest son, hardly recognizing him as his own. Beth just shook her head.

"Wolfgang..." she said, though it pained her to say it. She could feel the heat from her husband, and although everyone felt an incredible tension, only James wanted to die from it.

"He asked, I delivered," Wolfgang said, shrugging.

"It's about all you do," Lewis spat under his breath. Wolfgang just leaned back in his chair, taking a large gulp of his drink, smiling with very sad eyes. Rosemary pushed around her peas, glancing over at her parents. They had been quiet, but often were. Delphine and Henry stayed in their own world; it was always with a sense of superiority, whether they intended to emit that or not. And their daughters had grown up lawless with a sense of enormity about the world. They had explored almost everywhere, scraped knees and bruised hearts around nearly every turn, but nothing had ever felt so mysterious and dangerous as that long wooden table in the farmhouse's dining room. Heidi gave Rosemary a wink from across the table when she finally looked up; she smiled.

"We could attempt civility, for one night I would think," Sara said, her words shaking the table as everyone turned to look at their matriarch. Of course no one argued, and the conversation drifted to small talk, short stories with brief overviews about what everyone had been up to the past year of their lives, and eventually, a few quick comments about Ramone. Everything about the Pennyfathers was short and precise, especially in those early weeks at the big house.

"Ramone loved this time more than any," Sara said after a

moment of silence fell over the table. She held up her glass in front of everyone, waiting for them to do the same before taking a sip. She had loved that he loved it, the big gatherings. She wasn't sure why she didn't anymore. Everyone finished the wine in their glasses and helped take away dishes to make way for dessert. There was an abundance of sugary treats on the counter, a product of everyone in town sending their most sincerest condolences. Dessert went on without a single hitch and then it was over. Officially, they were all moved in.

James was always the most invisible when walking through the house, so the others sent him in to smuggle out some of the alcohol from the bar cart in the living room. The cousins wanted to have a little toast to summer together at the big house, and perhaps a little toast to their grandfather, whose presence they weren't sure had disappeared. Armed with a bottle of rum, the four made their way to the old pole barn; climbing up into the hayloft and sitting in a rough semi-circle as they passed around the big bottle, taking different sized shots. They gave it a few before they started talking.

"Family dinners are strange without a mediator," James said, breaking their drinking silence. Wolfgang shrugged, not sure there had ever been a mediator. Lucy nodded, taking a big swig to compensate for her bruised feelings from dinner.

"Yeah, I need someone supporting my ideas," Lucy insisted, looking around for support. Rosemary tossed her a small smile, but Wolfgang had no time for it.

"You're too much," he replied. Lucy rolled her eyes.

"Too much? That's all you got?" she shot back. Wolfgang tried to wave her off, but Lucy had a very hard time lying down and playing dead. Her eyes smoldered at the thought of someone thinking *too much* was somehow also in the same breath, *not enough.*

"Alright," she snapped; he didn't reply. He had nowhere to go with it anyway, he was already constantly bleeding out. And they saw that, they did. But when it's a constant waterfall, it's easy to forget where it's coming from, that it's not just supposed to be there all of the time. The cousins kept drinking, kept looking at the moon, kept thinking about different things that were the same. Lucy and James grew invested in a game of clap back, and Wolfgang eventually grew tired of watching and started whittling old wood that was laying around the loft floor with his pocket knife, having probably been needed somewhere else. Rosemary looked out the large window, studying the house and the dark lawn around it. The trees whistled together as a light breeze drifted through them, pushing away leaves and branches as it moved forward. By light of the moon, she was able to see the outline of the old oak tree that stood guard over her grandfather's grave. It was hard to be sad all of the time, or to know when sadness was appropriate and when it needed to become personal. Rosemary had never known the difference, and still didn't know that sadness wasn't required to be bottled up to make those around her less so. She'd faced darkness, a grand nothingness, a plain of absolute void brought on by only the most extreme nervosa. And what brought on that painful over-firing of nerves? More nothingness. She hoped her grandfather was resting peacefully under that big tree. She knew she had always felt calm beneath it, touched by the way it shaded her from the sun, talked to her in the breeze, and held up against her waves of sadness and expected nothing. She thought long and hard about how much sadness she had felt under that tree, and now with real tangible sadness planted, she was back to the nothingness. She got drunk off that thought much quicker than the others did. They watched her, out of the corners of their eyes. They could feel it coming.

Rosemary started her short trek back to the house before anyone else did, but took her time under the moonlight. The farther out from the barn she got, she found herself continually looking up, searching the stars for answers to long forgotten questions. They were so bright above all that family land and they too, like almost anything else, seemed unreal, much too far to grasp onto. Maybe she did have hope, but she wasn't even sure for what. Wind whistled through the pines along the border of the big farmhouse as she walked the narrow path between the two that only she and sometimes a few deer walked. She stopped right outside the door for a moment, hand on the handle. She just wanted a moment to breathe, to still be outside, be free, be awake when everyone else was asleep. She didn't know.

Slowly, she crawled into bed after pulling off her jeans, already feeling a headache forming. She hoped she would get some good, solid sleep, wake up after the hangover had already come and gone. Maybe she'd dream something fantastical because sometimes she had film-like sequences play out in her mind and they usually made things better, more tolerable. She almost always wrote them down after she opened her eyes, if she could find that line, anyway. Head on the pillow, eyes fluttering before shutting, a gentle breeze wafted through the open window, a torn curtain dancing around it. She fell asleep almost instantaneously and still for hours more, did not know.

And then, deep panic raced through her veins.

Rosemary opened her eyes as wide as they could go, hands spread out on her sides, clutching the sheets around her. They were soaking wet and smelled of salt. Deep in her chest, her heart was pounding; trying to beat its way out of a bone cage. There was air all around her, yet she couldn't breathe it in, felt like she was gasping forever, or drowning.

Everything around her was darkness. She couldn't remember where she was, day or night, and she couldn't tell if she was awake or asleep. Somehow, it felt like a place in between, some kind of horrible limbo that was breaking her body apart, her mind failing to grasp the new set of physical rules. Eyes open or closed, it didn't matter, one moment there was nothing but darkness, the next, a racing set of images, horrible nightmarish things, faces, ideas, light. All scattered across the space her mind thought it was looking at, or standing next to. One moment, her hands were clutching the sheets of the bed; the next she felt sharp grains of sand wafting through her tightly balled fists. No matter what, she could not stay grounded. Every other moment she felt the horrible sensation of falling again and again. The entirety of it all was too much, and she found herself hoping to meet death and ask for finality.

It didn't subside; it didn't go away. For hours or days, she couldn't tell, the feeling of being lost in some kind of middle ground persisted. She wanted to cry out for someone, but she couldn't think of anyone to ask. Was she alone? Rosemary wanted to move her body; only faintly aware it still existed because of the great pains in her chest, the pulsating muscle spasms that were occurring throughout her limbs. She couldn't, though; it would not budge, as if it was no longer hers to command.

For a while she thought she heard laughter, then more prominently, screams. They started out softly, but got much louder, until they were ringing in her head. She tried to move away from them, think of something else, but nothing worked. She was forced through the nightmare her mind was experiencing, forcing her to be there. She thought her eardrums might explode, then everything got quiet, then an incessant buzzing started. Were they cicadas? Were they in her room, or was she outside? Was she even anywhere, at all? She kept trying to breathe, and kept failing at it.

Time didn't seem to matter, wasn't working in any linear way, but she knew she was in those clutches for a long, long while.

Finally things started to fade away, and her body was beginning to make peace. The noises eventually stopped, the muscles in her body began to rest. Her heartbeat slowed to a more regular rhythm, and her lungs caught a deep and pleasing breath. Her fingers loosened their hold on the sheets around her, no longer clutching for dear life, afraid of falling. When she opened her eyes, it was still dark, but the ceiling looked familiar, and a gentle breeze wafted in through the open window, and it felt cool on her face. She sighed. Had it been real, or a nightmare? She faded deeper into sleep, leaving the treacherous middle ground she had inhabited for only an hour, but had felt like almost eternity.

When her eyes finally fluttered open, she laid very still on her bed for a long time. She thought she might be paralyzed, but knew she wasn't. Daylight was streaming in through the window next to her, yet she still felt stuck in the dark somehow, a deep shadow covering her line of sight just enough that things were hazy – or at the least, behind a curtain. A deeply unsettling feeling was radiating throughout her entire body, trapped there, unable to go anywhere, unable to bother anyone. She wondered what time it was, but knew there was no way for her to care. Where was her sister? Already eating breakfast? Or was it too early still? She couldn't tell, and still, didn't feel like she could move.

Rosemary knew she was alone in the room after a while, yet somehow she didn't feel all the way alone. There was the strangest sense of something wandering around in the house, hiding behind a piece of furniture, an old necklace, a plate left on the table. Eventually, Rosemary sat up, her whole body aching deeply. She looked down at her arms, her hands. They didn't feel entirely hers anymore, either. A deep purple color raced down both arms, where light blue veins used to rest. She raised a hand and placed it on her chest, searching for a heartbeat. It was so quiet now, nothing but a low murmur. She shook her head. Was this the worst hangover ever? It couldn't be. Carefully, she crawled to the edge of the bed and slid off, pushing the curtain back from her window and stepping into sunlight. Looking out at the yard, feeling like breathing had suddenly become a new skill; she knew that whatever had happened, she'd escaped a dream only to have brought back a piece of it alive inside of her.

Two.

Rosemary spent longer than usual pacing the small space of her shared room, back and forth, back and forth, feeling caged, or as if she was the cage to something trying to claw its way out. She stopped. Was that the feeling, what she was left to contemplate? Caged or the cage? Prisoner, or prison? What kind of thought was that to have? Prisoner, or being the cage? Perhaps she was. She felt uncomfortable. A suffocating feeling at the bottom of her throat, like she might need air soon when it wouldn't be available. Also, there was a new sense of energy inside of her. Perhaps someday she would learn to call it power. But for now, it was just chaotic energy, dancing around in the pit of her stomach, wailing, wandering, wanting out.

She went on a walk that lasted for miles. There were no edges on that family land; the woods and meadows seemed to amble on forever, an old house falling apart or a car rotting next to a creek bed no matter the distance traveled. The trees never stopped growing. The water, a constant cycle of up and down. And the road? Had anyone gone down it far enough to claim it ended somewhere? It probably just brought its travelers back in one solid loop. So she walked, miles and miles, a fire burning in her that didn't seem able to be put out. She didn't get anywhere. Her aunts and uncles saw her, here and there.

"You think she's getting where she's going?" Some laughed. Wolfgang saw and watched her too, having never left the loft.

"Hey now! Whatever it is, you're not getting any farther from it," he yelled out, but Rosemary didn't stop. She wasn't sure if his assumption was correct, that she was trying to get away from something. The more she was compelled to walk, the more it started to feel like searching and less like running away. The energy was still there, her body still twitching and achy, needing to expand but not knowing how.

Rosemary walked seventeen miles before she finally stopped, collapsing a half-mile from the house, in the middle of the woods. And just like that, her body felt all seventeen miles. Lungs on fire, muscles tense and shaky, she laid on her back in a muddy section of forest, looking up at the leaves all waving to her far down below.

What would it take to burn it all down?

She was stunned at the thought. Had never considered something like that. Although many were blinded, she had always appreciated the immense beauty the woods had to offer. It was the only thing that kept her sane, solidified.

If it burned away, what could you see beyond it all?

Everything hurt. She shook her head, wanting to escape the thought. It wasn't accurate, that wasn't how she felt. Getting away was a pipe dream; an abandoned idea left at the bottom of a box much like a childhood toy. Get away? To where? *Everything* was an awfully large and impossible thing to avoid. She would know, she'd tried before.

Anywhere.

Rosemary tried to crawl back home, and eventually made it, hours later. Dirty and sweaty, she crept into bed, barely able to strip her clothes off her body. The sun was hardly setting, but she needed sleep. She had no dreams, felt no pain, simply let the energy deep in her chest radiate throughout her body, a fantastic imitation of a heartbeat. It would keep her going.

She woke to Lucy staring at her.

"*Jesus Christ*," Rosemary mumbled, her mind still half asleep but forced to stare into her twin's eyes. They looked nothing alike.

"Wrong. It's me, your sister. Are you okay?" Lucy asked. She had climbed into bed with Rosemary, the covers over both of them. She had her head propped up on her hand, and was intently examining Rosemary's face, studying every micro movement that passed over her. Rosemary stared back for a long moment, then stuck her tongue out to break the tension.

"A little weirded out how you're looking at me right now, but yeah?" Rosemary replied. Her voice went up at the end; it was a question. Lucy narrowed her eyes, not moving her body any farther away. Something felt different, a barrier perhaps. Her first thought was the void her sister visited. She didn't like the drifting; she rarely knew how to draw her back. There had never been any rope on board.

"You don't sound sure," Lucy insisted.

"Okay, well. I'm sure. Can you back off a bit? You have morning breath," Rosemary replied, pushing Lucy's shoulder slightly. She wanted it to be playful.

"Interesting tactic," Lucy said, still. Rosemary huffed, throwing the blanket over her face. She knew her sister was worried, could feel it radiating from her body, even though she was taking great strides to keep everything cool, calm, and compacted.

"You know, there was a funeral two days ago, okay? I'm sorry if I'm a little weird," Rosemary said, her voice muffled by the bed sheet. Her sister contemplated the response, feeling a deep pang in her chest at the thought of no grandfather in the kitchen boiling eggs for his grandchildren that morning. She'd never been friends with Ramone, like Rosemary had, but she had felt very loved.

"It's going to be hard for a long time," Lucy finally said, her voice soft and cracked. Rosemary carefully pulled the blanket away from her face, looking up into her sister's. There was no mirror image, but perhaps in some ways, a reflection.

"I know," she whispered. Lucy finally laid back, getting out of Rosemary's face. The two of them laid together for a long time, the sun still rising just outside the window barely covered by a tattered curtain. Soon enough, their breathing synchronized, and they felt calm and united like they did every so often. Little stars lined their ceiling, glow-in-the-dark plastic stickers that they had stuck there a long time ago, hiding their initials in the nightscape as their own personal constellations. A gift from Ramone.

"The boys want haircuts," Lucy said, just when the sun had reached the top of the trees, finally throwing direct light into their bedroom. Rosemary sighed but nodded, accepting it as her task to do. She didn't mind: it wasn't a chore. But it wasn't necessarily a hobby, either. Lucy patted her arm as she got up, getting dressed easily and heading downstairs without so much as brushing her long hair. She'd leave that to her sister while basking in sunlight on the porch, her favorite pastime.

Rosemary cut hair all summer long. She first cut her aunts' hair, then sometimes her mother, Theresa from next door, and then finally, the cousins. James always went first and she moved quickly. He didn't like being touched, especially with something sharp, but there was trust so he allowed it. Lucy and Wolfgang would fight for the next cut, but Wolfgang always let Lucy win. There was a lot of laughing and jokes while Lucy got her hair cut, it was easy. And Wolfgang, he would go last, and Rosemary would take her time as she did it, and everyone would be silent as she cut, listening to the snips, hearing her comb through his hair stroke by stroke. No one really watched, but sometimes they'd glance up for a moment, stealing a look. He would almost always have his eyes closed, his breathing slow and steady. Rosemary looked almost studious as she cut, being careful, taking her time, thinking. It was something he needed, to keep him human, and she wanted that for him.

Her grandmother always sat in the living room, cross-stitching a new project, and looking out spitefully as she cut. She had never much cared for her granddaughter's projects, and there always seemed to be one. She thought it was dirty, her fingers in everyone's hair, greasy, unwashed, shaggy. She never paid attention to what it looked like after Rosemary took her scissors and comb and occasionally water and shampoo to it. It wasn't so much about what she could do; it was more so what she was always willing to do. In a much-twisted way, she wanted more for her granddaughter. She thought she needed more than all this desolation that followed her. Not everyone could dream of a place outside the woods. Not everyone could see it.

"Hey now, don't cut it too short," Lucy teased, jerking her head away from Rosemary's scissors for a moment, always tempting fate. She laughed, but placed her hand firmly on top of her sister's head to hold it still.

"Got someone you're trying to impress?" she asked.

"No, just trying to keep a certain look," she replied as James scoffed, hair freshly trimmed, feet up on the porch railing as he carved up an apple for himself, a perpetual scavenger of many needed things.

"A little late for that, I'd say," James said, his fruit crunching loudly in his mouth.

"Yeah, we're not really sure what the look is, exactly," Wolfgang said, waving his hand over her entire face. Lucy rolled her eyes, but found the banter amusing. They heard distant yelling, but felt safe enough on the porch. The dogs in the yard barked back at the sounds, then ran to hide, enjoying the fear they felt because the sun was out and they could not see it. James slid his knife over the apple in sharper strokes.

"That old man of yours catch anything out there? Or is he just seeing ghosts? Skeletons in the closet?" Wolfgang asked, cupping his hands into fake binoculars, peering out into the woods as if seriously investigating the hunt. Wolfgang liked tossing ownership to his brother, though James had never owned something a day in his life. He didn't say anything for a moment.

"He thinks he can lure something out if he screams," James mumbled, looking off into the woods, the only one who truly had any idea of just how his father looked out there, wandering around in a mad stupor yet driven by something so intellectual and logical it was almost sinister.

"How noble to use himself," Wolfgang replied, swinging around on the railing. He was always antsy, full of possibilities, needing something to focus on that wasn't himself. He found a lot of dark amusement in the family's monster hunter. James didn't find the same joy in the subject. Joy had been killed a long time ago. He'd been forced on a hundred too many expeditions into the never-ending swamp, looking for something he didn't think his father would ever find.

"I got a twenty for whoever goes into the woods and screams back at the hunter!" Wolfgang sang out. They all knew how to taunt someone, especially during a wild summer, but nobody would go in that deep. It was a death wish. Though before, they had hardly known what death was. Living in the midst of decay had a way of erasing its possibility and when it did happened, it was shocking.

"Don't move!" Rosemary called out, finishing the last few snips of Lucy's side fringe. She stood up, brushing the back of her neck and waving to Wolfgang to have a seat. He made a big show about it, but as soon as she wrapped the towel around his shoulders, the other two looked away and out towards the woods.

His hair was always a mess, every month. She started by brushing it all out, and she took her time with each stroke instead of yanking it quickly through. Each tuff of hair she'd hold in her hand gently and brush out in her palm, moving around his whole head in that manner. He'd close his eyes, resting but not asleep, the only time he did so in front of other people. He couldn't help it, the need to rest was overwhelming all of the time, and Rosemary always created a safe place. And while Lucy and James watched the yard so he didn't have to made him feel innocuous enough to not be the beast for once, creating a moment to close his eyes. Who was their father screaming for, anyway?

She never used the buzzer on his head. It was too loud, too

fast. Instead she snipped away small pieces, here and there. Brushed it out a few more times. Sprayed on some water, using soap, washing it out with a washcloth. It was time consuming; her grandmother huffed at the notion of her using all that energy and putting it into someone like Wolfgang, but Rosemary would not be deterred. It probably amounted to an hour of silence, where just the wind in the leaves of trees overhead whistled gently. There was hardly anywhere other than around the house that one could look up, on all that land, and see a big open blue sky. Leaves, bordered up by trees, covered everything.

When she finally wiped away the last bit of cut hair off his neck, his head clean after a few weeks of not being so, he stood up. The silence was over. It was strange, the pause. It took a lot of energy to create. And then, the yard seemed to fill with the sounds of all kinds of whispers. Sometimes they sounded like vicious barks, made from a dog who had been tied up too long but still harbored fear amongst the resentment. Each yelp, each cry, were such loud whispers never truly lost to the wind. Their words always drifted in the breeze, falling on the ears they were meant for. It was amazing, what always lived on. She couldn't silence all of it. None of them looked at her when they heard it. Nobody ever really said the word, until someone finally would.

"*witch*!" her grandmother murmured, as if she had not been called the same before.

The cousins took that with them as they ran off, away from the house, the barn, the mowed grass, the big oak tree that shaded more than merely one person. They went deep into the woods, welcoming the brisk air that only the trees could keep ahold of. Easily, they found the trails they had made over the years, pushing fallen trees off to the sides as they came upon them. They owned those woods. As children they had fought all kinds of monsters and dragons lurking in hidden caves or treading in deep black waters. The land had been theirs, and they had always defended it. As they grew older, the threats seemed smaller, yet more vicious. Suddenly, monsters did seem real, but they weren't big. The trees didn't seem to trust them as much, but they still reached out for their branches. They all saw how easy it was to just let go. Some of them wanted to, and did so a finger at a time. Some of them only worked harder to keep seeing it, all of it.

The truth was, they needed those woods. It had housed them, molded them into the people they were outside of themselves, even though it was hard to admit. The world was very far away every summer they spent on those family lands, and yet the world had never been closer to their fingertips than when they walked those trails, swam in the small yet deep lakes, and looked up at the canopy of leaves covering them from the sun. In those woods, there didn't seem to be anything other than each other. And sometimes that was enough, but a lot of times it wasn't. And in those moments, it didn't matter, because they were still there together. No matter the grievance, they'd always be standing right back there with one another, an unspoken agreement in truest form. Was blood thicker than water? Or was it whomever you found yourself in the pot with, boiling?

"We could go boating with some of the locals today," Lucy offered, after they had hiked their way deep into the woods, to the ridge that overlooked one of the bigger lakes in the area. They had talked a little on the way, mostly inconsequential topics. A little light teasing, a few unremarkable questions, and a general sense of deep seeded judgment free thoughts. The four of them sat down on big boulders at the ridge's border, a few trees splitting through to create some shade among the hot surfaces of the sun-basked rocks.

"With who, exactly?" James asked, never sure how Lucy put herself out into the world so easily, when he felt so on edge of the opposite side. She shrugged like it was no big thing to gain anyone's trust she desired at the drop of a hat.

"Friends from awhile ago, I don't really remember how we met. You've met them before, but it's been a couple years since you've seen them last, I'd think. They go out all the time, and invited us out whenever," she replied, half her body sprawled out collecting all the warmth it could.

"You mean they invited you out, anytime you want," Wolfgang was quick to say. His tone was dark, uncaring, serrated. Lucy didn't cut easy.

"You too. Everyone loves the dark and broody type," she replied, lifting her head up when she said so to ensure he'd catch the wink she tossed him. He huffed. Rosemary eyed them both, before sharing a look with James. Lucy didn't believe her cousin to be anything other than a hard callus covering a soft, emotional shell. She didn't find him dangerous. Rosemary wasn't sure that was the truth. James knew it wasn't.

"I'll pass," he replied. Lucy huffed.

"What're you going to do today instead? Get high and sleep in the pole barn?" she asked and he nodded like it wasn't such a bad idea. He agreed too readily with people's disapproval.

"All summer?"

"Every summer so far, why stop now?" he replied, making sure she caught his wink.

"Come on, Rose," Lucy said, standing up and grabbing her sister by the hand, forcing her up. James stayed back with his brother, too nervous for outsiders, too nervous to leave him alone. Rosemary shared one last look with him before disappearing into the greenery. Just because they could always meet in the woods, didn't mean they stayed.

They all struggled, but Lucy hated summertime. She wanted to be with people and places, not face the isolation and personal disparities her family held. That year was going to finally be the year she didn't show up, but then Ramone had died. And once again, the woods were calling her name, whether she wanted to hear it or not.

She drove. Rosemary rolled her window down and let her hand slide about in the wind as she kept her head rested against the back of the seat, still looking up at the tops of the trees and noting the exact time they gave way to a big blue sky. There wasn't anything out there like that place. Warm air soaked into the car, leaving the sisters' skin hot and red to the touch. Rosemary knew

Lucy had forgotten sunscreen. As they descended down the forested hill, the big lake finally came into view, a small town barely shackled around the farthest edges of it. This place was all new money or no money. The Sommer sisters weren't sure they fell into either category. They both watched as sand dune grass whipped around in the wind as they sped past in their borrowed car. Rosemary looked out at the blue of the sky and the water, always having wanted to travel to that middle ground where the two masses met and see what it would be like to be connected, but no matter how far you went, the horizon line stayed very far away.

"I'm glad you came," Lucy said over the wind and music, looking over at her sister before darting her eyes back to the road. Rosemary smiled a little, looking back over at her sister. She hadn't really given her much of a choice, but didn't mind. Lucy looked out for her, and even when she didn't, she was still trying.

"It's interesting, having to get used to this place again. Even though it's never not been ours," Rosemary replied, pushing her sunglasses back up the bridge of her nose. Lucy didn't react for a long moment. She had different feelings about it.

"I guess so. You're happy to be back, aren't you? Even in spite of everything?" she asked, getting serious. There was only a short distance until they pulled up to the docks. Rosemary moved her head to the music before she answered.

"It's a strange place, but ultimately a good one. That's how I've always felt," Rosemary replied. She wasn't being entirely truthful, but didn't want to lay anything too heavy on Lucy as they pulled into the sandy parking lot, looking out at docks full of large and beautiful boats. Lucy sighed, but not out of despair.

"Are you sure you're okay? I just feel like something happened...you had a real hard time the first few days. I know you did," Lucy said, having parked in a shaded section under a tree. Neither sister moved for a minute, soaking up the scene and their most recently shared secret. It didn't matter what science said, Rosemary knew that Lucy could hear her mind. She knew it had been high pitched lately.

"This place feels, louder somehow. I don't know what it means," Rosemary confided, though felt terrible at her lack of description.

"Is it the dreams again?" Lucy whispered.

Rosemary hated that Lucy worried for her. But she knew about the dreams, the dreams that had always plagued her since she was a small child. The dreams of a fanatic, deep and vicious, somehow providing an abundance of intuition that nobody could explain other than coincidence or manipulation. And then of course there was the time it had all gone dark, and Rosemary hadn't moved her body for a week. Everyone knew about that period, and had acted as if it were only a matter of time before it came knocking again.

"I have them so often. But right now, everything's okay. The sun feels good, I'm sure being out on the water will be fun," Rosemary said, trying to be cheerful. Lucy studied her sister, then turned away – unsure. Lucy had always belonged everywhere, which had to be scary to some degree. If you belonged everywhere, then what was special anymore? What was home? And yet her twin felt worlds apart, and she hated that it was the only place she sometimes felt she didn't belong.

"Alright. C'mon, let's get this shit to the boat," she said, quickly opening the door of the car and letting warm lake air invade, breaking them from their point of uncertainty. It was a reminder of where they were, even if it was a façade. They stepped out and shut their doors in unison, a hard habit to break. Over the years, Lucy had made friends with a man named Beau and his family, who were arguably some of the wealthiest people to inhabit the lake. It was never talked about, and looking at Beau, it was very hard to see. It was interesting though to talk with him. Everything was available, every option open. The world held no limitations, and perhaps, even beyond that. It could be an enchanting perspective, at times.

"The Sommer sisters finally made their first appearance for the summer!" Beau called from the top of the boat as the sisters made their way down the dock, swaying a little as the waves pushed on the sides of the boat. It was a choppy day, a true favorite.

"You've been officially graced with our presence," Lucy called up, already teasing, already on for him and everyone else on board. It was amazing how she could weave together the past and present so tightly that it never seemed any time had gone by, no separation had occurred. It was part of her magic. Beau jumped down onto the deck, giving Lucy and Rosemary a hand up onto the boat before welcoming both of them with a large and gracious hug. He carried their bags to the back, and introduced them to the others, though none of them needed one.

"Liam is here, you guys remember him?" Beau said, as Liam and Rosemary shared a look. He gave Rosemary a small smile as they made eye contact, and she smiled back at him. He was a distant memory, but one she would always remember well.

"And Violet, she brought her friend Mia, she's down below somewhere. She'll be back up. But man, it's good to see you guys," Beau said, beaming, always happy and excited to have more crewmembers. Lucy glowed from the attention, reflecting it everywhere.

"You too, I'm sure you just dig a hole and hibernate until we're back in town," she teased and he laughed, pulling her in close for a moment before jumping over to the driver's seat. He nodded at Liam, who threw off the ropes as he revved the motor.

"Ready for a ride?" he asked.

"That's why we're here," Lucy replied, settling down at the front of the boat. Rosemary tried to follow, but there wasn't much room and while Violet gave her a crafty smile, she didn't move from where she was laying out. She sat next to Liam, immediately feeling the heat, though no pressure.

"How have you been?" Violet asked, looking over at Lucy from pushed down sunglasses. Rosemary watched as her sister shrugged, beautiful and caviler in the wind as the boat raced across the water. Beau zipped around in many quick turns, cracking jokes with Liam as he did so. Soon enough, Mia came up from below deck with a drink.

Lucy started talking a little about life back home, the city, how this summer was going to be different. She had a way about her that made everything she said sound interesting even when there was nothing to really pull away from her answers. She was secretive, always on the defense although no one had ever really come for her. And, she was beautiful. There was no denying it. Her hair was thick, layered, and long. Her eyes sparkled; showcasing so much life it was hard to believe they could contain it all. Her smile, however often she flashed it, felt genuine and pure each and every time. Rosemary's dark hair was a stark contrast to her sister's dirty blonde, along with her dark silted eyes, her sharp bones. She tried not to think about it too often.

Rosemary turned her head to focus on the water. It was brilliant and blue, little droplets splashing up into her face. The wind and the world seemed to rush by, her hair untamed. She did love the feeling of being so close to speed and sky. The boat was big, but still rose and fell quite a few times, battling the waves that only grew bigger the farther out they went. Rosemary watched as they glided past the tall ridge rocks, trying to focus on the spot they had all sat earlier. She hoped her cousins were okay, alone together, on their land. Not every spot was a safe one.

Nobody moved until the boat slowed to a halt, anchoring in a place fairly far off the shoreline. When Rosemary turned her head back to the group, she noticed everyone had opened up a drink from the cooler, and Liam tossed her an unopened beer when he caught her eye again once more, glancing away with a blush. Beau's parents kept the fridge in the hull well stocked.

"I tried to hit a couple good waves for you," Beau said as he joined the crowd, looking right at Lucy who smiled just as brightly.

"Appreciated," she replied with a smile, taking a sip of her cold drink. She hadn't eaten much that day, or any day, so it warmed her whole frame instantly. A conversation started, but

Rosemary found it hard to interject. She studied Liam, watching the way his bright eyes were piercing in the sun from under the darkness of hair and brows. His skin was tan and the scar that ran through his right brow was exceptionally defined that particular afternoon. He was covered in scars, actually, but somehow made it seem like they didn't matter.

"Are you talking to me again?" Liam asked, his voice low, breaking Rosemary from her thoughts. She looked over at him, a sly look on his face. Neither of them treated it like a big deal and in retrospect, it wasn't.

"It's not that I ever wasn't..." Rosemary replied, naturally trailing off. He absorbed that before speaking again. No one was paying attention to them.

"I think a year speaks for itself," he replied calmly, not upset. It was better that way, because nothing had really happened. Maybe that was the issue, but she sat fine in his presence. It hadn't started out that way. Then, for a long while, she hadn't been sure if it would ever be okay again. There were a lot of things like that for her. They always seemed important.

"I guess the year was talk enough, you just didn't like what it was saying," she gently teased. His eyes opened wide, but he smirked, leaning against the seat, wrapping his arms around the back of the bench. He seemed to be listening to the wind.

"Have you seen that one kid this summer yet?" Violet suddenly asked, breaking into the conversation with something that should have been trivial but wasn't. Lucy's eyes narrowed for a moment, but it passed so quickly nobody noticed.

"Who?" Rosemary asked, though she knew.

"Silas. You know him well, don't you? We see him when he's working around the marina, but he comes over your house a lot, doesn't he?" Violet replied. Lucy gave in instantly.

"Yeah, we know him. Does work around my grandparents' house sometimes. Haven't seen him this summer yet, though," she replied offhandedly. It got quiet for a moment; everyone had a different idea as to why.

"You guys hang out with him?" Beau asked. Lucy sat a bit forward, not enjoying the air anymore. She did it for her sister, and she did it because no matter what, she set the tone for the crowd. She never allowed it to go the other way.

"And if I did?" Lucy pressed. She was forward, curt.

"Nothing. He's just, kind of weird," Beau mumbled, easily taken down by a strong stare and tanned shoulders. Lucy hadn't leaned back yet.

"Seems fine when I've talked with him," she replied.

"You would know," Violet interrupted. Liam clicked his tongue, and Rosemary looked up at him. His eyes wavered back and forth from each person anxiously. He enjoyed complacency, more than anyone else. All of a sudden, Rosemary wasn't sure at all why it had been a year.

"Mmm, I would." It was nearly a growl, catching Violet off guard at how instantaneously her voice had shifted, and how easily she commanded the air. The seagulls overhead screeched as if they too had noticed the difference and were hoping to feast off scraps.

"Alright, alright. Everyone needs another beer. The guy's all right, high school was a long time ago. Take a drink, take a drink," Beau said, waving away the dark clouds and getting in between the girls' sharp words. Mia was the only one who didn't need another beer, because she'd already gotten one.

The conversation moved on, and all of Lucy's feathers smoothed down fairly quickly. She barely knew Silas, but he had been around the last couple years, and she knew someone who had enjoyed a conversation or two with him, a small smile here and there. That alone was something to defend. They all stripped off their clothes, exposing bare chests and newly bought bathing suits. Lucy could hardly contain herself and was the first to dive into the water.

"Rose! Come in!" she called after she resurfaced, throwing her hair back away from her face and treading water near the side of the boat. She always fit into the world so well. She did things effortlessly; very in tune with her own body, and it worked easily to fill her desires as if there were no need for reserve or resistance.

Rosemary jumped off the side and plunged into the water, feeling a momentary freeze pass over her skin before adjusting to the much cooler temperature of the water. Bubbles whizzed past her towards the surface, moving faster than the buoyancy as her body naturally carried her up. Calmly, she broke the surface, almost laughing. She floated on her back, splashing her sister a time or two before going back under. She liked to attempt touching the bottom even though there was no feasible way to do so. It was too deep. When she broke through the surface once again, everyone had jumped in alongside her.

"I forgot you're such a good swimmer," Liam complimented as he treaded water next to the girl he had thought about all year, yet hadn't called even once. He only wanted to talk to her when she was around, a fault of his own. In other spaces, he found other company. It had taken Rosemary a long time to understand that, see it as something outside of herself rather than something her own soul was innately doing. It hadn't been easy, no one had told her how it was done.

"In comparison to you, maybe," she teased, splashing some water his way.

"You know, fishermen are never supposed to swim in the water they fish in," Liam reminded, looking around him as if something large would emerge from the darkest depths and bite. Rosemary looked too, but she wasn't fearful. She worked to stay afloat, to stay on that side of the water's surface. It was a constant task, and she found her body running hot with the idea. Something in her head murmured.

"Jump off with me?" Lucy asked, swimming up towards her and breaking Rosemary from her thoughts. She nodded quickly.

"I'm glad you came. And don't mind Vi, she's always looking for something to bite into, you know?" Lucy whispered as they climbed the ladder back up into the boat. Rosemary nodded as she waited for Lucy to climb the last rung and reach the top with her.

"I know," she said.

"If it's important to you, then I'm right behind. You know that, right?" she asked, her eyes watchful once more. Rosemary smiled, she knew. Together they carefully climbed to the tip of the boat and stood at the very edge, taking a moment to look out at all the space and water and sky around them. Wind rippled through their hair, pushing it back away from their faces. It was like standing on the edge of a great divide, and the way it felt in that moment convinced both of them they were powerful beyond any measure, and whichever direction they choose, they could withstand it. A hot summer sun and a murky lake could be convincing.

"Ready?" Lucy asked, grabbing her sister's hand. With her other, Rosemary covered her nose and together they jumped as high as they could into the sky, screaming with delight at the quickness of their descent, right into the rolling waves of the lake's water, submerged.

Three.

Mostly, it was like softly drifting.

Maybe like floating on ocean water, a salty support. Soft waves at first, just beautiful teal blue, inviting. Then, bigger waves, something to battle, but always suggesting the opportunity to turn soft once again. It was hard to see when exactly the waves got choppier, when exactly the last violent swirl of wind pushed the water higher than imaginable. Her eyes were like those waves, fluttering. She, drifting.

Rosemary found herself walking around an old house, but one she felt she was a stranger in. It didn't feel like it belonged to anyone, yet had housed everyone. There wasn't a sense of comfort or warmth; something passive was shifting around, wandering within the walls, looking out through bathroom mirrors. Sinister? Perhaps not, less likely than a simple pinprick, or a broken glass dish. Rosemary found herself compulsively painting on the walls; not knowing what it was until she took a step back.

Let lost friends transition through fine art.

She didn't understand it. Was she supposed to? It didn't seem to matter one way or another, because that invisible force whisked her away quickly before she could think about it for too long. Time was pensive. The house around her had changed. Still large, but all glass, a pink hue washed over everything. There was water in the backyard: a small pond only an inch or two deep, tables set up throughout it. It seemed to be a dinner party for the dead. Rosemary felt calm, the dead weren't daunting, weren't hiding behind walls. It was peaceful, and while hazy, still gentle and warm. Weeping willows decorated the sides of the pond, and there was nothing but calm laughs and soft murmurs. A big white screen came into focus at the front of the pond, and everyone turned their attention to the screen, finding a place to sit in the water and rest. Something played. Memories?

"papa!"

The sound of an alarm drew her sharply back to a reality she knew well enough. A reality that did not create interest, and one that did not seem unpredictable.

A cold shower, that was always first. She would stand under the stream, hands on the wall, holding her body still under such a shock. Almost always, she would forget just how long she had been standing there, bracing herself, hoping to be transported to some other kind of place. It seldom worked. And maybe, if the water had started hot, was given the chance to grow cold, she'd know how long she'd stood there. Time seemed limitless sometimes. She took a couple of deep breaths, nursing her sunburn, and finally focused. It was roofing day.

After brushing her hair out and getting dressed, she wandered down the two flights of stairs to the kitchen, most of her family already occupying the room, reading the newspaper, drinking orange juice or coffee.

"Good morning, sweetheart," her father greeted her, pouring her a cup of coffee without being asked. She took it with a spoon of sugar, resting against the long kitchen island before waking up fully.

"I heard you got roped into working on the roof today," he said, looking over at his daughter. It was the same way a lot of people did, never sure about what they were looking at, the person before them seemingly changing every day. Rosemary nodded.

"I volunteered," she replied.

"You shouldn't be the one too," her Uncle Lewis interjected from where he sat at the table with his mother, eating his breakfast, the paper spread out before him.

"I don't mind, I like being busy," Rosemary replied quickly.

"Don't mind doing what?" Lucy sang, coming down the steps happy and alive. She gave everyone a hug good morning, even showering her grandmother with enough love to make her smile for a moment. It was hard not to.

"Working on the roof of the pole barn," Rosemary said, her voice quiet, wanting to end this bit of the conversation. Lucy just laughed; grabbing some toast from the plate next to the toaster and spreading strawberry jam across it. Whoever started making food always made a heaping amount, because someone was bound to wander by and need something to eat.

"Yeah, that's all you girl. I'm excellent moral support though, if you need it," she teased, taking a bite of her toast and accepting her own cup of coffee from their father. She looked around a moment.

"Where's mom?"

"Heidi and her went on a morning run, they should be back later," Henry replied, patting his daughter on the back before making his way over to the table to sit with both his brother and mother-in-law. He made himself a plate of eggs and bacon, a staple for their family. There used to be hard-boiled eggs, but only a few people enjoyed them and they were the quiet ones. Rosemary watched as her father and uncle spoke to one another. They were very different people, but Henry worked hard to seem civil or even friendly with Lewis. It was the way the family was, accepting of their own, and only their own. Rosemary didn't hold too much contempt for the practice; she knew that her cousins did the same with one another.

"I hired some help for the roof," her grandmother said instead of a good morning.

"Who?" Rosemary asked, befuddled as Lucy elbowed her in the ribs, already knowing.

"Looks like you got out of your project," she teased.

"No, I still need you up there. I know you'll do it right. It's just the neighbor boy coming by for a few hours. He helps a lot around here while you're all away. I give him some jobs when I have them," Sara said, looking around. She acted as if the favor extended was all hers to claim. Everyone let it slide, including the neighbor boy. He knew her lifeboats were small amongst the waves. Heidi's husband had yet to say anything or join the in-laws at the table. And still, he didn't.

"Just letting you know, Rose," Sara said, waving her cup in the air for some more coffee, Lucy obediently grabbing the pot and walking over to refill the mug.

"Alright, thank you," Rosemary said.

"Don't thank me, it's a necessity," Sara replied. She battled loneliness, even before her husband had passed. Every summer, all these people came together because she gave them life, and still they chose to leave, wandering to places that seemed too far away to understand. They'd asked before if maybe it was time to sell the house and land, but Sara refused. She would die there. It was everything, even if they didn't understand. Part of that was her fault; she'd beaten the curiosity out of almost all of them. She'd thought it to be protection, but she'd just built a wall around herself, and the outside world didn't seem any safer than the one she knew she inhabited.

"Seth, anything going on in that head today?" Lewis called out, breaking everyone away from the necessity of a roof. They looked at him, still standing against the counter, drinking his tea. An espresso person he was not.

"Just enjoying my morning," he replied, loving Heidi so much he was willing to subject himself to three months of this for her. He repeated that mantra all day long.

"Beth, will you wake those boys up already? How much daylight are they going to waste?" Lewis called out, catching Beth as she drifted between doorways, bringing up her second load of laundry that morning. She stopped, smiled gently at her nieces, and then nodded her head that she would wake her sons. Lewis was taking them somewhere for the day, out in the woods maybe. It was always secretive, always working towards some grand objective in his head that he could never verbalize to anyone else. It was why they couldn't help with the roof, but they wouldn't have offered anyway. Both girls knew Wolfgang would get out of it somehow, and hide away so that he could be all but forgotten. The summer was still young; he had plenty of time to disappoint the people who expected it, almost wanting him to.

The sun already felt sweltering when Rosemary made her walk from the house out to the pole barn, packages of shingles littered around the building. She caught a glimpse of Wolfgang sauntering off into the distance, disappearing somewhere, anywhere other than there. She waved as Lewis and James got into the car and drove off, just to be polite. She didn't know where they were going. And slowly, she began to feel alone out by the barn, under the sun. She wasn't, but it felt that way.

While Lucy tanned on the back porch of the house, Rosemary started ripping off the old shingles and roof covering with the edge of a hammer, sweat pouring down her face and back as she worked. She didn't mind the heat, or working in it. Some people needed rest, like Lucy, and some people needed to move their bodies and force anything uncomfortable upon it to become comfortable. She avoided a lot, but this wasn't one of those things.

"Working hard, Rose!" her mother shouted up as she and Heidi finally made it back up the drive, sweaty and red from their late morning run. She waved down to them but didn't say anything back. They both disappeared into the house, but Heidi came back out with a small bucket of ice holding a couple of glass bottles filled with water.

"For you," she called up, setting the bucket in the shade. She watched her niece work, noticing how she made up for almost everything with determination. She hoped she was doing so for the right reasons. Not every glass was half empty.

"Careful you aren't throwing nails into the grass, that would be the worst thing around here," Heidi teased but with a thread of honesty. There were a lot of animals and barefooted women who walked around the place.

"I know! Thank you for the water, I appreciate it," Rosemary yelled back down, giving her one more wave before continuing to yank up the old weather-beaten shingles. Eventually, Heidi wandered back into the house, joining Seth in the kitchen to work on prepping for lunch and dinner. It took a lot of forethought to keep the family of eleven fed all summer long. She did what she could. Outside, Rosemary worked for another hour before she found herself almost done with one side.

"Hello," a voice said and Rosemary nearly jumped off the roof at the sound. She turned around, one hand holding her chest as she looked at the top of the ladder and saw the neighbor boy looking over at her, welcoming.

"Silas, hey. You scared me," she replied, standing a little straighter as he continued up the ladder and stood up on the roof with her.

"Sorry, I didn't mean to," he said, surveying the roof for a few moments before meeting her eyes again. He looked different than last summer, older maybe. They were all older, but there was that line of emerging adulthood that they found themselves standing on that seemed to make it different, unique.

"How've you been?" he asked, signing the question with his hands as he spoke. He meant it, he wanted to know. They studied each other for a moment, taking in the sharper faces, the longer hair, the callused hands, and darker eyes. They'd always felt connected in unrecognizable ways. Though they had never talked about it, they seemed to see the same hidden things, and feel them in the same ways. Both of them observers.

"I've been okay, yeah. The past year has been alright," Rosemary said with a shrug. He nodded, like he could read in-between the lines.

"I'm really sorry about your grandfather. He was a great man; it must be hard without him around. I know I miss him," Silas said, breaking into something she had been trying to keep at bay. She nodded, wiping salty sweat off her face and out of her eyes.

"Yeah, it's rough. But thank you, I appreciate the thoughts," she replied. They stood there for another few moments, silent, accepting that silence.

"Ready to lay down new shingles?" he asked and Rosemary nodded. She was.

With Silas's help, carrying up the packages of new shingles was fairly easy, and not as dangerous as she had imagined it to be. They moved at a decent pace, falling into sync quickly. She enjoyed working with him; this wasn't the first project they'd taken on together, but it was her most involved role. It was simple, working with Silas. He was calm and compassionate, and always thought before he spoke. There was no tension or heat, but a tight bond, much like a safety net if anyone were to fall.

A few people watched them work. Wolfgang watched, from the large oak tree in the yard, up in the branches. They were big enough to support him and let him lay down, and he did. He was someone who could work, but hated all the eyes on him. He always created chaos, and not everyone could tolerate it. Sara watched the two work also, wanting to go out and correct them in some way, but finding their work pattern to be unbreakable and in need of no criticism. She knew why, but she tried to push the thoughts away. It was the same reason her daughter Heidi could hear the things she did. And why she herself, could feel the things she did. Superstitions, all of it.

"Have you done anything fun yet, while you've been back?" Silas asked, almost using the word *home*. Their pace had slowed down after a few hours, the sun hot over their heads. It was on its way down, though Lucy long ago had abandoned her activity of basking for something else more entertaining.

"Lucy and I went boating a few days ago, it was fun. You know how easily she makes friends around here," Rosemary

39

replied, looking at him directly while she spoke. The cochlear implants worked well, but she liked to be helpful where she could.

"Ah, boating down off of the marina? I'm sure it was fun, there's some nice boats docked there," he teased, knowing how Rosemary would feel. She laughed, nodding as she nailed down another row of shingles.

"It's the nicest boat I've ever been on," she replied.

"Can we take a water break?" she asked. Silas nodded readily. They climbed down the ladder, standing on the side of the barn that provided shade and each finished an entire bottle. They sat in the grass for a few minutes, stretching out and taking a different position than hunched over rough shingles and shiny nails. Silas seemed lost in thought, looking out over the Pennyfather land.

"Are you okay? Do you want some more water?" she asked, trying to be polite. He didn't respond right away, just kept looking out at the fields that eventually met up with the woods. His house was right over the ridge, but it couldn't be seen from that particular spot. He turned his head to look at her, his eyes soft. It wasn't strange, it was almost as if he were trying to remember something, or figure out a novelty. His eyes were always kind. Finally, he shook his head.

"No, I'm okay. I just have a feeling about this place, this moment. I can't understand exactly why..." he stopped short from finishing, his hands falling silent before his voice did. Rosemary looked up at him, feeling those vibrations in her chest again, not sure anymore if they were heartbeats. It felt louder than that.

"I kind of feel the same way. You don't know from where?" she asked, wondering. She thought she might know. The memory seemed faint; the edges soft like a dream leaving as eyes fluttered open. It had only been for a second. She couldn't believe he might remember too. He seemed nervous, uneasy to finish his thought.

"It feels like there should be water here," he said, immediately regretting his words. He didn't know if that made sense, could ever make sense, or if she wanted to consider any of it further.

"Like, a beach or something?" she asked. He was still looking intently outward, grasping for threads to bring it all together. Her eyes were little glistening windows, and they were looking back at him with such intensity he was having a hard time concentrating. It was something he'd always known about, but it seemed for once she was right there too. The idea of the memory was there, but fuzzy, almost completely faded. Still, he found it harmonious.

"Yeah, like a beach. The sky was a brilliant pink, wasn't it?" he asked. She froze. It was like he was wandering her mind, coming up with the details before they had even surfaced, before she could make sense of them and put them out into the world as normal thoughts, not just fantastical ideas. She had never had someone understand a dream before, only one person had understood the darkness.

"Pink?" she asked.

"Yeah, wasn't it?"

It had been. Pink and swirling, almost upsetting, but there had been that strange calmness that comes from knowing you're dreaming, if that is where you are.

He laughed. "I mean, maybe. It's just a feeling, not real or anything…"

"It wasn't?" she asked, her eyes narrowing, looking confused, losing her cool and confidence. It was almost unsettling. She didn't know where she was pushing this to go, but he had brought it up and now she couldn't stop feeling something about it all. It was as if there were an edge, and she was now following it along, standing on its slanted surface. Maybe she had never seen any of it, simply wanted to.

"I might have seen you there. It feels like just a dream, though. I don't know why this moment brought that up. I'm sorry," he said, trying to air out any wisps of dreaming. He could see the wind had been knocked out of her, and that she felt like she was falling. Falling like you do when you're about to enter a bad dream, and your body wants out, so it wakes you up, throws you away from the idea before it can form and you can exist in it. She clutched the empty bottle in her hand; she didn't want to wake up from this yet.

"It's all silly. This is why they call me strange around here," he laughed, trying to push off the heaviness. She knew he meant much farther places than her family's house.

"You're not strange," Rosemary said softly. She didn't know if he heard her.

"It's all just some banter. I had some wild fever dreams from all this, I've never seemed to shake them," he went on, moving his hands around his ears as if he needed to continue to explain. She put her hand on his shoulder for a gentle moment until he stopped justifying.

"Let's finish the roof?" she offered and he gladly accepted. They climbed up the ladder and immediately went back to nailing down shingles. They skipped dinner entirely, not wanting to go inside before they were finished. They knew they were filthy, dripping in sweat and dirt. They didn't speak the rest of the time they worked, just thought about the dream they'd both had, wondering if they'd had it at the same time, and if they would have recognized one another in the shallows of pink water. Nothing felt sweeter than the last nail pounded into the last shingle, the pole barn's roof complete. Rosemary took a few minutes to admire their hard work, then looked over and noticed Silas at the edge of the barn, sitting down and looking out at the sky.

"What are you looking at?" Rosemary asked. Her breath was finally starting to catch up to her as she sat beside Silas, all awkwardness having melted away after their second round of hard work. He sat on the newly shingled roof seemingly like he had barely exerted himself at all. He looked over at her before letting his eyes focus back at the view in front of them.

"The sunset is nice," she commented, feeling like that was what he was admiring, watching the sun paint the sky in dripping wet oranges and pinks, watching the small golden orb fall gently below the tree line of the woods surrounding them. Silas shook his head, almost laughing.

"Nah, that's not what I'm looking at. But the sunset is nice, yes," he replied, almost mumbling by how quietly he spoke. He used the sign for sunset, to show her. He didn't want to disrupt the moment; he hadn't felt so peaceful in many days. Rosemary furrowed her eyebrows, looking over at him, studying his face.

"Then, what?" she asked.

"You don't see it?" he said, barely paying attention to her as his eyes were transfixed on something else.

"See what?" she asked, turning her head to face back out towards the sky and the woods and the bare land before them. Her eyes searched all of it, but she didn't know what he was looking at, what was making him so calm and grateful as they sat up on that high roof surely sunburnt with opened blisters on their hands. She wanted to see it.

"You just have to witness it for yourself," he replied. He looked down for the first time since he'd sat down, all the work completed. Her grandmother didn't pay for breaks, but he was glad they had taken one. He hadn't been sure, but thought maybe she would be able to see it after all, someday. She didn't ask again, sensing she wasn't going to get an answer better than that. But something about it, the way his eyes lit up and were calm all at the same time enticed her. There seemed to be some great magic out there, some feeling that was manifesting itself so close, yet outside her reach.

"I want to," she nearly whispered, dusk officially setting in, the sun having gone under so quickly, dragging purples and dark blues into focus. Silas nodded, with a small smile and little laugh.

"Ah yes, they all do," he said, standing up and giving Rosemary a hand before they headed over to the ladder and back to solid ground. They each dropped down, feeling the sturdiness under the soles of their shoes from the ground, not slanted for the first time in hours. They looked at each other, a strange goodbye.

"Thanks for the help," Silas said, tossing her a little wave. He was already backing up, grabbing his water bottle and bandana from the ground.

"We're here all summer," she said. It was an invitation. He nodded.

"See you around," he replied, accepting it shyly, and taking a few steps backward before turning around and walking quickly down the dirt road. It seemed a matter of moments before he dissolved into the air, just like everything else that summer, and maybe all summers.

"Great lengths, you're going to. I like a game of chase myself, but roofing the pole barn in this heat? You're running a marathon," Wolfgang's voice accused, emerging from the darkness. He'd been crawling around the property ever since the afternoon, not sure what to do with himself, whether that be small or large. Rosemary rolled her eyes, but finally found his shadow and walked towards it, following its edges to meet with his body.

"That's not my game," she replied, reaching over for his joint and taking a puff, simply because she could, not because the crushed leaves did anything for her. She watched as the end of the paper lit up brightly, casting a small but pivotal light on Wolfgang's hardened face. For a moment, she took in his eyes, then blew the smoke in his face. He let it all slide. Without discussion, they both leaned against the barn, sliding down to sit in the cool grass and look out at the house, bright light radiating from most of the windows in the three-story house.

"It's like watching television, sometimes," Wolfgang commented as they both watched the same show of their mothers, fathers, aunts, and uncles wandering around. Only sometimes did it seem like they were chickens without heads, or snakes slithering in tall grass after small mice that did not see them.

"Where's Lucy?" Rosemary asked.

"Probably skinny dipping in the lake. Isn't that what all the cool girls do?" he asked, blowing his own smoke in her face. She didn't choke.

"What even is being cool anymore?" she mumbled.

"I don't know, you tell me," Wolfgang replied.

"And James?" Rosemary wondered, looking over at her oldest cousin. He didn't react right away, just kept watching the television show in slow motion. It was such a painful episode; he wondered when the season would end, when the series would be pulled. Rosemary took a deep breath to remind him she was still sitting there.

"I don't know. Off, hunting maybe. Staking out the land, preparing for the good fight. What do men do, you tell me," he said, voice hollow. Rosemary nodded, thinking about her uncle out there in the woods, wandering, trying to uncover some darkness, trying to hunt the things his son was named after. What did that feel like?

"Do you ever, I don't know, see anything out here?" she asked, diverting. He laughed.

"Not that kind of drug, cool girl," he teased. Rosemary shook her head.

"No, not like that. Just...do you ever feel anything out here? Something that, maybe you could see, but don't?" She wasn't sure what phrasing to use. Truthfully, she'd been feeling something for a long time. Was it Ramone's death, summer blues, the heat? Now, she was starting to feel that was all just covering up the real, true feeling, deep in her chest. Silas had seen it, out there in the distance. It felt tangible now, physical. And with that realization, came the notion that something was pulling her, but to where, she didn't know. Wolfgang didn't know either.

"What're you doing, trying to get me to talk about my feelings or some shit?" he asked, relying on his age-old tactic of brashness. His youngest cousin, by just seven minutes, let it slide off her like maybe a cool girl would out at the lake.

"Do you have any to talk about?" she asked, her voice quiet. He snuffed, used to the game. He didn't expect it from her, though. A new sting.

"Yeah, I see a lot of things. Like a girl out here pretending," he said. Carefully she nodded her head, back and forth a few times. Her nails dug into the sides of her knees, which were pulled up to her chest loosely.

"Pretending what?"

"You aren't a tough girl," he said.

"Screw you," she shot back. He let out one breath – short, ironic.

"Didn't your parents teach you not to poke a bear?"

"There isn't a bear to poke. Just a puppy who won't bark," Rosemary said. She stood up, brushing the grass off the back of her legs. She looked down at him for a moment, but he wouldn't meet her eyes, committed to keeping them focused on the show, no curtains having been drawn yet.

It wasn't like his house. She hated her words.

"They're not hunting you," she whispered, almost annoyed she said it, then all of a sudden, wasn't. His eyes became glassy in the dim light from the stars, the moon, the pieces of lit paper in his hand. He shook his head, a sad smile dancing on his face before he said anything more. He licked his lips.

"Whatever's out here, it's watching us differently."

Four.

Lewis Pennyfather was a hunter. He had always been one, even since a young child. He sought out the weakest of the pack, even when there wasn't a pack to observe. He'd pull his sisters' hair and look innocent when his parents asked him why they were crying. At school, he'd push the smallest kid to the ground, or prick them with a pin and have no reason to give the teacher, no facial expression to explain the urge. It wasn't necessarily an urge; it was more curiosity. He wondered about a lot of things, but mostly *why*. The need to know *why* continued, and Sara watched her son grow up with less worried eyes than her husband. Ramone wanted his son to be good, and Sara wasn't convinced he wasn't. She also wasn't convinced there was a narrow way to understand the term *good*. He just had a much different way of approaching anything; he valued strength, and couldn't comprehend why someone wouldn't inherently have it. Maybe it had something to do with the land. He was attracted to it, like everyone who lived in that house. So what, if he went to the other side? Sara argued the point. There were two sides for a reason, after all. Weren't there? It was all about balance. All her children went somewhere different. Lewis hiked deep into the woods. Delphine had always climbed to the highest point, wanting to see the sun and the water touch at the same time. And Heidi, well, nobody really knew where she went, but she always came back with wildflowers. Lewis came back holding squirrels with pierced hearts.

It surprised no one what kind of man Lewis became, or husband, or father. Wolfgang was born to them young, and he grew up in the very striking way that Lewis did, but his actions, however similar, were always in spite of his father. He wasn't any less a Pennyfather. And the thing Lewis wanted to discover, felt was owed to him by blood, wasn't in his possession to pass down. Wolfgang would always be a step closer, even when he seemed not even in the race. Wolfgang's attitude only grew worse when James was born much later, planned and welcomed, and grew up to be quiet and respectful and included. It didn't make sense; he clearly wasn't born a hunter.

Heidi and Rosemary sat on top of the pole barn's new roof, breathing in the dusk air of summer as they watched James follow his father out into the woods towards one of their many blinds. They didn't say anything as they watched them walk out, one trying to keep up with the other, not knowing where the need came from.

"Lewis is always out there looking for something," Heidi said, leaning back on the roof to lie down. She'd come up to the roof often as a child, finding the solitude that existed so close to the open sky a good perspective shift. She liked that she wasn't the only one who could feel that and chased it down. Rosemary nodded; unconsciously searching for the exact spot the sky met the tree line.

"So is everyone," she replied. Heidi chuckled.

"I guess they are. I feel bad for James, I don't think he likes to hunt at all," her aunt said, looking for recognizable faces in the clouds. She missed her father.

"He's good at it," Rosemary said.

"Yeah, he is. But that's not the same."

They laid in silence a while longer. They often didn't have to talk, it was a lot of work to always be on, ready to go. Instead, they spent more time in solitude together. It was comforting to journey forward as a self, but have someone to look back at over your shoulder to let you know you weren't alone if you happened to fall.

"Have you been having a good start to summer?" Rosemary asked.

"It's all relative, I guess. Have you?" Heidi asked, looking over at her niece. She watched as she tucked a fly away from her ponytail behind her ear, the profile of her face lit up miraculously by the sunset's last flares of light. It was still hot, and the sweat on her face only highlighted the sharpness, forcing her to look more ethereal than Heidi already thought she did.

"Relatively," Rosemary replied with a grin, looking her aunt in the eyes for a brief moment before turning her attention back out to the vastness.

"I feel something… *greater* about this summer. I don't know how to put it into words, but everything feels…very different," Rosemary continued. She aired on the side of caution when speaking to her family about things far above the tangible. She had a record of going comatose, and it had become an unshatterable reputation.

"Things are different this summer," Heidi replied, her voice soft and emotional.

"They are, I know. But it's about everything. Almost like everything that should be familiar is separated away from me by frosted glass," Rosemary said, honesty pouring from her soul if only for a moment. She quickly tried to bottle it back up.

"But you know," she started; wanting to fill up the space with something she thought would make more sense.

"I hear it's like that, when someone's gone."

Heidi looked at her niece with sad eyes.

"How you see the world is okay. If this summer everything is hazy, that's okay," Heidi replied, trying her hardest to stay open. Rosemary felt that.

"I know. It's not really hazy though…" Rosemary stopped,

trying to find the words to continue. She wanted to be accurate. Heidi waited for her, feeling no rush to push the conversation forward, or finish it up. They never really finished any of their conversations; more so, they just continued them when they laid their eyes on each other again. It was easy, especially with living together the past few years. The commanderie had lifted them both up, kept both of them whole. Finally, Rosemary found her comparison.

"It's more like a rift."

Heidi nodded. She knew. Rosemary looked at her aunt, seeing something cross her face, some kind of acknowledgment that went much deeper than words or conscious thought. Instead, it all drifted into memory. While Rosemary looked at her aunt, whose eyes laid focus on the setting sun, she started to think. She thought about how Heidi had married young; to a man she thought she loved. And it turned out she did. Because no matter how badly he hurt her, she stayed. There was always that morning glimmer after a bad night, when the sun would filter in through cracked shades, his hulking form still beside her on the bed, a soft innocence appearing on his face as he slept. She would watch him sleep for hours, fascinated by how calm he could be, how soft his breath could come. She wondered what made a man as violent as him. Heidi had told her nieces all of this over the years. They had many late nights of deep conversation. There was no reason to hide the world from them. Heidi had rather they learn the dark secrets the world held for them from her, rather than from themselves. After five years, she had left with a firm sense of finality. There was something to be said for that.

"I've known a few rifts," Heidi replied finally.

"This one feels like a place," Rosemary said, watching as a car drove up the long drive, her parents' laughter and voices spilling out the open car window as they pulled past the pole barn and closer to the house. They'd gone out for dinner, just the two of them. Heidi took note.

"You should hang out with your parents this summer, at least a little," Heidi said, breaking into their silence once again.

"I will," she replied.

"Don't lie to me like that," Heidi said, stretching out on her back before propping herself up on her elbows to have a more involved conversation.

"Okay, you're right, I probably won't," Rosemary said.

"How long are you going to carry this grudge?" Heidi asked, her question hanging with open ends.

"How long are you going to carry yours?"

Rosemary and Lucy's parents were journalists, but more importantly, they were after something. It had many names, the *truth* being the predominant one. That's what got them started. Rosemary, before knowing any better, had found it to be perhaps one of the worse kinds of addictions, because it had been prized over almost everything throughout her life. It had started off as many one-week trips every month, then it grew to several weeks, and then suddenly it was two or three months of just being gone. That was the worst time, the uncertainty when they had been young. The girls were surrounded by a constant rotation of people, and then one time, no one showed up. They were only eight. Heidi stepped in then and took her nieces to live with her for a long time; there were no definite dates. Heidi had a long talk with her sister about it, and things got better. They moved around a lot still, but took their daughters with them. They sold the house and lived from one grand apartment to the next. It was fine, for a pair of eight year olds. Constant adventures seemed to be the building blocks of life, but after a while, it felt more like being a balloon lost in the sky than a bird with wings.

When the out of country trips started happening, they came to live with Heidi for those months. Months however, started turning into a year. It was a year here, in a house with Heidi, and then it was a few months with their parents in a big city in the states. Their passion wasn't lost on Rosemary, but sometimes she felt lost from them. Rosemary never spoke ill about any of it. She had taken each rotation, each move, with silent grace. And then when

Allison Astorino

she was fifteen, she had simply said no to moving again. Lucy stayed too, for her sister. No one really fought. It seemed natural, the way for things to be. They had graduated from high school in Heidi's small town. Then Lucy went off to a college town and made her friends with the money and looks and big egos and small ambitions. And Rosemary moved from Heidi's house into the backyard's guesthouse, and liked reading more than she wanted to admit, and wanted to tell stories more than she felt comfortable. And they were okay with it, for now.

"None of us have ever been typical, you know," Heidi replied, knowing the exact narrative her niece was mulling over in her head. For some reason, the universe had never allowed Heidi to conceive. She'd always felt that perhaps there were other ways to mother creation, even if not its direct creator.

"I know. It's all right. But it doesn't make me want to extend any grand gestures," Rosemary reminded her. Heidi accepted the response, fair enough.

"Save those for someone else, huh?" she asked.

"I guess," her niece replied. There was an air of quietness for another moment. Then, Heidi did what she often did, asked her niece for council. Their relationship was one of partnership, and Heidi never pretended to have all the answers. She couldn't.

"Why do you think that is?" she asked, her voice almost getting lost in the evening breeze, her choppy hair flowing into her face. She held a freckled face, her hair more clementine than strawberry blonde.

"Think what is?"

"We are how we are. How did we all decide this was who we'd be?" she pushed, the humanities professor in her bubbling to the surface. The leniency of summer sabbaticals was something she'd always appreciated.

Rosemary thought about it, not sure why she would know. But, there was a pulsing inside of her chest that thought it might have something to offer. Perhaps the ability to give it a home had always resided within her and that's why, that summer, it had finally chosen to enter and become known.

"If you're looking for uniformity, I think you picked the wrong family," Rosemary laughed, hugging her knees up to her chest. She rocked side to side, her body constantly seeking out a safe position to be in.

"I think we're probably all more alike than we care to admit," Heidi replied.

"Not even my twin and I are the same," Rosemary replied, attempting a joke.

"Yeah, I see that. But also, somehow we all became extremes of one another. I guess what I'm trying to get at, is we can understand each other more than we initially think we can. Give your mother a chance, perhaps. Delphine has a lot to offer, even if she's messed up in the past," Heidi said, looking over at her niece who was finally looking at her. They felt so alone on the barn's rooftop, a place of invincibility as everything that had ever affected them stayed below that horizon line.

"Sounds like you're talking from experience," Rosemary replied.

"Siblings always have tumultuous relationships," Heidi said with a smile. It was true.

"You know that, and with your cousins, too."

"So, what? Should I ask her about the latest big trip?" Rosemary asked, begrudgingly entertaining the idea of extending the first hand.

"No, you're not interested in that. Try just asking her how her morning has been, and if she'd like some toast," Heidi laughed, elbowing her niece in an attempt to liven her up. Rosemary stayed even, at least on the outside. It was a trick; Heidi had learned to look for the small cracks to avoid a catastrophe.

"Your father, too," Heidi reminded, as if she had to. That relationship was somehow a little easier, because they were more similar than they weren't. Really, Rosemary and Lucy were a perfect mix of their parents, exuding the possibilities of both.

"I hear you," Rosemary said. Heidi nodded, letting it go at

that. It felt honest enough for the moment, no grand gestures needed yet.

"What's your brother doing out there?" Rosemary asked, nodding her head towards the woods. Something unsettling shifted in the air when she breathed the question, Heidi felt her skin shiver. She'd known her brother a long time. Her perception was cloaked in darkness.

"Searching," she said simply.

"For what?"

"Something he thinks he's lost, but never had."

The sound of a shot pierced through the evening air. It silenced them both as they looked out over the trees. Something about the echo of the shot ripped apart and frayed them both. It did every time.

Nobody really knew how hard it was for James to hold up the façade of the hunt. He wasn't driven like his father, didn't feel the pull that Lewis did to be outside and looking for something, anything, to possess. He didn't feel entitled to any of it. James had spent long hours every day of his life propping up his father's wild delusions about what was out roaming. At first, when it had been very dark and very cold, his father's calculated chatter would turn sinister, fanatical. He had preached about there being something out there, in those woods. Something bigger than either of them could comprehend. He would talk about the glimpse he got of it as a child, and from that brief touch had been passionately trying to invoke that energy once more. But he wasn't satisfied with simply seeing it again, he wanted to capture it, kill it, take it for himself. Now, his father talked about it all the time, because all of their time was in those woods together. James never talked about those kinds of things. Somehow, he'd become roped into hiding away his father's malevolence. He was an accomplice in his own victimhood, or so it felt. He could write off the cruelty instead of becoming angry at it, because he knew the truth. He knew his father was a fanatic. James knew others had their suspicions, but Lewis was precise, and never let loose any of his delusional thoughts around anyone other than James, and only in those brief moments that feel so far removed from the world it seemed anything could be a possibility. Until that monster was found (because Lewis was sure that was what it was, a monster) he would not rest or lay down his weapon. And neither would James. To James, the woods had always been and truly become a thing of deep pain, brutality, and toxicity. The vastness led to no escape. His father's violence extended far outside his words.

But there was a monster on the loose, and James knew he'd have to kill it.

The house was dark, quiet at the latest hours of the night when Lewis and James finally returned from their hunt. Everyone had long gone to bed, but Rosemary heard the footsteps as they crept up the stairwell and the way each sound traveled felt tired. She stuck her head out of the doorway, Lucy asleep and breathing deeply on her side of the room. James made his way down the hall, his face only half lit up by the moonlight trailing in from the uncovered window at the end of the hall. He barely saw Rosemary.

"Hey, how'd it go?" she whispered, stopping him. He didn't meet her eyes, just shrugged off the question. He was tired, sure.

"We got a coyote," he replied. His voice didn't sound like his own, but rather some mix of other people and otherworldly sources. Perhaps a version of him that lived everywhere else but his own body.

"How was that?" she asked.

"Well, it's dead," he said. There didn't seem anywhere else to go from there, especially not for the coyote.

"How was it?" she asked again, her voice a whispered hush. She didn't know where her uncle was, if he had already plowed up the steps, or if he had stayed down in the living room.

"It's dead," James said, looking up at her finally. She couldn't really see his eyes, but winced anyway. He could feel her trying to peel back one thin layer, but if she wasn't willing to crack the shell entirely, he couldn't do it for her. It would crush him.

"Yeah, it is," she said, nodding like she understood. He took one moment to study her eyes, only pity living in them. To her, his eyes looked tired. But he knew what they really were was hopeless. He'd always wondered when it would be too much, when the secrets he carried would become too heavy, too much of a burden that his soul would simply refuse to go on any farther. When people looked at him, when they talked to him, no one ever seemed to understand what he meant. The same was true in that moment, although Rosemary was trying. Her own soul could feel it, maybe only on the edges, but it was growing.

For now, that didn't amount to anything, so he kept walking, slipping into his room quieter than any creature in any stretch of woods.

Five.

It sounded like rain.

Swooshing down, smacking hard against the windowpanes. Pattering away at the wood of the windowsill, creeping in slowly and deliberately, running down the wall once it had finally beaten past its barrier. Rosemary turned her head to look at their bedroom's dark window. She couldn't see any rain, she couldn't really see anything; it was so dark outside. A few glitters of light flashed up in the sky, like a shooting star, or a ship being shot down in brilliance. She wondered what it was, but there was no way she knew to find out. There was a knocking at the door, she turned, didn't answer it, and the sound went away. Did the person?

She was sweating. It felt incredibly cold in their room, all that darkness around her, but her body still radiated warmth. Maybe the rain was coming from her. The drops running down her skin, was that the rain she was hearing? Still, she felt drawn to the window, and finally crawled out of bed and over to its glass surface. It seemed like a lot was happening outside, inside the darkness of the night, and the momentary flashes of light high above. Setting a hand, palm open, on the glass in front of her, she could feel the screams from down below of coyotes. What had they found? What did they miss? She yanked her palm away. She didn't want to hear it. The knocking started again, but this time it was coming from inside her closet. She didn't want to answer it, couldn't let it out. Eventually, the sound went away. Did the thing?

Feeling unsteady, she wandered down to the kitchen to get a glass of water. She had never sipped down something so cold in her life. For a moment, she felt okay. Looking around, everything seemed fine. Stars could be that bright. The moon could be reflecting sunlight that brightly, perhaps. She walked over to one of the large windows in the wall of the living room, but she was having a hard time. There was something grabbing onto her, holding her back. Her legs felt uneasy beneath her. She didn't know why, but she pressed herself against the glass again, trying to hold herself up. Why couldn't she stand? The sweat came back at the touch of the cool glass. The temperature difference was striking; she couldn't miss it. She let out a soft moan, something hurt. Then, she heard it. The knocking. Her heart seized as she realized it had moved again. This time, it was under the couch, scratching at the wood, knocking on the frame. She turned away, still holding herself up against the window. She was so hot; it felt like an ocean's wave was hitting her over and over. She could taste the salt in her mouth. A deep pain ignited from her leg, and she moved her eyes from the knocking sound to her own body. Her breathing heightened as she noticed deep fiery red claw marks on her legs, swelling up, oozing over, as bright as the slashes in the night sky. The knocking didn't stop. Why wouldn't it go away?

At some point, Rosemary made it back to bed, only able to open her eyes after a restless sleep. She couldn't hear any knocking. She looked around; the sky only as bright as early dawn would let it be. She felt down her leg, her fingers gliding over her smooth skin. How bad had they been last night? She shook her head, confused. A glass of water stood at her bedside table, half drank, condensation on the exterior. So, there had been ice. When she turned over again, Lucy was staring at her.

"What's going on?" her sister asked.

"I don't know what that means, I just woke up," Rosemary replied, keeping her voice as clear as it could be. She didn't know what she was trying to hide, but she felt pushed to keep something inside of her, deep down, out of the way. Lucy narrowed her eyes at her sister, feeling that resistance in the short space from across the room.

"No, you didn't," Lucy said. Rosemary displayed genuine confusion in the most believable way.

"What?"

"You've been roaming around this whole house all night, saying crazy shit," Lucy said, not moving a muscle in her body. In waking up, there is a moment of complete honesty, of having no skin. She didn't want to muddle the waters and bring the day upon too soon.

"Oh. Wow, I must have been sleepwalking," Rosemary said, stunned, not sure where to go from there. She turned inward, thinking about what she last remembered. There wasn't much. Just a strange noise and a fiery pain in her leg. She couldn't place how it had gotten there, or where it had gone.

"Sleepwalking? It felt a little more involved than that. What were you dreaming about last night?" Lucy pushed. She wasn't letting go.

"I honestly can't remember. I was really hot, that's all," Rosemary replied. She studied her twin; always grateful it wasn't her face looking back at her. She watched as Lucy's mind worked, trying to decide what she believed and what she didn't. Rosemary didn't want to lie to her, but there wasn't anything concrete to say. It was just a feeling. It was always just a feeling.

"Okay," Lucy said finally.

"Okay?"

"Okay for now," she corrected. A loud knock rattled their bedroom door as it opened, the person behind it not waiting for an invitation.

"What the hell was all that last night?" Wolfgang asked, standing before the two girls wearing his boxers and a sleeveless shirt that was basically ripped to shreds. His dark hair lay unkempt, sticking out at all angles. Deep shadows caressed his eyes.

"Uh, good morning," Rosemary said, pulling herself up from under the covers and leaning against the headboard of her small bed. He didn't shake.

"It would be a good morning if you could convince me right here right now that you're not possessed," Wolfgang said, his voice serious and still. Lucy watched, for once quiet and cautious. Rosemary felt stranded on a raft.

"Possessed? That's ridiculous..." Rosemary replied, trying to laugh it off.

"Is it? Because you scratching at windows and asking me if I think something's watching me under the cloak of darkness isn't sitting right," he replied, his own voice tripping over his words, unmoving from the doorway he stood in. Rosemary looked at him for a moment. She didn't know how to defend herself. She hated how it was always a trial. It was tiresome, and made her want to hide.

"You think something is watching you?" Lucy asked, her voice cracked.

"What? No. It's out of context. You're both looking at me like I'm crazy. I am not crazy," Rosemary defended, pulling the blanket up tighter against her waist. She wanted to hide, crawl even deeper down a hole she had never realized she was digging until she felt their pressure. There had to be an escape.

"I didn't say crazy. I said possessed," Wolfgang clarified. She rolled her eyes.

"Not much better."

"Listen. Figure it out, because anyone else sees you acting like that, you're gonna have a much bigger problem than me performing an exorcism and salting doorways, understand?" he asked. As he said it, his eyes involuntary darted back, thinking of the exact people he was referring to. Maybe everyone, maybe no one. He didn't want to admit it, but ever since he'd thrown dirt on his grandfather's coffin, he'd felt something too. He hadn't

allowed his mind to travel farther than *something*, and he was fine
settling for that. It was a word he knew well; people said it a lot
about him. *You're really something, Wolfgang.* And sure, they
didn't mean it well. And this feeling he had didn't really feel like it
meant well either. What was so wrong with that? But now, looking
at his cousin, watching her face hide both fright and wonder, he
felt forced to face it. Whatever it was, she was only diving in
farther. She'd never heeded a warning a day in her life. Lucy felt a
similar way, he could tell. Maybe they'd talk about it later, maybe
they wouldn't. Either way, they would both watch.

"I've just been having bad dreams," Rosemary finally said.
Wolfgang rubbed his eyes, exasperated. His teeth found the side of
his tongue and bit into it deeply, needing the sharp pain to feel
grounded.

"Whatever you say, dude," he mumbled, walking out and
remembering to shut the door behind him. The girls sat quietly for
a while, neither of them knowing what to say, so eventually Lucy
just stood up and started getting dressed for the day. Rosemary
followed suit, each step she took her body surprised that there was
no pain in her legs.

They sat together at the kitchen table and shared breakfast,
listening to an impassioned political argument between Seth and
Lewis, who even after a late night was still the first person up in
the kitchen, making espresso. James eventually made it downstairs,
groggy. He sat at the table across from the girls, who took
sympathy for him and fixed him a plate of food so he wouldn't
have to exert the effort. The women were already on the front
porch, chattering loudly.

Everyone had a slow morning, eventually drifting off as they
did. Rosemary found herself sitting up in her room, looking out the
window and trying to sketch the scene before her. Something
wasn't right though, and every time she looked down at her paper,
there was a divide in the land that she didn't see blatantly out the
window. Her hand just felt like it should be there. She pushed past
the feeling of uneasiness. After a short while, she started to hear

the sound of a steady pounding. Looking out the window, she finally found the origin. Silas was over, and he was chopping wood.

Rosemary walked out the back door of the house towards him, approaching him from an angle so that she wouldn't be sneaking up on him. When he saw her coming, he stopped swinging the axe, wiping the sweat off his brow as he smiled hello.

"Hey, stranger," he greeted.

"Hello," she replied. They stood for a bit, looking at each other.

"Cutting wood this early in the year?" she asked, looking at the tree he was dismantling. It had died a long time ago, dried well in the summer heat.

"It's an all year job, easier that way. Always have to be ready for a long hard winter, no matter what," Silas replied, surveying the work he still had left to do. He pulled up dead trees from the woods when he could, giving a few hours a day to split and stack it against the old house of his neighbor so that there'd always be a steady supply come the colder months.

"You sure do a lot of work around here," Rosemary commented, beginning to notice it all.

"Just keeping it together for your grandmother," he replied. She nodded, appreciating the effort he put in. She knew he did more than Sara would ever ask of him, more than she even realized at times. Rosemary wanted to know more about him, but settled for the fact that at least she knew he had a golden heart.

"Can I split some?" Rosemary asked. Silas laughed.

"Be my guest," he replied, setting her up with a log and handing her the axe. He directed her on a good stance, and exactly how to throw her body weight into the motion. After a few misses, she hit the wood perfectly, causing it to split halfway before she tapped it again with the axe and it split perfectly in two.

"You're a natural," he replied, smiling. She liked the feeling of the motion, pleased with the results. She decided to tackle a few more while he grabbed the chainsaw and began cutting the rest of the tree up into sizeable chunks to split. They didn't talk much as they worked, both very intent in their actions. But within an hour, all the wood had been split and was ready to be stacked. They looked out at their work, breathing heavily.

"You don't always have to help me with my jobs, you know. It's your summer vacation," Silas said, sitting on one of the logs, legs out and crossed in front of him at the ankle. He was deeply tan, his mop of brown hair sweaty at the end of each soft wavy curl. She shrugged at the suggestion, like she was pushing it away.

"It's summer for everyone," she replied. He accepted that.

"Do you want some lemonade?" she asked. He thought about it, eventually nodding. He didn't really like going inside the Pennyfathers' house.

"Sure, that sounds nice. Can we drink it on the porch?" he asked.

"Yeah, that's fine. Ready?" she asked. She didn't know.

"I am," he replied, grabbing his bandana off the ground and wiping his face dry. He wasn't ready at all. The thing about dreams is sometimes you don't always remember them. Not until they happen again, or you see a shape or hear a noise and suddenly you're back, standing somewhere you didn't realize you ever were before. And one good dream didn't mean the one before it hadn't happened.

They started walking up the lawn, past the barn, up to the house. Rosemary first, Silas right behind. The wind blew past them both, and Rosemary turned her head to hear the leaves whistle from the fruit trees near them. She heard something else instead.

The hinges of the barn's doors around the corner screeched open. The sound, familiar only in a memory that had yet to happen, made Rosemary spin to look. It was around the corner from them, quiet, but nonetheless she heard it. And without thinking, without even the briefest moment of analyzing, she stepped quickly in front of Silas who she knew would never hear it coming.

Neither of them did, not really. It bounded quickly across the lawn, body flattened, ears back, no reason behind the attack it was so invested in carrying out. It was just a cat, but relentless. Rosemary let out a scream as it first jumped on her, digging its claws into both sides of her exposed calf, ripping the bottom fabric of her shorts as it latched onto her thighs with razors under toes. She went to kick it off of her, but its dagger teeth had already sunk deep into her muscle, and she let out another howl comparable to the one the small cat was simultaneously letting out. Her shoe fell off as she moved about the lawn, and she hit the cat with it as hard as she could, backing away from it as it fell down to the ground. But it didn't stop. It jumped at her again and again, no matter how much she yelled or kicked or batted at it. Silas ran over to her what seemed hours later, and grabbed it by the neck, tossing it as hard as he could towards the barn. It landed with a thud against the wall, momentarily stunned. It tried to slither back, dazed, but Silas picked it up again, tossing it through an open window of the barn to keep it back as long as he could. Rosemary could still hear the cat howling from within the barn's walls, wanting to come back out and finish the job it had started. She sank to the ground, her leg muscles contracting; blood flowing freely from open wounds and slashes in her skin. She had five bites total, amid the deep and lengthy gashes down her legs.

"Bring her here!" Sara shouted from the porch, having materialized from nowhere. She said it with such authority that Silas simply acted without any forethought or hesitation, just confidence in the instruction. His arms were shaky as he grabbed up Rosemary, holding her to his chest like something precious as he quickly carried her up the lawn and into the house. Tears were streaming down her face but she had yet to make a sound past the initial screams of battle. She didn't feel pain yet, just fear. Her broken heart was pounding.

"Here, set her down right here," Sara instructed, her voice calm but stern. Carefully, he set her down in the kitchen chair Sara had pulled out, placing her legs on another chair opposite. One of her legs was much worse than the other, swelling up rapidly around each deep puncture wound from the bites.

"How'd you know it was coming?" he asked, kneeling next to her as Sara got together warm water and towels. He let her hold on tightly to his shoulder.

"I heard it," she said, looking forward, thinking about something else.

"Oh."

He held onto her as the pain began to rise from the wounds, and Sara began to clean them out with the warm water. She grabbed some peroxide and dabbed at the wounds, causing them to sting and swell even more than they already did. Rosemary's whole body began to shake at the pain and adrenaline, but she remained as steady as she could. After all the efforts to disinfect, Sara went through her pantry, coming back out with some glass bottles filled with her own remedies harvested from the land. She'd lived and survived in that wild place long before western medicine had set up practices and called them clinics. Carefully, she applied a few different balms on the wounds, each one calming the redness, reducing the stinging, and cooling off the heat. Rosemary finally started to breathe normally again.

"You're lucky that cat didn't climb up your legs to your face," her grandmother said, her eyes pulled deeply into the work she was doing. There was no gentleness as she worked, instead exuding a very stern and confident motion. From her, it was comforting. Rosemary liked that way of working.

"Where did that cat come from?" Rosemary asked. Her grandmother looked up, her eyes meeting her granddaughter's perfectly. They had the same ones; it was like looking into a mirror sometimes.

"They wander," she finally said. Rosemary nodded, knowing somehow what she meant. She couldn't have verbalized it, but the knowledge added to her feeling, that deep-seeded feeling that only knew how to grow.

"Alright. You need to sit and rest somewhere. Maybe out on the porch where it's cooler. Silas, can you help her to the bench?" Sara asked gently, having finished wrapping large bandages across the most vicious parts of her attack. He nodded quickly, helping Rosemary up and wading over to the large patio bench, lowering her gently onto the overstuffed cushions. Sara disappeared back into the house.

"Are you okay?" Rosemary asked, looking up at him as he simply stood over her, not sure what to do next. He was too quiet. The sun was beating down, but beneath the shade of the porch, they both felt cool for the first time in a very long time. It was a jointly created space.

"I should be asking you that," he replied, a sad smile. She shook her head.

"Trust me, I'll live," she assured. He didn't seem immediately convinced.

"You don't have to stay. Thanks for carrying me to the house, but don't feel like you have to hang out with me since I'm stuck up here now," she said, giving him an olive branch. He gave it right back.

"I'll stay for a while, if you'll have me," he replied.

"That sounds nice," she replied. There were a few minutes of quiet, as he settled on a chair across from her on the porch. She had her legs stretched out in front of her, elevated to help the swelling. She had yet to absorb the attack; it didn't feel quite real, even though the pain seemed to have an everlasting ache beneath those bandages. She wondered vaguely where the rest of her family was, but didn't miss them. She liked Silas's company. Her body was still coursing with adrenaline.

"I propose a game," Rosemary said, surprising even herself with such a suggestion.

"What kind?" he asked, a small smile peeking out, better than the last. It gave her courage to continue.

"One with stakes. The rules are simple. Ask a question. We answer wholly, honestly, and without hesitation," she said, looking at him. He nodded, accepting the terms and responsibility of entering such a game.

"You can ask me something first," he offered, glancing down

at her ravaged legs. He felt like he owed her something for that.

"I accept your offering," she laughed, thinking of her question. They both knew it wouldn't consist of favorite colors, or best desserts.

"What's your relationship like with your parents?" she asked. He breathed in before answering, looking right at her. They were going for it.

"I don't really know them. My mom left when I was really young, so I only have the vaguest memories of her. Sometimes I think they're just ones I've made up in my head to have something to dream about. My dad isn't around a lot. He had a hard time growing up I guess; his father died when he was young. And then he had a hard time when he was left alone with me. We moved in with my grandmother a long time ago, and she's basically raised me. My dad doesn't come home often. Rarely, ever. I see him around sometimes though, we say hello. Do the whole nod thing men do, I don't know why they do it. But I'm not angry with any of it. It's really been all right. Suffice?" he asked. Rosemary nodded, taking in everything he'd said. She didn't want to make it seem sad, that wasn't the point of the game. It surprised her; somehow, that this person she'd known of for a very long time was also someone she didn't know much about. She liked the game already, but felt a nervous flutter in her chest for whatever he was going to ask. The warmth in the air sweltered around them both, but they still couldn't quite feel it. Sara came out with a drink that would supposedly help fight infection, looking over her granddaughter with cautious eyes, then whisked herself inside again. She didn't spend much of her time with company, anymore. Perhaps, ever.

"Mmm, okay. What's one of your biggest insecurities? Not physically," he asked, adding the last stipulation on quickly. She wished she could simply say her eyes were too narrow, but this was her game after all.

"I guess...I feel like not enough? Like people run away too easily from me. I'm a good place holder, a fun Rubix cube, but one that no one takes the time to finish because nobody ever really finishes those things. There's better things to do than align all the colors. I'm not even really who I want to be. I thought I'd be different at twenty-two, but here I am, not exactly what I was expecting either. So I just feel like not enough. A work in progress. One that's past due on the deadline," she said, mumbling near the end, though trying not to because she didn't want Silas to miss out on any words. That wouldn't be fair to the game. He nodded, making it okay to be said.

"Alright. Who's your best friend, and why?" she asked. He thought a moment.

"I've had friends over the years," Silas replied. She looked at him, confused why he stopped. He breathed in deeply for a minute, before looking out at the sky and continuing. He didn't know how much to say.

"I've had a lot of friends over the years. Still do, guys I went to school with. Guys I work with. I don't know if you know this, but your grandfather spent a lot of time with me, especially growing up. He taught me a lot. He was kind of like a father to me, but also a friend. Ramone was truly good, and he's who comes to mind when you ask something like that. I just thought you should know, thought I should be honest," Silas replied. When he looked back at Rosemary, her eyes were watery, but she held herself tall and simply nodded, a small smile on her lips relaying her appreciation for the honesty. She liked hearing people's stories of her grandfather, how they saw and related to him. It kept him whole, in front of her.

"My turn I guess? Okay, how often do you lie? And when do you do it, if you do?" he asked, after she nodded.

"Oh, damn. Um, compulsively. Though please don't let that worry you. I just tend to tell people what they want to hear. I can make the story anything it needs to be, the statements believable. It's not hard. Because it's what they want to hear. Finding someone who only wants to hear the truth? Well, I don't think I've ever really met someone like that. I only do it because it's hard to get someone off your back. They don't care about your journey, no. They just want their checkboxes ticked. And I can do that easily, by saying what they want. Then everyone can move on, have a drink, and be merry. Or whatever," she replied. She knew she sounded like a bad person. She hated that. He could tell, from the way she bit her lip and wouldn't look at him after her big declaration. He was wary of her.

"I don't want any specific answer," he said.

"That's not a question," she replied, though he could tell she was happy he'd said it. The porch seemed smaller, it was beginning to become the whole world and they were the only two people in it. Neither of them could lie even if they wanted to. They'd have felt it, in that small space, the whole world.

"Your turn," he reminded.

"Okay. What's your biggest fear? Whatever comes to mind," Rosemary asked.

"Well, what comes first to mind is drowning. I know there are all kinds of horrible ways to die, but for me, being somewhere underwater without hope of escape, without being able to give yourself that breath of air your body is demanding. Ugh, just talking about it gives me chills. Is that okay, or were you looking for something more?" he asked. She shook her head.

"No that's good. Your turn again, sir," she said.

"What's your biggest regret?"

"Mmm, that's a tough one. Maybe missing out? I don't take a lot of chances; I often find myself paralyzed. I guess that's not a good answer, it's not one exact thing. But this summer has so far brought up a lot of it. I miss not striking out in front of myself, do you know what I mean?" she asked and he nodded.

"That is tough, that feeling. I can relate. Really," he said. She believed him.

"Have you ever had your heart broken?" Rosemary asked, after a pause.

"Ah, no. I don't think I would say I have. Got my feelings hurt a time or two. But nothing really ever rocked my world. If that's how you mean it, anyway," he mumbled, not sure anymore what she'd asked. He was lying.

"Have you?"

"I think the world has broken it, somehow. Before I even knew," she replied. The world didn't seem very vast. It never had. Her spaces had always been small, even during summers, all that family burdened to just one small piece of the world, and there was never anything outside of it.

"Did you really hear the cat coming?" Silas asked, looking at her. There was no more ice to break between them: they were comfortable. As he asked the question, one of her bites began to sting deeply, and she hoped she wouldn't get an infection. There were secrets though, between them. Neither of them could tell how much the other knew or felt in this place they called the woods, the lake, people, their small little town, *home*. It was so much space and yet, very contained. Silas knew Rosemary had been searching for something the very moment she spread dirt over her grandfather's coffin. His death had opened the door for her to see that there was something greater than all of this, and it could be felt, not just dreamed of. She'd always been in the fog, but now someone had turned on a light. She wanted to bask in it. In fact, it demanded to be felt. Would she be able to find its source? That was hardly guaranteed.

"I heard it before it made a sound," she replied. He nodded; it was the only sound he could hear.

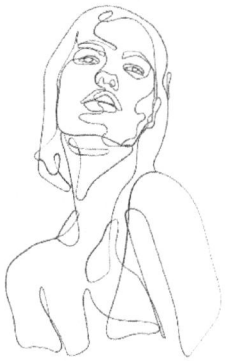

Six.

It jumped from person to person, leaving pieces of itself behind that grew.

Because James was quiet, people regarded him as calm, easy. This might have been true as a child, but a lot had happened to him since then, and there was a tipping point. His nineteenth birthday had come an exact month before his grandfather found his way into the ground. Everyone in the family still treated him as the child, and while that may have been observably true, it was no longer accurate. Something was watching everyone. It was calling out, beckoning for them to come find it. Wolfgang and Lucy felt it, deeply resonating in their chests even though they pushed it away, refusing to embrace it immediately as others had. They thought Rosemary was the closest to it, whatever was out there. They were wrong.

James was no longer taking the injustices dealt to him as personal sacrifices. He was turning them into a deep-seeded need to escape. It was a dim fire, but a hot one, and whatever was watching felt that, blowing oxygen readily to the flame. It happens sometimes, the most desperate searchers will stumble upon the wrong answers and claim it as the light that brought them home.

Everyone in the family had different ideas about what summers were like at the house they all called home. Delphine and her husband felt like it was time well spent as it made up for being abroad the rest of the year, and most of that time inaccessible. Deep down, she only half believed that to be true. Heidi enjoyed seeing her family, craving time with them, but was only able to handle small doses, prescribed seasons. Seth, again, loved Heidi. It was his mantra. Her charms had long ago bewitched him, and the best part had been her lack of effort in doing so. It left some envious, though they forgot the pain that had brought her to that point. Lewis came because he was fixated. Beth came because she was told to get in the car.

Wolfgang showed up half because he was forced into it, and half because he was worried what three months alone would look like for him. Lucy came because she enjoyed the lake the way birds do, and Rosemary always followed her sister – to the edges of the earth if need be. But Sara knew why they all really came. It was why she stayed. They could hear it. They all could. Ramone's death had started the rumbling; the echoing only growing louder. She'd felt the vibrations in every surface in her house; on the ground she stood on. Her granddaughter's screams as a rabid animal sliced away at her skin had only confirmed her feelings. She hoped her husband was safe. She hoped they'd all be.

James stayed quiet, while he listened to Wolfgang breathe heavily, sweat pouring off his body in bed as he lay under the moonlight in their room having what James recognized almost immediately as a fever dream. He didn't know what to make of it, but something in him always reminded him to be quiet and watchful. It was the only way to stay safe but also stay ahead. He never said much about what he saw.

Wolfgang's body trembled in his sleep, his lungs begging for cooler air but none seemed to be able to waft in from the open window. Heat rose, and being at the top tier of the house didn't help, no matter the breeze from the far off lake. He thought he heard growling, low howls, and the clashing of teeth and nails as if coyotes were in his room, ripping each other apart just to be the first to pounce on him. He didn't know if that were real, he couldn't open his eyes; his mind seemed too scared and threatened to vacate itself into the real world around him. Whatever was outside his body, his mind decided it wasn't worth discovery. It was like his body was high, but his mind wasn't. It continued for hours, which felt like days in his dreams. Weeks, even. He thought he heard the tapping of sharp talons on glass, but could see nothing. His dreams were auditory, never visual. It felt a lot like the rest of his life.

He woke early in the morning, his clothes and sheets soaked in sweat. He glanced over at his brother, his turn to watch him sleep. James was breathing softly in bed all curled up in blankets. He never looked softer than in the morning hours when he had finally given himself up to sleep. Wolfgang suspected it was the same for everyone, but would learn that it wasn't. Carefully, he stood up, stripping his bed and tossing the sheets into a basket. He went downstairs to shower. He always took a cold shower, even in the winter. Something about the tingling on his skin always woke him up, made him feel alive in ways nothing else in the world did. He didn't know what his constant was, but he knew it was more than just depression. They'd labeled him so early; everyone had. And while he was down more often than up, he knew that something in him was still searching for a lost piece. It was more than just depression, because he wanted it back. Whatever it was, he wanted all of it back.

He looked at himself for a long time in the mirror. He was in a constant state of trying to recognize himself. He was older now, twenty-four. He thought that might have to mean something, but all it did was make him feel the same – trapped. He studied his eyes, a brightness that shone from the rest of his darker features. He'd dyed his dirty blonde hair black all throughout high school and when he finally let it rest and the roots grew out; they'd stayed dark. Lines of ink decorated his skin in meaningless ways.

He knew when people looked at him; they expected to see all

the marks of living a hard life, of living some dark and twisted basement dwelling. But it wasn't the case. He was smooth, if not shadowed. His life hadn't been spent under the hardships of a controlling man. They'd been spent being neglected. And so, nothing had happened.

When he finally slid the bathroom's pocket door open to step out, he almost jumped back as it revealed Lucy, looking him dead in the eyes.

"Good morning," she said.

"Uh, morning," Wolfgang mumbled, squeezing past her. She hardly moved, just studied his face so directly that he felt he couldn't do anything else but let her.

"Did it happen to you too?"

"Did what?" he asked.

"You know. The dreams. Did you have one too?" she pressed, her eyes wild in her face.

"What are you asking about?" Wolfgang mumbled, trying to walk past her, away from her. Something about her certainty derailed him, making him want to go out and climb a tree and hide all day. It was what he often did.

"Stop it," she said, running up to him and pushing him, hard. He took a long look at her, but she didn't back down from her older cousin. She wasn't afraid of him; she knew whatever he could become was hardly treacherous.

"Lu…" he said softly.

"You had a dream, didn't you? I know you did, because you were in mine."

Wolfgang looked at Lucy for a moment, taking in all of her energy. Her hair was pressed against her forehead, damp. She was carrying her own sheets in her hands, a crumpled mess. Her eyes seemed wild, darting around expecting anything to rush out.

"What happened?" he asked, voice reserved. They heard footsteps on the stairs and both of them darted away from one another without another word. Lucy headed off to start a load of laundry, Wolfgang waited around the back of the staircase to head up to his shared room with his brother. They'd meet later, with no one else around. He wondered what her dream had been like; if maybe she could put images to the sounds he had heard howling in his head. He still wasn't convinced it was anything more than restless sleep on a hot summer day. In his room, James was still sleeping, still curled up in the farthest corner of his bed that touched the wall, away from the door. Because he was quiet, nobody saw all of his marks, but Wolfgang did. His brother was living a hard life and it wasn't hard to see at all.

"Mmm, hey," James mumbled sleepily when he finally woke up, half an hour later. He stretched out his body before rolling over to look at his brother, sitting awake and dressed on his stripped bed. James narrowed his eyes for a moment, noticing the missing sheets, then looked up at him.

"You're up early," he said, not ready to sit up just yet. Wolfgang shrugged, not sure if that was entirely true.

"I have no idea what time it is, but the sun is up," he replied, leaning back to look out the open window. The room was small, two beds and a dresser barely fitting in the space. They weren't used to being so close to one another, it certainly wasn't that way the rest of the year when their distance could be measure by yard after yard of silence. It didn't feel uncomfortable though; there was more a constant yearning. Invisible, thus easy to deny.

"Is everyone else awake already?" James asked.

"Maybe. I've heard some noise," he replied.

"You didn't want to go down yet?" his brother asked, looking at him with big eyes. Maybe there was something else in the room that morning, having crawled in the open window, well lit by the moon.

"Nah, you know I can't take all that noise too early," Wolfgang teased, finally standing up but not knowing where to go after he did so. James got up too, grabbing a shirt and pants before opening the bedroom door.

"Hey, has anything felt, weird around here lately?" Wolfgang asked, not sure how to phrase his question. When he was forced to use words, all his ideas seemed to vanish. His mind operated in visuals, but his dreams made him blind. He thought.

"Feels the same to me," James replied, shrugging. Wolfgang took that as an answer, but he read it entirely wrong. They walked out of the room together, Rosemary still asleep in her bed, but everyone else downstairs starting breakfast. Her mind was light and soft and easy.

In the kitchen, all the siblings and their spouses were debating how to spend their day. It had been discussed a while ago to compete in a bocce ball tournament, and because the weather was finally a little cooler, they decided today was that day.

"Kids, do you want to join us? It's going to be fun," Beth said, hoping her sons and nieces would say yes. They looked blank as they thought up excuses. They each murmured different things, and after a little back and forth, they were happy to sneak away from their parents.

Wolfgang and Lucy didn't discuss it, but somehow they both knew to meet each other at the edge of the woods by the back of the house, their parents' loud shouts and excited laughter from their tournament carrying farther than they thought. It only pushed them in deeper. The edge of the woods met them quietly, untouched by trivial games. Lucy trudged through the tall grasses slowly, making her way to the dark form that was her cousin, standing in the shadows of the trees, hardly noticeable until he moved. It startled her heart every time. She took him in as she walked up, not sure what to say. They'd never had to talk like this before, but after her own wild dreams, she knew she had to. She'd seen too much.

"Hey," she greeted, meeting him. She stood facing him, her body cast in sunlight, his shaded by hundreds of hundreds of leaves. He nodded at her, blank-faced.

"You can't act like this isn't important," Lucy said, giving him a hard look. He nearly laughed at her, but was trying his hardest not to push her away too soon. He was good at that, having someone choose to stand in limbo for him. It was something he really wished he wasn't, but continued to do, anyway.

"Important, coming from you," Wolfgang said, arms crossed. She rolled her eyes, hating the persona of her he was perpetuating, always without thought about the consequences. She knew he knew there was more to her than parties and boys. She hated that everyone forced her to prove it.

"Yeah, this summer has been far from normal. *Something* is different this year. I know it, and I know you do too. Maybe we're the idiots. Maybe Rosemary and James have known a long time now..." Lucy said, spinning off, just as more laughter erupted from their family as the game started wrapping around the house and moving into their view. Wolfgang looked out at them for a moment then tilted his head towards the woods and led Lucy in deeper. They needed privacy to have an honest conversation. Isolation removed barriers in ways they never could on their own.

"I don't know what your *something* is," Wolfgang said, a few minutes down the trail. Lucy shrugged behind him as they walked, not sure what she meant either.

"Well, so far it's just...a feeling. And I can only see it in my dreams. But my dreams aren't even that spectacular, or out of the ordinary. I can just sense that there's something in them now, creeping around. It's the only way I know how to describe it. It feels like..." she started but stopped quickly. Wolfgang stopped walking.

"Feels like what?" he asked, turning back to look at her. Lucy looked up at him, towering over her. She noticed his eyes, so bright. They were hopeful. It was why he never scared her. Hope, however fleeting, always reassures. She shivered in the heat.

"It feels like the fringe of Rosemary's dreams. It feels like her dreams are big and dark and wild and I'm standing on the edge of them. At least, last night it did," Lucy said. To her surprise, Wolfgang didn't immediately cast aside her statement. Perhaps like her, he was momentarily entertaining the idea of something largely intangible yet connective. He felt the feeling, too. Especially out there, a place as equally vast as the mind.

"You said I was in your dream?"

"Yes. Well, sort of. I saw you in the dream. It didn't feel like you were in it though," she corrected. They'd both stopped walking, just standing in a space between a few trees, the greenery wrapping them up warmly, protectively.

"Is there a difference?"

"Somehow, yeah," she replied.

"Alright, well what did you see?" he asked. Over and over in his head, he heard the howls, the scratches of nails on floorboards, slanted glass in windowsills. And still, the harder he thought, no visuals came to him. Lucy looked down at the ground.

"There was something about... dogs. I think. They weren't very physical, so they were hard to spot. It was more like, a lagging shadow. They were running everywhere and barking. And they saw you, I think. But they went right through you. Whereas James, they wouldn't go through him. They circled him," she replied, her eyes watery even though she wasn't sure why she felt so instantly sad, so horrified. Wolfgang felt the shift in her aura and didn't like it, taking a protective step back.

"James was in it too? What about Rose?"

"James, yeah. I don't know about Rose. But like I said, somehow it felt more like her dream than mine," Lucy said. For momentary sanity, she chalked it up to a twin thing.

"Don't you think if there was something more to see out here, James would have been the one to see it? He's the one whose been combing every inch of this place for years with a lunatic," Wolfgang spat, feeling resentful. Lucy stood still, knowing that her uncle and the life he cultivated for his family was full of complexities that were kept intentionally hidden. Best kept were family secrets.

"Well that's what I'm asking you. Is there something...out here? Do the dreams mean something? Is it about the woods? Is it about something else?" Lucy asked, pushing forward. She could tell that her cousin was becoming guarded the harder she pushed. She didn't care though, whatever this was now lived inside her too.

She could feel it itching away at small pieces of her soul. Did it want out? Did it want to be acknowledged?

"I don't know," Wolfgang mumbled.

"Well neither do I. What was your dream?" she pressed, exasperated.

"I don't really remember. It was really dark," he replied, rubbing his forehead and no longer meeting her eyes. Lucy had always intimidated him. She intimidated everyone. There was nothing soft about her; she was all hard edges and absolutes. She went out into the world with confidence stolen from everyone else because they fumbled with claiming it. Whatever she wanted, she sought after and gained. The idea of a barrier had never been something she'd been forced to contemplate for long. And to Wolfgang, who lived his whole life amidst unknowns and dark subtleties, he couldn't compete. He hid.

"Really? That's all?" she pushed harder.

"Really. I never said I had a dream worthwhile of this. You just came yelling at me after I took a shower," he grumbled, pushing himself even farther back from her. He knew she was getting angry with him, but he didn't know what to do with that other than hide away. People did see hope in his eyes, but he rarely looked into a mirror.

"It's a hard summer, with grandpa dying. I think we just leave it at that," he muttered, turning away from Lucy, starting to walk away. He could feel her upset.

"Really? That's all *you* have for me? Nothing about this feels off to you? Like more than just grief, more than just some dreams on a hot summer night?"

"No," he was quick to say.

"I don't believe that for a second," his cousin replied, her words tense.

"Maybe that's because you just want there to be something more," Wolfgang said, cutting his words short, but not for long. Lucy didn't know how not to push.

"What's that supposed to mean? Of all of us, I'm the least

dramatic," she said, her arms crossed, looking Wolfgang up and down in a way that was supposed to make him feel small. She succeeded, he felt thoroughly demeaned and so he laughed, looking away from her, hiding his sideways grin. It was perhaps his only viable defense.

"I don't know why you won't be honest with me. No one ever will be. What's the big secret, huh? What's everyone got to hide that's so big and dark and scary?" She was really asking. He just started shaking his head.

"You have nothing in there, do you?"

"Screw you," Lucy spat.

"Well, I'm zero for two," Wolfgang replied. Lucy thought of her sister.

"I bet she apologized immediately."

"Of course she did. And she was out here asking me the same type of questions. And you know what? It wasn't because she was standing alone on the edge of anything. Oh no, she was standing directly in the center. And I don't know that because she told me. I know it because your sister has secrets, just like everyone else. Why don't you?"

Lucy felt the sting of the last words. It was an implication, like everything else. People saw Lucy and thought she had no secrets, they saw her and thought to themselves, *what does a girl like that have to hide*? It was hindering, having people assume they knew everything, that all the cards were on the table because of a pleasant attitude or the ability to do a couple parlor tricks that wowed the crowd. It was all theatrics. She was a person too, owning a soul existing deep down in the crevices of her perfect body and it screamed too, it cried, it wailed, it rambled on and on with dark insecurities.

"I guess I just hide them better than you. Because unlike you, my secrets are secrets, and I'm not looking for someone to find them," Lucy replied. He looked at her, eyes heavy as they raced side to side. It could be a terrifying look; Wolfgang held an infinite amount of possibilities.

"You're cruel, you know that?"

"I'm being honest because you pushed," Lucy replied.

"No, you're being decidedly cruel, because I won't give you what you want," Wolfgang replied. He watched as Lucy took that in, deeply. She wanted several times to fling something quick and witty back, but bit her tongue each time. He was right.

"Why don't you trust me?" she finally asked, quietly.

"It's not about that," he said. It felt like it.

"What are we doing here?" he asked. They both looked up at the same time, remembering where they were, standing in the middle of the woods, greenery all around them. Hundreds of thousands of leaves whistling in the wind above their heads, a canopy like no other. It felt like they were alone, and it also felt like something was holding them there together, wanting the conversation to finish on a certain note.

"I don't have it in me to entertain these far-fetched theories, alright? I just don't have the energy for it," he replied, feeling that exact energy buzzing inside him. Lucy looked at him, her eyes growing sad but for once, not pitiful.

"I think you have a lot more going for you than against, Wolfgang," she said so, wanting to be decidedly kind. Her words were honest, a piece of her inner mind revealed to him. He could feel the honesty of the words, and they were hard to swallow.

"Better not throw it away," he laughed, then choked.

"So don't," Lucy begged softly, but it was too late for her cousin, who saw every act of kindness as bait. He'd never been caught in a trap, but knew he'd gnaw his leg off to crawl away before being found.

"Wolfgang, please!" Lucy shouted, her voice growing quieter, because Wolfgang was already walking away deeper into the woods. He had no idea where he was going, but the pressure he was beginning to feel was becoming too much and he needed to push it off and often for him that meant walking away.

"Think about it, Wolfgang!"

Eventually, he couldn't hear her voice at all.

Wolfgang didn't know what he felt. He didn't like to entertain ideas about a greater anything, let alone something in his backyard. He didn't believe in god, a higher purpose, or nirvana. There was no escape from life, it just finished when it did and that was the end of it. Was there a purpose? Wolfgang thought not, because the alternative meant that he was failing, that he wasn't whole like everyone else. And perhaps, that was what angered him most.

Why had the shadows moved through him, in the dream? Why had they moved around everyone else? Wolfgang didn't believe in anything greater, but he couldn't deny the energy pulsating throughout his body, growing louder with each step deeper into the woods. All it did was confirm what he feared most. He was angry.

Maybe there was something greater out there, something universally bigger. Everyone else could see it; they all seemed to feel it. And here he was, empty, blind to it all, left with nothing but the growls of creatures moving through him, not even bothering to go around his body. It was his greatest fear; being born so empty he had and would always simply be, nothing. The thought echoed.

Seven.

Rosemary offered to help her grandmother in the kitchen a few days later, for Saturday night dinner. The family was together so much over those three months of summer that they often ventured out in small groups and couples for meals. Sara insisted, however, at least once a week they all make a big dinner and feed the whole family together. Nobody could complain or push it, and often it ended up being on Saturdays. Most of the time, Rosemary couldn't stand being trapped in the kitchen. She felt like it was such a harsh place, full of heat and bloodletting and a lot of manipulative bereavement. But that evening, she was feeling a sense of complete calmness. Her grandfather had liked to cook. So that Saturday, with his face in her mind, she wandered into the kitchen and started carving up potatoes. At first the two women worked in silence, neither quite sure of one another. They were very alike, but used their similarities in opposite ways. They seemed unrecognizable to an untrained eye, but to Ramone, he had always seen the way their eyes glittered the same, how they moved in step, and how they muttered the same little phrases under their breath. Bursts of magic, here and there. He'd always smiled seeing them together.

Eventually, the two women started talking. It started out simply about the food, what to start preparing next, and the oven rotation schedule. Then it drifted to little tips on how to adjust the heat and when, what herbs to add for a little extra flavor or create the right type of atmosphere. Perhaps how to cure an illness with onions. Or remedy a broken heart with a little extra garlic, followed by a little thyme. There were always a few whispers about how to keep the dead buried, and how to set out a pie by a shaded windowsill to bring about good memories and happy tidings. There were questions about knives to use, and the right occasion. When to wash your hands with soap, and when to rub them clean with salt. Lucy would walk through the kitchen sometimes, grabbing a slice of warm bread without being able to wait and laughing about superstitions and black cats. When she'd leave, Rosemary and her grandmother would share a look, knowing the cats sometimes showed up white and brown with their fangs out.

Eventually, others would join in the kitchen and help finish cooking. They'd talk and laugh, but Rosemary and Sara always stepped together and apart perfectly in tune with one another, never raising their eyes from their work. Sara had cast away the word a long time ago, but Rosemary had never seemed to shy away. Her eyes always held wonder, no matter who tried to snatch it from her. It was what it was, that's what Ramone would tell her every time she was scared. Then he'd give her a small and sometimes wilted wildflower, pulled from the depths of his pockets, under a disapproving look from his wife.

"The world isn't sweet, Ramone."

"It can be."

Beth didn't like the family's cilantro rice, it always tasted bitter. She wouldn't even touch the bowl, instead carrying the plate of chicken into the dining room, placing it just so at the head of the table where her husband now sat, the eldest male. She looked around for both her sons, but only found one.

"Where's your brother?"

"He went out a while ago, said he'd be back," James replied with a shrug. In truth, Wolfgang had stormed out after breaking a couple bottles in the barn. James hadn't known what to do, but at least he knew to slightly cover for him. Lucy eyed him, taking a sip of her pre-dinner glass of wine. He shied away from her intensity.

"You don't know where he went?" she asked him, out in the parlor. The spirits of the dead seemed ever-present in that room, her skin shivering. Her voice was low, because she wasn't a snitch. He shook his head.

"I really don't. But he was mad earlier, I'm not sure what about this time," he replied, wishing he had his own glass of wine to sip. Lucy nodded, thinking something over. She wandered away from her youngest cousin, peeping into the kitchen to watch Rosemary finish the last touches on the side of roasted vegetables for the table. She hadn't talked to her about any of her ideas yet. Part of her was fearful Rosemary would think she was insane for trying to say some cosmic force was calling her name from out in the hills of the woods. But, perhaps a bigger part of her was worried that Rosemary wouldn't think it was a wild thing to say at all. To be substantiated made Lucy quiver. Her world was easily conquerable, because she could see everything that lay in it. But this new sense of energy, drawing her out, drawing all her family out there didn't make logical sense. It frightened her. She'd never remembered a dream before in her life, and this one she couldn't forget.

"Are you okay? Do you know something about Wolfgang's mood?" James pushed, coming back over to her, watching her eyes dart back and forth as they contemplated a response.

"No, not really," she replied. James hated the lie.

"Really?"

"Mmm, I don't really know. We've both just been having some bad dreams lately. Maybe someone poisoned the water," Lucy teased tilting her head back as she said it then walked off to refill her wine glass before dinner. She left James feeling ignored, and it wasn't uncommon at all. Moments later, Sara called everyone to the table and after she took her seat, they all took theirs.

"Pass the potatoes, would you?"

"Does anyone want more than one piece of chicken for now? There's plenty of it."

"God, who salted this?"

"I'm so glad it cooled down this evening, it's been one of the hottest weeks I can ever remember up here."

"That's a lot of bread, why don't you have something to go with that?"

"Yeah buddy, put something red on that plate!"

"Did anyone want to go to the docks tomorrow? It might be a good lake day."

"Maybe. We have to go to town anyway, there isn't much food left."

"Wow, this rice is delicious. Have some?"

"No, no thank you."

"Come on, don't hold out."

"Rose, have you seen Wolfgang?"

"What are you whispering down there?"

"Nothing."

"Wolfgang? Where is Wolfgang?"

Lucy was sorry she'd asked her sister, but she knew they'd notice the empty chair eventually. The table quieted for a moment, everyone's eyes darting from Lewis to Sara, shooting over to Beth, occasionally James, and back to Lewis. The upset was palatable, and wherever Wolfgang was, he could probably feel it too.

"Missing again, huh?" Lewis muttered, ripping apart his meat and chewing loudly. There wasn't much else to say.

"Kids are always on adventures," Delphine cut in, the least bit concerned about her nephew's disappearance. She didn't find his lack of companionship all that alarming.

"He's not a kid anymore," Lewis reminded. Delphine laughed.

"If twenty-four isn't a kid, then how old are we really?" she asked, genuinely curious what her brother thought. She was like Lucy, in the way that nothing intimidated her from asking the question. It was why she was such a good journalist, and why she had given her parents such a hard time as a child. Everything had to be negotiated, understood, leveled. Her brother didn't scare her, either. But maybe he should have. Somehow, she always knew to dodge any lashes.

"You wouldn't know how to parent a child, you're never home to do it," he said, trying to quickly cut her short. It was violent, but his sister was used to the fire. Delphine didn't miss a step. A sibling feud was nothing compared to the wars she'd run through.

"And yet my girls are here, making the food and wiping your dish afterward," she replied. Henry touched her leg under the table gently with his hand. Her eyes were fire, but Lewis's were smoke. She'd been dealing with her brother the longest and something in him had always reached deep inside her heart and squeezed.

"Heidi gets the credit on that one, not you," he shot.

"Maybe. Not much a defense for you, though," his sister replied.

"Enough of that," Sara cut in, no longer appreciating the route they were taking. Sometimes she'd let the fighting go on, especially if she could jump in with her own jab, but this particular quarrel never went anywhere. They'd all heard it several times.

"Pass the breadbasket, would you, James?" Seth asked, sticking his neck out to try and change the topic of conversation. He never seemed to realize he would always end up the sacrifice, even after all this time.

"Oh, the bread, Seth? You need the bread right now?" Lewis asked, grabbing a roll from the basket and tossing it to his brother-in-law who missed the throw, the bread making a thud as it hit the floor. Delphine rolled her eyes at the show.

"Lew, c'mon. We're just trying to have dinner," Heidi interjected, as her husband crawled over to grab the roll from under the side table in their dining room. He got it eventually.

"Don't I know it. Butter, Seth? Do you need some butter with that bread?" Lewis continued, his face begging for applause.

"Why are you always like this?" Heidi asked, exasperated. Lewis laughed at his little sister, always giving up too quickly, always begging for it to stop before it even really started. He'd pulled her hair plenty of times growing up. He hadn't known what he'd been doing then, but he did now. And maybe, he liked it.

"Beth, *gently* hand Seth the butter, would you? He's a bad catch," Lewis said, his opinions rotting even the smallest of phrases. He elbowed his wife as she tensely grabbed the tray of butter and handed it to Seth who flashed a sad and sincere smile at her. It only sent the hair on Lewis's neck up higher.

"Is the butter too cold, Seth? Do you need my wife to – " Lewis went on. Lucy had long ago stopped listening to the adults and their fighting. It was childish, but never in the ways her sister and cousins bickered. Maybe they'd already seen too much. James felt his mother's tension, and sat beside her wishing he knew what to do to make it stop. He thought the darkness in the living room moved, but every time his eyes would rise quickly to check, it was still.

Rosemary heard the phone ring first and jumped up to answer it. She heard people saying she could leave it, but she insisted. Anything to get up and take a breath. She rushed into the kitchen over to the old mint-colored landline on the wall. The cord had long ago lost its bounce, now nearly hanging on the floor.

"Hello?" she answered, slightly hesitant. Rosemary heard a whooshing sound, a grateful sigh of relief from whoever was calling.

"Rose? Hey. Thank god it's you. I really thought no one was going to answer, then I realized no one might be better than someone. But you're the right lady for this," an extremely familiar voice teased and Rosemary felt her brows narrow in confusion.

"Wolfgang?" she asked timidly. He laughed.

"The one and only. Having a nice family dinner?" he asked conversationally. She nodded even though he couldn't see;

surprised he even remembered it was happening.

"It's just fine. What number is this?" she asked.

"Listen, I need you to come pick me up in a few hours. And you need to bring two hundred and fifty dollars cash, please. Think you can manage to get that clunker into town?" he asked. Rosemary was trying to understand. He sounded sickly chipper, which usually meant someone was listening to him and he wanted to get under their skin. Something was wrong. This wasn't the kind of involvement her cousin usually went for with his antics on display.

"Uh, yes. Okay. What's going on though? Where are you?" Rosemary asked, a bit of worry creeping into her voice. She couldn't help it. She felt like she knew the answer before he even spoke.

"Yeah, I'm at the jail right now," he casually replied, almost whistling his words like a bad tune.

"You're in prison?" she asked with disbelief, her voice getting high at the last syllable.

"Prison? Who are you talking to that's in prison?" Rosemary heard another voice mirror equal disbelief and turned to see her mother standing in the doorway with her plate in hand. Rosemary just shook her head, laughing it off.

"No, no, it's a joke. Sorry," she mumbled, moving into the pantry. The cord was long enough.

"Oh, is that Aunt Delphine? Is she proud of my life choices? Maybe she can do a piece on me," Wolfgang snickered as Rosemary peeked back around the corner to see her mother looking at her worried, but carrying the cake out to the table anyway.

"You're in prison?" She repeated, her voice lacking any color.

"Jail. I am in jail. C'mon Rose, prison is where the real criminals go," he replied, his voice so carefree she hoped he wasn't giving up. He did that sometimes, care so little that he just began wandering around, saying anything, all lax.

"Why are you in jail? What did you do? Are you okay?"

Rosemary rambled quickly, suddenly feeling like they were running out of time.

"Alright, this isn't exactly a metropolitan area. Listen, I really need you to come down here with that money. I'm using my one phone call on you. Please make sure that I am not wasting my one phone call on you," he replied, quite seriously. Rosemary snorted.

"That's just offensive," she teased, a little forcefully. If he didn't want to waste a phone call, maybe he wasn't giving up. She hoped deeply that he wasn't.

"Mhm. See you soon, cousin. Have fun with the family. Sorry I couldn't make it, you know I'd die to be there. I'm a great instigator," he mocked. Rosemary didn't want to push, but she thought about saying how that was just like his father.

"Be safe," she whispered.

"A little late for that," he said, his voice going cold by the end. Rosemary opened her mouth to say more, but was greeted by the click of the phone being disconnected. One phone call, over. She looked up, seeing everyone looking out at her through the doorway. She sighed heavily, taking a moment to decide what she would say before going back to the table.

"What was that all about?" Lucy asked, looking concerned. Rosemary shrugged, sitting back down at the table. She could see the dessert had already been brought out, and helped herself to a slice of cake.

"Just a stupid idea of a joke," she lied.

"What were you guys talking about?" she asked the table, biting into the soft cake, looking around and waiting for someone to continue. Eventually, someone did.

Dinner ended better than it started, and because Rosemary had cooked and she had a twin to help clean, she was able to steal away upstairs. She knew where the money was, all four of them did. They'd started their own little bank years ago, for more innocent things like candy and meaningless celebrity magazines. These summers they spent their collection of cash on drugs, alcohol, and sometimes birth control. Apparently, it was also bail money.

Rosemary slid her fingers over the old tin container as she brought it up from under the floorboards in their bedroom. It was rusty, but still had a visible image of two women dancing on the front, the letters of words almost lost amongst the red paint of their dresses. Everyone contributed to it, and no one ever questioned how much was taken or how it was used. There was enough for the bail, and plenty remaining. Rosemary never thought to wonder how it truly accumulated so much, deep down in the dusty flooring of her bedroom.

She shoved the money into her bag, walking over to her shared dresser for the keys. The old car was just another member of the family, free for any youth to use. Ramone had liked it that way, always figuring it helped entice family to stay for long summers if they had even the smallest amounts of freedom given to them before it had ever been taken away. He hadn't been wrong. She reached for the keys, and found a small and delicate wildflower laid next to them. Rosemary paused. She hadn't received a gift like that all summer. She thought this summer was going to be her first without the random small gifts, but maybe she'd been wrong all along who'd been placing them. Was that possible?

There didn't seem to be time to ponder it any longer. Without another thought, she ran her fingers over the velvety petals of the flower, noticing its deep purple hues. It was her favorite. Carefully, she walked down the flights of stairs, sneaking out the back before anyone noticed amongst all the chaos. Her family always grew loud, so loud that the sound of the car starting and rolling down the hill wasn't heard by anyone. She didn't turn the lights on until she was completely down the hill, almost off family land. Once she hit the road, the lights went on and she felt completely transported to a different place. The dark trees that boarded the sides of the street into town didn't wave the same as the ones in her woods. She shook her head, wanting to be free of those thoughts for a night. Going into town usually did that for her, because town was a part of the world, even if it was small. The Pennyfathers' land seemed to be its own entity entirely; maybe that was why she'd cherished every summer. A place away from a place.

There were parts of the town that remained how they had always been, but now the mostly vacation season driven city was filled with modern stores, small boutiques, and franchise ice cream stores. On the fringes of the town lines were still small stores filled with people Sara knew well. But the rest of it was created for people like Lucy, who felt less on the outskirts of the world with a mall so close. Rosemary grew a little sadness in her heart when she passed by the small stand she and her grandfather had gotten ice cream and farm vegetables at all on the same trip.

Driving through it that night, she didn't stop to take in too much of the town. She was just trying to remember exactly what street the police station was on, and when she finally found it, realized it hadn't grown young like most of the town; it had stayed old.

Rosemary's headlights flashed through the parking lot as she pulled into a spot far from the glass door and parked. For a moment she sat still, looking up at the large brick walls of the building. She didn't want to go inside, she felt very unsure of what she'd be going into. Her cousin hadn't even said what he'd done. After a few deep breaths, her chest settling back into a normal routine, she grabbed the money and shoved it into her pocket and got out of the car quickly before she had to battle her mind anymore. She walked into the small office with purpose, though as soon as the officer behind the desk looked up at her, she lost most of her momentum.

"What can I do for you?" the man asked. He looked tired as he spoke, the words simply falling out of his mouth.

"I'm here to pick someone up," she mumbled, taking a few steps closer to the counter. He studied her for a moment before looking over slowly to his computer. It was another long minute before he said anything else.

"Name?" he asked.

"Wolfgang Pennyfather," she replied. His eyes glistened as he typed in the name and a few other things, yawning before looking back at Rosemary. He was trying to seem casual, but there was something about her that he found unnerving. He could tell she was nervous to be there, and young. There didn't seem a threat. But then again, something about the way she stood in the room made it seem like they weren't the only two present. He rolled his shoulders back, trying to push the feeling away.

"There's a bail of 250 dollars. Are you prepared to pay that in full now?" he asked. She nodded, grabbing the crumpled money out of her pocket and setting it on the counter. He took a moment to count it, a variety of bills before him, then wrote out a receipt and stapled it to a document he printed.

"Make sure he gets this. Wait over there, he'll be out in a moment," the officer said. She nodded her thanks and went over to the back wall and took a seat. There was another length of uncomfortable silence. She could feel the man's eyes on her, but it wasn't in the usual way. He seemed tense, like her presence was creating something uncomfortable in the dingy waiting room of the small police station. The space felt less than lonely. She didn't have too long to ponder why, because Wolfgang was released through the side door soon enough, and his presence often took up an incredible amount of space when he wanted it to.

"Alright, end of the rope for us my man," Wolfgang said, his eyes lighting up when he saw Rosemary. She stood up. She tried to see how they might view her cousin, tall and solid, sarcastic and bitter. Did they think he was worthless? That he was just another problem? Did they find him dangerous at all? He could be, she knew. But he never wanted to be. That had to count for something. She watched as he turned around for the officer who'd brought him through to uncuff him.

"Don't be a smartass. Make some better choices," the man grumbled, pushing him forward with harsh intent. Rosemary knew her cousin has probably been yelling back there for hours about the injustices of the world against him. Everyone was probably sick of him, but that was the game Wolfgang had learned to embrace. He

was a malignant force, or so he thought. So the world around him
had made him think.

"Yeah, I'll pick a different bridge next time. Later," he said,
giving him a two-finger salute before wrapping his arm around
Rosemary's shoulders and pushing her outside with him. He cursed
a little under his breath, out of annoyance.

"Does anyone know you're here?" he pressed as they walked
up to the old beater. It was like a warm hello from an old friend as
he slid into the passenger side, waiting for Rosemary to get in and
shut her door. He cranked the window down for a breeze.

"No, but I can't say they haven't noticed I'm gone by now,"
she replied, being honest. He shrugged like that part didn't matter,
pulling an old carton of cigarettes out from under the seat. He
turned to Rosemary for a lighter, and she fished it out of the door
and handed it to him. He was quiet for a moment as he smoked.
Rosemary just watched him, not driving. He looked upset; like
none of this had been the big fun time he liked to portray.
Truthfully, Wolfgang wasn't a comic by any stretch of the
imagination, and his humor fell on the ears of those who always
wanted him to conform. He didn't know another way of protest.
About halfway through the cigarette, he looked over at Rosemary.
He thought she was too good for all of them.

"Thanks for picking me up."

"Of course."

"Thanks for answering the phone."

She started up the car and backed out of the parking spot
carefully, then pulled out onto the dark road and headed back
through town, around the lake, then up the hills with wide
expanses of both land and woods. Everything seemed quiet as she
drove, the world very still except for the sounds of water lapping at
the beach and the wind that flew past their car. It was as if they
were very alone, together.

"I don't know how to say it, but something is different this
summer," Wolfgang said, breaking their silence. She'd felt him
tense up before he said it, nervous to become real for a moment.

Rosemary didn't know what to say. She'd never felt such openness between them, a place so free of judgment or preconceived notions. She knew what he was trying to say, but still felt too fearful to simply agree. He had to say it first, all of it.

"Well, things are different this summer," she started but he cut her off. He couldn't deal with any more formalities that night. He'd had enough of them. He wanted to say what he meant and he wanted Rosemary to understand that. He wanted everyone to, really, but chose her first. She was the way in.

"This doesn't have anything to do with the funeral. Or maybe it does, I don't know because I don't know how to explain what I'm feeling. But there is something… out there. Something is out there, and everyone can feel it. I can see it on their faces. And I know you know this too because I don't think your dreams are just dreams," he said, looking at her desperately as he talked. She remained focused on the road, not breaking her eye contact from the pavement as they sped down the two-lane highway alone. She wanted to take the bait, but Wolfgang could be cruel sometimes.

"You're talking crazy," she whispered.

"Crazy is a circle," he said.

"What did you get caught doing tonight?" she asked. He breathed in heavily, but had already decided to drop all pretenses.

"Vandalism. Nothing too upsetting," he replied.

"Why?" she asked. He didn't know what she meant.

"Why? Why did I do it? Why do I do anything I do? Because I felt like it," he said, leaning back in his seat and changing his view from her to the road in front of them. It truly felt like they were the only ones out there, surrounded by tall walls of trees and the biggest, blackest sky.

"Why'd you do it?" she asked again. There was something different about the way she said it that time. It almost broke Wolfgang's heart. She wasn't asking because she was mad about it, or being protective of herself. She wasn't asking because she was disappointed or frustrated and defaulting to the common, *you're something else* everyone placed on him. She was asking for something much larger from him than to practice more civil obedience.

"Do you know what happened in my dream last night?" he asked, voice stone cold.

"I didn't know you had a dream," she replied, glancing over at him. He nodded.

"It wasn't actually my dream. It was yours, and I was just a part of it. And Lucy watched it happen because it wasn't her dream either. And she saw some wild things happening. But for me, I could only hear it. Wherever I was, wherever I'm going, it's just...nothing. A whole lot of nothing. And I have to wake up to that every single morning," he said. His voice didn't break once, but Rosemary didn't know if that made her feel better or worse. She took her eyes off the road for a moment to look at him carefully; wanting him to really see the light she knew was there. He only saw it reflect off her.

"You're not going nowhere," she whispered. It was almost too late. He didn't really care.

"Are you admitting there's something?" he asked.

"Somewhere," she replied.

As the words left her, a huge crack of lightning brilliantly illuminated the sky above them, splintering out into many small arms before disappearing back into the darkness of the sky. Rosemary and Wolfgang were mesmerized, quiet. Another fissure followed, louder and brighter than before, the entire sky cracking and showing daylight before closing back up again. There were a few more splits of lightning before eventually settling down, disappearing from view. They stayed quiet.

Neither of them had ever seen lightning before in an absolute cloudless sky.

Eight.

"What are you all doing today?"

The four of them looked at one another, not sure what to say. They were doing something; it had been a long time coming. Somehow, secrets passed through walls and windows, they each had agreed to meet and talk about the enigmatic thing that was happening to all of them. It was a feeling, at the very least.

"Maybe head down to the lake, jump off the cliffs if we need a little adrenaline," Lucy said, giving Heidi a broad smile as she nodded, only half accepting the answer. She knew when her nieces were lying to her, but didn't hold resentment for it.

"Sounds fun," she replied simply, looking over each one of her nieces and nephews. They seemed harrowed by something, but she decided not to press it, especially as Delphine walked into the kitchen looking for coffee. Whatever they were up to, they didn't want to be interviewed about it.

"Morning," Delphine said, grabbing her cup of coffee and taking several gulps as she leaned against the counter next to her sister. Everyone nodded their greetings.

"Quiet bunch this morning," she commented, leafing through the papers on the kitchen island and finding the newspaper she'd ordered specifically for her three-month stay at her parents' home. Service was spotty at best, and while that was nothing new to her, she didn't want to miss out on any events or spectacles happening in the world. Constant communication had only sped things up, but it wasn't ever something Delphine shied away from. She liked the constant motion. It gave her no time to dwell, only the drive for action.

Eventually, she wandered out to the front porch and sat on the old swing with her husband, reading through the different articles together and talking their usual politics and science. Sometimes, in the earliest parts of the morning, they'd talk about each other, what was inside. But none of that was left for daylight. Heidi left minutes later to change into workout clothes and make a run to town with Seth, both eager to continue their training for their next marathon. It was something Lewis teased her relentlessly about, even though he was no stranger to hard work for a mostly self-serving cause.

The cousins found themselves alone, if not for a moment. None of them really wanted to be the first to break the silence, agreeing to talk about the feeling most were still in denial about. They were surprised by who did break that everlasting silence.

"So, what's going on?" James asked, looking out at everyone. However it had worked out, conscious or not, he was often the one on the fringe of their group. Family was never chosen, and something about him had kept him separated from the others early on. Sometimes, he felt he was marked by his father's interest. Other times, he just felt he didn't drink as much as they did. He didn't know what they wanted to talk about, but he could see it on their faces.

"Just wait 'til we get out there," Wolfgang said, standing up and putting his breakfast plate in the sink. James took a last bite of egg before following suit. His brother had been acting strangely for a few days now; it was impossible not to notice. He wasn't sure what was haunting him. Quickly, the girls finished their toast and eggs, rinsing off their dishes and putting them in the dishwasher before turning around and heading out the side door, towards the back. They had considered climbing up into the hayloft to talk, but the woods seemed the more obvious choice. It wanted them there.

They walked a fair way out in silence. It never hurt, to be quiet in the woods. It was beautiful, an uneven landscape filled with greenery and the threat of a short cliff down to the lake, or just trails and trails of small footpaths leading out for miles, hardly ever seeing sky. As they walked, James trailed behind, familiar with all of it. He had spent the most time out in the woods, feeling comfortable enough to almost walk with his eyes closed. His father had instilled in him that ease among a great set of trees. It was woven deeply with the need to protect it at all costs. Still, he wasn't sure what the threat was that his father saw, but he had grown up with the fear. Now, to him, it didn't seem as if it could be anything other than real.

"Is there a certain spot you're trying to get to?" James called up to the front. Wolfgang shook his head, but didn't say anything more about it. They kept walking.

Perhaps there was something to feel out there in the trees. It wasn't like James had never noticed it before. But he'd never said anything about it, mostly because the feeling came when he was out with his father, wandering the darkness, having ghost stories told to him as if they weren't fairytales. And, it had always seemed as if no one else wanted to know. Their silence kept him silent. Everyone knew Lewis was harsh, and something about that generalization kept people from asking any other questions. They thought that because they knew he was harsh, that was all there was to know. But it wasn't. James knew a lot more than just harshness.

He lagged behind the others. It wasn't intentional, it was just exhausting being as observant as he was used to being. He'd been trained to look out for everything. And sometimes, he saw something. It wasn't anything he could put into words; those experiences weren't for life outside of the woods. But every so often, if he was looking very hard, he'd see what he only knew as shadows running through the woods. Dark, amorphous forms racing between trees, chasing one another under heavy brush, or sometimes creeping close and staying as still as they could for a look to see who was traipsing through their land. At first, he'd feared them. Considered their sighting observable evidence of his father's insanity passed on to him. No one else seemed to see them and when they ran around, it was more in play than a hunt.

"James, are you coming or what?" Lucy yelled for him, having noticed how far he'd fallen behind. The shadows whizzed under small plants along the trail, hiding, evaporating.

"Yeah, I'm on my way," he called back. He blinked, and they were always gone. He jogged up the hill for a few moments to catch up and meet them. They'd found a spot to sit, their usual place among the boulders that were deeply embedded into the earth, their large exposed surfaces only the smallest pieces of them. No one wanted to be the first to sit, so eventually, Wolfgang did out of spite. All it meant was that he wouldn't be the first to talk.

"Alright, what is this?" James asked. The girls looked at each other, then him.

"We don't really know," Lucy started to say. James looked at her, brows furrowed. They weren't very good liars.

"All this secrecy about…nothing?" he asked.

"Well it's not nothing, it's something. We just don't know what, yet," Rosemary tried to explain, but wasn't sure where exactly the starting line was. James looked at both of them, then his brother. He was already staring deeply at James, almost daring him to dismiss this. He didn't know what James knew, but he had grown up in the same household. He knew there were secrets.

"Alright…what makes you feel like there's something to talk about?" James asked, playing along. He was trying to be diplomatic, but also some part of him he hadn't known existed was bubbling up, demanding he hide anything that he knew, that any words out of his mouth would be death. That was always the fear, wasn't it? Death as a finality, as a consequence.

"Well. Rosemary's dreams, for starters," Lucy said, glancing down at her sister, forever protective of her. Nobody knew how to touch the statement. They'd all heard about her spells of nothingness, and no one wanted to be the person to tip her back into it. For some reason, no one ever protected her secrets, so she had to create large expanses to hold them all on her own.

"What about them?" James asked. He was starting to feel nervous.

"They've just been different since being here. And I…I'm not sure how to explain it exactly. But the first night we were here, I had a dream that was out of body. My whole body experienced it. It was like a raging fever tore me apart, and then put me back together again before the sun rose. But differently. I feel different," Rosemary said, her voice growing unsteady by the end of her explanation. To put it into words was to truly claim the experience, and she didn't want to sound disturbed.

"I had a dream too. I couldn't see anything, but I could hear howling. And my body felt torn apart, and when I woke up I felt different. I still do," Wolfgang said, quickly throwing his experience under Rosemary's words to support her. He suspected she felt it all much deeper than he did, but still, it was there. He was a part of it. James looked at the two of them, then Lucy.

"You too?" he asked.

"Yes. I haven't felt torn apart, but I keep seeing these flashes of moments. I don't know what they mean. It's a brilliant light, and there's howling and it's painful but also really beautiful. I think it's the fringe of her dreams," Lucy said, tossing her head towards Rosemary who was sitting on one of the boulders next to Wolfgang. Neither James nor Lucy had resigned to sitting yet.

"Have you not had any dreams?" Lucy asked, desperate.

"No." James shook his head.

"And there was the cat, too," Rosemary threw in. Everyone glanced down at her legs, recovering but brazen with scratches and the marks of healing punctures. The wounds were still pink and bright.

"What about the cat?" James asked.

"I'd heard it in a dream somehow, and I knew it was coming before it did. I can't explain it, I just feel like I know things now. I can feel them as they start to think about happening. Does that make sense? There's just this feeling around here. We all feel it, you really don't?" Rosemary asked, almost exasperated. No one wanted to admit it, but they all felt that James was the one they needed to validate these feelings. He was the one who would know if something was truly out there.

"I can't say I feel anything differently..." he stopped talking. They were all looking at him so earnestly. He didn't even know what he was trying to protect, but he felt suddenly on display. His body turned to its familiar feeling of being cut open and bleeding for someone else to find something they wanted. Their need for him to join them only caused him to shut down deeper into himself and think. It was a maladaptive trait.

"Grandma has always been superstitious. And what about our parents, when they were younger? They have all kinds of stories about the woods and doing certain things. I mean think of...well, you know. And last night, Wolfgang and I saw lightning but there wasn't a single cloud in the sky," Rosemary pressed on. James looked at her deeply, trying to be empathetic but he just found that his eyes were beginning to go blurry.

"I don't know what you want me to say. If there's something you're all feeling, I'm not denying it. I just can't say I have..." he stopped.

"Really? You can't say you have?" Wolfgang stood up as he asked the question. Everyone felt the shift, like the pressure had bottomed out. It was so instantaneous; hardly anyone had a chance to react, to push the anger back into the box. Lucy started shaking her head slightly but it was too late, he wasn't going to listen to subtleties.

"You're going to stand here and tell them, tell *us*, that we're all crazy for this? You live with crazy. Tell them what dad says, if you have nothing of your own to contribute. Go on, tell them what he's training you for. What all your little father-son camping trips are *really* about." Wolfgang was pushing, and pushing hard. James couldn't meet his eyes, but his whole body wanted to lash out at him. He was so much bigger than James, it would never hold. But he wanted to.

"You don't even know what you're talking about," James finally muttered.

"You're right, I have no idea. Fill in the blanks for me," Wolfgang replied. It was almost cruel, the way he spoke. Utterly dismissive, though it was because he was defensive. He sounded disgusted with even the mere possibility of being told anything, because he thought he knew it all. He had a hard time realizing that he wasn't the only one suffering. He thought he was in a box with no windows. Maybe he was. But he couldn't fathom how his brother felt with open skies and open land and nowhere safe to lean against. The girls didn't move, just looked at the two brothers, two very different forces.

"There's nothing to say. He's just a mean old man who feels better out in the woods than around other people. He's fucked up. We all know it, they know that," James replied, waving his hand at his cousins. He was right to a degree; they weren't naïve. They'd seen his mood swings, heard his angry taunts. Everyone knew about his obsessive nature. They blamed the screaming on the liquor. But they didn't hear anything more than what they saw, so like most people, they didn't ask. Wolfgang wasn't accepting it though; he wanted more. He said his next words with malice, because he wanted an answer and had learned that's one of the only ways to get one.

"Yeah, but what is he saying?" he asked.

"What is he having you do?"

James had to go to a different place. He thought about the first time he'd had to go to a different place. There were always going to be things that he'd keep a secret. But maybe it didn't have to be everything.

The first time, he'd heard it before he'd seen it. Scuffling behind him had caused him to spin around, catching a full glimpse of an animal he had chased before it vanished into darkness. Doglike, and eerily and obviously not alive. The term monster had risen in his mind, but it hadn't scared him. What were the places he went with his father anyway? Were they real? What existed there?

He'd been in awe, mostly interested. It was something to focus on, distract him. Time had passed, and he didn't see anything for a long time. Hope had filled him though, and he had felt if he just concentrated hard enough and waited, maybe he'd see another. And he did. He saw quite a few. All different, most resembling dogs. They were unlike anything he'd ever known before. All black, with bright eyes and silky bodies that moved in ways unimaginable. They had no hard edges, no solid parts.

Bright, green and yellow eyes.

That first time was the day James had felt he had finally figured out what there was in life, and that was darkness. They kept going out into the woods, and he didn't always see them. His father never did. He was looking so hard, but they never showed up for him. After an exceptionally hard trip, with watery eyes and an unlit night, James finally reached out and touched one of the shadows. His skin had felt icy and cold, but there wasn't any pain attached. For a while, there seemed to be nothing more than seeking out those things only he could see. It was his life. Everything else was background noise. James was numb, but he didn't want to be. He just had to go somewhere else.

After a while, he began to see them all the time. He learned about them. They got closer to him. He began to rely on seeing them, giving him some type of high so he could be anywhere other than where he was. They changed though, as everything does. He'd been drawn into this new place, and it wasn't somewhere meant for escape. For a moment, he wanted to. Then, he surrendered. The shadows were mad, they growled and barked. And one night, they didn't leave. They stayed.

It was a night that changed him. It showed James that everything was real, whether he wanted it to be or not. Existence was an eternal membership, not a sideshow club. This was his life.

It was a night he felt wild, seeing things, black forms that would run up and push him down, then dart away. All those eyes glittering out from behind trees staring at him. Whenever he'd move, they'd come back out and push him down again. He wasn't special; he wasn't allowed to do what they couldn't. It was the first time he'd felt so pushed down that he'd broken through another side. And there was something in the woods, underlying it all. Maybe it was old, something that had always been there but was just now becoming awake. James remembered he'd wanted to scream. He never did.

He always woke up, sunlight streaming into the woods. No monsters or shadows, just his father cooking bacon over a campfire, eyes averted. That had been the day, when he felt different. He felt the weight of it every day. Darker, more attuned. There was a new look to his eyes, one he couldn't stare back at for very long in a mirror. People noticed, he thought, but they didn't care enough to really see what it was. James had realized early on that almost everyone wanted things to be okay so badly; they accepted blindness as a shield from seeing extraordinary things. It was a game, where everyone had a motive, to gain the most by hurting the most. James always tried to figure out people before they could know him. That way, when it came time to push him over, he was already a step ahead, hiding in the shadows, hoping they'd walk right past. And then, maybe he'd be able to breathe.

Wolfgang repeated himself.

"What's he saying? What is he having you do?"

"A rift," James said, looking up.

"He doesn't know it, but he's looking for a rift."

Nine.

An hour away, there was a city. Every Friday night, a club downtown hosted different performances to draw in new crowds. Lucy's friends from the lake had invited her to go and she had readily accepted the invitation. She always would have, but she eagerly did so because she wanted to be far away from any ideas about a rift. Instead, she preferred to be close and personal with her chosen perception of the real world as she thought it was. If only it were that easy.

She'd invited her sister to come along. And somehow, Beau had run into James at the store in town, recognized him, and insisted he come along too. He'd agreed; it was nearly impossible to decline an invitation Beau presented. Out of anxiety, he'd seen Silas working on patching a hole in the pole barn and talking to Rosemary, and had invited him along as well. Somehow, he'd also agreed with little hesitation. Wolfgang heard the talk and purposely created a space where no one would ask him to come and he was happy when they didn't; he was tired of dashing all the hope.

Rosemary stared at herself for a long time in the mirror before getting into the car. She didn't understand how the group they'd gotten together had formed, and she wasn't entirely sure if it was all that great of an idea. She was nervous to be out in the world and every time she thought of Liam she found herself digging her thumbnail underneath the skin of her forefinger's nail, deep. She already knew how it would go. Lucy would be off, partying in an effortless and natural way. James and Silas would stick together. And Rosemary would be left looking down at the dance floor, or possibly on it, alone. She couldn't believe this was what she was worried about.

"You look so cool," Lucy said, walking into their room to grab her small purse to store a couple items. She looked her sister up and down, admiring the way her long sleeve dress fit, appreciating her boots, and wishing she could wear blue and gold glittering eye shadow and look ethereal.

"I don't know about that," Rosemary mumbled. Her sister smiled.

"Good thing I do," she replied. Rosemary threw her phone, keys, and cash into a small sequenced bag and followed her sister down the steps. She almost forgot her ID, then stopped to take one last look in the mirror. She didn't know if she felt like herself, but she did feel good about who she was looking at on the reflective surface. Was it even her? She wasn't sure if mirrors worked in dreams. She was over pinching herself awake; it hardly worked anymore. Instead, she would just ride it out, see if anything other than airplanes and birds could fly. Her chest ached from nerves, from people and places whizzing by her, from needing a drink.

The girls said goodbye to a few family members, then met the boys out on the porch. Lucy was excited and welcoming when she saw Silas, giving him a warm hug before having everyone follow her out to the car. Silas flashed Rosemary a small smile as they walked, getting into the backseat with James and giving her shotgun.

The whole drive downtown, Lucy chattered away and had the music up loud in the car. She was excited to be away from the house, the land, the small town, even the lake. She wanted to be in a dirty city, a dirty club, and dance dirty. Rosemary couldn't get it out of her head that none of it mattered.

After they'd left the woods that day, speaking their feelings into existence, they'd talked more about what James meant when he said a rift, after he had cooled off from Wolfgang's harshness. When it was darker after dinner, they'd gone out to the tire swing and spoken more about the dreams and the strange occurrences, the feelings and of course, what a rift would mean.

"It's like, a slash of energy. Where our reality should line up and just continue, there's a rift splitting open, and there's just...*more*. I don't really know how else to describe it. It's just an idea," James had said, pushing Lucy higher and higher on the tire swing. They all let that idea sit for a moment.

"Like, the other side?" Lucy had asked.

"More like, a different side," he'd replied. Wolfgang hadn't said anything, just absorbed their words and smoked a cigarette. He'd spent hours on the computer later that night, after everyone was sound asleep. He read about quantum physics, about how time isn't permanent and can be crushed together. He read about different realms, alternative realities, and the astral plane. *A rift?* He couldn't believe it. *Here?* Absolutely not. Rosemary had wandered in on him while researching; she hadn't been able to sleep. No dreams were keeping her awake that night, nothing more than her own mind contemplating what was truly possible. They talked about it, but neither gave in. It was all theories, at the end of the day. What was possible?

They made it to the club quickly with Lucy's driving. It was a place that was hard to miss. Big flashing lights, a long line, and almost no parking. But for Lucy, everything worked out. It was part of why she was so attractive. It was absolutely intoxicating to be around her because everything always went smoothly and effortlessly. There was never a better time to be had than when with Lucy Sommer. She checked her reflection in the mirror before stepping out.

"James, did you bring your fake?" Lucy asked, looking back at her youngest cousin. He was the only one who needed it.

"Hell of a time to ask," he replied, nodding that he had remembered it. She laughed, opening her car door. The four of them walked out of the parking garage, running across the street between whizzing cars, and jumped into line. Lucy texted her friends and immediately received a reply telling them to skip the line and meet them near the front.

"Hey! You made it! Wow, you look great," Beau greeted, giving Lucy a warm hug. Her chunky heels were at least six inches tall. Lucy was beautiful, undeniably. It just radiated off her being. It was rather conventional, but there were all these small things about her that were different, sometimes feeling off, sometimes just unique. People often got caught up for a long time in her aura, but Lucy had been captivated by it for her whole life, and now at times there were visible cracks. She hated seeing them.

"Thanks," she laughed, saying hello to Violet and Mia as they walked up.

"How do you walk in those things?" he asked her after breaking away from her engulfing hug. She laughed like it was nothing.

"You just tiptoe. Anyway, are we ready? Where's Liam? And you guys remember my cousin, James? And our neighbor, Silas?" she asked, pushing the two boys forward. Beau was genuine in his hellos, and Mia was already drunk enough to be giddy. Violet kept her face even and nodded a greeting.

"Liam is...oh, there he is!" Beau shouted, pointing to his friend darting across the street, running into them and pretending to jump on Beau's back.

"Hey man," Beau said, clapping his hand onto his friend's shoulder. Liam looked around at their group, his eyes excited and warm. He said hello to everyone, then settled his eyes on Rosemary for a moment longer.

"Hello," he said directly.

"Let's head in, we have a booth ready," Beau said, ushering everyone into the door, greeting the bouncers as if they were old family friends. He was a lot like Lucy, utterly magnetic. They had walked past the entire line, people staring at them as they went. Rosemary felt her cheeks grow red, but Lucy didn't notice any of it. And just like that, they were transplanted to a place that was very different from the drab of the world outside. Inside the club was dark, but the flashing lights lit up different sections at different times. There were three distinct levels, one with all booths and a bar, the second more open with booths just along the sides, and another step down was a long bar with an open floor. It wasn't filled yet, but would be soon. The DJ was excellent as he warmed up, the beat already resonating and building momentum. The music radiated small promises of the possibilities of the night. Everything felt very real, except Lucy.

"Over here," Beau said, leading the crowd to a reserved booth with bottle service. It was at the top level of the place, a giant corner booth with a great view of the stage and dance floor. They all assembled in slowly and Liam patted the seat beside him for Rosemary. Her heart nearly burst on the impact.

"Hi," she finally replied back, tight-lipped.

The crowd started talking and ordering drinks, and Rosemary tried to keep up but found her eyes wandering. Her body was very aware of where she sat. She glanced over at Silas, who had given up trying to follow the main conversation at the booth and instead was talking to James about something entirely different. She looked at them closely, never having guessed they were friends. Maybe they saw each other out in the woods.

"So, are places like this fun for you? Like, can you hear the music?" Violet asked, her voice breaking Rosemary out of her thoughts. She whipped her head back to the table, ready to say something, but Silas just laughed at her.

"Sure. But also, there's a lot more going on than just the music, right?" he asked her coyly. She sucked in her breath and nodded grudgingly. Rosemary felt light-headed.

"I'm going to get another," she said softly, standing up and walking over to the bar to order another whiskey soda, hoping this time she could get a lime. She sat at the bar for a long moment, taking in two deep sips of her drink and then just twirling the straw around, watching the carbonated bubbles rising to the surface and disappearing into the air. She couldn't help but wonder what that transition was like.

"Already hiding from us?" Liam asked, coming up behind her. She almost choked on her next sip, then drank half the drink in one go to help recover. He sat down next to her, looking at her as he smiled. It had to be a dream, because her heart had completely stopped beating and she was still sitting there, looking at him, awake.

"I'm not hiding, just getting a drink," she said, holding up an almost empty glass, rattling the ice. He nodded, pretending to believe her.

"Let me get you another," he said, already holding up a hand. He was quick to fey off her insistence not to.

"I'm getting one too, it's efficient," he replied, putting in the drink order, not needing to ask what she was drinking because he already knew. The club was filling up, people were crowding around, but Rosemary felt very much alone in a dark room with Liam, who was still looking over at her with bright eyes.

"How've you been?"

She didn't know how to answer. Was he asking about the past year? Last summer? The most recent month? None of her possible choices of an answer seemed allowable, seemed good enough to say, or sane enough to give comment.

"Rose?" She'd gotten lost in her head.

"I've been good," she settled, taking another heavy sip of her freshly delivered drink. Dinner had been a long time ago, so she was waiting for the slight tinge of alcohol to hit at any moment. She wasn't usually this person, but then again, she'd shown up as someone not quite herself. She supposed it was all a dare to the universe, if that was actually what was after her.

Find me now, she thought. *Do something now.*

"Oh, okay," he said, but he was teasing her.

"How're you?" she shot back.

"Good, yeah. My master's program is a year in, just one more to go. I'm happy it's almost over, that I'm so close to really finishing," he said, his words so honest, they cut. She nodded, finishing her third drink in record time. She raised her hand for another before he had the chance to.

"Well, that's great. I'm glad you're in a good place with all of that. Any idea what you're going to do post-grad?" she asked, not sure why she was asking. Finally, she had reached a place where she didn't care anymore, had stopped wondering almost completely. Her memories of last summer had mostly faded from her mind, any remaining ones becoming eclipsed by the current summer. Now, it all seemed like little tiny dreams, slight fantasies, and nice moments rather than grand expenditures. But she wasn't back at the house, thinking about it. She was there, sitting next to him, his presence overwhelming every sense she had the longer they shared such close proximity. Why was he seeking her out? She was starting to feel her third drink.

"I'm not sure if I'm going to stay here. I might, I love it here, with everyone. But I was contemplating the west coast maybe," he said, again meaning it. She blinked.

"Much different than the Midwest, huh? Big tech is in full bloom out there though, so I get it. Makes sense," she said. It didn't make sense.

"Yeah, it would be a change. But that can be exciting," he agreed. She shrugged, she wouldn't give him that much. He noticed it immediately and felt entitled to ask.

"Do you not think it would be a good opportunity to take?" he inquired, his eyes steady on her face, taking a sip of his drink.

"I don't know. Have you thought about it enough?"

"Yeah, I've made time." The words stung harder than the liquor on her dry throat. She didn't have a follow-up.

"But you're just, totally fine?" he asked, moving past what he could not see, wanting instead more from her. She wanted to give more, especially to him. She still had always considered him one of the deepest people she'd ever met, but for the first time in a long while she felt like she wouldn't know where to begin talking, especially with this stranger. A body she recognized, but a person she did not. It was more than just the alcohol bubbling up.

"There you guys are! C'mon, we all want to dance!" Lucy yelled, running up, indeed tip-toeing, and grabbing their arms.

"Finish your drinks! We'll get more down there," she shouted as the volume of the music turned up, and the night officially started. The DJ had successfully built up energy that was starting to boil over. Quickly, Rosemary downed her drink, grabbing her sister's hand and running down to the bottom floor. Liam followed with everyone else, but she wanted to hide away from their crowd. She wanted a moment to feel at peace with her sister that she hoped to make last longer than just a moment's time.

"Drinks!" Lucy said, getting them quickly at the bar. She was hardly ever ignored. Vodka for her, whiskey for her sister, and together they made it out onto the dance floor and started moving. They were at it for a while; laughing and talking, teasing men and then disappearing from them, getting another round later on. They had a big enough group that it was easy to let loose, because everywhere you turned there was someone familiar. It was fun, together. Each sister could tell the other was having a good time from the light in their eyes when they'd look at each other.

Time went by, they all did a round of shots, and then another. Lucy kept getting drinks for the two of them, occasionally getting some guy to pay. Rosemary had stopped looking out, stopped following her movements or patterns. She was having a good time, Liam was only showing up on the fringes, but the music was so loud and so good she was able to maneuver away.

"Do you want to sit down for a minute? I need just a little break," Lucy yelled in Rosemary's ear, holding onto her arm. She did seem winded, tired in her body. Rosemary nodded, helping her over to their top booth. It was much quieter there. It was a nice setup, the corner of the third floor, overlooking the main floor packed with people dancing and banging their heads in time together.

"Are you having a good time?" Lucy asked, smiling, sipping her drink instead of swallowing it quickly. Rosemary nodded, breathing in deeply. She was definitely drunk, but still okay. It was a rare place to be.

"This is a lot of fun, I see why you do it," Rosemary replied, eyes wide.

"Yeah, you're always welcome to come. We should go out more," Lucy replied, checking her phone briefly, then looking back up at her sister, taking in her wide eyes. She smiled.

"Really?"

"Of course," she replied. Rosemary didn't think it would last into morning.

"Have you been able to sleep, since we all talked last?" Lucy asked, her voice changing. Rosemary's eyes snapped up towards her, recognizing the *all* immediately.

"Yeah, I guess," she replied. Lucy laughed.

"And where are you going these days, when you dream?" she asked. Rosemary looked at her, figuring she was probably being casual because she was drunk. They hadn't talked about it between themselves alone yet. It felt like a strange time to do so.

"You talk a little in your sleep," Lucy said, a soft smile.

"Do you believe in it? You've never said," Rosemary pushed.

"A rift? I hardly understand what that even means," Lucy laughed, but her face was solemn. She looked out at the crowd, wondering what each person felt down there, dancing as one big entity. Were they able to effortlessly cast aside unsettling feelings, or did they embrace them, wonder about them? She didn't know how far she wanted to fall down that particular rabbit hole. The more she thought about it, the more she realized that she was afraid. To the cosmos, she was but a mere particle.

"I've always dreamt a lot, you know," Rosemary said; trying to comfort her sister, make it seem less extraordinary, less meaningful. Lucy didn't bite.

"Yeah, but now it's been more than that, hasn't it?" Lucy asked. She looked her sister in the face, reaching out and fixing some of her smudged eye shadow. Together, at that moment they realized there was no escaping. All of it was energy, and they felt it radiating towards them. There was nowhere to run, no way to deny it. Even there, a place so far away from the woods, they could still both sense that the music was louder to them; the heat was hotter for them.

"Yeah," Rosemary replied. "Lately, it's been hard remembering if it was a dream or if it really happened. Like, where the two realities meet and where they each end. I feel like that's a rift," Rosemary continued, her eyes watering as she spoke about it. Lucy sucked in a deep breath. She didn't want to be subjected to that, an utter lack of control. It was her greatest fear, innate or not.

"I never dream," she said.

"Wait, never?"

"No. Just that one time I felt yours. I had never even realized what a dream would be like before," Lucy said, a sadness in her eyes. She was chasing after it, though never sure what she was running towards. This didn't feel like what she wanted, but it was there to stay. She'd come out that night wanting to escape it, but it demanded to be felt by both of them, sitting drunk in a booth with loud music in their ears. When they looked at each other, it was all they could feel.

"So, what do you mean you can't tell the difference? Like, do you feel trapped?" Lucy asked. Rosemary wasn't sure how to answer. They did experience the world differently, and the way Rosemary felt about the world and its possibilities were always a different diversity than Lucy's. Still, she knew the cliff they stood on now was scary; the space before them was full of uncertainties and lawlessness.

"No, it feels very expansive. Like so many things...overlap," Rosemary said.

"So it is real," Lucy whispered. It was more for her to take on than her sister. But Rosemary nodded very slightly. She was teetering too but denying it felt meaningless.

"I think so," she replied.

"I need another drink. Do you?" Lucy asked, jumping up. She was looking around panicked, like she was feeling sick. Rosemary nodded, her own drunkenness allowing her to break from the severity of their conversation easily.

"Sure," she replied, staying seated and watching her sister walk off into the crowd towards the bar. She sat alone for a while, waiting. Vaguely, she wondered where the others were, her cousin, Silas. And then as if he'd heard her, she spotted Silas leaning against the railing looking down at the dance floor and stage alone. She stood up, feeling the alcohol swoosh through her body warmly, and walked over to him.

"Hey, are you having a good time?" she asked, a little drunk, but still on the right side of it. He looked at her, smiling with his eyes. He knew she meant it honestly.

"Yeah, I am. Places like this are cool sometimes," he replied. She nodded, agreeing. She looked down at the floor, spotting the others, James among them. He looked to be getting along with everyone, needing just a few drinks to seemingly erode all his walls. He was the best at illusion.

"I'm sorry about what Violet said earlier. She's the one I can't stand," Rosemary said, swaying a little against the railing. Her body was beginning to feel so light that it seemingly wanted to float away. She almost wanted to let it.

"It's alright, she doesn't really matter," he replied.

"Still," Rosemary said. He accepted that.

"I do like music. It's just, something about the feeling. You feel it right here, all the time, no matter the sound," he replied, holding his hand over his heart and lightly thumping on his chest with his palm. She watched him do it, still not sure what he meant.

"You can't separate the feeling from the sound, but for me, it's easy. Actually, it's one of the only ways I can experience live music. You can do it though, you just have to be the one to try, for once," he tacked on, a small teasing smile on his lips.

"Like this," he said, just as the lights went low, a rumble flowing through the audience and bouncing off the stage. A new song had started up, and Rosemary started bobbing her head to the music almost instantaneously, and then she felt a hand on hers and looked back.

Silas took off his cochlear implants, sliding them into his pockets. He held his hand over his heart again, tapping it to his chest to the beat of the bass. He held up Rosemary's hand to her own chest, trying to get her to feel the feeling instead of hear the music. She looked into his eyes, darker than usual in that light. They were so serious. Not in an upset or desperate kind of way, rather in a true plight of communication. She wanted to feel what he was feeling. She looked back out at the crowd, and kept her hand over her heart. After a few moments, she felt it too.

It started as a shiver over her skin, pickling at the new sensation. The shouts from the crowd weren't words or noises, but vibrations, and she felt connected to each one. The music was nice, but the beat was more than that, it had a physical quality to it, one that caused her body to pulse in unison. Everyone in the room was pulsing with it. And that was the feeling, the big connection, the whole room. It was beautiful. Rosemary wanted to cry. She watched Silas for some of it, his eyes heavily on the DJ, the crowd. A smile on his face, pure enjoyment. She felt that, too.

"Let's go!" Lucy shouted coming up to them, putting a drink in Rosemary's hands and then her arms around both her sister and her friend. She seemed much different from her uneasiness ten minutes prior, and much wilder than their sobering conversation in the booth. As Rosemary followed her out to the first floor again, she watched as Lucy's whole body stood much taller, her eyes bigger, her smile wider.

Something seemed different.

But they danced and got lost in the crowd, and as they drank more, the faces were all a blur and no one could tell if the music was good anymore or not, but it was loud and it was pounding, and everyone wanted to keep up with it. Someone floated over to Rosemary, and when she looked up, it was Liam, smiling down at her. They danced together for a long time, first respectfully as friends, then as people who had shared a bed a few times over a hot summer. Rosemary got lost in that thought. She had been wrong. She wasn't thinking about him alone in a dark room, she was instead alone in her drunken mind, walled off by very loud music, forcing herself to dance with someone she thought she'd loved but had not loved her back. Lucy was always after a good time. Rosemary had always been after something more painful.

She didn't know what it was about him. He wasn't the typical person she went for. He was much too clean-cut, way too driven. She liked someone slower; who looked around, thought it was okay to like two contradictory things. Liam hadn't. He had always been someone to choose. But as they danced, the music so loud it was washing over them, pushing them together like angry waves, she couldn't help but just feel it. Deep in her chest, that ache, the yearning. She wanted to touch him more than this, in sunlight even. She loved the way he looked, the way he carried himself, the way he talked in the early morning before their alarms had gone off. The energy he had, she wanted. That's all there had been to it. But she had never found out what he had wanted from her, and what he had decided he couldn't get.

Nothing could stop them, until the lights flipped on.

"I know of an after-hours place," Lucy yelled at their group, somehow all closer than Rosemary had thought. Under the bright lights, she felt very disoriented. She didn't want to go home either.

"Let's go," Rosemary agreed, draping an arm around her cousin's shoulders, looking into his face to see if he was okay. He drunkenly smiled at her; grabbing her hand and helping her walk out to the car. Liam drove, though he probably shouldn't have. It was just a few streets away, and at two a.m. the streets were vacant. She sat upfront with him, watching him drive. She liked that, too. She kept glancing back at Lucy who was laughing and talking a mile a minute in the back seat, shoved together between everyone else. It was funny in the moment.

"What's after hours?" Rosemary asked, her words slurred. Liam grabbed her hand; Rosemary's breathing halted.

"It's not technically legal, but Lucy always gets us in. Just a bar running after hours. It's fun, you'll like it," he whispered, pulling into a parking spot. They seemed to be in the middle of nowhere, large city buildings looming darkly overhead.

"Okay," she mumbled, squeezing his hand. He let go when they got out of the SUV, all eight of them. They stumbled down the street, laughing and running around, dancing to music that was ringing only in their heads. Even Violet was loose. Soon, they made it to a single man standing outside a brown door. He hugged Lucy, then knocked and the door opened. Down a flight of stairs, they made it to a dark basement that was lit up with small lights and was filled with people and music. What was deemed the bar were merely tables in the back filled with a random assortment of possibilities. When Rosemary asked for more whiskey, the girl replied with, "I'll see what I can do," and handed her a red solo cup. She took a sip of it and didn't feel well. It was bitter.

"Where's the bathroom?" she asked Lucy, grabbing her arm to steady herself.

"Oh, this way, follow me," she replied, carrying her sister along with extra strength. They made it to the front by the stairs again, and Lucy talked to one of the guys standing there, who let them in a side room. It was an office, and very quiet. A different place entirely.

"It's around there," the guy said as Rosemary made her way to the door.

"Hey, did you want toilet paper?" he asked, before she shut the door. She looked at him, nodding, wondering what she would have to do to get some.

"Here, hold on. Some people can't handle it," the guy mumbled, walking over to the mini-fridge in the room, and pulled out a roll of toilet paper. He handed it to her without hesitation.

"Thanks," Rosemary laughed, and then locked the door. She looked at herself in the mirror for a while, finally settling on splashing some water on her face. She looked like herself again, but hot and sweaty, with too much dark smeared under her eyes.

She used the bathroom, put the toilet paper in the fridge, and walked back out to the floor. She had set her drink down, but didn't go to pick it back up. The mirror had been sobering. She didn't need another one.

She danced for a long time there, mostly alone. No one she didn't know tried to talk to her or dance with her, and she liked that. Lucy was having more fun there than she had before, but Rosemary wasn't sure why. She'd lost track of Liam. It didn't matter. She danced with her eyes closed, trying to go somewhere else, be herself again somewhere else. Maybe this was the dream, and at that point, it felt like it could be.

Silas drove the girls and James home. It was past five in the morning when they finally pulled up to the house. Rosemary couldn't believe the time, didn't know how she'd be able to wake up the next day and be normal. Everything felt hazy as she got out of the car. She said goodbye to Silas, embracing him in a long hug and telling him to drive himself home and she'd get the car later.

"Are you happy?" she'd asked him through the window. He'd laughed.

"Yes. And tired. Goodnight, Rose," he'd replied. The three walked in, barely making it up the stairs, all drunk and overtired.

"Drink some water before you pass out," Lucy said, roughing up James's hair. He waved at her as he stumbled over to his room, disappearing into the darkness. Rosemary tried to help Lucy change into pajamas, but the farthest she got was unstrapping her sister's heels before she fell down on her bed and passed out. Rosemary stayed up a little longer, trying to replay the night in her mind. It was hard to stitch together. Had Liam held her hand at the club, or in the car? She pulled her dress over her head. Why was Lucy so interested in her dreams, was the rift real? Her tights magically had no rips as she shimmied them off. Why did he have such nice eyes? She climbed into bed, under the covers, forgetting to drink water.

When had he floated over? Had he floated over?

She felt like the floor was moving but she wasn't. And the

lights were still going, though it had to be much too late for that now. Or was it early? There were no clocks on the walls; she wasn't sure why she had even looked. Liam was standing in front of her. Her whole body ached, wanting to pull towards him, but there was some kind of invisible force holding her back. Maybe it was Lucy, but when she looked around, she could never see her, just a small dark shadow darting around.

What had he said to her?

"I still care about you, you know."

Long wisps of white started sashaying around them, and when Rosemary tried to turn her head to look, to break Liam's gaze, she had a hard time. The man at the front was involved. Maybe it was the toilet paper. Maybe it was something else.

"I still care, you know."

Where was Lucy? Why was she suddenly darting around? She didn't eat enough, or sleep enough to have this kind of sustained energy. Usually, she showed up when Rosemary felt desperate. It had always been their code. But in that moment, she could just see shadows; behind doors of rooms she wasn't allowed into. She could see the light from each door, before it shut against the wall, leaving her in darkness. A piece of her was trapped in every room. She felt stuck; she didn't know what to do. She just wanted to walk through this and be on the other side.

"I care."

Not enough.

Ten.

The only thing she could feel by midmorning was one side of her head throbbing. Her headaches always came in concentrated lines, swooshing above her eye, through the bridge of her nose, up across her forehead, and back behind her ear. Carefully, she laid the side of her head that hurt the most down on her pillow, putting pressure on her skull. It relieved the pain; though she wasn't sure for how long.

Her body was begging for water, and she'd never wanted something so desperately. Wanting to get up to go get that glass of water, she tried to rise, but something felt wrong. Her face felt smashed, her sight skewed wavy on her left side. She stood up, and wobbled to the dresser, but couldn't shake the feeling in her face – all that pressure.

She blinked, opening her eyes, on her bed again. Really, she wanted that glass of water. Pushing up from the bed, she rubbed at her eyes, trying to see clearly, get rid of the swirling of black stars racing through her mind. Her fingers glided against the side of her face, and although her skin felt smooth, her body knew it wasn't. She stood up again, just as dizzy as before.

And again, eyes open, face pressed into the mattress.

Rosemary wanted to stand up so badly, her tongue was dry and felt like sandpaper as it ran across her teeth. Her chest ached, her stomach rolled. She couldn't pull her tongue back into her mouth, her face firmly pressed into the side of the bed. She tried to stand, but couldn't. Couldn't even lift her body to sit. Her breathing grew more desperate. It was the only physical thing that would react, because somehow, for some reason, her body couldn't leave from where it laid; her face couldn't straighten out; her eyesight wouldn't come back clearly.

Another blink, her breathing still rapid, but this time, something was different. Her mind cleared, alert. A weight she hadn't noticed before was suddenly lifted. She sat up, stood up. Finally, she was able to leave her bedroom, walk down the hall and stairs and go into the kitchen. She poured herself a glass of water from the pitcher in the fridge, and leaned against the counter as she sipped, thinking about the bed she hadn't been able to leave, hadn't been allowed to get up from. Had she?

"Oh, good afternoon," Wolfgang greeted her a little too loudly, walking in from outside. Rosemary closed her eyes as the bright sunlight streamed in past his body, finally dissipating when he shut the door.

"What are you, my mom?" she grumbled, rubbing her forehead. Still, something didn't feel right, but she was trying to chalk it up to the alcohol. She was having a hard time understanding what had happened last night.

"Good one. But somehow I managed to be awake in the morning hours after helping my brother throw his guts up all night. Did you guys show him a good time or a bad one? I honestly couldn't tell," Wolfgang said, pouring himself a glass of water.

"You've never drunk too much and paid for it the next day?" Rosemary teased, trying to give him a light smile. He shrugged his shoulders.

"Is he alright?" she asked.

"Yeah, he'll live. Just sat with him in the bathroom and made sure he didn't choke. He was saying some crazy things about shadows moving when the people weren't, or something. Sure it was just drunk talk," Wolfgang replied, his voice growing low at the end. He wanted to believe his brother's ramblings were just drunk words.

"Yeah, I'm sure he was just wasted," Rosemary said. Neither of them believed it.

"Ugh, good morning family. How are we feeling today? Wolfgang, you missed an excellent night," Lucy sang as she came down the steps feeling almost perfect. It was her secret weapon, somehow she always rallied.

"You're way too chipper," Rosemary said, walking over and making herself a piece of toast as Lucy easily downed a glass of water, then went about making more coffee. All the breakfast food had long ago been cleared and stored away.

"It's the best way to be," she replied innocently.

"My parents are going to kill James, you know that, right?" Wolfgang said, leaning up against the counter away from the girls. He'd felt different since they'd talked out in the woods. He wasn't sure what was real and what wasn't. There was a lot of fear.

"He's allowed to sleep in," Lucy said nonchalantly, watching the water boil.

"Like hell he is," Wolfgang muttered. All at once, the three of them looked out the kitchen window towards the big garage, their fathers in view working on the old grass-cutting tractor. Their voices were loud and energetic. For the most part, Lewis and Henry got along and enjoyed each other's company over the summertime months. In the real world, they had conflicting views, but in the world of the Pennyfathers' land, their energies lined up and usually synced. It caused conflict in Rosemary's heart, but she didn't know the half of it. Nobody did. It was all by design.

"Well, go drag him out of bed and get him some juice and toast. We can cure a hangover no problem around here," Lucy said, already searching the refrigerator. Neither Wolfgang nor Rosemary moved, however. Their eyes were focused on their fathers, sweaty and greasy, talking loudly at the head of the open engine.

"What do you think it was like for them to grow up here?" Wolfgang said, his voice nearly a whisper. Rosemary didn't know, but she realized her mother had married someone who resembled her uncle if he were good.

"Do you think they ever felt...more?" Wolfgang continued. Lucy tried to move the conversation back to saving James from certain death, but realized that her sister and cousin were frozen in time, trying to go back and remember memories that weren't theirs to know. She looked out the window. She felt a certain way about it, too.

"Judging by everything, I think they must have," Lucy finally said. It felt like more proof. Nobody brought up the idea that was on their minds. Should they go and search for the rift? Would they be able to find the source of all this energy that was creating possibilities and situations unable to be explained away by simple rationalities? What would happen if they did?

"I don't understand how they could just, not think about it anymore," Rosemary said, wondering vaguely where her mother and aunts were.

"Some of them still do," Wolfgang replied.

"Hey," James said, his voice hoarse as he walked into the kitchen, a mess.

"Oh dude, you need a shower," Lucy said, looking him over a few times.

"I need water first," he replied walking over to the sink and simply sticking his head under the faucet and turned it on. Wolfgang laughed.

"You'll be okay, just walk it off," he said. James shook his head at the seemingly impossible.

"I think I died twice last night, at least," he replied.

"Well, you look pretty good for a dead man," Wolfgang said, clapping him on the back as he walked past. He hurried James back up the stairs when he noticed his father and uncle walking up to the house. The girls stayed behind as a distraction.

"Oh, good morning girls. How was your night?" their father

greeted, giving each of them a kiss on the forehead as he walked by to the sink to wash his hands. Lewis looked up at the ceiling.

"A lot of fun," Rosemary said quickly.

"Are my sons awake?" Lewis asked, a stern voice.

"Oh yeah, before us," Lucy said, her voice cheerful and eyes sparkling as she spoke. He nodded like he believed her, and maybe he did. She was hard to deny.

"I don't know if you have other plans, but your mother and I were wondering if you wanted to go to one of the restaurants down by the docks for lunch. We haven't spent much time together just the four of us this summer. Are you hungry?" Henry asked looking back at his daughters. He was always diplomatic. They were surprised by the invitation, but for different reasons. In unison, they both nodded in agreement, but spoke different words.

"That sounds really nice, I'd love to," Lucy replied, finishing up her mug of coffee and setting it down in the empty sink.

"Yeah, that's fine," Rosemary said. Her sister eyed her. They agreed on a time and the girls followed each other up the steps to change and get ready. Rosemary's head was still pounding but she hoped after some food it would simmer down. Lucy seemed unabashed after she came back from a shower to put fresh color on her eyelids and lips. Perhaps the distractions really worked for her. Rosemary was too caught up on feeling like something was still watching her from under the bed as she got dressed, and moving through time and space was becoming cumbersome.

Something about going to lunch with her parents was sobering. In more ways than one, it seemed to immediately drain the magic from the air and from Rosemary's fingertips. She knew they'd talk about her future, about the world outside of summertime at her grandparents' house. It was a hard topic for her to keep up with. Often, she noticed how she didn't fit into the routines everyone else seemed easily adjusted to. It hadn't bothered her until she got older and people expected more from her, and without it, were disappointed. She knew it was a silly thing to allow weigh her down; her own cousins faced much greater stresses from their parents. Yet still, it was a weight she carried, and nobody liked it when her answer was to hole up in Heidi's guesthouse and work at the restaurant bar just down the road and write poems in the hills.

"Ready?" Lucy asked, looking up from her phone.

"I guess," she replied, grabbing her bag. She'd checked her phone a few times that morning, but no one had texted her. Truly, she was back on summer's time, alone in the world among tall grasses and old trees. At times, it felt mundane, but when faced with having to part with it, she wished they could stay and didn't have to go into a place with buildings and cars.

"It'll be okay," Lucy whispered, squeezing her shoulders before heading down. It was like a burst of energy radiated into her body, and for a moment she felt the confidence and luster Lucy felt daily. She appreciated the moment, breathing in deeply to hold onto it for as long as she could. Then, she followed her sister down. They walked out onto the front lawn, one of the dogs coming up and barking at them, barely knowing the direction he was headed he was so old. The girls waved to their parents who were already beside the car, a beautiful new SUV far different than the old beater they drove around. Rosemary was grateful they'd already had their moment.

Heidi waved to them all from the porch, screaming to have a good time as they piled into the vehicle. Rosemary tried to put aside any foul feelings she might have had accumulating over the past couple of years. Immediately, Delphine and Lucy started chattering away about last night, and Lucy made it seem grander than it had been. They beamed when they were together. For a moment, Rosemary felt like she had a family, a normal one, a fantasized one. She felt like she too had adventure and agency and kindness.

"Rose, how are you? Did you have fun last night?" Delphine asked happily, turning to look at her other daughter. Rosemary hadn't been listening but she nodded and flashed her mother a smile to give her a moment to think of an answer.

"It was a lot of fun, it was good to see everyone," she replied.

"I noticed you got James to go out. Good for you two, he needs a night out like that," she said, turning around again to look out the windshield. Henry laughed, knowing it was true. Neither of them saw much need to parent. It was a combination of things probably, a culmination of having chosen to prioritize other things, and after seeing so much of the world, molding other humans into anything other than worldly beings seemed worthless. They wanted their children to be powerful and truth-seeking. It would play out some way.

"Lewis and Beth still have no idea," Henry laughed.

"About him going out, or his fake?" Lucy teased and they all laughed.

"Now your other cousin..." Delphine started but Lucy rolled her eyes.

"Lost cause, never wants to have any fun," she replied. Nobody said anything for a few moments. Rosemary didn't entirely know if that was true, and wasn't entirely sure why Lucy had said it. After everything, it didn't seem fair. She started to feel far away again, and Henry felt it instantly. As a photographer, he'd become extremely sensitized to a shift. Delphine had taught him a lot. He looked in the rearview mirror at his daughter as she looked out the window, and he could tell she felt herself drifting in that cloudless sky above them. It was just a feeling.

"How was South America? We haven't really talked much about it since you got back and we've all come here. I want to know everything," Lucy said, chattering away. Her excitement was obvious as it wove throughout all the high notes in her voice. Delphine started talking about their time overseas as Henry and Rosemary listened, often used to walking in others' shadows. Their conversations continued as they parked and walked into the restaurant, finding good seats on the back balcony overlooking the water. It was a pristine day with a cool breeze.

The refugee crisis was a massive situation, and they were gathering all kinds of stories from kids and women to young men and old men alike. Rosemary could see just how excited her mom was when talking about how close they were to compiling something so substantial and painfully worded accompanied with stunning photography that they were going to *change minds* about the whole ordeal. That was her catchphrase for everything. She wanted to change minds, and if it hadn't so readily excluded Rosemary's youthful mind, she might have been more into it. It was hard though, to keep any of her resolutions when they were both right there, so close to her, talking excitedly about everything happening, combined with just how happy they were to be with their daughters.

"That's a beautiful bracelet, Rosemary," her mother said, breaking her out of her headspace as she quickly tried to detect where the conversation had gone while she had been drifting. She glanced down at the simple leather braiding, colorful beads strung on certain strands. It wasn't even hers.

"Should we have had Silas come to lunch?" Lucy teased, thinking it was an innocent comment. Rosemary immediately shook her head, feeling a deep ripple of anxiety in her chest. Or was it meant to sting? She was having a hard time telling. The smallest voice in the back of her mind whispered the question, *how did her sister know?* Their mom looked back and forth at the two of them.

"Wait, I want to know. Is something going on? I feel like something is going on. Last summer it was that boy Liam, wasn't it?" she asked, almost nosy to a fault, already supplying her follow up question.

"No, that's nothing. And we're just friends, that's all. We talk when I help him work around grandma's house. He's nice," Rosemary quickly replied. This time, Lucy and Delphine shared a look.

"Sounds like you're getting defensive," her mom argued. That's how it was, always an argument.

"I am not, you're asserting things," she quickly fired back. In only some instances, did playing dead work.

"I haven't said anything," she responded, holding her hands up, still tightly holding her forkful of uneaten salad greens. For some reason, that annoyed Rosemary.

"Yeah, but it's in your tone and the way you're looking at each other," Rosemary replied and to that, she didn't have much to say. Lucy looked down at the floor, like the punch line of her joke hadn't gone over well. She wrapped her arm around Rosemary, pulling her over for a quick moment. It hadn't been her intent. Rosemary let it go. She didn't want to fight with her sister in the summertime. They fought enough the rest of the year. In the summer, it was always different. She didn't know why.

She watched quietly as her parents talked extensively about their travels some more and all the adventures they had gotten themselves into the months they had been gone. It did sound absolutely wonderful, exciting, and adventurous. That was the other thing that always bothered Rosemary about how everything had turned out, she didn't know if she'd make a different choice than they had. And had it really been so bad? Maybe Heidi was right, count the blessings and move on from the pain. She almost settled on that resolution. Watching Lucy, however, chattering away, a million different pieces glued together, she could see that making a mental choice to move on, move past, move over something wasn't reality. Long ago, Lucy had moved on. But nothing seemed right about her, not usually, not always.

"And how has applying to your master's program gone?" Delphine asked, eager to hear about her daughter, the one who was willing to talk. Yin and yang, that was the kind of twins they were. Lucy chattered on about her schools of choice, her friends, the parties she went to and even occasionally promoted. She had a big name. Delphine soaked it up, enjoying all the details, all the extroverted energy her daughter had to give. And now, it was appropriate to ask what they were up to. They were adults now, not abandoned children. It was okay.

"Rose, how's being at Heidi's been? The bar still good?" her mother asked, finally breaking away from Lucy. She felt her sister nudge her foot with hers, trying to keep her positive any way she knew how. They were interrupted for a moment as the main dishes came out and the waitress collected their small salad and bread plates. She refreshed their drinks and headed out, leaving everyone to look back at Rosemary.

"Yeah, I like the space. It has lots of windows and Heidi has really let me do almost anything I want to the place," Rosemary replied.

"And the job?" her father asked. It was okay, the way he asked. She was most like him. The way he talked was slow and intentional, and it acknowledged that she didn't feel at home with them the way a family usually did. But it was also her father's voice, and it was honest. She felt herself opening up, like a caterpillar in the spring who somehow found its way into a child's warm hand, tricked into thinking it was summer.

"I like the people and the place. I won't stay there forever; I just don't know what I want to do yet. I think I have some time still to figure that out," she replied. She was worried she wasn't being direct enough, perhaps sounding too secretive. She didn't want to rock the boat any more than she already did: the true rebel.

"You ever consider journalism, not to be cliché? I know how much you love to write and explore," Delphine asked, hopeful. Her daughter shrugged. She was a lot like her father; she didn't give anything up easily.

"It's not off the table. I have always liked a good mystery," she said. Had she?

"Well, it's good to hear you're thinking about it. I want so much for both of you," Delphine replied, deeply meaning it. That killed her. She watched as her mother twirled around some seafood pasta but not quite bring it up to her mouth. Lucy copied her eating patterns, moving her rice around a bit as she looked around, waiting for the next exciting thing to come up so she could put the fork down.

"Do you think journalism is your thing, or is there something else?" her dad asked suddenly, surprising her. Rosemary felt like she'd been snuck up from behind. She didn't like that.

"I do like it a lot actually, maybe that's the surprising thing," Rosemary said, a small bite to her words. She let it sting for a moment before covering it up, pretending like she hadn't intentionally caused it to burn.

"But otherwise, I'm not sure. Something outside, something that involves thinking and moving around. Maybe the sciences. I'm sure it will come to me when it's time to move on," Rosemary replied, not even realizing she was describing her summers until the words left her lips. She wasn't sure if anyone else understood that. Suddenly, her food tasted cold and the weight of everything came crashing back onto her shoulders. Although there was a fear attached to this possibility of a rift, an opening, there was also a euphoric high that came along with it. She was finally admitting that to herself. The more she wanted from life wasn't going to come from some societal structure. She wanted more from the universe. She needed more from it, and as long as she did, her mind would always be at least half occupied by its ideas.

"Mm, well that's alright. As long as you're enjoying yourself for now. You're too young to be doing something you dislike," he commented and Rosemary let it slide, appreciating the out he was allowing her. They all finished up their food slowly, taking a few moments to chew in silence. Rosemary looked around at the bustling docks, the waitresses running around to take care of everyone's lunch order. Even though the street was on the other side of the large, multi-story restaurant, the cars whizzing by the road could be heard easily in between the whooshing of waves right below. Rosemary was always amazed how much a part of the real world the town was, when right up the hill where the land stretched out far and was split into family farms it seemed completely removed from anything she knew the rest of the year.

"What're you thinking about?" Lucy asked, breaking her sister from her thoughts.

"Nothing," she was quick to reply.

"Oh? If I think hard enough, I bet I could tap in," Lucy teased.

Rosemary rolled her eyes, not wanting to talk about anything in front of their parents who no matter their interest level, were always all eyes and ears.

"Telepathy of no kind exists," Rosemary replied, her voice a little tense. It went against what she was beginning to believe in, but for a long stretch of time she'd denied any kind of other worldly connection with her twin. It had come from many years of feeling like an unexpected and disappointing addition. Lucy's eyes grew fiery almost immediately, feeling her words across her face like a slap.

"Bold words coming from our manic dreamer," Lucy said, her words short and sharp. Rosemary tossed the words away from her before they could touch her skin, regretting ever discussing her dreams with her sister. She didn't know how to move on from them, she never had. Mostly, she didn't want to. She couldn't admit it to anyone, hardly herself, but she loved her dreams. Even as they grew more and deeply pervasive, even as she started looking forward to going to bed and dreading waking up in fear of missing out on a good time, she didn't want to deal with it, talk to someone, or push them away. Usually making a choice in a dream led something astounding to happen. Trying to make that same choice in real life fell short. The reality somehow always came out that you don't have any to make. Someone has already made them for you. The steadiness of life was too much for her, and often, she found herself unwilling to continue participating.

So, she went to sleep.

Her parents were staring at her, worried. Everyone always looked worried around Rosemary. They didn't push her too hard, in case she fell. She found it bizarre just how worried everyone was about her next move, when only Heidi had seen her unable to make one for a long time.

"What, you've never had a crazy dream before?" Rosemary said, leaning back in her chair and throwing her napkin in her plate. Lucy wouldn't look at her, and her father just shrugged and finished his beer. Delphine looked curiously at her daughter, her eyebrows furrowed as if she were trying to remember something wildly important, even though it was fleeting. She felt like maybe she had a dream or two like that, but couldn't seem to remember more than a hazy image for a second.

"Mom, what is it?" Lucy asked, staring at her mother over their empty dishes. Her upset with her sister melted away as they both realized she was thinking about something she didn't know how to put into words. That never happened.

"Not much, just dreams I've had. And this place. It's beautiful here isn't it? I'm glad we get to spend this time together," she rambled, bringing them back to a much less interesting and vulnerable conversation. The girls let it go but each noted it in their mind. She'd had the feeling before too, whatever it was. The waitress came up to the table.

"Are you guys ready for the check?"

On the way back to the house, the car was mostly quiet. Everyone was retreating into their minds about the world in some fashion. Lunch had been good for them, if not to continue pretending in some kind of tolerable and easily consumable way. But Rosemary couldn't shake the feeling that Delphine knew about the way that place made people feel, and that there was some extra element exposed out there amongst Pennyfather land. But if that were true, she couldn't believe her mother hadn't found it. Or was this why she was such an explorer otherwise? Needing to find the truth and motivation behind everything all over the world. Maybe her mother didn't understand the feeling any more than Rosemary did in that moment. Maybe she felt the feeling in more places than just the Pennyfather family land. And if that were the case, then why was Rosemary so numb the rest of the year? She vowed, in the back of their rented car, the smell of starch shampoo in her nostrils, that she would come to understand the abundance of this energy. She would learn the language of what was calling out to her, and make it so she could call back.

The car swerved to an abrupt halt, everyone slamming forward in their seats like dolls. Lucy yelled out, but Rosemary was quiet, staring. A stag so great was walking daintily across the road, stopping for nothing. It was immense, seemingly prehistoric by it's sheer size and the weight of it's antlers that draped out massively on either side of it's head, green moss and vines caught in the bone like a crown. For a moment longer than it should have, the deer looked at them. His eyes were black voids, containing a swirling of consciousness and vision. Then he turned and walked off, saying no more.

Eleven.

Sara didn't ask for much, and the older she grew there was even less she seemingly needed. Wanting, was a different thing entirely. That summer had aged her more than one summer should, and she found herself often secluded from her family. She preferred it that way, things were becoming difficult in her old age and she didn't want anyone to see her struggle, or see the things she no longer could hide away with ease. She'd yet to truly be alone. On the eve of fall when her children and grandchildren would pack their bags and head back out into the world, she knew she'd find herself alone for the first time, without Ramone walking around and mumbling his little incoherent phrases, or stumbling into a half-filled vase with dying flowers and then forget to pick up all the shards of glass. She was too old to get sentimental about the idea of loneliness. It was time to face that, and somehow the older she was the easier it was to sit with and be comfortable. Was it what she wanted? No, she wanted youth. But she knew that of her choices, she'd pick change over a halt.

None of this isolation stopped her from noticing everything there was to observe from those around her. She felt the hum of their souls far beyond the boundaries of skin and bone. It had always been that way for her, and for some above her. Some things were easy to deduce. Others were hidden secrets, and if shared too readily people would stop and look back and see horns from your head, or clutch their heart and say a prayer. Neither was accurate. Sara admired those who could continue on and be happy, radiant even. But she was not one of those women. Life had left her with a bitter taste in her mouth, and although sometimes she could taste sweetness it certainly wasn't what she was used to, so she resisted. No one bothered to ask. Some are bestowed gifts, but it is a choice in how to use them.

On a hot summer's afternoon, most of the family found themselves sitting on the side porch in the shade, trying to enjoy the day while also not succumbing to the heat. Rosemary and Wolfgang sat on the porch swing, lightly swaying from the force of one foot each. Sara rocked in the wicker rocker, while Lucy and James sat opposite from one another on the floorboards, their legs touching as their backs rested against the wall of the house and the side of the railing. Delphine and Lewis came outside with glasses and a pitcher of iced water and lemon juice, taking a seat on opposite chairs. Heidi was laying flat on her back near the other end of the porch, trying to keep the sweat from leaving her body, but was failing miserably. Seth, Henry, and Beth were some place no one really knew, but it wasn't questioned. It felt good sometimes, to be in that particular group over others.

"Wolfgang, will you pour me some more?" Sara asked, hand outstretched with her used glass. It still held a little bit of melting ice at the bottom. Quietly, he took the glass from her hand and poured more water. She watched as the water filled her glass, the ice cubes shimmering under his hand, almost restoring. He caught her staring and looked down at the ground, handing her the glass back. She took a sip; it was sweet.

"How've you been enjoying yourself this summer?" she asked him, rocking.

"It's been nice, as always," he mumbled. No one was paying

attention yet, their conversation routine, the shimmering ice in Sara's glass catching no one's eye.

"As always?" she asked, her words catching Rosemary's ear first. She rolled her head over to look at her grandmother, who was now eyeing her sitting next to her cousin. Wolfgang wasn't a friend with any of his family, but the two of them often coiled around one another. Gravity was unbreakable, as was blood.

"Well, there's been a darker cloud this time," Wolfgang tried to backtrack. Delphine and Lewis looked over at him, waiting for him to explain more. The heat was affecting everyone, making every action lazy, words sloppy. Not Sara, who seemed piercing as she took another sip of her water, sweet and icy. Youth served in a glass.

"It has. There's been a lot to process, a lot to think about and feel," she said, rocking back and forth much faster than Rosemary and Wolfgang were on their bench. Sara's eyes met Rosemary's, and she sensed her granddaughter begging for her to let it go, to stop bringing this thing no one had seen yet to light. But Sara didn't want to stop, she found it unfair.

"It really has," Wolfgang said, hoping they were still talking about the funeral.

"You seem different this summer," Sara said. Everyone's eyes rose from what they were doing and looked over at Wolfgang in unison.

"I do?" his voice was shaky.

"Yes, you do. Changed, in some way," she replied.

Something rippled; they all felt it. Heidi sat up, turning half her body back to look at everyone. There was an uncomfortable silence that fell over the crowd, but it roared nonsensical sounds. Only some could understand the message. No one said another word, but they were all thinking about it, pondering the change. Sara sat back and continued to rock, perpetually the provider, never the sacrifice. She sipped her water.

Lucy sat back against the wall of the house, her face hidden from the others. Her head began to pound from heatstroke, her body working too hard to keep up with all the mumblings she was gathering. She could hear what they were all wondering. It was like her sister's dreams, how she had simply watched from afar. She could hear her mom, lost in thought, wandering the grassy hills. She could hear Rosemary's worry, James's need to hide. Heidi was reaching out with a gentle touch, but it was being pushed away. Loudest, was her uncle. He felt ravenous, a darkness pulsing from his fingertips unable to be contained by his body. No one moved for an hour, they were paralyzed.

Finally, Beth came outside, asking if anyone wanted light sandwiches and pasta salad for dinner. It broke the spell for a long enough moment that Wolfgang was able to jump up from his seat and walk off the porch, disappearing out into the field. A few people accepted her offer, standing up and stretching their bodies before walking back into the house, a light breeze created only by a few fans and thin curtains over the open windows. Rosemary and Lucy shared a look; ducking off the porch the moment they felt it was safe. James didn't move. Rosemary looked back at him, giving him a questioning look that demanded he follow. He didn't know if he was able to, but he tried.

Wolfgang hadn't walked far. He'd wandered around in the fields, but eventually ended up in the pole barn, unable to even look at the woods without feeling a sickening resentment mounting in his chest. They found him pacing on the straw-covered dirt floor, a wild look to his eyes.

"They know," he spat when they entered.

"Know what?" Lucy asked, trying to be calm.

"Whatever the fuck it is, they know. And it's not…it doesn't feel like a good thing," Wolfgang said, his words fast and racy, his eyes unable to keep panic from filling them. He looked out at his cousins, his brother, and none of them seemed to mirror his own feelings. He didn't know why he always had to be the hollow one, defending the last bit of weight that kept him grounded before he floated off.

"It's going to be fine, nothing happened…" Lucy mumbled

but even she didn't believe her words. Because something had occurred, and she knew it. Rosemary shook her head.

"We're not going to get anywhere if we continue to act like nothing is happening. Wolfgang, something did happen. You're right. What made grandma say what she did?" Rosemary asked, her voice low, her cadence even. It was soothing, if not for less than a moment. Everyone waited for his answer, even James, who was tucked back against the wall in the shadows.

"Something about the water. I felt it. When I poured it into the glass, it changed. It was bright. She noticed it too," he replied, his thinking too sporadic for any clean-cut details. Rosemary nodded; she'd seen it without realizing.

"I don't know why she said that in front of everyone..." he muttered.

"Because she is who she is," Rosemary said, not having a better answer. He looked up at her for a brief moment, acknowledging that this was something she'd always dealt with from her, even though they all ignored it. They moved on.

"Something is changing for all of us," Rosemary said, looking over at her sister. Her eyes were red, glassy. Arms crossed against her chest, protective. She didn't want to dive into this world, these ideas. Rosemary was demanding she face it. There were no strobing lights, drugs, or men to blame her experiences on this time. She'd felt something for once all alone, in the middle of sunlight and bright, deep heat.

"Yeah?" Rosemary asked. Slowly, her sister nodded.

"Yeah. I feel right above it...on the outskirts. I could feel what they were thinking...I could just barely *hear* it..." Lucy whispered, her voice cracking as she desperately tried not to cry. The feeling was too much sometimes.

"What were they thinking?" Wolfgang pressed. Lucy shook her head like she couldn't remember it, but rather she wished not to repeat it.

"What did they think?" he asked again, though he wasn't asking. He took two strides and was in front of her, looming over her usually confident body. He placed his hands on her shoulders as if to shake her, but stopped. He wasn't his father.

"It wasn't so much words. Mom was, walking around in the grass. And James felt like he was hiding. Heidi felt so bright and warm, not like the heat of summer…" she rambled, trying to describe it in a way that made sense. It was hard to extend her experience into reality.

"And my father?" Wolfgang asked. Lucy looked up at him. He wasn't dark or cruel, he was desperate. She felt it deeply in her soul, absorbing all of it without intention.

"It was foggy, but a black fog. Like billowing smoke. I'm sorry, that's all," she said, voice low and steady against the dirt floor. He took a step back from her.

"I'm fucked," he moaned, running his hands violently through his hair.

"No, you're not. This is something, but nothing any of them will act on," she said, waving her hand back to the house where their parents were.

"We just need to keep this to ourselves and figure it out before anyone else. We can do that," Rosemary promised him, a beacon between their insanity and terror. James said nothing and did not move, focusing on being so still he hoped to melt into the wall.

Each of them took a step back, paced around, sat on the floor, looked out a window and thought. Anxiety was racing through all of them, but most didn't know why. They'd never felt such impending doom before from something they could not see, only feel in the smallest nerves of their fingertips, or the deepest cavities of their beating hearts. For several long, strung together moments, they existed together in contemplative silence. They didn't know what was beyond the horizon, but they wanted to.

Beth kept fitfully looking out the kitchen window, wondering if the kids would ever come in for sandwiches. She knew they weren't children anymore; none of them had been for quite some time. To her, they'd aged too quickly. Childhood had been a fleeting idea, and she didn't know how she'd allowed any of them to miss out on something that was supposed to be the foundation. Nervously, she bit at her fingernails, thinking about her own childhood and all its bounds.

"What are you hoping to see out there?" Lewis asked, bringing his plate over to the sink where his wife stood. All of her in-laws still sat around the dining room table, food spread out before them as they talked and laughed, sharing wild stories and even wilder ideas. She hadn't grown up around so much noise before. Her life had been all about order and work, a very stern sense of conduct in her household. Perhaps her most treacherous mistake had been wandering into the kitchen after that first time meeting Lewis's family and offering to dry the dishes.

"Just wondering if the kids were coming in any time soon, if they wanted food," Beth replied, her voice quiet as her hands were gentle grabbing the plate from the counter and washing it. Lewis chucked a little, leaning against the counter, blocking most of the drying rack with his body. He didn't notice.

"They're not kids. They know how to make themselves food," he replied, a soft smile on Beth's lips as she nodded and grabbed some utensils to wash as well.

"I know. I just like to do it."

Some yells erupted from the dining room, Lewis walking in to see what the excitement was for. Heidi sounded passionate as she battled some outlandish political policy with Henry, simultaneously trying to win an arm wrestle with him. Lewis stood in the doorway, cheering his little sister on as Delphine and Seth laughed and took bets on who would persevere. It was interesting to Beth, what bonded the Pennyfather siblings together, and what pushed them apart. Still, more than two decades in, she found her guesses of unifying moments less than accurate; she was still doing dishes.

"Thank you for making dinner, Bethany," Sara said, coming into the kitchen from one of the many sitting rooms. She'd taken her meal elsewhere, only coming back to deliver her dirty plate and glass. Beth smiled warmly, taking the plate from her mother-in-law with soapy hands.

"Of course," Beth replied. Sara meant to walk away, but the commotion in the dining room was mildly feigning her interest. The loud voices drew her in, something she never realized she missed until it was happening.

"What are they having fun about?" Sara asked, rooting through a box of chocolates for a little dessert before her evening wine. It was a routine, by then.

"Oh, something political. Then art was brought into it, and Henry had to add historical context. Honestly, a little too over my head," Beth replied sweetly, rubbing the plate back and forth with a sponge, all the crumbles washing away. Sara nodded, with no smile on her lips. She looked out at her family, the ones she had raised and made last in the world, then back at her daughter-in-law.

"I'm sure you could understand, if you were in there. Thank you again for dinner," Sara replied, walking off with achy limbs. Sweetened water only lasted so long. Beth felt her comment had been a little backhanded, as she often did, but instead chose to continue washing the dishes, glancing out the window as the sky darkened and still no sign of her sons, or nieces. She wondered what they were talking about, under a setting sun, and if she would understand their conversation. Perhaps, she was too old.

She flinched as she heard clanging plates as they fell onto the floor, nobody caring as the arm wrestling came to a close – Heidi somehow ahead.

"Again! My point's stronger than yours," Henry called out, fitting in so well with his brash feral cries and his rolling muscles. He was somehow the combination of perfect tranquility and thought, mixed with the wild and reckless energy of a young man. It all came out in different strokes, different moments. Beth wished for such self-assurance, but she didn't have the intimacy of Delphine's smile coaching her every step of the way.

With Lewis turned away, she stared openly at the back of his head. There wasn't much confidence in how she felt, her ideas about it waxing and waning like the sun did every day. Did it contemplate how much it loved the earth? Probably not – assurance because it never moved, instead forcing the earth to spin. Beth never felt she was the sun; she had no light to give. She'd given life to sons who were benevolently dark, even though one of them tried with all the life in him not to appear so; the other couldn't. Sometimes, she felt Wolfgang hated her for creating him out of his father's blood. Other times, she thought maybe he pitied her for her own.

"Are you going to come in here and spend some time with everyone?" Lewis asked, looking over his shoulder. He was a little startled to catch her eyes, but she quickly averted them.

"Yeah, Beth! Put the dishes down, they aren't going anywhere!" Heidi called with joy in her voice from the other room between anxious yelps of cheating as Henry tried to win their fight. Beth considered it, as she picked up another dish to wash. The thing was, the dishes wouldn't go anywhere. No one would come in and pick one out of the soapy sink and wash it clean. She didn't know exactly when she had felt the only way to hold it all together was to wash the dishes, but somewhere along the way, she had. And now, she was obsessed with the work. It freed her, she convinced herself.

"Beth, come sit with us," Lewis said. It was stern.

So, or not.

"Okay, okay," she whispered, wiping her hands and draining the sink. It was clear of dishes, for now. She took one more glance out the window, the last pieces of light fading from the sky. Laughter erupted again, her own husband's voice among them, as the debating became more intense, the games were more competitive, and the sweet treats and red wine grew more bountiful. She turned away from the kitchen window.

She sat down in a corner chair, looking out at everyone spread across the room, their energies filling up the space in a way that almost suffocated her. She glanced at Seth, quiet like her, but the similarities stopping there. He was happy to sit and watch; happy to laugh when the other voices did, and contemplate when the other minds did. He was a little naive, Beth liked to think. At least she understood what she had gotten into, what this all was. But then again, she didn't have Heidi softly giggling in her ear during quiet parts of the day to let her know past the harshness there was unearthly bliss.

They didn't seem real at times, the Pennyfathers. She remembered when she'd first met Lewis, his middle sister in tow with him and his friends, a perfect gang. She'd found them to be a fantastic high, an interesting intensity she'd only known to exist in film and poetry. To that day, she couldn't guess what Lewis had noticed about her. And maybe that was the thing he'd noticed, her ability to be invisible. When Beth had met Heidi a few weeks later, she couldn't believe there was another one with such intrigue and the same set of eyes, even though at the time she'd been hiding blue bruises with purple halos. But maybe that too, was the thing she'd noticed: big eyes and soft skin.

"Beth, tell me you've heard of – ," Delphine started but Beth was already shaking her head slowly, a small smile on her lips.

"I haven't," she said simply.

"Okay, but really, it's all involved with..." Delphine continued, captivating her audience with a wild story filled with monsters and victors, almost insurmountable odds. She watched her husband's eyes as he absorbed his sister's story, sipping his wine. Heidi was rolling on the floor, her arm wrestling fight with Henry turning into something of a full-body wrestling match. It was childish and yet, more fun than her own children had ever had. She'd never join in. What she had was Lewis not seeing her, until he did. Beth still found him to be all the things she had first thought he was when she'd met him, years and years ago. The only difference was now she thought she understood what living with such brazen ferocity meant. She thought it could still be worth it, only because her understanding of Lewis fell short, like looking into murky water. Understanding had been forced onto her sons, as is the unbreakable path of father and son. It was a forced road to take, no matter the danger along the way.

That place had changed her. It had lent change to everyone. It had foraged Lewis, Delphine, and Heidi – the same abilities in different creatures. It had allowed Henry and Seth to assimilate, camouflage. And it had cast Beth aside, forced her to watch. She looked back out the window, this time from the dining room. She wondered what they were doing out there, amongst all that darkness, amongst all that wide-open land and sky.

Unlike inside the house, filled with booming noise, the barn had remained quiet and still; the only noise were hearts beating.

"Are you different, too?" Wolfgang asked after their shared silence.

"I think so. For a while, now," she replied. He nodded like that made sense.

"It feels like I'm somewhere else when I dream. Like I don't stay...*here*," she said, holding her hands to her chest. She meant her body. She didn't mean the land.

"What happens in them?" Wolfgang asked, his desperation too obvious. He was like a wounded animal, one that was showing the predator he had a limp.

"All kinds of things, but mostly when I wake up I just remember pieces of them and it seems like premonitions almost. I hear and see things right before they happen, and then I remember it was a dream where it first happened," Rosemary replied. She knew it sounded crazy, her words a small slice of irrationality. But what if they weren't?

"What things so far?" he demanded.

"What?"

"What things did you know were going to happen before they did?" he pushed.

"The cat. Your phone call. A conversation I had with Silas when we first got here. And I knew...I knew papa wouldn't be here when we got here," she said, holding back nothing. Lucy let out a sob, a plea for breath; she couldn't contain it any longer. It had been choking her.

"Do you see anything about us?" Lucy asked. Rosemary

shook her head.

"Not yet," she replied.

"That's great. Really," Wolfgang spat, again pacing around. He finally looked out at his brother. He wanted to shake him, pull him away from the wall. He wanted to demand something from him, but didn't know what he was asking for.

"You're great at this whole hiding thing," he mocked, spitting on the ground. James still didn't say anything. He wasn't as good as he wished. Some people still found him every time they looked.

"Look, we'll just be careful. And we'll keep talking about the things that happen to us. Maybe we'll have enough to put it together and make some sense from it. And if not, that's okay too. Because we'll always cover for each other. Won't we?" Rosemary said, looking first at Wolfgang, then Lucy, and finally shifting her eyes briefly back at James. Nobody said anything for a moment.

"Won't we?" she said again. Each of them nodded.

"This is serious," Rosemary said, and to showcase her point walked over to the workbench and grabbed a knife from a drawer. It was probably dirty, but she didn't care. She walked back over to everyone and made a small cut on her fingertip. No one said anything as she reached for everyone's hand gently, pressed her finger into their palms, a small red smudge left behind. She meant her promise. Wolfgang took the knife from her and did the same; placing his smudge next to hers. Then Lucy, with more tears. And finally, James took the knife and did the same, used to pain.

Each of them needed something different. But their vow was hopeful. There still remained so many secrets and individual experiences, but there didn't seem any way to say it all. Instead, they all wanted to protect each other, and be protected. Blood was as good a signifier as any.

When she went back to the drawer to put away the knife, she noticed a few deserted petals from a flower that no longer existed. They were wilted, perhaps there for a long time or no time at all.

Twelve.

Rosemary laid in bed for a while that night, watching the stars on the ceiling swirl. She didn't feel that drunk from the late dinner her sister and cousins had participated in the darkness of the kitchen, wild rumblings flowing out from the living room by then. The air had felt tense and warranted several glasses of wine, but it didn't affect her sight. Instead, she waved her fingers out before her and watched as the small glow from the dark stars stuck to her ceiling began to move with her fingers, dodging her touch. She looked next to her bed, but the room had slowly faded from darkness to something else, and all she saw was her sister curled up and sleeping nestled in tall green prairie grass and dressed in all white under the galaxy sky. The space between them felt so vast, but as she moved her body to sit up the land seemed to move quickly to catch up with her. She lost her breath. Then caught it again. She started walking, wanting a glass of water. She hoped there was one left behind unbroken. She looked back; Lucy was still behind her, asleep in a fetal position looking so utterly peaceful. She never looked like that, instead always having something going on behind her eyes. But shut? She was finally calm. A shrill sound rang out over the plain; it was almost an annoying ringing in her ears. She pushed against her face, trying to get it to stop. Eventually, pressing hard enough, she began to tune into the noise and it sounded like thousands of whispers. It wasn't horrible. There was no water. She sat down in the grass looking up, the sky moving so quickly overhead, the Milky Way an all-encompassing presence. It was such a stunning display of lights, at all frequencies. Her eyes had never seen more in such a silent place.

Somehow, mountains rose from the valley, and it grew cold, snow decorating the now rocky landscape. She started walking again, still alone, still among a very silent world except sometimes when in her mind. A train, artistically magnificent and thunderously large, pulled up around the next curve, and she ended up inside. It was easy to find a seat. She picked one in the middle of the car next to an open window, staring out as the train began to move. Soon enough, it raced.

She was up in the sky, and it was so incredibly vast that all she could do was look out at the utter enormity of it and cry. It was magnificent, a beauty so stunning she could never have imagined it all on her own. The stars shined brightly in the sky, a decoration of light in a number of different patterns, far greater than just a few pinpricks in a dark sheet. The train swirled around a valley deep in the mountains; perhaps a small town down there, a few bits of light escaping a window. It seemed inconsequential when the sky was a mere arms reach away. She was so close to it, and wanted to go up and be with it, but wasn't sure where she would go if she did. It had been quiet until then.

She wasn't alone. She turned her head and saw someone sitting across from her, and he hadn't been there before. He smiled at her, welcoming. Tears welled in her eyes, an entire sea of emotion finally breaking through her storm walls.

"papa!"

He didn't say anything for a long time, just smiled gently and looked out the window at the sky with her. He seemed hazy, but she knew it wasn't her, she hadn't forgotten him at all, not a single trait. She missed him greatly. While she was like her grandmother in being, she was like her grandfather in mind. And they had rejoiced in that for her entire life, because he had been there for every moment. It had always been a gift.

"It's vast, there are no edges," he finally said, his voice sounding like a song she knew well. She nodded, her eyes torn between the night sky and glittering cosmos and the twinkle in her grandfather's eyes. The train was still marching forward, swirling around the valley, destination unknown. She wanted to speak, but found herself not having a voice. He nodded that it was okay.

"It's when you stop looking for an edge, that you can find it," he continued. She nodded like she knew what that meant, and in the moment she felt that she did. Her soul did anyway; it resonated deep within her being, understanding the tune to the song long before she did. It had been humming for a long time, since the beginning.

"I'm sorry I missed this summer with you. I was looking forward to being with you. Well, you with me. It's different, but you will see eventually," he said. His words were a puzzle, one she was trying to remember so that she could put it together later. She had a feeling that in a moment, she'd only have a small piece of it and he nodded as if that thought were true. It probably was.

"It's close," he said and with one large breath, her voice returned.

"I can feel it," she said, her shoulders twisting as if her body were in pain. It was close, she could feel it. The feeling was becoming indescribable, because it was everything and nothing all bundled together. She couldn't understand it on her own.

"It's everything, moving. It's all alive. I am so happy you can feel it," he said, a sigh of relief as he leaned back in his seat, looking out the window with her. The darkness was an overwhelming and engulfing blackness, the contrasting sparkles of light so bright it would burn through anything it touched. Miraculous.

"I don't know what it is though. None of us do. Do you? Have you seen it?" she asked, her voice childlike. She'd never had to put up any kind of front with her grandfather. He was understanding, patient, and kind. He was not without fault, but faultless to her. He wanted to show her the world because he loved her. She was worthy of everything.

"You don't like the world because you think it has limits. There are walls and borders and boundaries. You come here, and you love it because it seems limitless. But I am here to tell you that both places are one in the same. And what you feel is the door. What you feel is a rift between the places. The energy that creates also destroys. Its circular, self-sustaining. You've always wanted it, and so it's reached out to you," he said, a smile on his face, his expression still warm and comforting. She felt very much at peace with him, almost abandoning the idea of there being anything more. Rosemary didn't want to get off the train; she didn't mind the confines of this place as long as he was there; it was love.

"Where do I find it?" she asked.

"Wherever it is," he replied. It didn't seem like anything more or less than the truth. She nodded, needing no further direction.

"Did you find it?" she asked. He nodded.

"We all do at some point," he replied, his voice a little sad as he looked at his granddaughter, the edges of her much more defined than his. Time was a ravenous force, a fickle being, an insistent foe.

They watched the sky for a little bit longer, but it wasn't passing by as fast as it had been. The train was slowing down, but she didn't feel ready to get off. All of a sudden her grandfather was standing, but he offered his hand.

"Come with me," he asked and she accepted. Together they walked off the train and into the snowcaps of the mountains. The further they walked, the warmer it grew and eventually they found themselves in unfamiliar woods. Tall dark trees loomed over them, and although they were imposing forces, she wasn't fearful. Rosemary didn't know where they were going but it didn't seem to matter. The destination wasn't a part of it at all; all there could be was a journey. Out of the corner of her eye she saw something move, then a few more pieces of motion. She looked around her, curious, but only seeing vague shadows running around, mostly hidden under dark hefty leaves. She looked up at her grandfather, the bites on her legs burning.

"Those aren't for you," he said. She didn't understand.

"Nothing is pure, and they can bite," he continued. Still, she didn't understand but watched as the creatures darted around beside them, their eyes bright like the moon and holding the same calming sense. She wanted to reach out and touch one, but he had said they bit. She felt like they wanted something from her.

"What are they? Where do they come from?" she finally asked.

"They come from need," he said simply, letting it go. The creatures fell back, leaving them alone as they continued to walk. Something bright laid before them, down the trail. Every step they took didn't seem to get them any closer. Eventually, they stopped walking, standing above a darkened cliff. The sky overhead was hidden by the tree line, and the ground beneath them seemed bottomless as she glanced down the cliff. It wasn't the same as the sky, and her grandfather didn't seem as happy there.

"I want to go back," she cried.

"I know. But that's the thing you have to understand. And please, remember it. It's not always about what you want to do, but more so what you have to do. For others. They can't do it alone. It's been hard," he said, his voice becoming a whisper, his body seemingly fading more than it had on the train. She grew panicked, wanting to reach out and hold him, keep him there with her. She did not realize where she was.

"It's not time yet," he reassured. She tried to steady her breathing, keep herself calm and cognizant. She felt a sense of control wash over her. Sometimes she could claim a piece of power, understand where she was and hold the world accountable to her whim. It wasn't easy, it often overpowered her, but this time she felt she could hold on a little longer than ever before. Her grandfather smiled gently at her efforts. He'd always felt her holding on. It was love.

"I want to tell you something. I think you already know, but it's good sometimes to be reminded. The world is steady. It's monotony. You're tired of it, I know. You've held yourself back because you're worn-out of the constant waves beating you down in a well-rehearsed rhythm," he said, his eyes looking upon her sadly. He wished she didn't feel that way already, so young in her own life. As years past though, he knew it only grew.

"I don't..." she tried to say but he held up his hand. There was no room in that space for frivolous defense. The woods around them only seemed to be growing, the trees lengthening, the valley deepening. The leaves of the plants surrounding them were becoming larger than her life alone.

"What I am saying is this, you need to be the steady one. Be steady, and you'll get it. You can evolve into something more. The constant of the world is okay, it's what keeps all of it together. Without it, you wouldn't have the tools given to you to build something grand. And you can create something grand," he said, reaching out for her hands. She gave them to him, feeling the pressure of his being against her, but unable to grip as hard as she wanted. He was fading to somewhere else.

"You just have to do it. Choose it! Believe it, my dear," he said, his words now a hushed whisper, a message only for her. She held onto his words, even though she wasn't sure it was what she wanted to hear. There had to be more than this.

"*Papa*," she said but he shook his head. They started walking again, back through the woods, the plants around them so large they seemed like an entirely different creation. Everything was changing around them and suddenly they were back out in the valley; this time down the mountain and standing in the depression, the sky above them bright but not as bright as the light coming from a few windows in darkened homes.

"I have to warn you about something," he said gravely. She

153

wasn't focused on his words, her eyes honing in on one window in particular. She felt she could see someone moving around behind the glass.

"Are you listening?" he asked.

"Yes," she replied, though her mind was drifting. It was hard to stay so still there, hard to learn anything among the constant shifting of her setting. It didn't want to stay as one form, instead transforming.

"You can find the rift, you need to. For everyone. But don't let it blind you," he said as she moved her head to see better through the window, almost able to recognize the person behind it. There were two people, now that she thought about it.

"People won't tell you everything, they can't."

Something about the way they moved was familiar, but it wasn't benevolent. Preparation was happening for something that had already occurred. Was it to make them feel better? Or was it all just darkness, no more defining line? She felt like it was something she shouldn't see with her eyes, but had already seen with her soul.

"*Rosemary*."

The shadows from the woods were crawling back, roaming around the house, howling deeply. Their eyes were closed, but they cried. It was woeful, as a witness laments after a vicious crime. Their dark forms didn't know how to break in, but they wanted to. They bit, but weren't cruel without noble intention.

"You have to pay attention," he said.

"No matter what happens."

With hesitation, she took a step forward towards the house and the open window, her feet crunching in the snow. The shadows continued to howl, their voices almost drowning out the noises from inside. A candle fell, a fire rose up. There was only one sound she could hear, maybe. Vaguely, softly.

"Don't let it overtake you."

She wasn't tall enough to see in the window, but it didn't matter. She closed her eyes as a feeling so painful came over her, knocking the breath out of her chest. She was meant to see this way. It hurt, everywhere. There was no reason to see it, she had always already known. Opening her eyes, she turned back to look at her grandfather. A handsome man standing before her. Dark black hair slicked back, a smooth face with bright blue eyes smiling out at her. He was larger than life, and yet almost translucent. The sky around them was vast once more, the valley such a small part of it all. He was right, there were no edges. The outline of his body began to blur, but maybe it was the tears in her eyes. She mouthed the only thing she knew to say. *I love you.*

"Steady, you'll find it."

Thirteen.

Her head was beginning to swim. She didn't know why, what was causing it. She had vague memories, deeply embedded feelings. Her eyes were swollen; she'd been crying. Was there some kind of raging infection in her bloodstream? Was it her parents' sharp view of what was important and what wasn't? Perhaps it was her sister pulling away from her, wanting to be separated from the extraordinary and just be ordinary for once in her entire life. Or her cousins, whose sorrow she could feel from across the hall as they slept, peaceful looks on their faces. She didn't know. Rosemary stood up abruptly and walked over to the window, opening it up to let in the morning breeze off the sunrise's ascent. It was cool for once and it calmed her eyes. She walked out of her room and down the stairs, sitting out on the porch in loose clothes, needing to breathe in the cool air, absorb the early morning rays. Her body needed to wake up; she'd spent too long on death's side. At least, she wanted some air.

The porch was pleasant that early in the morning and she sat on the damp railing, not minding the dew absorbing through the cotton of her clothes. She just watched as the birds pecked away at the earth, hoping it would offer them something. She admired their faith that it would, singing to each other as they worked.

She didn't want to admit it, but as she rubbed the pain out of her leg, being gentle around her healing pink skin, she felt the acknowledgment bubbling to the surface of her psyche. Something hadn't been right for a long time. It wasn't just the dreams; it was far more. She liked those wispy places so much she hadn't bothered to understand them, settling for only enjoyment. Her grandfather might have tried to warn her about that, if he were there in front of her. Somewhere, she had stopped trying to figure messages out and instead live inside their orbs, carrying those feelings around with her wherever she went.

It was how they made her feel powerful.

It was that she wanted a break from the mundane and the constant. She did. It seemed that however often the world gave her enough of something new to keep going, it also gave her more than enough to keep her small, forcing her to bend down and crawl. She held a lot of hurt within her heart and nothing seemed to take that away, the world merely giving her more to carry around. She had to carry it around, always. The birds kept pecking at the grass, golden and glistening in the sun's rising light.

She wasn't sure why she had always been so obsessed with the destination, when it was the journey that mattered. She had been allowed to make many different choices, and they had led her to this particular moment in time. She wasn't sure why; it seemed so overwhelming. It was much bigger than something as fleeting as happiness. Rosemary realized she wanted something bigger from the universe, to feel small in an important way, not small in a forgotten way. Maybe that was naïve, or egotistical, but she couldn't help the desire, and she was willing to follow any path to get to it. But also, she didn't want to go alone.

Her eyes didn't have any more tears to shed that morning, but her body rested in grief as the sun rose, warming her skin, drying both tears and dew from the world. As it warmed around her, she felt embraced, if just for a moment. She knew he had never left; that the body in the ground she'd thrown dirt on the day she'd arrived wasn't what she missed, not really. Understanding and navigating the world was difficult, but her mind was expanding with each breath she took. She wanted to keep taking them.

"Are you okay?" Lucy murmured, walking out onto the porch with a cup of coffee for her sister. She felt very muted, and Rosemary let it be.

"Thanks," was all she said, as she took the cup from her sister and tasted a sip. Just enough sugar, how she liked it. Lucy climbed up onto the railing's edge next to her sister, looking out at the morning sky and noticing the way the golden light made the fields around their house look like a place she'd never been before. They didn't speak as they sipped their drinks, sitting so close to each other they could feel every breath, each heartbeat. If someone was to stand out and look at the two of them side by side, they would think the girls looked like sisters, the profiles of their faces lining up perfectly, each girl's different colored eyes molding together to become a swirling golden just like the sun. Truly, they were complementary.

But no one stood out on the porch that day to see them, instead they sat together alone, welcoming another day into their lives because they wanted to, not because they had to. When the sun was fully up in the sky, surrounded by a brilliant blue, they went inside leaving the birds to sing to each other.

Rosemary eyed her cousins as they bounded down the stairs, pushing each other around and laughing a little before entering the kitchen and becoming somber. They each nodded a good morning to the crowd and grabbed some food and coffee before making their way to the table. James sat across from Rosemary, offering her some jam for her toast. She shook her head slightly, and he set it down away from her. She felt something about him, her body aching at the sight of him, but she didn't know what it was from. It was the feeling of a haunting, more than anything. Knowing something was there, feeling it, almost anticipating its next move and then just – not moving forward.

"Are you alright?" he asked her, voice quiet so no one could hear. Wolfgang did and looked up and over at her, then back at his brother. Rosemary yawned.

"Just tired," she offered, hoping that would calm him, keep him from asking anything else. At the moment, it did work. He felt the stress too, but he hadn't had any dreams. She was caught rubbing her fingertips into her forehead, desperately searching for the images and words that had belonged to her dream. She knew she'd had one; there was always a feeling when she opened her eyes, a weary weight to her eyelids that a traveler carries. She knew the message had been important, she knew someone had told her something she needed to remember and carry with her. All she had left were feelings, and James sent a deep tremble down her spine. Wolfgang was quiet, observing her. She smiled at him slightly, then stood up and set her dish in the sink and walked off to take a shower, close her eyes and feel some cold water and think. She was tired.

After a long shower that never ran out of cold water, she spent some time in her room brushing out her hair and looking out the window just enjoying the silence. Lucy had bounded away for the day to be with friends, wanting to be normal and ordinary for any day she had left to hold onto. Rosemary didn't press it.

She heard a hammer pounding on wood, and after a short while put a little perfume on the sides of her neck and walked downstairs and outside into the hot sun.

"Hi," she greeted, perhaps a little too cheerful. It didn't match her eyes.

"Hey, how're you?" Silas asked, looking up from where he was crouched at the base of the steps that led up onto the porch. The wood had rotted, and he was ripping it up and intending to simply replace it, initially wishing to not find anymore rot underneath the slits of the actual porch. In the new moment, he was no longer sure which he hoped for. He had his dark hair half pulled back, and she liked that.

"I'm good," she replied, taking a seat on the floorboards, her back up against the railing. He was already sweating from pulling up two planks of wood, beads of saltwater decorating the crown of his head.

"What've you been up to?" he asked.

She wanted to talk openly. She wanted to tell him about how vast the sky was, how her cousin had frozen water, how she had cut her finger purposely to make a promise in blood, how she missed the sound of her grandfather's voice but heard him whispering in the darkest corners. But she found herself simply chiming in, "not much." He looked at her. She was avoiding the intensity they had already built. Even though she had put it on hold, gone rouge for over a week, she had agreed that she wanted to see him. It didn't matter if she'd said it or not, there was already a place they met sometimes, even if they both couldn't quite remember it without the help of the other. They both wanted to share space in whatever way they needed. It changed, but somehow was steady. She felt that in her chest. He, in his heart. It was an ache to be heard and understood – vulnerability. She didn't know why all she could muster was a simple *not much*. She shook her head.

"You know, just..." she trailed off, not sure how deep to dive. She didn't know what spaces were safe to enter with him; what he would find too much. The decision of being known was mortifying. She found that to be true regardless of the subject matter. He nodded, a soft smile on his lips as he turned his head back to the wood, ripping up a third step and getting ready to crawl under and see how far the rot had spread. She hugged her knees, feeling her own sweat absorbing through her white sleeveless shirt.

"You can start with the smallest thing, you know," he said. She thought about that, maybe she could, maybe it wouldn't be so bad to talk.

"My sister and I are a little tense right now," she started out. He nodded, yanking an embedded nail out from the sideboards. He reached down and felt underneath, hardly devastated when he found more wood that needed to be removed.

"Is that unusual for you two? The twins," he laughed, though didn't miss the way her eyes furrowed. He waited to hear her complaint.

"People like to know we're twins, they act surprised if I don't mention it. But then they're always annoyed that we're fraternal, not identical," she said, looking at him, wondering why he had mentioned it. He didn't seem like the rest. He nodded.

"It's weird sometimes, how obsessed people can be with certain things," he replied. She knew exactly what he meant.

"We don't look even remotely related, and we're hardly the same person. It's like, damn, no parlor trick now. When I look at her face, it really isn't mine at all. But I like that, because we still...click. And right now, we haven't been. She hasn't liked hearing about certain things from me lately," she continued, again not feeling sure where to send the conversation drifting. It was nice that he was working while she talked, his focus on the motion of something other than her face giving her a sense of freedom.

"Are you looking to do a parlor trick?" he asked her.

"More than that, I think," she replied. She remembered the pink sand around her toes with him standing there, yelling out at the sky and having the glass in the sea ring back the same notes. It was an odd memory, but it felt right in that place.

"You seem tired today," he commented, bringing their conversation out farther than she noticed in the moment. She rubbed her forehead again, pushing her short hair away from her face. The sweat slicked it back easily, her baby hair curling under the stickiness of moisture. She rocked her head back and forth, weighing her options.

"I haven't been sleeping very well," she finally settled.

"You haven't been sleeping? Or you haven't been resting while you sleep?" he asked her just as he ripped a massive board off the porch. When he turned it over he showed her all the places it had gone soft and was beginning to give out. She ran her fingers over the spots, feeling the soggy wood with interest.

"You know a lot about fixing everything," she commented, leaning away from his worksite as he pitched the wood behind him. He shrugged his shoulders, wiping sweat away from his forehead with the sleeve of his shirt. Soon enough, he stopped to grab a bandana out of his back pocket and tie it around his head, both holding his thick hair back and also keeping the sweat from dripping down and stinging his eyes.

"I've lived here my whole life," he replied. It felt like a guarded answer.

"What does that mean?" she pushed. He wanted her to be honest with him; she wanted the same in return. It was the only way to be known.

"This place is unforgiving. It's not somewhere to rest. It's a place that constantly demands your attention and your time; otherwise, the woods might just grow up and engulf your house. You know?" he said. She had no idea.

"I didn't mean for that to sound crass," he mumbled, almost an apology.

"No, I liked it," she said quickly, still thinking about the idea of being swallowed whole by the woods. Did they really move that fast, in a blink you could vanish?

"Do you want some lunch?" she asked suddenly, standing up. He nodded, ripping out more wood without looking up. She went back inside and fixed up a couple sandwiches and something cold to drink. It took her a while as she listened to the sounds of his tools breaking apart the rotten wood and putting something much sturdier in its place. Maybe there was some way he could help. It felt like he might be able to.

"Here you go, take a break," she announced, coming back out with a plate and glass. He stood there for a moment, then slowly pulled himself up onto the porch and into the shade, sitting next to her on the floor. He took a large bite of the sandwich, his hands dark from sun and dirt. She watched him eat.

"What're you doing after this?" she asked, looking down at the hole in the porch flooring. He shrugged his shoulders, taking his first bite of the second sandwich.

"What did you have in mind?" he asked.

"Just a walk, through the woods."

She waited the full two hours for him to finish the job for her grandmother the right away. She watched him work the entire time and as she did, they chatted about mostly inconsequential things. She told him about living with her aunt, and how strange it was being there for the summer and pretending to be someone's daughter and someone else's niece. He told her about being raised by his grandmother after his mother left and his father couldn't always bring himself to remember the steps back home. He seemed a mere ghost when sighted, about as infrequently as a haunting. Rosemary mentioned sometimes she went down for weeks, her mind going dark and stormy and her body unable to rally. Silas said he understood how big the waves could be sometimes. He taught her a few new signs, a little phrase to use here and there. She was a natural. Maybe nothing was truly inconsequential.

Once the porch repair was finished, Rosemary jumped up and down on the steps to test out his handiwork. Silas laughed as she did, watching her do a silly dance along with each pounce to fully showcase the sturdiness of his fine work. He packed up the tools and placed them back in the barn, washing the sweat off his hands and face by the hose Rosemary held up for him. She let some of the water run down her legs, feeling her shaved hair prickle under the burst of coolness. They started walking out away from the house and all its many buildings. The farther they got, the less noise she felt she could hear even though the house had remained mostly quiet all day.

She started hearing cicadas singing, their hissing unmistakable above their heads. For some reason, she hadn't noticed them once that whole summer until then. Silas watched her head tilt up looking through the leaves of the trees above them.

"What is it?" he asked.

"Cicadas," she replied. He decided to be vulnerable.

"What do they really sound like?" he asked. He watched as she took her time thinking about it, wanting to get it right. They continued to walk into the woods, becoming completely engulfed by the greenery. The woods always created a feeling inside of her, but that day it was a new feeling. One of great vastness, of endless bounds and unlimited energy and movement. She almost felt restless, like she had when she'd woken up from her first dream back on her family's land. She looked over at Silas, still waiting for her description. He did look different that year, older, wiser. More worked. Less softness, more hard edges and callous skin. It went deeper than that, his brown eyes were more watchful, less inviting. But she had never felt closer to him. He still had the bandana tied around his messy dark hair, holding it away from his face. She'd found her answer.

"Kind of like this," she said holding out one hand in front of her. He watched intently as she rattled it side to side her fingers outstretched, then swooping it up into the sky. It felt about right, how they sounded if she could see it. He smiled.

They kept walking along the trail, stopping to look at the big trees that housed porcupines, the little creek where the frogs hummed, and the strange patches of weeping grass that dotted a certain part of the woods before a large hill rose up full of mostly uncovered rocks. It was more a casual amble than a walk; time was being held between them more closely than around them.

"When you leave in September, do you go home with your parents?" Silas asked, watching as she tiptoed across a large fallen oak, her arms outstretched to help keep her balance. She shook her head, feeling so hidden in the trees she didn't try to hide from anything else.

"No, I've lived with my Aunt Heidi for a long time now," she replied looking up at him after she'd jumped down from the trunk of the tree, having reached the end where the roots had been pulled forcefully from the earth by storm.

"How long have you lived with her?" he asked.

"Since high school. It was the year I decided I wasn't leaving anymore," Rosemary replied, watching his eyes ask the next question before his hands did. He was looking at her deeply and she felt confident about it for the first time. Maybe becoming known was okay. Her heart pounded at the thought, a deep ache in her broken body. But, it was still beating, and loudly, strongly. Did that mean it would be okay?

"*Leave to go where?*" his voice was quiet; his hands were not.

"Wherever my parents decided they wanted to go next. I didn't want to leave anymore, so I stayed. And I still haven't left," Rosemary said, allowing him to think what he wanted about that seemingly permanent choice. It had been a big moment, but she had done it so silently that she had always pushed away the idea in her mind that it had been any kind of monumental.

"Parents are tricky," he replied, a sly smile. She chuckled.

"I do like Heidi, though. She's a good one. We talk sometimes. At your grandmother's house, or when she runs past mine in the mornings," Silas said, his hands in his pockets as he swung his feet slowly forward, digging the toe of his boot into the dirt here and there. Rosemary turned her head to one side.

"You see her in the mornings?" she asked. He nodded casually.

"Yeah, she jogs in the mornings. Didn't you know? Her route goes through my land. She knows it well," he said looking over at his walking companion, not wanting to miss any of her next thoughts whether they were verbal or visual. He could tell something had been flagged in her mind.

"I know she runs. What do you guys talk about?" she asked. She wasn't entirely sure why, but something about her worlds overlapping in such obvious yet unseen ways was forcing her to consider something.

"Not a lot. Just the weather, if I'm coming by to work on something, how my grandma is doing..." he replied, shrugging it off. She thought about that.

"Did Heidi know your grandmother, when she was growing up here?" Rosemary asked. He nodded, but looked at her curiously.

"Yeah, pretty well. Our grandmothers were friends, sort of, a long time ago. And of course, Heidi was around, she was a kid.

You didn't know that?" Silas asked. They'd stopped walking for a moment; standing in one of the small patches of grass that were unlike any she'd seen before. It was long, curling over from the weight of itself and laying out in a variety of different patterns. Like a sea without water.

"I guess I didn't," she replied. She didn't say anything else about it. Somehow, she had forgotten that Heidi had an entire life before hers had ever begun. Looking up into the trees, the leaves moving gently together creating a soft symphony, she started to think about how much of her aunt's life she had never considered, never thought about even though it was probably all that Heidi did. Her mind forced her to consider the same for Delphine. She wasn't sure what her mother had been like at ten, sixteen, or twenty here in the very place she now stood. To the woods, had time passed at all? Did all the trees surrounding her recognize the moments that had molded them?

Silas and Rosemary talked some more, about silly things, more inconsequential things. It was nice though, the small talk. It was comforting in a way she had never known it to be. It was trivial, until it wasn't. It was bound to happen.

"What do you have?" Silas asked, eyeing her hand. They were sitting in the grass while they talked, and without realizing it Rosemary had fished a stone out of the pocket of her cutoffs and was rubbing her finger over the shiny surface.

"It's a gemstone, I guess. They call it a tiger's eye," she replied, holding up the small orange and brown striped stone, trying to gauge what he thought. Carefully she handed it to him and watched as he ran his finger over its surface, turning it over, finally resting it in the center of his palm, the weight perfectly distributed.

"Where'd you get it?"

"An old woman was selling a bunch of stones at a place I was visiting once," Rosemary replied, smiling slightly. She hadn't been able to place the feeling before but since it was growing, she was starting to know it. Her realities were always shifting, but it felt good to have someone else wandering through them. It almost forced a kind of order, one she rarely knew where to meet when on her own.

"By the water," he murmured knowingly, thumbing the stone. She nodded.

"It was loud," she replied, though wasn't talking about the water at all. He nodded as if that made sense. Suddenly, there didn't feel to be any space in the woods at all. In fact, all that space around them had shrunk, and she felt pressed into his being from an outside world that didn't seem to exist in any way that was within reach. It was far more than physicality; it was a space created and only accessible from an internal being. It was sudden and quick, but she felt a buzz in her arms and hands, saw a momentary gasp of light radiate from the life around them, and then fade away just as quickly. She trained her eyes back on Silas, who was just looking at her calmly, waiting for her to return.

"So, is this sleep? Because it doesn't feel like being awake," she said, her voice skittish, her breath quick. He seemed even closer than she thought.

"I thought you weren't sleeping well?" he asked again, but the question wasn't really from him at all. She thought about it for what seemed like eternity.

"Is this a dream?" she whispered. The world around her felt too familiar that she had to ask, but too different to not know the answer.

"The only people who dream are sleeping good," he replied, only half answering the question.

"I'm not sleeping."

"Me either."

It might not have been a dream, but she was comfortable, waking to find herself curled up next to him, his arm wrapped around her. At some point, they had drifted. Whether it was the heat, the work, or the excess of energy, it didn't really matter. She watched him sleep, his head turned away from her, his breathing deep and even. She'd always thought he was attractive, from the first moment she saw him. Whenever that was, she couldn't recall. But in that moment all constraints vanished, it was just him against the green grass, natural light spilling through the leafy canopy to light up his face. She found him handsome. A piece of life. A nice thought. Someone who deserved it all.

The rift was real.

She'd seen it.

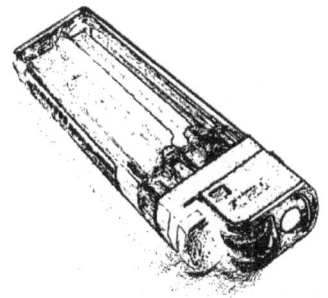

Fourteen.

They always came back in the fall, after everyone else had left and was gone. It was so they could be alone.

That was his father's favorite part of the year, being isolated on all that land. It always seemed so different, even though just weeks before it had been filled with the entire family. Well, mostly alone. He always had James follow him out. Something about Wolfgang had never worked, never seemed right. He'd been born when they were too young, he was too loud, too easily agitated. He used to scream for hours as a child for no reason at all. But when James had been born, Lewis knew he would be the one he'd teach to hunt. He was quiet and thoughtful; he wanted to please everyone. And his father used that, taught him how to make it useful to other people, and useful to him.

There wasn't much to hunt in the summertime except birds. Sometimes small predators. Mostly Lewis forced James to spend time with him preparing blinds and surveying, hiking out great distances to property James was sure they didn't own, but was also sure nobody owned. The places Lewis sought out were the most remote and the most removed. He wanted utter quiet. It was the only way he thought he'd be able to hear it.

Lewis was preparing for another trip out, feeling a sudden and absolute need to wander out there, farther than ever. He said he wanted to scout the best places to build a new blind. He told James to pack a bag and get ready for a long weekend haul. When he said those words, James hesitated for the briefest of moments, and Lewis loomed over him, daring him to look. He didn't. After he left, James got his things together slowly, a deep sense of exhaustion in his pace. He didn't want to go, he never did, but lately a growing resistance was building in his bones. James didn't know how to act on it, and thought he probably never would.

After securing his bag, he stepped out into the hall, shutting his bedroom door carefully. He heard muffled sounds, and tiptoed quietly down the first set of stairs to the second-floor bedrooms. The voices were louder now, more recognizable. He stood still, his ears straining to catch each muted word. His parents were fighting, something they often did but rarely made verbal. James curled up on the bottom step, sitting down, pressing his face against the wall and closing his eyes to listen intently. It was one of the worst fights he'd heard from them in a long time. It started out about the house, how Beth felt forced to live in a space even he didn't want to be in. How large a place it was and she was the only one taking care of it, and why should she? She missed her life back home; she didn't want to be stuck with his family in the middle of nowhere any longer. She felt trapped, isolated. She sounded so angry; her voice sharp like it never was around her sons. James shrunk away from it, feeling very alone on that bottom step.

His mother continued. She was upset with her life, having no idea how she stood where she was. She felt like a failure. She felt alone. Lewis didn't let her sharp words continue much longer, before biting in and yelling back, anything she said immediately washed away and buried under his anger. He called her ungrateful and unappreciative of the family and the life they had built. She mentioned something about all the hunting, but Lewis was quick to interject about the importance of building character, providing for a family, and learning how to protect.

"Who are you really protecting?" Beth shot back, her one

stance. James didn't see her face, but could feel the heat in his own cheeks. She yelled some more, not letting Lewis's own anger stop her. They continued the argument. She accused him of not loving her, and he challenged her idea of love. James felt dizzy under their words, a headache forming at the base of his skull. He wanted it to be over. The fight became about other things, Lewis growing more volatile as Beth's words raced further out of his control. Finally, the door yanked open and Lewis jolted out, James standing at attention so quickly he nearly fell over. His father looked at him for a moment then pushed him forward. Beth looked out at them for a few moments from the doorway, her face red and tear-stained, but she said nothing and shut the door quietly behind them. She'd never defended him.

Lewis nearly ran down the stairs, James moving quickly to keep in pace. James had hoped Lewis would forget about the hunt, forgo the excursion after such a fight with his wife, but he hadn't even come close. He was more invested than ever. They were almost out the front door, but Sara stopped them momentarily.

"Where are you going?" she asked, her words halting them. She had that power about her. They looked over at her, sitting at the kitchen table peeling potatoes for a big family dinner. Lewis just shook his head.

"Going to practice, perhaps set up a new blind for the fall. We'll be back in a day or two," Lewis replied with utter decision, his son silently behind him, focusing on the floorboards. Some of them were new.

"There's still land to conquer out there?" Sara asked.

"There's always more," Lewis replied quietly, then walked out. Sara looked at James for a long moment but said nothing, so he followed his father. Heidi and Delphine sat on the porch, talking and drinking minty cocktails. They stopped when they saw their brother and nephew, all packed up for a trip. They asked the same question.

"Hunting practice," Lewis replied, giving them even less of an answer.

"Do you have to go?" Heidi asked, trying to get James to look at her. He wouldn't. He couldn't take it, the way everyone wanted to give him a reassuring glance, a pep talk of resilience with their eyes, a silent farewell. They had no idea, and they only continued to prove that they didn't want to know. Lewis and James walked down the porch steps, passing Wolfgang on their way across the lawn. No words were exchanged, but Wolfgang reached out to touch his brother's shoulder. James jerked away from it as if the touch were poisonous. He didn't want his brother's pity, his mild attempt at comfort. He sulked around upset he was the unchosen one, as if he even wanted or knew what it was like to be out in those woods in the dark with *him*.

They started walking. At first, the hike was familiar. It was the same path to the end of the first hundred acres. Then, the trail split a few different ways, and it was always a surprise which turn Lewis would choose to take. They walked for hours, the first few in silence as the sun faded throughout the sky, the heat taking hold of them firmly then letting go slowly as time passed. They stopped at a stream to refill their water bottles. A few deer watched them walk, too timid to even run. It was only as the sun began to set, their destination an hour away, the heat and exhaustion having hit James's overworked body hard that Lewis started talking again.

What no one seemed to realize about Lewis was his anger was the only thing that anchored him to reality. He was only able to navigate the world around him by being firm, aggressive, and perceptive. Out in the woods away from everyone and any type of civilized societal pressures, he uncaged his mind and let all of his wildest delusions and ideas run rampant. And they were wild.

"Are you keeping your eyes open? We can't let them sneak up on us again. I know they found us last time, but we have to be the ones to find them this time. You know that, right? Your mother has no respect for this work. Your aunts have no idea about what's really out here. They take it for granted they can walk through the woods, use the trails for *leisure*. They're only safe because I've been out here, always looking…" he rambled, though his ideas would grow far grander about the dangers of the woods the longer into the night, the more he drank, the more pills he took. His drugs had been Lucy's first taste. She'd found them the summer she was fifteen.

James nodded his head when appropriate, but mostly he kept silent. His father liked him that way, until he didn't. James was well trained by that time. He could shoot a target no matter the conditions. He could find shelter in nearly every climate, find a water source, find food, and make heat. James knew how to survive because the threat had always been within view.

"Do you see anything?" Lewis asked, stopping. The liquid in the flask he held splashed as he turned suddenly, looking back at his son. His pupils were dilated, almost engulfing his entire eyes. James shook his head.

"You're not paying attention. They're close. Through there, I heard something," he muttered, walking on towards the noise he thought he'd heard. James followed, pulling his backpack up higher, the muscles in his back beginning to ache.

"Have you been talking to them? The beasts out here? You've been hiding from me, I know it," Lewis said, his eyes wide as he continued looking around, hoping to see something move so he could follow the noise. James kept a mental note in his head of where they were going so they wouldn't become lost. So far, they hadn't gone anywhere he'd never been before, but they were certainly going out farther than he had thought they'd make it.

"We should make camp soon, it's getting dark," James said. Lewis stopped, turning around to stare at his son, eyes wide and dangerous. James could hardly look.

"I asked you a question," he said.

"No, I've never told anyone," James mumbled.

"We'll stop to make camp when I find the spot," he said, turning back and continuing to walk. James looked out at the setting sun, hiding behind a large hill before even reaching the lower tree line they were hiking through. Something felt off about his father, worse than other times. He seemed particularly keen about finding something out in the woods that night: a pressure that had been building up inside of him had become too heavy a burden. James's mind raced with the idea about the rift, how everyone was feeling something that summer and maybe it was something Lewis felt too. James had lived in his father's insanity for a long time, grown up in it for so long he had never stopped to question it or find legitimacy. It was always about survival, and as long as it was about that, there was no energy to think about a rift, where it could be, what it could do for him, and how it was changing the world around him.

"Here, we'll make camp here," Lewis mumbled, finding a small clearing in the woods by large hills. James nodded, as good a place as any. Carefully, they each set up their tents, unloading their sleeping bags and clothes into the tents and keeping a small pack out only for hunting. The food they'd brought was strung up on a farther out tree and a small amount of wood was collected for a cooking fire. It took almost no time at all, a well-practiced ritual.

"Let's go," Lewis said, his voice desperate. James carefully followed behind him as they started another long walk, this time specifically searching for what he wanted most. He'd refilled his flask before they started their night hike. Another couple of hours went by, filled with manic thoughts as they searched for the unnamed beasts that populated the woods. Lewis was so sure they existed, he had felt their presence his entire life, feeling their violence as a burden he was hoping to win. He had raised James in that violence, and he thought James could take it because so far, he had. He always had.

At some point, they stopped, finding a high place to sit and Lewis demanded they wait, maybe something would come out in the last bit of twilight and they'd finally be able to take a shot. So they sat and waited. James had to go to a different place, his mind beginning to wander like it did a lot of the times he was out there in the dark woods. He was tired; he wanted to go home. He wished he was with his cousins, his brother, back in the barn or even the dirty bar. He'd had fun getting drunk and not thinking a single bad thought. Always, he wondered why some liquid turned his father into a monster but made him feel celestial.

James saw what he thought his father was looking for. The shadows, dancing around in the brush, swirling behind trees. It was too dark for shadows to exist, but they somehow still did, coming out to tease, bark, howl and laugh when Lewis remained wide-eyed and silent, always looking for them. James struggled to keep them a secret, knowing his father was keeping track of every muscle he moved. But as the time passed, he became entertained by his little beasts, and they were entertained by him. It was easy, to be somewhere else when they were around. Even their glowing eyes, the only thing alluding to a shape, didn't cause him any fear. He'd already met the monster; he remembered the night he first had.

"We're going back," Lewis grumbled, standing up abruptly and walking off, the shadows around him scattering into the air. James jumped up to follow him and tried to keep pace with his father as they hurried back to camp. By the time they arrived at the tents, James was exhausted and with his father seemingly in a stupor, climbed into his tent and zipped it up, hoping for a solid night's rest alone. He'd misjudged.

James thought, tucked into his small tent in the dark, his father had forgotten about him. He had thought his mind was running miles around the woods, thinking about a monster roaming around, something evil lurking in the shadows that needed to be taken down. He was the monster hunter, or so he thought. That's what he called himself, that's what he hoped to be. As James began to drift into sleep, he felt it. The stillness. It wasn't right. Something was happening, worse than before, but he wasn't sure what it could be. He stayed motionless, clutching the edge of his sleeping bag, hoping for a warning of what was going to happen before it did. Sometimes he wanted to know; most of the time he didn't.

Light invaded the thin material of his tent in one massive wave, then died down to an enormous simmer. It was bright, yellow and red, and one glance through the mesh of the tent showed that Lewis had lit a dead tree still standing on fire. An unmistakable smell wafted through James's tent walls – aide from an accelerant.

The ground shook as Lewis stumbled over to James's tent, the side of the wall being slashed with a knife so quickly James's heart skipped a beat, his breath halting. Lewis yanked him out by the crown of his hair, dragging him as he half crawled to keep up. Lewis threw him down in the dirt as he staggered around the fire, shouting at it with his arms raised. His head whipped around to face James quicker than he'd moved before, and James shrunk back away from him as much as he could.

"Look at it!" Lewis screamed poorly, beyond intoxicated. The awareness of the roaring fire hit James fully. Never had he seen such a fire before, so out of control and powerful. It seemed blue at its core, rising up to become the most vibrant and threatening shades of yellow, orange, and red. Lifting his eyes to the sky, he watched as the thick toxic smoke rose and darkened even the moon's rays that just barely hit the hidden ground of the woods. James knelt before it, as if some angry god was demanding his acknowledgment. Shakily, he moved his head up to look into the bright flames that flew towards him then darted away, teasing him with a dangerous pain. James glanced over at his father, worried what was next.

He watched his father as he moved around the fire. It didn't seem like enough for him, and he continued to throw almost anything he could find into the flame. He was on a ravenous rampage, causing James to cringe every time he heard something break. The smell burned his nose and his eyes watered fervently, but he didn't dare move and call attention to himself. His father was on the hunt, alone. It was only them and the fire, everything else was cast in darkness, safe darkness, only the circle of light signaling where there was danger. In horror, the dead tree began to collapse in on itself, sending brilliant small embers by the hundreds flying out, several hitting James in the face and chest, burning him with small specks of pain. A scary yell came from his father's throat as he walked around it looking almost pleased with what he had been able to summon.

And then suddenly, all attention was on James. Lewis began to focus on his son's kneeling form with watery eyes and ambled over to him angrily, kicking him unexpectedly in the ribs so that he doubled over and rolled onto his back in pain, never having seen it coming. He tried not to make a noise.

"It's you!" he yelled into James's face, pinning him to the ground with a solid hand around his throat. Lewis's face was so close to his, the liquor rolling off his tongue into James's face. James couldn't speak, no words would form in his head, just his constant gasps as the air he took in became less and less.

"You're one of them! You've turned on me!" he shouted over and over, and just as James started to close his eyes Lewis's hand left his throat and James winced as he gulped in air, rolling over onto his side. He'd been hit before, he'd been tested with lack of air before, but this wasn't measured. This was wild, uncalculated. His father wasn't on his side, training him to be better. Not that it mattered; it always hurt. But now as James looked up from the ground into his father's eyes, he saw resentment. Somehow James had been turned into the enemy. A traitor.

Lewis walked off for a moment, James struggling to see where he went as he tried to get up. His side twisted too much, a deep pain radiating through his body. He hoped a rib wasn't cracked or broken. Painfully, he dragged himself closer to the darkness, hoping for some kind of escape. Whatever had made his father move on was only a small distraction, because he came back quickly as James scrambled away.

"How could you do this? It's all your fault. You make me do this," he shouted, grabbing onto James's legs and pulling him back towards the fire. James reached out to grab onto anything, but found himself doubled over after another kick. His father paced around his crumbled body, not sure what he wanted to do this time.

"I tried to show you the way through these woods, through this *place*. And you deny that? You go off and get with *them*?" he shouted as James continued to try and crawl away. His attempts were pitiful. He was always rendered weak by his father.

"Why is it always you?" he asked, a sound of begging in his voice, as if asking why James had made him do this, all the time, every time. It didn't mask the anger though; the unleashed fury that drove him into those woods in the first place. He dragged James to his feet but he could hardly stand for long.

"Stop, please," James whimpered, the first words out of his mouth. The air had been knocked out of him, his side throbbing so heavily it was an effort to breathe, to even try and move. His face pounded and the fear in his blood was rising, making the need for air that he wasn't able to reach even more alarming.

"You should have thought about that before you told!" Lewis yelled. There was a fear in his own eyes, one that persisted even under such a large ego. He was afraid of the souls he'd killed. Sometimes, he thought he could hear them howling, too.

"Told? Told who, what? I've said nothing to anyone!" James yelled back, his voice cracking as he cried. He saw no way out of this, and was so confused by his father's abandonment of everything he'd done to James for years. He had never seen this coming. Suddenly, a new wave of feeling hit him, swooshing through him like the wind in a grassy field. There was something out in the woods, and it had not turned on his father, but it had turned on James.

"You're one of them, I know it. You've *seen* them," Lewis hissed, his eyes darting around them as if something would come out and attack him. *But not by the fire*, he thought. He'd built it for protection, against the monsters, against his son. Wolves were scared of fire. Easily corruptible, he saw James for who he truly was: a coward, someone who had never been devoted to the cause, someone who had lost his way.

"Were you ever even trying?" he shouted with stored up malice, making another grab for James who managed to roll out of the way and take in a big gulp of air before the pain of movement could steal it away. Lewis was caught off balance for a moment, but it only took him seconds to reclaim his ground.

"Say something for yourself!" Lewis screamed, his voice causing a deeper panic to run through James's veins. His chest heaved with the weight of facing such hostility.

"What do you want me to say?" James yelled back, still crouched on his knees, the light of the fire illuminating his face. His father stared at him deeply.

"When did you see them? When did you see them and not tell me?" he asked, his voice turning calm and collected in such a swift and sudden turn that James's eyes widened, backing up even farther from the flames and his father. He wasn't where he thought he was anymore. He wasn't anywhere he knew. He looked around him but saw nothing familiar, no sign of anything that would bring him any grace. His father kept repeating the question, the fire burning his skin from excessive heat. James laid back, hands clutched to his side, watching as the flames seemed to reach higher and higher into the darkened sky, almost to the tips of the trees. It was a bad fire, made of things that should not be burned. It was releasing things into the air that rotted Lewis's mind even more, and James was to blame.

"When did you see them?" his father roared.

"The night I couldn't look at you anymore!"

Finally, Lewis yanked James up to his feet by his neck, walking around him as he stood, slumped, knees ready to give out, side heaving and face throbbing. His words were hard to hear. James's vision was blurred. There was a moment of choice involved, but James had never been strong enough to make it. He'd fallen into insanity when he was too young and too small to fight it off. Something about growing up with it made him complacent to it. Could he really blame anyone else for not fighting for him, when he wouldn't even fight for himself? Maybe there was always a part of him that wanted to be out in the woods, wandering around. Maybe he'd felt it too, the thing that was drawing them out there, that needed to be found even if it said it didn't want to be. He felt so small again, so young. He looked out into the flames before him and wished anyone were there to help him. He cried out for it. He wanted it. James knew he needed it.

"You always make me do it. You belong with them," Lewis whispered, somehow suddenly standing beside James who flinched away, still desperately hoping to retreat somewhere safely. There seemed nowhere, and no one. Lewis's statement echoed in his mind, sounding as if he had long ago truly put all his belief into that notion. James wondered about it for a moment, then felt hands on him. As always, he rarely had time to consider anyone else's fault but his own. He wiped at his eyes in a minute of panic so he could finally see what was happening to him.

One look at his father's face, and James knew exactly what he meant to do to him.

"No, no...don't!" James cried frantically but he'd already been dragged to the edge, feeling hands solidly on his back as he was pushed forward. The moment was burned into his mind, damaging him so deeply; he would never be able to escape.

The air James had desperately wanted before was shoved into his lungs, burning them from the inside out as the heat and toxins followed, filling them. His fall was a harsh one, his hands flying from his side to outstretching before him in hopes to catch his body from the fall. One foot still held onto the ground, and he tried to spin himself away from the blaze. Arms out, he hit the ground, one landing safely on the cool earth. The other landed at the bottom of the fire, completely engulfed in flame.

The screams that erupted from James's lungs were so loud and awful; he barely knew they were his. The fire melted away skin before James could whip it out of the fire. Rolling, crawling, dragging, James did everything to get away from the fire, the heat, *him*. Somehow, he made it to the edge of the light, reaching the point where darkness was stronger. With that distance, James collapsed on the ground, withering in agony and moaning every awful note that his lungs were able to make. The heat, so hot, felt volcanic in nature. He was consumed.

Lewis only stared, bewildered and sobered by the noise and attempt at salvation James was making to get away from the awful and incomprehensible pain. He thrust his hand into a pile of damp leaves, and while it took away the sting for a moment, it was hardly enough. The pain was horrendous, and even though he was so far from the fire now, it was still there, inside of him, burning away at his flesh with no mercy.

There were no more options. James's mind was lost as he lay there, rolling back and forth, screaming in agony and hoping it would end soon, somehow leave him. In that moment, James didn't care if death was the answer, something, anything, there had to be relief from the awful blaze consuming him.

Abruptly, something cool touched his hand, and James scrambled to grab onto it, that one single moment of sweet relief. Mud, cool and dank, was hidden under a vast amount of leaves. How had it survived the summer's heat? He grabbed handful after handful, setting it onto his arm, the coolness providing relief he could never have dreamed. Again and again, he put on more and more, scraping the entire section clean. The hurt, still present, was dulled enough for him to think outside of the pain and he quickly glanced around to see where Lewis stood. He was in front of the fire, which had somehow seemingly shrunk down to something small and less sinister, feeding gently on the fallen remains of the once upright tree. Lewis didn't move, another line crossed. Tears still streaked James's face, moans of pain still escaping his lips. Lewis took one step forward, but James was gone, fast as a shadow could be. He ran, ignoring all the pain his body was violently reminding him. Quickly, James found a trail and stuck to it, never slowing down, burning off all the adrenaline he held inside. Eventually, he had to stop.

James fell, stumbling, the pain in his body taking over. Between the burning and the throbbing, he was in agony, something he knew he could never recover from. Soft moans escaped his lips, darkness covering him like a blanket. His eyes began to shut, not that they could see anything in the darkness of the night. Something chilled touched his fiery arm and his eyes widened back open but still he saw nothing; he felt nothing more than an icy imprint that remained for only a moment before being consumed, melted away by heat. They tried, but it was too late. James had fallen through the hole, he couldn't continue on if he wasn't a part of it. His eyes closed and his fear left him.

Ash covered him.

When James woke, it was the first thing he noticed. White and grey, it speckled over his body and everywhere else around him. Then the pain hit again. It was dulled, but when he tried to sit, he found that he couldn't, and laid back down helpless. His mind was racing to recount everything, but there were too many holes, too many instances of such intense fear that he was unable to playback the late hours of night in any straightforward fashion. He closed his eyes again, sleeping a little longer.

The second time he woke, he was calm. His lips were dried and cracked, his mouth begging for water. There was none, so he moved on. Slowly, he took inventory of himself. His face was sore, but there seemed to be no tender spots that reminded him of bruises. His back ached, but it seemed more from sleeping a couple hours on the floor of the woods than cracked bones. James felt his side, a deep ache under his fingertips, and after pulling up his shirt revealed a large black bruise along his rib cage. A hiss of breath escaped his lips at the sight, but he gained control, letting his shirt cover up what his skin could not.

There was only one more thing to check.

James's arm was hidden under a pile of leaves and mud, something he only vaguely remembered doing to cool down what would never truly be able to be cold again. Carefully he tried to remove the mud but found it to be a lost cause without having to touch the burned skin beneath it. He needed water. He almost cried at being lost.

The sound of a rushing stream floated over to him in the wind like a whisper. It was visual words. James sat up quickly, looking around but seeing no one. He heard it again, a whisper, a promise of water. Was there a stream? He had no knowledge of one even remotely close to where he was.

There was a step, and the leaves rustled as James's eyes shot over to the noise, glancing quickly through the trees. His mind screamed danger, but his body felt oddly at peace as if recognizing something familiar. As he searched, his eyes finally caught onto it. A lone shadow stood tall and mightily, meeting James's stare with green eyes. It looked almost human; something James had never known a shadow to be before.

At first, he felt intense anxiety. But the shadow did not move, which was also something James wasn't used to. They were always moving. This one stayed in place, looking intently, watching, waiting. The blackness of its form seemed to ripple, like fabric in the wind. Brilliant green, speckled with gold eyes stared back at James, utter silence around them as ash continued to fall like snow from the sky. Nothing else seemed green but those eyes.

With one movement, it waved some of its silky form and turned around, disappearing behind a tree. There was an urge inside of James to follow. Maybe the voice in the wind hadn't belonged to the wind at all. Cautiously, he sat up and grabbed a tree for support as he stood, taking a few slow steps loosening the kinks in his legs before following sluggishly behind.

It seemed the shadow was lost from him, but then it made a reappearance, far away but still within view. James continued to follow. After what seemed like forever in silence, a noise broke through. Water rushing down a stream. His eyes blurred at the thought of such simplicity, yet such a gift.

"Water," he rasped, rushing over and drinking from it. The water washed away more than just the dirt from his face, it took away some of the heated memories, the fear that still resided in his being. He drank tons of it, then sat back for a moment before immersing his arm. The water would cool it down, clean it, but what would he be faced with? Before he stuck his arm in, he noticed there was a deer trail that led right to it, the hunted always knowing a secret way.

He looked down at his arm. It was red, the skin shining brightly under the water's surface, a sickening kind of sheen, bright and angry. James averted his eyes but kept his arm submerged. There was no reason to look at it anymore. He knew what had happened last night, and this was the last effect. Deeply, as he sat alone by the creek, utter silence around him, he was convinced his father had been right all along. There was a monster out there, somewhere. It was dangerous, evil. It had told Lewis about James's shadows, it had wanted him dead. Every moment of pain that had happened in those woods over the years swirled together, and James could no longer decipher them as different experiences, different causes. That was all it took, the final act for his mind to forever be lost to his need to survive. A dense fog fell over James's vision of reality, to protect him maybe, but his own fever dream had already occurred, a heated nightmare. It was probably too late, the haze over his clouded eyes would only thicken.

Fifteen.

"Why won't you look at me?"

James didn't have an answer. He was trapped in his mind, caught there for what seemed like forever. He didn't want to leave, so he wasn't even looking for a door. He just wanted to sleep and dream nothing, be nowhere.

"James, at least look at me."

He couldn't. He didn't want to. It was strange, how the person who seemed to care the most, who hadn't been sold on the story told to everyone after three long days out in the woods was the person he was seemingly always most upset with. He could feel his contempt growing against his will, and thought maybe if he kept his eyes shut and a blanket over his body, he would be safe.

"I'm not leaving."

James's intolerance had mounted, but he found once he was at the top, it completely dissolved. He didn't have the strength for such rage. It was probably why he'd always been an easy target. Even after wild abuse, he still just crawled away to hide under a blanket of upset and contempt, only to be found again and again, dragged out nearly every time. People took advantage of that aspect of him. Or worse, allowed his pain to exist in silence.

"Please, at least just look at me."

James barely could understand who was talking to him, trying to coax him out from under his bed. Because he was underneath it, having dragged the blankets below with him. It was unbearably hot, but it felt unbreakable. He hadn't realized he'd gone under there until he was faced with someone asking if he could come out. He didn't feel the question was fair. Wasn't it obvious? Why wasn't it ever obvious?

Tap tap tap

He didn't know what else to say, but he was continuously reminded that he wasn't alone in that moment. His fingers drummed against the floorboards, making sure he knew. James thought he might really have to open his eyes. He was feeling that maybe it would be okay, even for five minutes, maybe an hour. The space in the room felt calm, it felt open. The window was ajar and there was a breeze, the smell of cut grass wafting in and gently covering everything. He liked that smell.

Slowly, carefully, he pushed his way from under the bed and managed to get his head and shoulders out, taking a moment to rest. He turned his head to look up at the only person who was patiently asking to know something about it. James was surprised, but he also wasn't. Their eyes met, looking at each other without blinking for a long stretch of connected moments.

"Are you okay?" Wolfgang asked, his voice rough but quiet. He wanted to know what had happened out there, but wasn't sure James would ever tell him. He had never said anything about their hunting trips and Wolfgang had fallen into the trap everyone else had, out of sight out of mind. But now, as he was older, he was beginning to start actively thinking about all those trips, all those small little things James would murmur at seemingly random moments. Wolfgang was realizing his brother wasn't okay.

James shrugged. Wolfgang accepted it.

"Alright. Well, I noticed there was blood on your shirt. I brought some things up from downstairs, if you need it. If you need help," Wolfgang said, his voice so shallow that it was easy for his brother to stay afloat. James eased into that comfort. He crawled out a little further, but the more of himself he removed from under the bed, the less he could look at his brother's face. Wolfgang didn't press it.

They'd arrived back late the night before, his father and brother. It was dark when they walked into the house, everyone laying around and resting after dinner. The more Wolfgang thought about it, the more it seemed intentional, arriving back that time of evening when no one wanted to move, ask questions, look at anything too deeply. James had simply walked right up the steps to their shared room, crawling under the bed and slept the entire night. Lewis hadn't said much, but nobody really asked.

"The trip was good, we found a better spot for the fall. Got a little scraped up on a cliff, but he'll be alright," Lewis had said. Everyone had nodded, accepting. James hadn't been standing there to say anything different. No one went to look. They didn't think they had to, instead drinking their wine and continuing their conversations in the summer heat, a diluter if nothing else.

Wolfgang had gone up to his room to find his brother under his bed. He'd left the family gathering hours before anyone else thought about retiring. He could sense that something was wrong. Something had happened. James was asleep when he found him, but Wolfgang drifted between short spurts of sleep by choice all night, looking out for his brother and wanting to be there to protect him. He felt it in the air, the danger.

And now, before most anyone else was awake, he could hear the change in James's breathing as he woke up, and had crawled down onto the floor to face him. He didn't feel tired at all, instead very carefully monitoring himself as James continued to slowly crawl out from under his hiding place. Slowly, he fully came out, carefully sitting up and leaning against his bedframe, his legs crossed. His face was dirty, smudged all over. There were small cuts on one side of his face, and his eyes looked hollowed and as if they were drifting away in the sunlight. He was wearing pants and a long sleeve shirt, something he'd put on just before walking through the doors of the Pennyfather house.

"What did he say happened?" James asked, finally breaking his silence.

"That you fell and got scraped up on rock," Wolfgang replied. James just looked off, nodding. Might as well be the excuse. He could already feel his body morphing to that understanding of the situation. He had done it so many times in the past.

"Is that what happened?" Wolfgang asked.

"Sure," James replied coldly. He really couldn't talk about it any more than that, not then. It was too deep a wound, too fresh a memory. Any entry into it and he'd be unable to shake the fear. He wanted to never be engulfed so deeply in fear ever again.

"Do you want to clean up?" Wolfgang asked. James thought about it, attempting to stand up, but his body felt tense and sore, and he made it a short way before sitting back down on the floor, feeling overwhelmed. His eyes blurred over, but he didn't want to cry. He didn't even know what it was he was crying about. His body hurt, sure. But it was okay. It wasn't that bad. He'd walked all the way home, miles and miles right behind his father. He had done that. He was fine.

"I can help," Wolfgang offered. James finally looked up at him from under his bent head. He'd forgotten he was screaming for help. Suddenly existing in his body felt too loud, too shrill. His internal voice had been screaming all this time, and he'd simply gone deaf to it. Carefully, he nodded, unsure of how to accept help. Wolfgang didn't hesitate. He stood; picking his brother up and helping him walk over to the bathroom. He locked the door behind them. Gently, he helped James take off his shirt, trying not to stare too deeply at the bruises. The burn on his forearm was impossible to look away from. James let him stare. They didn't speak as Wolfgang turned the water on in the shower, sitting down and waiting on the bathroom's tiled floor as James let the water roll over his body, washing away the dirt and dried up blood. He took his time, and Wolfgang absorbed the steam. When he was finished, he sat on the lid of the toilet wrapped in a towel, making no sound as Wolfgang carefully disinfected the cuts and took inventory of the bruises on his side. He wrapped his ribs up tightly, hoping the support would help with the burden of breathing. From somewhere inside of himself, he knew how to give. Finally, he addressed the burn on James's arm, rubbing a burn cream onto it and then wrapping it securely with bandages to protect the raw skin from anything it might encounter. For the most part, James kept his eyes closed, accepting for the first time to be easily at the mercy of another's hands. He wasn't used to those hands being so gentle.

"I'll grab you some clothes," he said, disappearing for a moment and returning with a clean pair of shorts and a long-sleeved shirt, something he knew James wanted. He helped him back to their room, shutting the door once again behind them. He looked James over, his body clean, his eyes dead.

"You're gonna be okay. All right? You don't have to go on those trips anymore," Wolfgang said, watching James lay on top of his bed this time at least, before crawling under the sheets. He didn't say anything, because neither of them really believed the words. Wolfgang meant them; he didn't plan on ever letting Lewis take his brother out again. But James didn't believe Wolfgang had the power to make that a reality. James didn't believe much of anything on that side of the wall anymore. He'd been pushed through, and there was nothing on the tangible side that made him want to return, or made him feel like he could return and make a difference. Eventually, he wanted to make a difference but for now he just wanted to rest and have his mind blank.

Wolfgang turned the fan on and after giving him a glass of water and setting some food on his nightstand he closed the door softly to let James sleep the day away. He meant to walk away but he found he didn't know where to go. Instead he just sank to the floor, draping his arms over his bent knees and looking out the small window at the end of the hall where their room was. He'd always had love for his brother; the obstacles in their path had always been placed by someone else. It was by design, he was realizing. Even now, James wouldn't talk about anything. He was silent, his brother always having been treated as the enemy, the disgruntled one, the loud and unreasonable one. Wolfgang was beginning to wonder if he really was that way, or if that was just what he had been turned into. Now, it didn't seem to matter. They were the people they were going to be. Wolfgang was hit by a great wave of sadness at the thought. Was this all there was going to be? A small moment over what the fire had scorched?

Lucy stepped out of her room, jumping when she saw a figure sitting in the hall until she realized who it was.

"What're you doing?" she asked. Wolfgang shook his head.

"Just sitting for a while," he replied. She nodded.

"Alright. I'm going out to the lake," she volunteered but she didn't know why. He hadn't asked, and she wouldn't have invited him or anyone else. She was in a selfish mood.

"With Rose?" was all he said. She shook her head.

"No, I haven't seen her actually," Lucy replied, shrugging. She almost turned to walk off but stopped, turning back to look at the closed door Wolfgang sat beside. She couldn't bring herself to ask, but she was suddenly able to see just what lay beyond the door. She could feel it overcoming her. When she looked down, she was rubbing her forearm, tanned and unbroken. She looked over at her cousin, asking gently with her eyes. He barely answered her, feeling the need to continue to protect. Lucy simply nodded, heading off down the stairs. She tried to wipe away the feeling in her arm but it persisted while she packed a beach bag and grabbed a bottle of water and apple from the refrigerator. She left a note on the counter and walked out, grabbing the keys to the old car in one easy motion.

As she drove, she turned the music up loud, rolling down all the windows. She was done feeling heavy, over feeling everyone's hurt and harm. The house was beginning to close in on her, and that morning had been a tipping point. All night she had rolled around in bed, unable to sleep, dreaming of fire and hearing yelling that belonged to dogs. She wished she had never started dreaming. Rosemary had been silent next to her in their room for once. Her body still, her breathing even. Was she dreaming? Lucy had gotten up in the middle of the night for a glass of water, noticing Lewis passed out on one of the porch chairs outside. He was snoring loudly. She studied him. He seemed unaltered. Was he supposed to be any other way? She'd crept back to bed, trying to sleep. When she'd woken up to an invite to go out on the boat, she seized it. There was nothing, not even Wolfgang's sad eyes, or Rosemary's absence that was going to stop her from getting out there, away from everything else. She thought she could.

She whizzed down the road, leaving family land, and entering public domain. Once on the road that looped around the lake leading into town, she began to feel like a different person, more of the girl she was used to being. Her long blonde hair was trailing behind her, whipping in the wind. She let one hand fly around in the breeze outside the car, her braided bracelets and rings sparkling in the sunshine. Her voice was loud as she screamed along to the cassette tape she was playing, a classic because there were only four cassette tapes they owned. She let herself fall back into the girl who was after a good time, but not forever. It was easy. That girl was fun, calm, charming. She was kind with a sharp aftertaste. She was the cool girl everyone wanted to be, thought they could be if they skipped dinner once a week. She thought she could.

"My girl!" Beau yelled out from his boat, greeting her as he watched her walk along the sun-stripped wood of the dock towards her favorite place to be in the summertime. She smiled wide giving him a little wave as she approached.

"No sister today?" he asked as she got on board, setting her things down and immediately taking her shirt off and shoving it into her bag. She looked back up to see Beau watching her, shaking his head of any thoughts and smiling welcomingly.

"No, you're stuck with me. Is that okay?" she teased.

"We're lucky to have you," he replied, walking to the back where the others were sitting, all ready to go out. Violet smiled an unassuming welcome while Liam looked a little disappointed by which Sommer sister had shown up. Lucy felt that she was going to take advantage of that for the afternoon. She was on the edge. Of what, she did not yet fully realize.

She sat back in her seat as the boat slowly trudged out of the docks and out into open water, catching speed as it began to race away from anything else that existed close to it. Beau whipped the boat around, probably going too fast, making turns too quickly. But no one cared, there was no worry. There was always a sense of invincibility out on the lake, especially when young. It might not have been true, but nothing a splash of water in your face couldn't keep alive. Lucy laid back, stretching out her legs and taking in all the sun had to offer, enjoying each periodic spray of lake water. She felt awake and alive and completely in control of her own destiny. She laughed, reclaiming that feeling. She wanted it to stay.

"What's so funny?" Mia asked, leaning over, wanting to be in on the joke.

"Nothing. I'm just happy," Lucy replied, stretching her arms back over her head and stretching out even further. She knew Beau was watching her, but that was half the reason she did it. The other half was it felt good. That was what she was always chasing, a way to feel good. She didn't care if it lasted a second, an hour, or days. Her decisions mostly were about how she could keep moving up, moving forward.

"Did you bring anything?" Violet asked, her voice somehow carrying through the wind even though she wasn't shouting. Violet was another cool girl. Measured, an ever-even cadence. She never got excited or invested in anything. She wasn't anywhere near as fun as Lucy presented herself, but she'd never had a twin sister to keep her human. Violet did what she could to stay above water, as most people do. And people wanted her around, needed her to give them a look of approval. Even the most self-assured people found themselves smiling blissfully when she nodded at them. Lucy nodded her head. She'd taken some over the last three days, when no one would be around to notice.

"Now?" Lucy asked and Violet nodded. Together they took the pills, swallowing them with mixed drinks. They waited for the shift; it always came when they least expected it. Slowly, she began to feel her body tingling, the world around her bright and airy. Beau was still driving the boat out farther; they liked it best when they couldn't even see a shadow of land. His boat was big enough to spend all day on and not feel claustrophobic. And the water was deep and warm and calm. There wasn't anything to fear, the world was theirs because in those moments they were the entire world.

They drove out a while longer, Lucy and Violet sitting close to each other and talking and laughing about things they couldn't really even remember. Liam sat up with Beau, sharing a beer together as he drove. Mia drank alone, looking out at the water, feeling lonely but not knowing where else she wanted to be. Eventually they stopped, finding a place they liked, and throwing in the anchor. Lucy was the first to jump off the tallest part of the boat into the water. She found swimming to be easy. Her body always seemed to float, to move swiftly through any wave, to always naturally navigate to the surface. The depth didn't frighten her, she felt bright enough that nothing dark would venture up and want her.

"Feeling good?" Beau called down, the only one still on the boat. Lucy laughed, nodding. She beckoned for him to jump in too, but he hesitated. She splashed him instead, treading water around the boat, heading for the ladder. She did feel good, every nerve in her body firing off with such smooth force she thought she'd never felt happier. Quickly, she hiked up the ladder and found Beau, pretending to push him overboard a few times before taking his beer and finishing it, then actually pushing him into the water below. They all swam together for what seemed a long time; until everyone was so tired they felt it was almost impossible to climb back onto the boat. Eventually they did, Beau making sure he was the last one up and everyone was safe. The girls gathered their towels and climbed to the top of the boat, laying out in the sun and passing in and out of sleep. Lucy loved the feeling of each droplet of water evaporating off her skin as the sun claimed it back into the air. She focused on the feeling, her whole body still tingling. When every drop had vanished, her mind started to wander.

It happened sometimes, her intentions not met. Lucy had wanted to stay solidly present on the boat, under the sun, swayed by the water. But her high was beginning to take her downhill, as it always did at some point. She tried to resist, but the plunge down came too fast. Suddenly, she felt trapped walking around her family's dark wooden house, looking in all the rooms for her sister, for James, for her mother, for Wolfgang. Rosemary had succumbed to that pain a long time ago, but Lucy had always fought it, kicking and screaming. She wouldn't be left behind. It had never been about her, so she'd created an entire life that revolved around her exclusively. It wasn't fair; it wasn't kind of her. She knew she wasn't a good person, that every day she let Rosemary stay alone at her aunt's, or avoided James's eyes after a hunting trip, or stole his dad's drugs because she thought they were a good time, or let her mother travel unencumbered by thoughts of her children, she was betraying something that should have been protected. She should have walked through the darkness, but instead, she'd always chosen to take the long way around it knowing full well the path was too treacherous for anyone to follow.

"Are you alright?" Violet asked, shaking Lucy's shoulder to wake her up. She opened her eyes, blurry, shocked by the blinding light of the sun. She didn't know what she was doing, but Violet was looking at her with furrowed brows.

"Yeah, I got sunscreen in my eyes," Lucy replied quickly, rolling over onto her stomach. Violet accepted the answer, lying back down to ride out the rest of her high. She wanted more, and would probably not ask when she was ready to go again. Lucy always factored that in when she packed, Violet was an enigma to others, not her.

More awake this time, she looked out at the water, feeling the boat rock under her body. She wondered what her sister was doing, where she was. She knew something bad had happened to James, the way Wolfgang was acting, silent outside his door. Hell, she knew something bad had happened the moment he came through the front door. She had ignored it, but she had known. She didn't know what to do with this feeling that was wrapping them all up together. Her mind was so much more connected to everyone in her life that summer, and she wasn't used to it. Usually her mind was a solo space, her own personal arena. It was painful to care, painful to be ripped open and looked at fully. After a while of feeling inadequate, feeling like a failure to others, she stood up and walked down to the deck searching for any way to toss off that feeling and be a success once again. She wondered if anyone else could feel her soul wandering.

"Hey, I thought you girls would never wake up," Beau greeted, sitting in a big chair off the back with Liam, looking out at the water and drinking craft beer. It was an easy sort of relationship that they had, one strung along only by the promise of a good time. Lucy knew that Beau was a good person, deep down. It only made her resent herself more. Here he was, able to create happiness for everyone around him and himself, while she was only able to after stepping on the necks of people she told herself she cared about. Her failure to care for herself would do her in.

"I didn't know we were in a rush," Lucy replied, sitting down on the ground and leaning against the railing. She dipped her hand over the side into the water, cooling her legs down with a few splashes.

"Oh, no rush. We have all day," Beau replied, leaning back in his chair.

"How've you been? I feel like you haven't been out that often," Liam brought up, leaning forward a bit in his own chair. Lucy took her time answering, because the truth wasn't something she was willing to give. She also knew what he was after.

"Just a lot of family things going on. That is why we all come here for the summer, after all," she reminded, teasing him a little as she pushed her sunglasses back up against her head so he could see her eyes. It was hard not to notice, but everything about her sparkled in the light. Her eyes, her smile, her jewelry, her skin.

"Anything fun?" he asked. She almost laughed, but stopped herself.

"Do you have another one of those?" she asked, nodding her head at his drink. He nodded, leaning back and grabbing one out of the cooler, opening the bottle for her before handing it over. She took a sip, enjoying the way it passed through her entire body. She wondered if Violet was searching through her bag yet.

"If you wanted to see my sister this summer, you could just call her," Lucy said nonchalantly, taking a sip of her beer. Beau chuckled, bringing his head forward to look at the two of them. Liam didn't react right away, decidedly shrugging off the statement.

"Rose is always fun on the boat," he finally mumbled.

"No, she's not. She's intense. And you like that," Lucy replied. Beau whistled.

"But not enough to call her?" Beau replied, eyeing Lucy as he said it. She agreed, enjoying having Liam sit in the hot seat. It was a bit of silent revenge for someone who had never asked for any, or needed it. But if anything, Lucy was good at using other people's pain to fuel her own small projects. It wasn't what they needed, but it did keep her going, allowing her to project some valiant code she told herself she followed.

"All right, touché," Liam mumbled, leaning back, already giving up. Lucy laughed at him, adjusting her body where she sat.

"Beau calls me all the time," Lucy said, looking up at him. He blushed.

"Oh, if the sunshine didn't let us know the seasons had changed to summer, Beau certainly would," Liam replied, neither of them able to give Beau a hard time about anything for very long. Lucy chuckled, swishing her hand through the water a few more times before standing up and sitting on the last of the chairs on the back deck. She pulled her knees up to her chest, looking out at the water and up towards the sunlight, not feeling a need in that moment to showcase any part of herself.

"I hope you've been having a good summer, I know there's been a lot of changes for you," Beau said softly, looking over at her. Liam had since turned his head away from them, wrapped up in his own thoughts. She smiled, nodding, his genuineness always present, always reaching for the core of someone.

"It's been different," Lucy said, a moment of honesty between them.

"It's certainly felt that way. But, seasons change," he replied with a shrug. Lucy was taken aback by his casualness to change, his simple acceptance of something so encompassing as shifts. Maybe he was right, however. The seasons did change and with them, everything else. It was nothing if not anticipated.

"You've felt it too?" she asked, her voice a whisper.

"Mmm?"

She didn't ask again, fear striking her down. Instead she looked at Beau, eyes squinting in the sunlight. He was still smiling at her, he always was. She brought him joy and he didn't care who knew. Lucy had always felt if there were a true side to her, Beau would be the one to see it.

"Has he said anything to you, about her?" Lucy asked, changing topics but only slightly, because it was all interconnected. Beau turned his head to look at his friend, his chair farther away from them, his mind caught up in music and the rocking waves. Beau nodded a little, not wanting to give away too much, but seeking honesty.

"Yeah, but it's better for her this way, I think. Liam's my best man, but he didn't see your sister for all that she is, you know?" Beau replied and Lucy nodded, appreciating his perspective, thankful it matched up with her own. She watched as Liam watched the waves, and while there was nothing negative to say, she too had always thought he wasn't looking for all that her sister could give.

"You think you do?" Lucy asked, a smirk on her face, teasing her friend. It was the move she always made, pulling everyone out of the deep end. Beau often followed her lead, yearning for a genuine smile above all else, but in that moment chose not to escape the seriousness for one moment longer.

"No. There's too much to see. It's like a kaleidoscope," he replied. He meant it.

Lucy didn't say anything more, the wind knocked out of her small frame. She leaned back in the chair, just happy to be next to someone she deemed safe, though he had a way of pulling back the layers and looking in. She kept her breathing smooth and even, wondering if when she saw the color blue, did everyone else see the same hue.

Eventually, Violet and Mia wandered down.

"We're hungry," Mia said, Violet never able to admit a human need. The boys agreed, having felt like the girls would never ask. Immediately they started getting food out, setting a small stove on the back of the boat for Liam to cook some hamburgers. Mia sat and chatted with him a mile a minute, but he listened and took everything in that she had to say. Lucy watched him, knowing he was kind. That's what had hurt her sister the most last summer. But it was all right; Lucy knew it wasn't anything sincerer than a summer holiday. Reality was split into factions; it's how it felt, anyway. It was why it wasn't hard for the older Sommer sister to understand what this rift was trying to do.

"Did you hear that?" Lucy asked suddenly, looking up at a sky that hadn't made a sound. No one really acknowledged her question, continuing on with cooking their food and drinking. She sat back down where she was but something in her shifted, and an indiscernible noise floated through her once again. She couldn't shake it.

"Seriously. What was that?" Lucy asked, standing up and walking around the back deck. Liam looked over at her and shrugged while Beau fiddled with the radio and made a joke how the artist currently playing wasn't real music. The girls gave Lucy an odd look, not enjoying the disturbance. And that's what she felt like, the only one standing, the only one not continuing on: a disturbance. She walked out to stand at the front of the boat away from them, hearing something calling just for her, it seemed.

As she looked at the dark blue water, the rolling waves in the light breeze, she felt a sudden surge move throughout her body. A light she hadn't recognized before flashed under the water's surface, deep enough to be muted, but elevated enough to be noticed. She swung her head around as the light pulsated out from the center of the boat, gliding through the water with such speed she thought she'd missed it, thought she'd created it in her mind. Her heart pounded. It happened once more, the sounds of her friends talking and laughing never stopping. They didn't see it. The light was just for her, speaking to her from the bottom of the lake. When it met the sky, it radiated into the vast blueness, becoming sunlight. She marveled how it had found the meeting point, the part of the sky and lake that touched.

The thing was, Lucy knew the rift was real. She had never questioned its existence to herself. She had seen it long before anyone else. She had been okay with that, because although she had seen it in everyone around her, never had it been a part of her. She remembered all those times as a little girl, seeing something flutter, and Ramone right there to give her a little wink and laugh, telling her it was okay to see more than everyone else. She wished he were standing there with her, because now, summer felt dedicated to consuming her. At some point, she had let her guard down and that wild energy, the dust of stars, the ability to see far beyond a boundary had entered her body. Panic flew throughout her. She didn't want that kind of power alive and awake inside of her. The only way she got through her days, her life, was to be nothing worth protecting. There was no danger to someone who didn't hold value. Lucy had realized too late how damaging her twisted thinking had been, but that was often the cost of abandonment. For a long time she'd been a glittering ornament to look at, but now something was being demanded of her. She didn't know how it had happened, but somehow that summer was different. It reached out for everyone, and she'd allowed it to creep inside of her and make a home.

Lucy held her hand to her chest, trying to even her breathing, trying to not be cold in the wind even though the sun was still shining. She felt the light she had seen; it was touching her. The boat rocked back and forth as she stood at the very farthest point, her feet almost slipping down the side and dropping her back into the water. It seemed suddenly too deep, she felt too confused to find the surface. She knew she could not run, could not be anything less than who she had hidden away within her for so long. Pain was inevitable; empathy was required. There was no cool girl, untainted by the world around her. There was just Lucy Sommer. And she wanted to cry, because she realized that fate was inescapable, and existence was forever. It was something she had perhaps always known – between each breath in and each breath out an entire life happened.

She threw herself into the lake, water touching her like nothing else ever had.

Sixteen.

Rosemary took the time to silently rub aloe onto Lucy's burnt back before a late dinner, the sun already beginning to set outside their bedroom window. It had been days since Lucy had been able to feel any real relief, so she'd broken down and begrudgingly asked her sister to help her, having already collected the leaves from the aloe plant their grandmother had growing on the porch.

"How have you been sleeping with this?" Rosemary asked but Lucy shrugged off the question. She wasn't sleeping. She didn't want to disappear into herself like that anymore. It used to be mindless darkness and now it wasn't. It had been days before she'd allowed herself to close her eyes, the light from the water still pulsing in her mind, keeping her watchful of everything and nothing around her.

"You missed a good time," Lucy lied.

"Where were you?"

Rosemary shrugged. "Around."

James looked up at her from where he sat on the floor, staring at the wall, just listening to them talk. He didn't remember if he'd seen her at all since he'd been back from the short trip, but a lot of things felt muddled in his mind, so he didn't put much faith into his own inquiry. Wolfgang was laying across the other open bed, throwing a ball up into the air and mostly catching it, though every so often it rolled across the floor and James would grab it and toss it back over the girls' heads. More or less, they had all gravitated towards each other over the last few days, even more so the last few hours. It was in the air. It had been there a long time, but their proximity had become so close that it was no longer deniable, or something to escape. Still, they had a hard time finding the words to talk about it.

"Dinner's probably ready soon," Lucy said, fixing her shirt as soon as Rosemary had finished with the aloe. She looked around at a hungry crowd, and still no one wanted to go downstairs. She was finding it hard to rally.

"C'mon, let's go," Rosemary finally said standing up and stretching her limbs before walking over to the door. She'd never been more appreciative of having the third floor to themselves than that summer. She watched as everyone watched each other.

"It's just dinner," Rosemary said, trying to persuade them. No one believed her.

Carefully, they marched downstairs, the coolness of the evening air not extending into the hot kitchen, or the well-lit dining room. The space was loud and full of chatter as they arrived, immediately having questions thrown at them about needing help and where had they all been. No one had a good answer.

Sara kept an eye on her grandchildren, feeling a shift in all of them. She had known something was coming for a long time, finally admitting that her husband's death had perhaps been a sign. She was still waiting to see him.

"Lucy, get the chicken out of the oven please," Delphine delegated, handing her other daughter a stack of plates to set on the table. James silently followed behind her with napkins and utensils. Wolfgang stood back and poured himself a glass of whiskey from the bar cart, his eyes watching his father almost the entire time. Lewis had been avoiding his oldest son more than usual, actually feeling the hatefulness radiating from him. His father wasn't embarrassed like Wolfgang hoped; instead Lewis found his son's resentment pitiful. His oldest would never understand the work that needed to be done, the loyalties that needed to be foraged. James had been challenged, but he had clearly come out the other side by his continuation of silence. Lewis thought it was his side that his son had come back to, but that had always been Lewis's biggest weakness, his inability to see all sides. When he touched James's shoulder as he passed, he didn't flinch. Just stood still and waited for it to pass. Wolfgang fumed, but didn't know what to say and how to make it as impactful as it needed to be. The gag order was still persistent, and he had long forgotten who'd muzzled him.

"Alright. Are we ready to sit?" Sara asked, coming out of the kitchen and standing at the head of the table. She looked out at everyone standing around at varied points. There was tension between all parties, but instead of worrying her, it thrilled her. She wanted to poke the hibernating bear. She'd spent too much time alone; too much time hiding away the parts of her that sensed these opportunities. To finally let it out would be a thrill, and she didn't have anyone there to stop her this time. The sun was setting at the back of the house; they were eating later than usual.

Everyone chimed in to say grace purely as a ritual formality and then began passing around the bowls and plates of food, small clinking sounds singing all around the table as food was served. Lucy leaned forward in her chair, her back hurting. Delphine and Heidi started chatting away about how good thyme was in potatoes, Heidi holding on to every word her older sister offered her. Beth buttered a roll to give to her husband. Sara watched as James carefully put a scoop of beans on his plate, only taking what was within reach, not wanting to ask for anything. Seth offered him a piece of chicken, and he nodded quietly. Henry started up a conversation with Lewis that expanded across the table, talking about the tractor outside and how many other things they could try to get it started. It was an antique, a project they desperately wanted to bring back to life. The noise was rising.

"So, Delphine, where's the next big story?" Lewis asked, looking directly over at his sister as he loaded his plate with meatballs. She seemed to think about it, slowly chewing her food. Her brother tried often, but it was hard to disorientate her.

"We have a few places in mind. Some the journal wants us to go to, others we've felt drawn towards. But it's only midsummer, so nothing is set in stone yet," she replied, looking up at her brother, feathers smooth. Beth admired the way she could stare at him; challenge him without putting in any effort or energy. She didn't give herself away. After dinner, she wouldn't even need to rest.

"Outside of the country, though?"

"Most likely. There's a lot happening out in the world that needs light," Delphine replied, Lucy looking up at her as she spoke, her phrasing catching her attention in a way it wouldn't have just a few days prior.

"You going to travel too, Lu?" Beth asked, curious.

"Uh, maybe, actually. A couple friends from undergrad wanted to backpack Europe in the fall," she replied, moving around the vegetables in her plate in a way that imitated disappearance.

"Is your sister going with you?"

"Ah, I don't think so," Lucy said, looking over at Rosemary. Truthfully, Rosemary hadn't even heard about her trip. It was strange, how different they were. Out in the real world, it was easy to walk their separate paths. Sometimes they didn't talk for weeks. It was all right; they'd accepted it by now. And they always had their summers, where things felt like they didn't anywhere else. A reunion of souls on sacred ground.

For now, both sisters hated how their family tried to bring the real world into their space, cracking them apart. Because the resentment that passed over Rosemary's face was evident, and Lucy wanted to bolt.

"It's not really my thing," Rosemary replied, giving a tight smile before chewing a too large forkful of potatoes. She always made her food disappear.

"Yin and yang over there, well done," Lewis said looking over at his sister who shot him a bitter look.

"They're not the only ones," she replied. It was a childish remark, but came out almost involuntarily. She didn't know why it was always made out to be upsetting.

"Oh, don't we all know it," Lewis replied, giving a look to his sons. He was surprised to see his oldest staring back at him, a fire he recognized in his eyes. He was taken aback, as was Sara. The only difference was she was proud.

"Why do you need everyone to value exactly what you do?" Heidi asked, chipping in as she passed the bread rolls to her brother-in-law. She always pushed the conversation deeper, thinking they would perhaps understand and reflect. She fell into the hole they dug every time. Henry took a deep sip of wine.

"That's not it at all. It's about hard work, something you're not used to doing. It's not always about enjoying yourself," Lewis said. He went hardest on Heidi because she collapsed the easiest. Usually, it was harmless banter. Often, it was tough stabs, debilitating by the end. That night, she felt a bit tougher, the air around her keeping her awake and her eyes dry.

"Hard work? You wouldn't know a thing about it. You think hard work only means yielding an axe. You don't know how to talk to anyone, how to change," Heidi snapped back, something deep within her finally pushing its way to the surface. It wasn't their usual sibling script, both often opting out of the hard-hitting for small causal shots. Seth looked shocked she'd said so much and shared a look with Rosemary who sat back in her chair to watch.

"All right, well you just keep living on your island of grand ideas and special conversations and see how far that takes you," he said, aggressively cutting into his steak. James stared at his lap.

"At least I'm happy," she spat.

"You really seem it," he replied, giving her a harsh look. She took it deeply, an insult that radiated throughout her whole body. Her life had been overwhelmingly unhappy, but she'd put in so much work to change it, more than only for herself. Rosemary wanted to reach over and thank her for showing her that was a possibility, but the table that stretched before them was too long.

The feeling in the air tilted, and all balance was lost.

"Your whole family is miserable," Heidi said, and as soon as the words escaped her mouth, a deep silence filled the table, all forks set down. She couldn't back away from it, so she sat looking at her brother, unapologetic. Wolfgang wanted to break the table in half and leave, a void somewhere needing a good scream.

"Well, I guess your house only had so many rooms," Beth said, her voice quiet but each word coming out with such effort. Both her children turned to look at her, stunned. It was amazing what she came to defend. Heidi's mouth hung open.

"Pass the chicken, please," Lewis said as if he hadn't heard a word the past few minutes, waving to Seth who sat in front of the platter. He carefully handed it to Lewis, who looked shocked by nothing, and helped himself to more food. Sara sat watchful.

"Yeah, green beans please," Henry said, coughing a little as he took them from Lucy who had long ago lost her appetite. She hadn't taken much to begin with. For a while, nobody spoke, just the sound of forks scraping across plates and chewing filled the air. Until, Wolfgang reached for his glass of whiskey and accidentally knocked it down, letting the last small sip spill onto the table. Everyone was at it again.

"You're going to get drunk at your grandmother's table?" Lewis yelled out, his voice slicing through anything it touched. He threw his cloth napkin at his son to clean it up, even though very little had gone anywhere. Wolfgang almost stood up, but something kept him rooted.

"You think I'm drunk right now?" his voice tight.

"No one else is spilling their drinks," Lewis snarled.

"Sorry I didn't get your talent," Wolfgang replied, his words sharp. There was swirling energy between the two, a dark cloud with bolts of lightning close to the ground.

"What did you say?"

"You heard me."

"Say it plainer, go on," Lewis said, voice low. Every muscle in his body was tight, but no inch of him had moved yet. Wolfgang couldn't help but roll his shoulders, tilt his head. He had so much frustration inside of him that he had never mastered. That was his problem though; he had never wanted to become master of it. He didn't want to use it.

"Alright, alright. This is for a different time," Henry said, his voice even and strong, something Seth only wished he could come out and say. There was something deeply and innately respectful in the way Henry talked, probably a skill accumulated over many years of photographing the best and worst of humanity around the world. Either way, he was also tall and wide, his voice calm but deep. Lewis and Wolfgang both felt the weight of his request even though they didn't want to succumb to it.

"Henry is right," Sara finally said. Everyone turned to look over at her, ever silent at the head of the table. She was reserved, always had been. It was all in an effort so that when she spoke, her words were considered. The older she grew, the less her words were a suggestion and more a demand. She had learned how to evolve them.

"There's still dessert," she said, as if nothing plagued her. What did she think, of her daughter's words? What did she assume, about her grandson's accusation? They all wondered, every head at the table, and yet she gave them nothing. She simply stood up and went into the kitchen. Nobody said anything; forced into begrudging acceptance of the mystery. It was almost worse than a sentencing. A few people carefully started gathering dirty plates and avoided looking in anyone's specific direction. Carefully, the clean dessert plates were brought out and the pie was cut into thin slivers and served with vanilla ice cream. Most of the ice cream melted.

Surprisingly, everyone helped with the dishes. There was a general sense of disdain, but instead of pushing any one person out, the entire family circled together, no one wanting to break the ring first and be the weakest chain. When the last dish was put away, everyone wandered out at the same time. And then, they were gone.

Wolfgang left the house immediately, the door slamming behind him. Lucy ran after him out into the dark night. Rosemary started to head the same way, but went back and made sure James followed. He didn't look like he wanted to, already halfway up the steps to his room. Rosemary shook her head.

"Don't you feel it?" she'd whispered, grabbing his hand and pulling him down the steps. He hadn't known what she meant but followed her anyway. They snuck out the side door and started walking through the darkened fields towards the woods. Rosemary had faith she'd find them. There was a full moon lighting the way.

"Rose…" James started to say, feeling uncomfortable being in the woods so late, his arm aching as fear began to course through his body. She turned right around and looked at him. She seemed different to him, but he was beginning to think there was a lot about her he hadn't taken the time to know. Her eyes were bright in the moonlight as they looked into his.

"It's going to be alright. We're going to find it this time," she said. He didn't know what she meant. He only knew what he had heard about the energetic chasm, the thing that both created and destroyed. It had always sounded less like a place and more like an embodiment. But something about the way Rosemary's eyes twinkled like he'd never noticed before made him feel warm and whole inside, and that maybe there was something good over the horizon. Maybe she'd already seen it and that was how she could confidently promise something so sought for.

She grabbed her cousin's hand again and led him through the woods towards sounds they both heard and knew belonged to their brother and sister. Finally, they found them arguing in a small clearing, Lucy trying to get him to come back and not go any farther into the woods. She looked back at her sister exasperated.

"I'm not going back into that house. I never want to see *him* ever again," Wolfgang roared, lunging forward as he spoke to get his point across. Only James flinched at his motion. Wolfgang barely noticed.

"It'll be okay, we'll be able to go back," Rosemary said but Wolfgang started pacing, shaking his head. He looked back at her.

"How can you say that? Do you really not see anything?" he spat. He almost reached out and pushed her, but stopped himself just short of doing so. She had been ready for it, her feet planted, but only because she knew he wouldn't. He did not scare her.

"Yeah, I see it," she said, her voice nearly a whisper.

"I don't think you do," he replied. She breathed in.

"I don't think you did either, for a long time," she said with honesty. He stopped pacing.

"What did you say?"

"Listen, they can feel it too. And it's driving them wild. They were never able to find it, and they still can't see it now. But I know we can," Rosemary said, looking around at the three standing before her. Her words were offering them something, it was becoming tangible right before their eyes, and they didn't know how to accept that. Fear was an insidious feeling, their bones quivering. It was nearly impossible; to go beyond the bounds – to accept there was something past the wall. As they looked at her, a girl they barely recognized, their eyes grew wide and confused.

"Rose, what the hell are you saying?"

"C'mon, let's go," she said, waving them to follow her as she walked quickly through some brush and was gone. Wolfgang, Lucy, and James looked around at each other, not sure what they should do.

It was a moment. Life only gave out so many; a moment where existence presented a choice so pure and brimming with opportunity that to not accept was an utter casualty. The three looked at each other and had to decide. They had to decide if this was all it was ever going to be or perhaps they could have more, be different, see more, be more. Vitality was filling up in their chests, pushing against the walls of their rib cages, wanting to break free and unite with something deeply meaningful out there in the moonlit woods. They each had to decide, would they go?

Rosemary heard footsteps behind her as she walked through the woods, and she smiled as she counted. They were all behind her. After a few moments she began to walk faster, dodging low branches and uneven earth. Eventually, she was jogging through the woods, wanting to get to the spot she knew existed desperately. Everyone was breathing heavily as they tried to keep up, starting to feel an understanding pass through their bodies, naming the feeling that had been so deeply embedded for so long. Any feelings of fear, inadequacies, and resentment started fading from them as they ran through the woods, chasing after Rosemary who seemed to know a path even the deer did not. A tingling went through their bodies, something they had felt before but had never known what to call. Ice hardening, swimming in light waters, touching shadows that moved all on their own. It had been there the whole time.

Rosemary looked out around her, longing for more than dark trees and foliage in her line of sight. She wanted to see Ramone, wanted him to be there again like he had been before. Heart pounding, she continued, knowing that even though she couldn't see him, he was there. He was whispering the way to her, having wanted her to find it all along. He had known she was capable, only because she had the others to go with her. Alone, there was fear. But together, nothing could touch them. They kept on.

As they ran, things around them began to shift. At first, they didn't notice and then when they did, it seemed unusual at best. The trees shimmered. Light radiated from small pockets underneath their feet in the dirt. Animals raced beside them before climbing up a tree or jumping into a burrow. A herd of deer stood still and watched as they ran past, their eyes glowing. Something about the world seemed to shift, and when Lucy stuck out her hand, she was surprised to see how it moved. There was an otherworldly amount of air, their breathing catching itself even as they ran on, following Rosemary into darker parts of the woods but somehow seemingly brighter. Blues, greens, and yellows radiated from everything around them, usually hidden, now openly observable. Wolfgang wanted to call out and ask, *what is this place?* But he couldn't find the words to describe what his eyes had never seen before, yet his body was already welcoming back as home.

Suddenly, the ground rippled, but it didn't throw them off. They stood on it, perfectly invited, perfectly needed, perfectly grounded. Rosemary stopped running, her small body becoming larger as they finally all came to meet with her. No one wanted to let her out of their sight, she was the guide. She'd found the place. Her face glowed as she looked back at each of them, happy. With one finger she pointed out in front and they looked, their minds and souls open. Before them, surrounded by the darkness of the night, was a deep chasm, an energetic field, a hazy wall that wasn't a boundary at all. It was everything, all at once.

They'd found the rift.

It was miraculous, out of body, a sensation more than any physical sense could ever perceive. The body was almost worthless; the only thing that even remotely tingled was deep within, a spirit beaming at the opportunity of being so close to the line. Breathless, staggering, they stood right before it, a heavyweight holding them back from crossing. But the electricity was there, the energy was radiating, it was simply one more step away. There *was* more, and they knew that now because they'd found it.

Seventeen.

Time wasn't a good measurement for how long they stayed. Time moved differently around that force created by the collection of them, a swirling moment instead of a linear one. The four of them gravitated towards the energy, the large crack in the earth that held universal secrets, ones that floated all over the galaxy and were too hard to see all on their own. But there, before them, was an accumulation of it all, a small sprinkling. It was stardust and souls and universal laws. It was breathtaking and incomprehensible.

Each of them floated near it, but couldn't go into it. Their hearts still wanted to beat, even in the face of such exquisite that promised an existence far greater. It wasn't the right moment. They lost track of everything else. For as long as it took, they stayed, soaking up knowledge and warmth, feeling their bodies heal and become the best versions of themselves. They saw things that they had only dreamed of. They felt things they had only heard about. Only in euphoria could you be washed of all your human flaws and still remain human, if not with a small gift of etherealness.

At some moment, their minds slipped and their bodies slowly fell into sleep. It was only realized when they opened their eyes, having never noticed they had been closed. Dew covered them as they each slowly sat up; having slept sprawled out on the bedding of the woods. The sun was only beginning to suggest its rays were about to peak over the edge. The birds in the sky sang, and it was the only noise they could hear. When time seemed linear once again, they looked at one another, wide-eyed.

"I feel different."

"Me too."

There didn't seem words capable of quantifying their shared yet deeply personal experiences witnessing the rift. It was like a radiation zone, proximity defining the experience. They all wondered what it had been like for the other, what they had seen, felt, and understood. While most had simply laid back and basked in the universe's collective energies, only one of them had thought about reaching out to touch it.

"Do we go back to the house?"

"I guess so."

Carefully, they walked out of the woods towards the house. It was a slow parade; one covered in a daze filled with a general unsteadiness. They knew the woods, they were familiar and unchanged, and yet somehow that felt wrong. The path they'd walked a hundred times stood still, carrying them back. It was unchanged, but they were not. Even though they didn't speak, they were thinking the same things. Their bodies still buzzed with a newfound high, forever altered to want more, to want to be closest to the break in that reality. Already, they wanted more.

When they came up onto the house, their parents were mostly all together on the porch, looking out eagerly as their not so young children walked up slowly, their bodies aching and uncomfortable.

"Where have you all been?" they asked.

"Uh, we camped out last night."

"Oh? Where are your tents?"

"We slept under the stars."

It only felt like a lie, but neither group could clarify why. As they stood there in front of their parents, they knew the secret had to remain. It was imperative. It seemed undeniable to each of them. Each of their palms burned as if fresh blood were escaping them, a gentle reminder. It was good to have one.

Since there were no more questions, they all went into the house, following four separate paths. Lucy went to take a long hot bath. Wolfgang retreated to the roof to smoke. James made himself food and sat in the back room eating quietly, watching the rest of the sunrise. And Rosemary found her bed and threw herself on top, unable to sleep, but unable to stay awake. Instead, with eyes focused on the swirls of blues and greens out her window, her mind wandered over her last night there, but her last ten nights somewhere else.

It had all started out so miraculous that she hadn't been able to see anything. It started as a bright warm glow, something so stunning she'd had to blink, look away, fall back. Then, slowly, it had engulfed her entire body until she didn't need to see anything, she could just feel. That energy had worked its way over her skin, into her flesh, touched her bones and made them smoother and stronger than they'd ever been. Rosemary remembered laughing, then breathing, then almost singing. Just a few notes, like a bird does. No words, just the sound of a radiating soul coming from the chest. It had gone on seemingly forever. Then, she had opened her eyes.

Pink swirling waves had coated her body, coming at her from a vast sea. She thought she might have recognized it, but there didn't seem to be any prize in that. Instead, she walked along the shoreline, the water splashing at her ankles, a bright and soft pink, golden almost in certain lights. She had felt alone, but there was a certain song in her ears, a whistling kind of singing from all the life around her that made her feel calm and assured. She wasn't alone. There had been a lot of walking on that edge, water and sand. Somehow, she made it to a field of grass, walking up the bank away from the water. Out far, almost farther than she could see was a speck of white amongst the tall waving grass under a sky of dark navy blue. The grass was bright somehow still, as if the light came from beneath and not above. Curious, she wandered out to that small white speck, coming upon it rather quickly. She had been confused, recognizing it as a person asleep curled up amongst the grass in a white summer gown.

"Lu?"

Her sister hadn't woken up, but instead stayed curled up and asleep, her eyes dancing behind her closed eyelids. After looking around for a few moments, she deemed it a safe place for her sister to rest and wandered on; the sky shifting overhead so quickly the moment she took even a few steps out. Then, she'd been dropped into a sea of water, pushing against her body, floating her around in every direction. It wasn't frightening, there wasn't a need to breathe, no body to keep alive. Everything seemed based on ideas, on concepts, on what she wanted there to be, on what could be potentially understood and processed. Whatever she held inside needed a place to roam around. It was a whole world of stardust, a whole world of want. She surfaced, finally. There was a garden, flowers and trees and leaves in colors she had never seen before, didn't have the words to describe. She thought there was a rustling beside her, felt like she smelled the familiar musk of her cousin amongst the dense leaves, but didn't look into it. Her sister was still asleep, safe. She had walked on, through shimmery lives, the ghosts' breaths, missed opportunities that dissolved the moment she stepped forward. There was hope she'd see a mountain in front of a night sky so magnificent she'd remember each constellation, but the more she looked the flatter the space around her became, and she thought she might be lost. Her heart fluttered, so she took an intentional deep breath in to steady herself, to go back to that warmth that came from the very center of the rift. She'd wandered too far into the outskirts, the places where the ground shimmered but the light was dim. Rosemary knew it was important to understand that distinction, felt the calling of a familiar voice deep inside her bones. There was the center, and there was the edge. The middle was the only place that remained safe, calm, a place of neutrality and wonder. The other places required choices. Her humanness had resisted the responsibility of choice and the consequences that come with choices. She had turned, eyes focused back on the sun, a star among other stars – the light of fire and magma and energy and deep need. She'd blinked, and woken up back in the woods.

Now, she laid on her bed, replaying everything she could, her body aching from the withdrawal of such vitality. There was nowhere more real than that place of make-believe. Her fingernails raked over her skin, a seemingly new sensation. The way her eyelashes created wind was suddenly observable. While she lay absolutely still, everything seemed very much alive and awake. Hours past, as she rested and thought. It was what she needed, and even though she was becoming lost in her mind, she almost didn't care. There was always an edge, though. A choice to be made, if she wanted.

Suddenly, her phone went off.

"Hello?"

"Hey. Hi, you answered. Alright," a familiar voice greeted, a little strung out. Rosemary tried to reign in her thoughts and the way her body felt, attempting to begin and try to figure out how to be a person here and now. She looked down at the screen, technology an odd concept after the magic she'd witnessed.

"Silas?" she asked.

"Yeah, it's me. How are you?" It was something he really wanted to know.

"Uh, I'm alright. I'm good. You?" she asked, sitting up on her bed, allowing her blood to flow more freely than it had needed to all night. Vaguely, she wondered where her sister and cousins were, what they were doing. She felt a need to see them, but also a strange need to talk to Silas. She couldn't abandon the phone.

"We've all seen better days. Look, I know you don't know about it yet, and believe me, it's killing me to give up this secret, but there's an old tree fort in the back of your grandmother's lot. It's a hundred yards out from the pond in the northeast corner. Do you know what I'm talking about?" he asked, rushing through his words. Rosemary nodded her reply, then thought to actually vocalize her answer.

"Uh, yeah. I think so," she replied.

"I need your help with something, please."

"Okay."

"Thanks Rose. Come when you can," he replied respectfully, though his tone indicated to come as soon as humanly possible. Rosemary felt swirled by questions, but quickly stood up and changed into a clean shirt before heading to the bedroom door. She stopped, glancing over at her dresser. A small collection of the tiniest field flowers rested on the dresser's surface. She felt their little green leaves between her fingertips before she trudged down the stairs and walked quickly through the kitchen and out the door. The sun was now bright overhead, summer heat already sweltering over the land. It dulled her senses, making her feel able to walk where she needed to go and focus on finding the fort in the woods. If anything, the heat made gravity real for her once again.

After wading through the grasses towards the edge of the woods, she slithered between branches and limbs until she came upon the small pond that had once served as a man-made watering hole for cattle a hundred years prior. Now, taken over by nature, it was home to fish and frogs, turtles happily sunning in small patches of sunlight on sunken logs. She walked out from the pond in the general direction she knew to be north and sure enough, saw a small and sturdy shape of a square fort resting in a large oak tree. Confused how she had never seen it before, she trampled through the brush to the base of the tree where the steps started. They were steep, but she took a deep breath in and started climbing anyway. Still, it all felt surreal. When she reached the top, she realized the fort was much bigger than she had perceived from the ground and was also built well unlike any haphazard fashion she'd been a part of as a kid. There was a small ledge outside the door, and Rosemary carefully sat down for a moment, breathing in deeply to stay calm so high up before knocking.

"Silas?" she called out cautiously. This was no social call.

Allison Astorino

"You're not skittish around blood, are you?" he replied his greeting, his voice muffled. Rosemary closed her eyes and commanded herself to stay steady. She was actually rather calm around blood and needles and broken bodies.

"Yeah, I'm fine with it," she assured, resting her open hand on the door. It felt like several minutes passed before he responded again. She wasn't in a rush.

"Okay, come in," he finally said and carefully Rosemary pushed the door open and crawled inside. A few moments passed before she could absorb everything around her. The place was packed with things, essentially a small home. There were real windows and carpet on the floor. Against the back wall was a small cot only a few inches off the ground covered in blankets and pillows. There was a small table next to the door full of dishes and plates and a couple bottles of water resting on top of a cooler.

"Like what I've done with the place?" Silas teased, shooting her a shy smile. He was resting on a beanbag chair closest to her; holding a washrag over his left eye, blood seeping through it from a cut across his brow. It was a large gash, and it was littered with small reflective pieces of glass. Rosemary stared at it too long; Silas lost his grin.

"You said you were fine with blood," he reminded, his voice dark. Rosemary quickly cleared her head. He was running the show; she was allowed merely a small view past the curtain.

"It wasn't a lie," she assured as he looked away for a moment.

"I need you to pick the glass out. I have some things in that box over there, to help. Can you do that?" he asked, voice edgy. His whole aura seemed unrecognizable to the person Rosemary knew, and she watched him with a nervous eye. Still, he looked hopefully at her, his face still soft and unnerved in the right places. She crawled over to the cot, pulling the box out from underneath. It was filled with first aid. She spied a towel on a shelf by the table and grabbed that as well as a bottle of water. Then, she made eye contact with him once more. He looked defeated.

"Why wouldn't you do this at home?" she asked quietly.

"It's not a good time," he replied. It was all he wanted to say for the moment.

Rosemary crawled to the middle of the room, the biggest empty space. She knew quite a lot about the wrong time. Sitting cross-legged, she laid the towel across her lap and set up the water and tools beside her, then looked back up at him. He didn't seem like he wanted to move.

"I think it'll work best if you lay your head in my lap," she said, her voice short and curt, assuming her role. It had to be that way. After a few moments, he carefully climbed over and rested his head in her lap, the top of his head pressing into her stomach. A grimace passed over his face as he moved; she waited for it to pass.

"Built this whole place, never once thought to bring in a mirror," he laughed, his voice strangled. She chuckled a little at the joke, then looked back down at him.

"All good?" she asked as he gave her a weak nod. Silas allowed his hand to fall away from the washcloth he had been holding against his eye. Rosemary felt her stomach knot up, not having considered that maybe his actual eye was hurt. Gingerly, she took away the cloth from his face; dyed a deep red. He tried not to move, but it hurt.

"Well, your eye looks fine. Does it feel alright?" she asked, almost imposing what she wanted him to say. He nodded, taking inventory of just where the pain was coming from. He could see, that much he knew.

"Yeah, I think that's how it went down," he replied. Rosemary washed some blood off his face carefully, feeling more hopeful about the situation as she continued. She needed a clean surface to work, her mind entirely transfixed on her task. The world could be incredibly sobering at times.

"Of all the things…not one damn mirror," he grumbled as she finished wiping, grabbing the tweezers for the real work ahead of her. The glass was small, dotting the gash that ran through his eyebrow and around the side of his cheek, just under the sensitive skin of his eye. She tried to stay even, knowing she was under watchful eyes, more watchful than most.

"It doesn't look too bad..." Rosemary trailed off as she pulled out small pieces. They glittered in the sunlight from the window, a dazzling display amongst the damage they had created. Silas grimaced a little as she pulled out another shard. There seemed to be so many. As she pulled out another, he squinted his eyes shut, moving.

"You can't move your face," she whispered, picking up his hand and setting it around the top part of her arm. When the next shard came out, he squeezed it tightly, his nails digging into her skin. All of it was an anchor.

"So," Rosemary said after a few minutes of silence and heavy breathing.

"Your small talk has never been very good," Silas teased as he squeezed her arm, feeling a sharp pain radiate deep into his skull as the glass fought to stay embedded.

"That hardly seems fair," Rosemary defended, her voice clear.

"Yet very accurate," he replied.

"Well, if you wanted good small talk, maybe you should have gone to see a real nurse at a clinic instead," she replied, remaining meticulous in her work. It was helping Silas focus on other things instead of the pain, on all fronts.

"They don't have service like this, my friend," Silas replied, looking up at her. He recovered a small grin before she started pulling out the largest piece. Blood gushed up around it and spilled down into his eye causing him to shut them tighter. Rosemary quickly started wiping it away and looked around to make sure there were no more remaining pieces before she applied pressure to the laceration to stop the bleeding.

"I don't think there's any more glass..." she mumbled, looking under the rag after a few moments. With that, he started to sit up but she pushed him back down.

"Oh no, I'm finishing this up," she insisted, out of need or want, she didn't know. For a moment he grumbled, but then switched his attitude to tolerance. As she poured some peroxide onto the cut, his nails digging deeply into her arm, she wondered about how this had happened. It seemed deeper than an accident, more secretive than just an uneasy story. He could sense her pondering and opened his eyes to look back up at her.

"The first thing I'm doing tomorrow is getting a mirror," he declared, hoping she'd laugh. Instead she just shook her head, reaching for the antibiotic cream.

"Oh really? Is this going to happen again?" she asked rhetorically. He didn't say anything as she spread the cream on the wound, finding some small Steri-Strips to hold the cuts together. It didn't look half bad when she had finished.

"All done?" he asked.

"I think so," she replied, wiping the last bit of blood off his face. He carefully sat up and crawled back over to the beanbag chair, sitting down and tilting his head back, rubbing out his neck. He felt mobile once again. Rosemary started cleaning up the triage center she'd created in the middle of the floor. When she was done, she looked back at him. His face seemed a little more rugged than usual, some bruising decorating the side of his face in deep swoops and swirls. He watched her look at him.

"You want to ask," he said.

"Of course I do," she admitted easily, unabashed.

"You seem very normal today," he said, his eyes suddenly looking at her in an entirely new way. Her hand reached up to touch her face, half expecting something to be different. Her body still tingled with discovery, but it was like the last small pieces of flame clinging to ash before the fire extinguished.

"Shouldn't I be?" she asked, voice quiet. There was a great space between them, somehow only moveable by action and never by declaration. Neither knew why it had to be that way, but it was. At least it kept them honest.

"My grandmother had a rough time last night. It happens sometimes. She gets what some people might call confused. It builds. And she lashes out," Silas said, using words he reserved for people who didn't wonder about anything past what they were presented. Rosemary didn't fit that category. She nodded, thinking about what he had said. He could see her mind dissecting those words, knowing the true meaning was lying right beyond them.

"Confused? Like dementia?"

"Yeah, like that," he replied.

"But not that?"

"No, not that."

Rosemary breathed in deeply, only letting the air escape her lungs in small releases. She was thinking about that pink rolling water again, the gold that glittered throughout the body of that sea. The songs of the seashells on the beach, each a life, always still alive. Her thoughts wandered farther than she realized.

"You're not the only one who can feel it," Silas said quietly, his voice only half breaking her from her thoughts. She looked up at him, eyes blurry.

"What?"

"You're not the only ones to have gone looking for it, either," he said. She didn't know what to say. Could she admit to him, that she'd found it? Had her discovery cost him some blood, caused him a wound by shards of glass? Somewhere deep in her chest, she'd always known he'd felt it too, but something about him had always stayed away. Whereas she ran towards that light, begging to see it, Silas never seemed to move. He stayed in place, orbiting around it, perfectly content. But he couldn't remain that way, because every orbit becomes closer and tighter over time, involving everyone whether they wanted to be or not. Silas didn't know if Rosemary would ever understand the history behind what she was seeking, or perhaps what she had already found. Looking at her, he thought she might have found it. And if that were true, he'd stay another night in his little cabin, letting his own grandmother who had lived there a long time beg the skies to open up for her alone.

"Sara make anything good to eat lately?" Silas asked, breaking the tension in the room momentarily. Rosemary was caught off guard by the question.

"Are you hungry?" she asked.

"More or less," he replied, giving her a warm grin to set her at ease. There was a small amount of tension in the fort, a line the two of them had crossed that they were not entirely aware of the consequences before doing so. He saw her making herself small, so he waltzed through the stifling air, wanting it to evaporate so she could breathe again. He looked out the window at the trees looming over the small pond. He'd thought he'd found such a unique place when he was younger.

"I can bring something back," Rosemary offered.

"I would love that," he replied. He watched as she slowly walked down the steps nailed against the tree and wandered off through the woods back to the fields that surrounded her grandparents' home. It didn't take her long to get back to the house, everyone still scattered as she made her way into the kitchen and started packing a basket. She hadn't realized it before, but she was starving. As she was about to leave, a voice called out to her from the living room, asking a question.

"How's Silas this time?" Sara called out, her words fizzy. Rosemary froze. She'd never acknowledged him so personally before, never called out so brashly, never seemed to realize there was a small house at the back of her sprawling lawn.

"Uh..." her granddaughter started, not sure what to say, peaking over into the living room to see Sara rocking in her chair, staring out her own window, a drink beside her.

"It's about time he went to someone about it all. Be a good friend to that kid, he'll be one to you. Yeah?" she called out, even less direct than before, becoming lost in a combination of summer heat and dulled senses and forgotten memories. She had made that mistake before, and in her muddled regret, hoped her granddaughter wouldn't follow in her footsteps. She could feel it in the air. To Rosemary, she didn't sound like she knew what she was saying. A falsified friendship was something Rosemary knew little about, and Sara had Ramone to thank for that because it wasn't a lesson she could have taught.

Rosemary said nothing, hardly able to take in her grandmother's words, only nodding her reply before she crept out of the kitchen, running across the grass with the food in hand hoping no one else saw her, and they didn't. She managed to calm down before she had to climb the steps again up to the fort.

"That was fast," Silas greeted as she unpacked the food and spread it out before them. Quickly, they both started eating, a comfortable silence between them as they chewed and swallowed. Their bodies needed it.

"You act like you haven't eaten in days," Silas commented, handing her a cup of water he had poured for the both of them. She took it.

"Days would be an exaggeration," she mumbled, reaching for another dessert that had been dipped in honey. She split it in half, offering him the remaining piece. Her comment wasn't lost on him, but he had decided a long time ago that it was best to not say everything all at once. Ramone had decided that had been best for him too, a long time ago. There had to be a gradual cadence to learning, otherwise, there was resistance. And he wanted to do this the right way. He owed Ramone that, at the very least. Forever entangled in its history: the new keeper. It was hard to warn people about power, and how destruction was the price of creation.

Once they finished eating, their stomachs full, they each sat back and rested a moment, the heat finally reaching them after all the adrenaline had dissipated from their shared space. Silas yawned, stretching out his shoulders one at a time. He'd been folded up for too long. He'd had a long night on the other side, and rest now seemed important. He glanced over at his cot, pain pulsing from his eye socket.

"I think I'm going to close my eyes for a short while," he said, moving over to the stretched material and laying down carefully, adjusting the pillows and blankets out of his way. He didn't need them that afternoon. Rosemary nodded, accepting that. Without a word, she came over to the cot, sliding in beside him and wrapping one arm around his chest, his arm already perfectly placed behind her head and around her shoulder. They laid there for a while, not sleeping but not really awake either, the skin of their bare feet touching. After a very long while, Silas started breathing peacefully, thoughtlessly. Rosemary gave into that feeling too. Her eyes fluttering closed, finally letting her mind finish its wandering, her body safe to rest in a bed that wasn't hers.

Eighteen.

They found themselves naturally gravitating towards one another. When one of them thought to grab the milk for coffee, another was already holding out the carton. When someone realized they had misplaced their shoes, another was coming out of the hall closet with the sandals in question. There was a natural rhythm to the way they moved around one another, it was respectful and smart, and felt too practiced to sit easily with any of them. Still, they had not talked about their individual experiences, only contemplated them in solitude. It was almost easier to understand it that way, to create a reality and a truth that conformed to what they were individually searching for, because each of them was seeking something different. Regardless of any secret thoughts, their time together had grown.

There was a new sense of watchfulness from their parents and it pushed them to run to the ends of their land almost every day. When Lucy suggested they go to the beach by the rocky shoreline, everyone eagerly agreed. Together they grabbed towels and food and started the long trek through the woods to the cliffs, then down to the rocky shoreline beneath. They each picked a boulder to sit on, lying out in the sun, getting high, whistling at birds that flew by curiously. Their land met up with a small enclave of the lake, an even smaller passageway to another bigger and less explored side.

They laid out a long time, everything feeling larger than life. The sun was brighter, warmer. Their bodies felt rested and ready to move at any notice, but also calm as they sat along the water's edge. Leaves crackled behind from small woodland animals up on the ridge, and they heard each and every sound of their exploration. They had never felt better, never felt more in tune and a part of something as vast as the blue sky above.

"There's only a month left of summer."

"Mmm, I hadn't noticed."

No one had, not really. Summertime had that strange air to it, a feeling of invincibility and longevity. After all, nothing passed slower than a hot day. Time didn't pass in any way they noticed, but the sun was shifting places in the sky above. All they did was move their bodies slightly in tune with its rays. From far out, they all heard a low rumble, and as the sound grew louder, they recognized it as a boat engine. It snapped them out of their sunshine filled daze, grounding them back in a reality where there were more requirements than simply existing. The boat came up closer, and when it was still a fair way out, they recognized it.

"It's Beau," Lucy said, holding her hand over her eyes to get a better look. Rosemary laughed at the chance of that as she propped herself up on her elbows, the boys sitting up to look at the boat.

"Someone has a rich daddy," Wolfgang said, a low whistle under his breath. It was more an observation than anything else, which was unlike him to not pass any judgment. The boat came closer, and eventually stopped its speedy sailing right before them on the rock jetty they occupied. Beau waved his arms in the air and shouted only a few words that they could hear. A few others gathered with him on the deck.

"Come out!"

Lucy looked back at everyone, somehow the invitation open to all even though it had never seemed that way before. Rosemary shrugged, James looked over at his brother, and Wolfgang nodded.

"Sure," he replied easily. The surprise should have hit them harder, but they only mildly felt it against their skin as they stood upon the boulders. Cheers erupted from the passengers on the boat as they carefully climbed down to the water's edge, leaving their clothes up on the rocks. One at a time, they jumped into the water as far away from the rocky edge as they could, swimming out to the boat and reaching for the ladder that Liam had already extended for them.

"I didn't even plan on coming out this way, but we felt like seeing the other side of the lake today. Awesome that we saw you guys," Beau greeted, looking each one of his new guests in the face and smiling warmly.

"Fancy that," Lucy replied, smiling back.

"Have you guys met my cousins?" she asked, looking around at the usual crew Beau took out. Mia nodded, while Violet only said, "James went out with us once."

"Ah, yeah. Well, this is his older brother, Wolfgang," Lucy replied, tilting her head to her oldest cousin. His family watched as everyone took him in, having never truly seen him before. There was a cautious air onboard, as if someone they didn't know had boarded the boat asking for a plate. Violet looked him over closely.

"Do your tattoos have any meaning?" she asked.

The sisters looked over at him, taking in his tattoos as if this were the first time they were seeing them. To a certain extent, they were. Never before had they really stared and looked at them, Wolfgang never inviting that kind of attention to himself. But also, he'd always had lines of ink on his skin. Ever since he'd been a young child he had taken a ballpoint pen and drawn intricate creations all over his body, wherever he could reach. His first stick and poke had been done in a friend's basement at fourteen, and his first one at a shop on his sixteenth birthday. From there, the last eight years he'd collected many more, his body filled with random drawings, little patterns, small phrases and words, symbols and scribbles. There wasn't necessarily a consistency with the markings he'd chosen to afflict onto his body, but they were all done in black ink, sharp lines, and with a somewhat serious sense to them. Wolfgang chuckled at her question.

"There's always a reason," he replied.

"Well hey, nice to meet you," Beau said, a bit nervously, sticking out his hand for a handshake. Wolfgang took it easily.

"Welcome on, all of you," he said, walking over to the wheel and turning the motor back on. Everyone settled on the cushions as the boat lurched forward, whipping back and forth in a few zigzags before taking off speedily forward. Liam sat behind Beau, sharing a few comments with him as he drove, eyeing Rosemary as she looked out over the side of the boat. James caught her eyes, nodding back and then smiling. She nodded, already knowing. Wolfgang sat between Violet and Mia, who were each trying to keep their cool for different reasons. Lucy claimed a whole section of the bench for herself in the back, elevated from everyone else, her body lounging in the sun and looking best all stretched out, not hiding a single inch of who she was or what she encapsulated. It was an easy thing for her to do.

They drove on for a long while, into mostly uncharted waters. That particular side of the lake wasn't as popular as where they usually drove, but something was calling all of them to drive out just a little further, go just a bit deeper. It took them a while to find the perfect spot to throw an anchor. On the ride there, the friends were taking in the Pennyfather cousins, all for different reasons. The energy was mounting in a way that was undeniable and all encompassing. Violet had begun counting the tattoos Wolfgang had, staring intently at everything from a huge honeybee on his lower stomach to the intricate line work of a bouquet of dead flowers on his calf. She'd gotten to thirty-seven by the time the boat slowed down, stopping in the very still waters of the east side of the lake, a place that was far out from seemingly everything except a very small and dense tree line that could be seen from a sheltered viewpoint.

"Does this spot seem okay?" Beau asked as the boat stopped propelling forward, gliding softly through the lake water with a new sense of calmness. Everyone looked around at the quiet spot, and it did seem ideal even though it was far unlike any place they'd stopped before to spend their time. The quiet didn't last though; it was uncomfortable, pushing for too much recognition. Instead, to drown it out, Liam quickly turning on the boat's speakers and had a well-curated playlist ready. While Beau made sure they were anchored tightly, the rest of the crew spread throughout the large vessel, Lucy showing Wolfgang and James around the lower deck. Liam came to sit beside Rosemary, having already climbed to the highest deck with a towel she'd grabbed from a cabinet. She'd been able to bring nothing with her.

"Hey, how've you been?" Liam asked, feeling a little awkward. Rosemary looked at him for a long time, sitting opposite from her. She'd never felt like the one with any power before, but the way Liam was looking at her now mirrored intimidation. Something felt different in their dynamic, and Rosemary didn't know if that difference was between them or inside of her.

"Good, yeah. I guess it's been a while since I've come out on the boat," Rosemary said, echoing what he was thinking. She'd only just touched the surface though, because he was also thinking how it had been a long time since she'd called, since they'd gone out, since they'd talked under a dark sky with pinpoints of light. It happens that way, when the other finally moves on, the first one wants to run back towards a moment they thought would exist forever. And those moments did exist forever, but they couldn't necessarily always be alive.

"Yeah, a few weeks. Has your summer gotten busy?" he asked, curiosity dripping off his voice. He wanted so badly to know what she had found that was better than all this, but if he was being fair, anything was probably better than constantly running towards something with no stationary target. It had all been amicable, until it wasn't.

"Honestly, no. It's been very slow, and I have been enjoying it that way," Rosemary replied. She wasn't sure if slow was the right way of putting it, but she did feel like she'd been given more time for experiences than a usual summer holds. There wasn't an easier way to explain it, and in a rare moment of craving a revengeful feeling, she liked watching Liam's face fall as he was given only half an answer, half a truth. Did he deserve that? Did anyone?

"That's nice. A lot of family time then," he stated, though it came out much more like a question. She tilted her head back and forth, thinking about that. It had been a lot of family time, a lot of time and energy spent with people she was tied to no matter the supernatural forces of the universe. She had never viewed any of them so tightly woven together before that summer. Even from the beginning, standing around a hole in the ground and letting dirt flow through a loose fist, she had felt all their strength and need behind her. Never had it mattered as much as it did just then. But he wasn't asking just about her family. He never just was.

"Yeah, we're never all together, not even for winter holidays. Only the summer, when the sun is scorching above us," Rosemary replied, looking out across the crystal surface of the lake, trees decorating the horizon so far out they could be shadows of something else entirely. Liam shifted from where he sat, feeling like he was talking to a different twin.

"Hey, this is a nice boat," James said, climbing up the ladder and breaking the bond between Rosemary and Liam. He didn't seem to notice as he crawled over to them sitting on the top of the deck, laying out beside his cousin. He hadn't been on the boat before, but he liked it too much already. It felt wildly secluded, far away from any kind of land roaming beast or monster. There were no pressures while sitting on that huge hunk of metal, swaying softly in the breeze, cradled by water. There didn't seem a place like it, one where he could relax and feel sunlight for once, not moonlight.

"Yeah it is," Rosemary laughed, looking down over at him and smiling. He was all stretched out, his muscles loose and sprawling. It was the most relaxed she'd ever seen him, his bruises seemingly invisible under such a filter.

"Lu give you the full tour?" Liam asked, remembering James only vaguely from the night at the club. He nodded his head, not bothering to sit up to answer his question. The way his skin burned under the sun's widest rays was so unlike the burn he'd felt that one forever night. He glanced over at his arm, out of habit. Mostly, it had healed. Faster than he thought it would, better than he could have dreamed it would. Still, it ached, a shooting pain lighting up his entire arm at different moments in time. Maybe that meant something, maybe it didn't. Cyclical pain was built into existing, so he had been taught. He realized he'd taken too much time to answer.

"She did, yeah. It seems really great, I can't imagine having one of these to use all the time," James said, looking down at the lower deck and the people who mulled there. Liam laughed.

"Yeah, it's great. A lot of work though, more than anyone realizes," he replied.

"I'm sure."

Rosemary pushed James in the shoulder for saying it the way he did, but stopped herself from really putting in any force. Just because they felt so light now, so curious about the world, didn't mean that James didn't know what was a great deal of work. His whole life had been a great deal of work.

"Is Wolfgang behaving down there?" Rosemary asked, looking down at her cousin talking to the two other girls. Mia was chattering away, laughing loudly at jokes he was probably making at her expense. Violet was laid back, chill. Her eyes were the only active part of her face, holding everything she refused to allow her body to express. It was the reason everyone had a hard time meeting her stare, but Wolfgang appreciated such a challenge.

"We can only hope," James replied, not bothering to take a look at his brother. Liam glanced down, a little uneasy. He felt thrown off in a place that was supposed to be his domain, a place he always felt sure-footed. There was part of him that knew why, but there was also a very small part of him that held a growing voice making sure he knew it was also something else, something he had not met before.

Lucy and Beau were watching the same interaction take place but from much closer. They stood in the shade of the small captain's room, the windows wide open. There was honesty there that always existed. It was easy and very natural. The two of them were similar people with similar energies. Everyone was drawn to them like they were gifted with something extra upon birth. It wasn't fair, and they weren't sure if it was real, but they lived their lives as if it were.

"That's really James's brother?" Beau asked, and it wasn't lost on Lucy how he separated Wolfgang's relation to her even farther by wording it just so. Lucy laughed, leaning back against the railing, water still dripping from her body from her initial swim out to the boat.

"It really is. Why, what were you expecting?" she asked, curious. He shrugged, but she pushed for an answer. He thought about it for a moment, always taking the time to be honest with her.

"I'm not sure, but he's so big, and dark, and the tattoos are a lot," Beau replied. It was true, he was a lot taller and broader than James would ever be, and he certainly didn't look like his cousins in any obvious way. The tattoos, she barely saw.

"I feel like you're more disappointed now than when you found out Rosemary and I weren't identical twins," Lucy teased, elbowing his side to get him to laugh. He did, but kept looking out towards the front of the boat. He felt something about Wolfgang, and maybe he had always felt it with Lucy too, but it was easier to detect something when not over showered with affection.

"I think you need a drink. I think we all need drinks," Lucy said suddenly, walking below deck to the fridge to start assessing their inventory. As always, the bar was fully stocked. She grabbed a variety of drinks, walking around and passing them out to everyone. She convinced the three up top to come hang out again on the lower deck, and started giving drinks out to Violet, Mia, and her cousin. She shared a look with Wolfgang, one she recognized from him but hadn't seen in a long time. She wondered what he was like, out in the world. If he even existed outside of summertime, or just hibernated in the walls of his house when he wasn't there with them. She couldn't picture him anywhere else; though, he didn't fit in there, either. An enigma, always.

"I see why you come out here so much," Wolfgang said, sipping the beer she'd handed to him. She laughed, watching as Violet stalked out their entire interaction.

"You haven't seen anything yet," she replied. She held up her beer, freshly opened. Together, they knocked their bottles together and then raced for first place. It was a close call, the excitement growing as the bottle tilted higher towards the sun. Friends cheered, and the music grew louder somehow. Lucy finished mere moments before Wolfgang lowered his and with one swift motion, threw the bottle back behind her and jumped off the side of the boat. Her cousin plunged down next to her without a second thought, thrusting both of them into an almost absolute silence. For a few moments, their bodies sank downwards, deeper into dark water. They could see each other with blurry vision, both of them waiting for the other to move first, to propel themselves higher and surface. It was calm, in the water. The floor was hidden by a dark shadow, rays of sunlight pouring in fractured ways. It didn't feel like they needed air, or to ever hear sound again. From somewhere, bubbles rained up, and with them came their need to push upwards again. Their heads broke free at the same time.

"Were we under long?" Lucy asked.

"Barely seconds," James replied. It hadn't felt so brief.

They swam to the ladder, splashing each other on the way over, climbing out of the water easily and walking over to the front of the boat where everyone else still was. Both of them grabbed another drink and continued. They all did.

Easily, the game became drinking and jumping, the water a welcome coolness against the heat of the sun beating down on them almost mercilessly. The music played on, evolving into a different kind of sound as everyone began offering up their obtuse requests. Some of it no one had heard before but they all felt connected regardless. Even though things had been tense in the beginning, the longer the day stretched on, the more everyone grew used to the energy, and mostly, it was an okay collaboration. It was a lot like it had been at the club, almost easier on a boat far away from anyone or anything. Secluded to themselves, the stakes felt higher, but also the world wasn't such a weight on their shoulders. With more time to focus, it became easier.

"I bet I can hold my breath longer than you," James teased, spitting lake water out of his mouth as he treaded water next to his cousin. She laughed, a little buzzed.

"Are we little kids?" Rosemary asked.

"You tell me, Rose," he replied. She looked into his face, sunny for the first time in a while. Even before, it had never shined. And past that day, it might not again. But she felt happiness for him, deeply in her chest. She knew how hard it was to find, how it evaded people for long stretches of time that created moments that felt like it would be the only way. She didn't want to deny him anything. And, she thought she could hold her breath longer.

"Ready, set, go!" she shouted, plunging under the surface quickly. She opened her eyes briefly as she went down, watching him sink down with her, and then she went limp and numb and shut down everything but the fire in the middle of her chest. Her mind wandered in that silent, dark place. Her body seemed gone, completely detached. It swayed in the water but wasn't a part of her, or anything she was responsible for. It could have completely floated away from her and she wouldn't have noticed or cared. Instead, with eyes closed and her breathing stilled, she lived an infinite amount of time within that last gulp of air. She was on a beach, or walking through the woods behind her aunt's house, or sitting on a park bench in a city with a really beautiful sunset. Some words came to mind, but they held no sound to them: only meaning. She felt herself drifting in between all those moments, all those possibilities. She heard cicadas. She liked it.

Suddenly, she was lurched upwards, the colorful moments whisked away from her as a deep darkness spread over her consciousness, then absolute brightness as she was thrust upwards.

The moment her body left the water, she felt she had a body again.

"*Rosemary!*"

She looked up, utterly still, her first breath back after resurfacing merely a small inhale. Everyone was looking at her, Liam and James beside her treading water.

"Did I win?" she asked.

"Win? Rose, are you okay? You were under for *minutes,*" Liam said, looking at her with a certain kind of crazy in his eyes. She didn't share in the panic, and even Lucy and Wolfgang still up on the boat looked down at her with confusion, but not panic.

"Yeah, a couple of minutes," she tried to justify.

"No, more like ten," Liam insisted. She shook her head, it didn't seem possible, especially because she would have stayed longer, roaming around, living off that one gulp of oxygen for eternity if she'd wanted. She looked over at James. He seemed surprised, if not a little wary. She didn't want it to be that way.

"I'm sorry if I freaked you out," she said, looking at Liam. He just shook his head, still treading water right beside her. The rules of his box were small.

"Freak me out? I don't want you to die," he said. It was defensive, shifting what he really meant away from himself and back on to her. She looked at it heavily. It wasn't the time to say anything, but she had never seen it so clearly before, or known about it with such certainty. He didn't like showing his hand, and he'd been forced to act on her behalf. There was something different about her: a light in her eyes, a tint to her skin, a way she spoke without such a nervous tone. Maybe it had all happened over the past year, or maybe it had simply switched overnight.

"Well, thank you for that," she replied as kindly as she could, pushing off away from the boys and gently gliding over to the ladder of the boat, pulling her body up easily, as if she had never split away from it. No matter its vacancy, it would still never belong to anyone but her.

"Are you alright?" Lucy asked, her concern extending to something different.

"I'm just going to layout for a while," she replied. Her sister nodded, accepting that, looking around at the others to see how heavily they were watching. The truth was, not much. Lucy and Mia took a few dives off the front of the boat together, and Beau had long ago gotten in and was floating around in an inner tube he'd tied to one side of the boat. James and Liam picked up a water game.

"Tell me what one of them means," Violet asked Wolfgang, once they were again alone together, sitting on the tanning benches. They were both very good at playing the game, both very well trained in being cool and collected and not caring about anything too deeply. Which meant they were both open to hurt, entering a dangerous game usually reserved for late nights.

"You're the only one who cares about any of these," he replied. She was laying much more stretched out than he was. Wolfgang was sitting next to her, cross-legged, leaning back against the boat. The distance between them was close. She shrugged.

"I doubt that," she said.

"You're the only one who's asked me in years."

"That doesn't mean I'm the only one who cares about them," she said. He nodded. Perhaps people did notice them. He didn't, they had started out as a distraction from loud voices and lack of attention. Now they served their purpose as a hobby, a thing to do when the alternative was worse but still tempting. Glancing down at the array of them, he wondered which one he would pick and tell her about, if they really didn't mean much of anything. He found it harder than he thought.

"Well, I got this crow after we read some Poe poems in the eleventh grade," Wolfgang said, pointing to one side of the piece across his chest of a crow with his wings outstretched and feet positioned outward as if about to grab onto something that would fight back.

"All right, and the other?" she asked, nodding her head to the second half of the entire piece.

"It's a sparrow, I had them do it in watercolor style. I got it probably a week later. I thought it was a good opposition, I guess," he replied, looking down at it. He hadn't considered all the reasons he thought something in opposition would be good companions. It seemed to echo a lot of things.

"That's interesting you thought of that," she said. If Wolfgang had known her longer than just that day, he would have thought her use of the word *interesting* was remarkable. Because interesting meant interested, and that was something Violet avoided at all costs. But she had never met someone like Wolfgang before, and he wore that difference very plainly across his face. She'd noticed it the moment he'd stepped on the boat, the last one up the ladder. She felt like maybe they had known each other before, in a place different than the one they shared, and in circumstances far more similar than the ones they shared now. He knew what she was thinking.

"I also got this honeycomb because I ate *Honey Nut Cheerios* for breakfast that day, so there's some perspective on depth for you," he replied, wanting to drag her out of any serious contemplation. She laughed, but still the look she had didn't leave her face. It was comforting, in a way, how it stayed.

"Everyone's allowed a good time, in the middle of it," she replied, taking another sip of her drink. They'd both lost count of how many they'd had, the fridge below seemingly never empty. He thought about those words for a moment, considering them. He didn't know the last time he'd had a good time. Everything was jumping from one boulder in the stream to the next.

"What's your idea of a good time?" he asked.

"Don't be crass," she replied. He shook his head.

"Oh, I don't mean it to be. I mean honestly. Like is this it for you? Do you really enjoy being out here all summer long? I'm curious," he asked, looking at her, hoping that he'd see some emotion flash across her face. She was a master at a blank expression, something he longed to achieve. His face was constantly angry, constantly threatening violence over discovery.

She thought about it for a long while, surrounded by the happy yells of everyone in the water, of the music dancing around them in the air, of the warm feeling across her skin of a good tan that wouldn't burn the next day. Water splashed over both of them from below as James and Liam pushed Beau off his inner tube into the water, laughing.

"I guess it's all numbing, which is a somewhat positive direction to take, from where I'm standing" she replied. It was an honest answer.

"Is that all we get? Numb instead of..." he couldn't finish the painful acknowledgment.

"Maybe it is," she replied. They'd entered some type of emotional chasm, a place where they both stood, looking down into a ravine of something that people had and needed to live, but they didn't possess. It was hard, realizing they were both still searching for that feeling even after so many years of denying they needed it because they couldn't have it. Perhaps that was the most painful part of living, acknowledging the absence of something your whole soul knew you needed, no matter how much it was denied again and again. There was comfort in standing on that edge with another, some small semblance of unity when at all other times it was just loneliness scattered far across the galaxy.

"It can't be the end of the road yet," he finally said. She nodded, smiling a little, letting him say his small well-rehearsed line to take them out of the dark place they both acknowledged was home. But there was a little more hope in his voice than she thought there should be, and when she looked over at him, his eyes glittered in a way that did resemble true hope.

"You're convinced, huh?"

"There just...it just has to be. Never feeling whole means there's a piece missing. It has to be out there, somewhere, in all this. Why can't it be found?" he offered. She didn't like to talk like that, where there had to be some great amount of personal effort to just be okay. It wasn't her fault something was lost; she hadn't been careless. The world had constantly shown her that she was unworthy of it; she would never be given an end to her wandering. She didn't want to hike some challenging trail to nirvana. She didn't want to go to therapy anymore. She didn't want to have to pretend that food made her feel good, or new things made her feel joy. Mostly, she didn't want to pretend until she found it, and that's all anyone wanted from her. Her refusal to play along was uncomfortable for most, but Wolfgang sat with it well.

"I'm sure with some personal growth," she huffed. Wolfgang shook his head.

"No, legitimately. There has to be something for us to just find..." he said, grasping for the words. He knew what he felt, that he wasn't whole, that he was missing some vital piece of himself. It wasn't even that shiny, or loud, if he had lived all this time without being able to find it. But days ago at the rift, he had seen it, glittering there, moving and pulsing in the life around him. He hadn't been able to reach for it then but he thought he might still be able to go back and have it.

Violet had closed off, her narrow window of introspection over before it could really even begin. Mostly everything was too painful, and at that point in her life, she would probably never move forward in any outwardly measurable way, only the optics of onward movement. She needed to spend too much time with herself, and it was impossible when the world kept demanding things all the while. Wolfgang looked at her, sadness in his chest. He wanted to go back and say something else, give her some of the hope she was yearning for even though she felt dead inside. He'd always felt it too, but now he wasn't sure if it was forever. He closed his eyes, wishing he could.

He looked over at her again; she was back lying down slouched on her chair in the sun. She looked over at him, shrugging at something, touching her collarbone absently where his crow sat, as she had been a little while before.

"Maybe it is," she said. He felt a pang in his heart. She looked open again, receptive for a moment. Water splashed over the edge of the boat in his face.

"It can't be the end of the road yet," he said, trying it. She nodded at him, a small smile on her lips. He watched as she looked at the hope he held, not yet deciding if it were real or not. He decided to give it all to her.

"You're convinced, huh?"

"I've seen it, out there. Pieces of you are not lost at all. It feels impossible to grab onto in this moment. Maybe it is, but at least it's there. The chance exists," he said, trying to do better. He didn't question why or how, but he was thankful for the chance. He wasn't used to many second chances. Her eyes stayed bright longer than they had before, the honesty and certainty in his voice giving her a small piece of golden string to follow in the dark forest her mind was stuck wandering.

"I'm tired of looking," she finally said, but it wasn't bitter or hopeless. Simply, an acknowledgment. He nodded, letting the moment slip.

"Cheers to that," he replied darkly, holding his drink to hers, clinking the two before they finished up the rest. When she stood up to grab more, Wolfgang jumped up, grabbing onto her as she screamed with a smile across her face and tossed her over into the water. Then, he cannonballed next to her, surfacing easily. Everyone cheered as Violet came up, rarely taking the time to swim. She couldn't help but laugh, finding it strange that the darkest person there had given her so much noticeable light. But she took his advice, if not for a moment. Maybe it was there, around, even if she couldn't grab onto it just yet.

They swam for a while longer, before climbing up into the boat and drying off. Together they all went to the top deck and laid out in various places to watch the sun begin to set, a new kind of warmth radiating from the lowering orb. It brightened their faces. Rosemary glanced around, looking at everyone. There seemed to be a calmness that had settled over the group, even though it had been far from a seamless integration. If asked, no one would have been able to put it into words, how the strange new feeling that had entered when the Pennyfathers boarded no longer felt fearful but instead felt strong, beautiful, almost the essence of life itself. Everything was silent as they watched the sky change colors, their bodies turning pink and orange along with it. Somehow, everyone had been given something that day. It was a rare gift. Something about the day ending didn't make them all that sad.

"We should head back before it gets dark," Beau said softly, moving down to the lower deck to start up the boat. The motor roared to life, but nobody moved as the boat slowly turned around and headed back towards home. The breeze felt good in the evening air, the smell of lake water lapping at their faces. More than one of them felt as if tomorrow that spot wouldn't exist anymore; it would simply fade away into that dreamland that was nowhere and everywhere. Such moments could never be recreated.

"I'll get as close as I can," Beau said to Lucy as he pulled over to the big rocks on their land, their clothes and towels still scattered. Lucy shrugged, she didn't mind another swim. They said their goodbyes before jumping into the water, their skin tingling at the cold sensation. Slowly, they swam back to the rocks, waving at the boat as it left. Without talking about it, each of them sat down on their towels, drying off slowly, finishing watching the sunset before heading back to the house. There was a stillness in the air; a green sky before a storm.

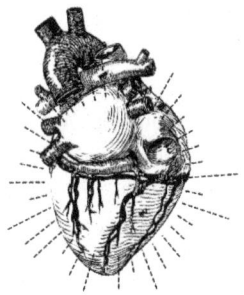

Nineteen.

"Lemonade?" Beth asked, coming out onto the front porch where Delphine and Heidi were sitting, wrapped up together on the big porch swing. They each happily took a glass from her without thinking what it meant for Beth when she served. She took a seat opposite of them, a book in hand. She'd done a lot of reading that summer, snuck in a few pages here and there between chores and maintaining a household of eleven people. But some days, when everything was finished and the other women were out resting, she would join them and relish in being restful in the heat, instead of working against it. There was a certain sisterhood among them, one that always struck Beth down with awe at times as she realized that no matter the waves that crashed between or over them, they could remain together, she just had to learn to give herself to it. She glanced over as Heidi worked on a crossword puzzle, and Delphine read a lengthy magazine article.

"Six-letter word for constellation twins?" Heidi asked.

"*Gemini*," Delphine responded without missing a beat. Of all the things she had done, gone, and seen, Heidi always told her sister that her most interesting accomplishment was having a set of twins. She laughed at the quick reply.

"Of course it is," she mumbled, filling in the letters.

"A lot of people know that," Delphine was quick to say, not

wanting motherhood to ever fully define her. Heidi liked to push that, not sure exactly what it was rooted in, where the need to become such an outlier had started.

"Of course," Heidi replied, light-hearted. She rubbed her legs methodically as she continued finishing her puzzle, completely encapsulated in being outside. A little bee flew around her and she didn't swat it, instead allowing it to crawl around on her stomach unharmed and not rushed. Curiosity was a beautiful thing, and she had been sheltered from ever realizing that sometimes it did kill the cat. She took a sip of her lemonade.

Beth turned her attention out onto the fields around the house, enjoying the breeze on that humid summer day. She wondered where the kids were, even though they were hardly children anymore. It was hard to adjust her thinking. She hoped they were having fun, enjoying each other's company, and safe. Her eyes wandered to the garage, hearing her husband and Henry talking loudly as they rattled the metal of an engine that needed repair, but would rather take all day to tinker, even though it required such a small fix. She didn't mind how long it took, how much they drank, how long they talked. She enjoyed the peace and quiet to herself, with her sisters-in-law on the porch. Beth found the place hard to be in, but she didn't know why. There was no extra special reasoning for why; most places were hard to exist. Beth tried to understand the feeling in the air, but she never could. To her, the breeze was a welcome relief from the everlasting heat. But to Heidi, it made her think of when they were young.

There were a lot of different moments that encapsulated being young in her mind. Different life stages, different time periods, different seasons of life. When she was very small, she remembered helping her dad fix all the broken things around the house, in the garage, out on their land. Later, she helped him fix other things like strained relationships, paralyzing fears, and a sense of violence. Those things were harder to fix, and at some point (a point she never realized) he'd started fixing those things for her, and not bothering her as his little accomplice anymore.

Delphine didn't have very concrete childhood memories of her father, the way her younger sister did. She remembered a more youthful and cunning Sara, above all else. She'd been tough and confident, never faltering. Delphine had loved watching her in action, even when that pressure was applied to her. She felt it only made her stand taller, forced and created her to be tough in the face of the opposition of the entire world. They were different, but mostly it was okay. And yet somehow their brother hadn't found value in either. Instead, Lewis had felt the need to find every secret that had formed, to suspect they were there all along, and even felt privileged to them. They weren't easily given, so he hunted for them. Adolescence had only sharpened the corners of the blade into adulthood.

And what were those secrets?

At first, he wanted to know why Heidi's hair glowed golden when it was brushed. She insisted it didn't. Then he wanted to know why Delphine always said something before the person who was supposed to say it, did. Delphine didn't know what he meant. Lewis had felt ordinary until his sisters joined the world. Then, all he could focus on was their seemingly extraordinary. He didn't take time to think of himself, what he was enacting, rather entitled to whatever he wanted to take from everyone else. When Ramone died, it had been nearly a year since they'd spoke.

As the three grew older, there were more curiosities. Vivid dreams, answers to unasked questions, strange occurrences in the kitchen, or to the plants on the porch. There was a weekend of a rampant bat infestation in the attic, rooms no one in the house had yet to use. And then there were the woods and all the trails that had been left to grow up and become entangled in the thick of the forest once again. Some of them noticed and some didn't. Heidi was too small to stay alone, and spent a lot of time at Sara's friend's house, just a short walk away, working in her garden, learning all kinds of things about nature and creation and how to pickle vegetables. She thought the changes in the air were as common as the seasons.

Delphine felt them, and of course wanted to know everything about it, what caused it, what was the impact, the goal, the wish, the need? Lewis wanted control; so like something with no corners, whenever he got close to power's edge, it retracted from him, never revealing itself for as long as it could. Like magnets, they naturally repelled. Nature's innate need to protect itself.

When they all became teenagers, there was a different set of alliances. Sometimes, Delphine would choose Lewis, enjoying the thrill of danger that hanging out with him and his friends gave her. She learned a lot about protecting herself and being the more intimidating force while driving out to farm fields and getting drunk next to sleeping cows in pastures hardly visited by farmers. She started writing then, carrying around little pieces of paper in her back jean pockets and scratching small words and phrases she thought gave meaning to the otherwise meaningless encounters she was having, the ordinary drunken nights with the cool kids from high school, whatever that meant. The qualifications were always changing, the dynamics always begging for something new and fun and interesting. Heidi never went out with them. She was too young, too trusting. She didn't want to fight or be on guard, rather simply exist and be happy enough with that. When things got too rough out in the fields late at night, Delphine would come back and spend her Saturday mornings with her sister, appreciating how gentle the rolling hills looked in the daylight. Heidi taught her the value in exploration, if not in the least about understanding how the smallest parts of the world that lay directly in front of her could also be the biggest. Together they read books and talked about plants and agriculture and politics and music and art and sometimes boys. It was easy to do that, then. Youth was blissful, until it wasn't.

It was interesting, to see their childhood curiosities blossom in their young adult bodies. Lewis's obsession with danger and lurking monsters came out as he began hunting, fighting, becoming paranoid of so many people that eventually he found himself alone, more dangerous than it was worth to be around. Heidi thought nature was so intricate that she eventually found herself unable to leave the sprawling woods and fields around her house. She couldn't understand it all, and it became overwhelming to attempt. Her sister couldn't stand that. Delphine had to get out, move about the world. She wanted to know what every person out there had to say. She always thought she could hear their whispers, their cries. It was all written on small scraps of paper she eventually put under the floorboards of her bedroom and left. Eventually, they all left. And it was years before they came together again, all at once.

There was more though, of course. The three Pennyfather children only knew so much about the place they grew up. Some of it was by design; some of it was by sheer will and determination. And some of it, perhaps, by luck, if there is such a thing. Ramone and Sara did what they could as young parents, and as their own individual people. Their marriage was much like a river, flowing steadily in some parts, swiftly in others, and more stagnant along rocky beds. Ramone's heart wandered, his attention spent everywhere around him. Sara was more withdrawn, deeply involved with her own self. There was nothing wrong with that, she spent more time with herself than most people do, and her level of understanding was only strengthened because of it. It served her, on the lonely road she was forced to walk. Everyone was forced into something.

It was because something had happened many years ago, on a very specific night. No matter her age, that night was something that refused to fade because it had been burned into her mind deeply. Only a few people knew about it, those who had witnessed it, because otherwise it was never spoken of after its occurrence. There was nothing to say. Things always had a way of being unearthed, however, and Sara found herself watching it unfold from her bedroom window, her family sprawled about on the land as if they had no idea, no sense of feeling. Maybe they didn't. She certainty had never been forthcoming, not now and not then. It had been too difficult to face, the only part of her she'd never been able to make peace with. Her own husband hadn't been able to look at her for many years, having lost so much to her ache to claim power outside of herself. But she hadn't been able to look at him for many months without a pang of upset and hurt, knowing how far he'd wandered from her. She had allowed something to happen because of simple curiosity, and it had ended certainly and irreversibility in death.

Lewis, Delphine, and Heidi's childhood had been littered with many defining moments, and they all remembered pieces of that night. If they had ever bothered to talk to one another, to put their pieces together, they would have been able to see the answer their bodies were aching for, instead of the fractured feelings they carried around in their souls. But they never came together, and so they were stuck with a feeling, and eventually, the feeling was numbness.

Because one night, a pot boiled over. The water seeped down the sides of the stove, staining the wood as the hot liquid dripped onto the wooden planks, mostly unnoticed. Marigold Reid was making a pot of tea to calm her nerves, or so she'd told her son right before she'd offered him a *goodnight, sleep well*. Anxiety was something she usually felt in place of excitement, but her mind was excited that night; it was feeling a pull for once, towards the thing she thought she wanted and had worked so hard to reach out and hopefully touch. She had smiled at the thought, then burned her hand when she finally went to clean up the mess, not bothering to pour herself a cup of tea at all.

Her husband, Nicholas, had been outside late that night. He wanted to blame Marigold for a lot of things, including that night, but he would realize at his very last second that no one acted all on their own. And he had been out, often, always, more so than not. He told her he was working, which he was. He told her he was building a life, which he thought he was. He told her he saw some friends on occasion, which was a lie. He only saw one.

When he wandered home after an unusually late night, he had looked up at the dark night sky, seeing lightning without clouds over the woods that stretched out far on their land and touched all the neighboring farms and town. There was an external road to drive on, but there was a more secretive and complex internal roadway filled with trails and passages used by those who had lived there the longest, unable to remember a time before that land of rolling hills and lakeshore. That night, Nicholas had taken the common roads, a little too drunk to bother wandering muddy footpaths. When he walked into his house the pot was still on the stove, the liquid beneath it haphazardly cleaned up. He barely noticed. The house was dark, and when he wandered upstairs he found his son asleep in his room, but his own bed vacant. For a moment, he didn't really notice that either. Not while he untied his boots and pulled them off each foot slowly and intentionally. He didn't notice it as he changed his shirt or stretched out one last time in front of the window overlooking the backyard, the glass panes closed tightly so that a slight breeze came only from the ceiling fan, moving the lace curtains like small motions to a dance. He made it all the way back to bed before he felt the stark wind touch his skin one last time, and all of a sudden, he knew.

It was a combination of things. He felt them all at once, the way that breeze chilled his skin from above, the way the smell of something that wasn't tea at all had slowly climbed its way into their upstairs bedroom, the sight of lightning over one singular spot far out in the woods. *She's finally done it*, he thought. Nicholas tried to jump up, but the herbs his wife had boiled in the pot on the kitchen stove had been no accident, and his mind felt hazy as he struggled to make any bold movements. With great intention, he grabbed his boots and wandered back out into the darkened hallway, holding onto the walls for support as he continued down. For a moment, he thought of his son, asleep in the bedroom next to theirs. He did love him, and because of it, he was able to muster the strength to take off his overshirt and tuck it underneath his son's bedroom door. As he threw himself down the stairs, he hoped it would make a difference. Reaching the kitchen, his mind hazy, he fought to crawl across the floor begging to make it to the side door before passing out. He thought about everything, all that he knew, all that he had felt, and he knew he had to keep going no matter what. Somehow, just as everything seemed too dark to navigate, the door opened and a gust of chilled air rippled through the house, cleansing it of the dangerous fumes and giving Nicholas back his senses. He still thought he blamed his wife. After gulping in a few deep breaths of clean air, he took off into the woods, not sure what trail would lead him to where he was headed. He thought he knew what he was looking for, but he was yet to have an idea. People had been searching the woods, searching all the land there was for something more, some explanation of meaning, of fate and destiny. Nicholas had never been very occupied with those questions of existence, but he wasn't occupied by loneliness. Marigold was, and she had been for a long time.

While he wandered, searching desperately, hoping he wasn't too late, Nicholas didn't at all think about Marigold's loneliness. It was something she had been forced to confide in others about, and only one woman really listened to her, the neighbor down the road. She wasn't lonely, instead finding solace in her independence. Marigold wished for some of that confidence and ability to fight and persevere. In the end, it was Sara's curiosity and need for more mixed with Marigold's loneliness and need for more that created a friendship built on encouraging one another to seek it out, find that missing piece. Eventually, cost became no object.

Sara knew things she never told Marigold. It was easy for her to spot other people's secrets, even when they themselves didn't realize there was something to hide. Sara suspected Ramone hadn't quite realized yet, but the way Nicholas refused to look at her was evidence enough to her suspicions. The most unsettling thing about Sara was her anger was utterly untrustworthy. Never did her anger leave her body at an issue that would usually warrant it, instead she lashed out when everything felt resolved. So far, resolution felt like a distant oasis yet to be discovered, so in the meantime she came over to Marigold's house often, helped her tidy house and lace it with positivity and encouragement. Sometimes Sara brought her youngest daughter with her, and they watched as she would mess around in the garden, first catching toads nestled in the dirt, then growing old enough to actually contribute to growing the vegetables, the flowers, the herbs, and the magic. It was always there, subtly, glittering in the sun. Marigold felt comfortable with her company, sure her husband was at work, and sure her son wasn't getting into too much trouble. Sara didn't tell her otherwise, whether to protect her or use her; somehow the intention didn't matter, and the meaning got muddle throughout the years. It was something Sara had learned was regrettable, in her old age. Perhaps there was a cost to not knowing, to feeling too much in one moment and not enough in the next. She thought about that sometimes now, reading her daughter's stories.

As Nicholas continued to walk through the woods, shouting her name, he wondered if he would be too late, if he were alone in his search, if any of it would make a difference. He was kind, but self-centered, an imperfect human. They all are. It felt like hours went by, but the darkness indicated it could not possibly have been that long. He began to feel like he was no longer alone, that his cries for Marigold were being drown out by someone else's cries for another. And when the shadow of a man stumbled into the dark space Nicholas was in, it was no coincidence.

"Ramone?" Nicholas asked, squinting his eyes even though he would recognize the man anywhere. His friend nodded, coming up close to him. He was looking all around at the surrounding woods, an uneasiness everywhere.

"Something is happening tonight," he replied, his breath hot against Nicholas's face. They stood so close to one another, it made the world feel safe.

"I know," his friend replied.

"My daughter is out here," Ramone cried, his voice breaking in pieces that cut.

"This late? Why?"

"She felt something. She wandered."

They headed off together, realizing the entwinement of everything almost too late, but still late enough that there would be casualties, costs, final seconds. It wasn't a thought that entered their minds lightly, or with very much form. It had to be kept at bay to continue, because Ramone loved his daughter, and Nicholas loved him.

Together, they searched. Nicholas told him about Marigold's disappearance, the tea, the cool breeze he knew came from somewhere other than the depths of the earth. Ramone knew too, much in the same way everyone else did; he had just chosen to pay attention sooner and for longer. He marveled at his own wife, sitting up at their house, knowing she was looking out the window not hoping for anything in particular, just to catch a glimpse of the thing she hoped was real. He felt the cold air too across his cheek, breath from the universe. There was something to be said about forgoing personal gain to be a protector. When he looked at Nicholas, he didn't know if he was ready.

"Do you think she found it, what she's looking for?" Nicholas asked timidly.

"She's close," Ramone responded, voice quiet and even. They continued to search, the world around them shifting. It was hardly noticeable at first and then slowly, everything shifted. The trees buzzed with an electric force, their aura's changing at such a speed the eye had a hard time following each movement. The ground beneath their feet felt soft, each step at a slower pace than the previous one. They saw the bounding shadows of creatures physically not there, wandering in-between realities suggesting the one the two men stood on didn't exist alone. Deep fear filled Nicholas and then, when he saw it, he was empty.

At first, there was nothing but light. A kind of light he had never seen before, a force and energy so warm that all he wanted to do was slide into it, comfortable, and dream. There was such enormity to it that he could not process all of it, but he knew exactly what it was before he had a chance to think. A *rift*, a whisper between women, a small breeze on a cloudless day, a pang of electricity through the body when there was no ghost there to cause an itch. It was power and chaos and beauty. Simply, it was everything all at once.

He wasn't sure how much time it took, but he slowly turned his head to see more, see what Ramone had been focusing on from the beginning. His daughter laid beneath the light, lost in her dreams, pieces of her turning bright gold as they flew up into the chasm like embers from a fire. Ramone was trying to reach her, pull her back, protect her from scattering. She was a beautiful accumulation of stardust; Ramone had always thought so. She needed to be connected awhile longer still. Nicholas saw that passion. Then, he turned his head slowly to his wife, her loneliness evident as she stared back at him, the last to be seen. It all felt too far along, the sound of all that energy suddenly such a loud culmination of atoms he couldn't even open his mouth to speak: it would be lost. He had never been very good at action, his own wants and desires started and completed by someone else in the room. But for once, there was too much at stake, and that realization hurt Marigold the most, because she realized she wouldn't be the one to die for anything, and she wouldn't be the reason to live, either.

Ramone had reached his daughter, holding her tightly, his own strength being sucked away into the entity that was everything and nothing on its own. Nicholas sobbed at the sight, the realization finally that these were the final seconds. Everything seemed infinite until a choice had to be made. He stared longingly at Ramone, a dear friend. Then, he looked at his wife who begged him not to, pleaded for anything else. *Let me go*, she mouthed, but Nicholas couldn't do that. Even amongst that much glory, he could still feel the power behind their own lives. He wanted to protect that for her, give her the chance to live a life of fulfillment. He realized how they had all arrived there, standing in the middle of the eye of the universe, and it was because he was self-centered. And now, it was time for him to be kind.

He foraged ahead, a whisper of a goodbye, dust.

They all awoke at different moments. Marigold first, the darkness surrounding her like loneliness only wished it could. She cried, sobbing, her heart breaking harder than it ever had before. Somehow she managed to crawl home, a broken mess, more of her trapped in that great rift than was left to sustain her. Over time, it would ruin her son. And he'd leave his son in her care, unable to hold up the world for even himself. And sometimes, that loss would become too great, and his son would be forced to feel it, too.

Ramone woke next, the darkness comforting him, causing a great calmness to pass over his body. He allowed his eyes to adjust. There was a great loss that swept over him, a part of his soul sacrificed to give his daughter a chance to live and grow and not die at the hands of someone else's loneliness. He touched his sleeping daughter's forehead gently, then carefully stood up to go, wandering the woods till sunrise, alone in his grief.

Lastly, Heidi woke up in a field of rosemary, basking in warm sunlight from a brilliant sunrise. As she stretched, yawning, she felt she'd had a stunning dream, but couldn't remember it exactly. She skipped home.

It was just one night. One night of everything coming to a breaking point, and then simply splintering off, not ever knowing how truly connected they all were. Ramone finally began to understand something about the rift; they'd really discovered the crack in the air, the deep chasm one could fall upwards into. They had all touched the energetic light. Maybe this was why the three Pennyfather kids never truly knew what was out there. It wasn't necessarily for them. Ramone and Sara worked very hard to hide it from them, to keep that deep earth magic hidden and unfound. Power always wanted more, spirits always wanted a body, and knowledge came at a cost and a sacrifice. Nicholas died to protect Ramone's own. Was it fueled by love? There was no way to see the bounds. Marigold Reid's husband loved Ramone Pennyfather very much, and thus any extension of him. So when the rift beckoned, he dove in someone else's place. And Heidi didn't know, she'd simply awakened and continued on. And Sara couldn't look Marigold in the face, having tempted fate. And Ramone knew he couldn't ever walk away from such endearment.

He knew one day he'd have to go, too. He would want to. It was both a debt and a favor. When Ramone later died, it was for nothing less than the cost of a very good friend.

On the porch now, three women sipping their lemonade in the heat of a summer day, they had no idea how deeply Ramone had fought for all of them. How much he had fought for everyone. He had braved the universe for Heidi, given Delphine the keys to the entire world to explore, and tried his hardest to teach Lewis discipline and ritual if nothing else, so that Beth might be able to predict him, at least. Heidi took a sip of her lemonade as the porch door swung open, her mother coming out to join them, the taste suddenly bitter in her mouth.

When the breeze blew across their skin, they felt the cool breath of the universe.

Twenty.

Close it.

It was a whisper, her own voice but not her own intentions. Rosemary moved her head back and forth on her pillow in her sleep, her heart racing, sweat dripping off her brow onto the sheets. She heard it again and again, her own voice mirrored back to her. When she opened her eyes, her own face looked back at her earnestly.

Close it.

Was it begging? Or insisting? There felt like the need to differentiate. She didn't want to talk to herself about it though, not at all. She waved her phantom limbs in front of her face, both her faces. Her sister vaguely heard her whine from her own sleep, peaceful that night with the warmth of an entire sun beating in her chest. The words wouldn't come out, but Rosemary wanted to tell herself to go away, vanish, become nothing so it could become everything. The thought surprised her other self, looking down at her, eyebrows cocked. She tried to look away, but it was hard to do in a room made of mirrors. Something howled, causing both faces to turn and look at the bedroom door that slowly opened halfway. A creature scurried past the door, a person racing past it. Rosemary jumped back, suddenly finding herself standing right in front of the door. When she looked out, carefully peaking her head, James was standing there, looking for something. It was deceiving him.

"What are you doing?" Rosemary whispered, her voice hoarse as the two images of herself folded together just in time for James to look back at her and only see one. His eyes were deadpan; he was asleep. She looked at him a while longer as he scurried around in the hallway, looking for something that was moving. Rosemary rubbed the sleep out of her eyes, trying to better focus. Wolfgang came out of their shared room and stood between them before she could look too closely.

"Hey it's fine, go back to bed," he muttered to his cousin, gently leading his brother back into their room. Rosemary didn't move, still looking at the two young men. Wolfgang met her gaze for a moment longer than was comfortable. She got the message, fading back into the darkness of her own bedroom and shutting the door securely behind her. She laid back in bed, eyes fixed on the stars sparkling out her open window. She watched them twirl around, move throughout the sky, and slowly disappear as the sky brightened and the dark blues and purples were mixed with bright pinks and oranges.

A new day, a sleepless night.

"Hey, good morning," Lucy mumbled as she stretched under her covers, pushing her long hair out of her face. She had always slept deeply. She yawned again, blinking as her eyes adjusted to the light. While she looked at her sister, she took in how still she was, how perfect she looked on top of her covers, arms folded over her stomach, her dark hair pushed perfectly away from her face and laid around her head like a shadowy halo.

"Did you sleep?" she asked.

"Yeah, I woke up a little bit ago," Rosemary replied, her eyes darting around her sister's angelic face. It was so golden in the morning light. Lucy was too groggy at first to wonder how honest the answer was, instead rolling over and shoving her face under her pillow in protest of getting up, though no one was making her. Time was almost meaningless out there on a summer's day.

"I think I had a dream last night..." Lucy mumbled from

underneath sheets and pillows. Rosemary almost laughed at the declaration, but instead asked her about it.

"Oh yeah? What happened?" She expected she already knew, but she was wrong.

"I'm not sure, but we were all there and there was this big, soft, shallow pond before us," Lucy mumbled, her voice slowly becoming more awake but with that, the fragments of her dream began to fade. Rosemary sat up quickly, surprised it hadn't been anything she'd seen during the night. In fact, it was much different.

"Whose *we*?" Rosemary asked.

"Us, Rose. And Wolfgang and James. It was just some silly pond, and Wolfgang walked into it when James splashed him. It was a nice place... I don't really remember anything else. Why? What did you dream about?" Lucy asked, still laying flat in bed. She felt warm and protected, never wanting to move ever again if it were possible. She knew the feeling wouldn't last, slowly her legs would begin to tingle and she'd have to go out and move around if only to take the edge off.

"Oh, nothing really. Just about the sky," Rosemary replied. She was surprised by the different perspectives, and found herself wondering what it meant. For the first time, she contemplated that maybe the dreams meant nothing. The thought didn't sit well with her. For her entire life, she had always followed her midnight messages and they'd always taken her somewhere. What if she'd been misguided, lost to her own desires?

"What did you say we were doing in the dream again?" Rosemary asked, trying to place the scene, thinking about her cousins having such carefree fun in a shallow pool. Lucy shrugged like it didn't matter.

"I don't know; I think we were just sitting together, laughing at it all."

They laid around for a while after that, not really talking or doing much of anything. Taking the time to not do anything was harder than it seemed. Procrastination was one thing, but carving out time simply to exist was another entirely. Neither girl moved until they heard their cousins across the hall begin to wake up and walk around. Their door was cracked, and Wolfgang knocked before he opened it wider.

"You're both still in bed?" he asked, hardly able to believe it. They laughed.

"Lazy morning," Rosemary said.

"We're finally taking pointers from you!" Lucy teased. Wolfgang rolled his eyes, but it was hard to resist a smile as he raked his hand through his messy hair, sleep still needing to be rubbed out of his eyes. He stood there as if he didn't know what to do or where to go next.

"James awake?" Rosemary asked, thinking there was another reason she felt like asking about him other than random curiosity.

"Yeah, he's hogging the bathroom right now," Wolfgang replied, looking over at his cousin for a long moment. There was a faint memory in his mind, one that was fading away with the quickness of sand running through a clock, only in the way a dream ever did. It was just sounds, dark shadows moving about even though he couldn't make out the edges. He thought he heard a voice, but wasn't sure what it had been saying.

"Plans for your day?" Lucy asked, finally sitting up in bed and stretching out her back. Wolfgang sank to the floor, leaning again the wall by their bedroom door. He was antsy in their space, but it felt safer than any other part of the house. He heard the water from the shower turn on and settled in.

"Smoke and take a nap," he replied with a devious grin. It was a common activity for him, but something about the honesty of it didn't seem all that true on that particular morning. Things were different inside of him; he knew it. Now all his body wanted to do was go outside, move around, roam the land for lack of a better understanding of the motive. His mind was constantly trying to catch up, understand this sudden change, and know what it was like to be awake after nothing but sleep. He could hear that voice again, mumbling, but what were the words?

"You know we never..." Lucy started to say but stopped

suddenly. She didn't want to be the first one to bring it up, but they knew immediately what she was talking about, or at least trying to. There wasn't any concrete reason for not speaking of their experiences, of its possibility or what it meant. Some of the time, it felt like if any of them spoke about it, the power would dissipate and cease to exist entirely. That's not what they wanted. It was like holding onto a dream, if you focus on it carefully alone in the morning, the entire thing is memorable. The moment you start to share its details over eggs and coffee, the most important pieces vanish, and you're left with fragments at best, a feeling at most. For now, they all wanted more than that, for different reasons but a common goal. So Lucy didn't elaborate, didn't talk about the sun pulsing in her chest or her ability to seemingly move about unencumbered by friction.

"Should we make breakfast?" she asked instead.

"I guess we can," Wolfgang said, shifting back to his more routine way of acting and speaking. Uninterested, distant, and vaguely dissociated. Oddly, it was comforting to all of them in that moment when at the start of summer it always seemed cold, with the ability to grow into something dangerous. They couldn't see the storm on the horizon yet. The water turned off.

"We could eat on the porch," Rosemary offered, continuing off her sister's suggestion. Something about it seemed nice, normal even. A normal they could only have now that everything else had been so erratic. Wolfgang shrugged, which meant he wasn't opposed.

"I'm pouring some milk into a bowl of cereal and that's it," Wolfgang said and somehow, that seemed better than cooking up a whole meal. The simplicity was kind.

"Well, all I'm doing is spreading peanut butter on a banana," Lucy shot back, teasing him. She threw one of her pillows down at him, but he caught it before it could make an impact. When he threw it back, it smacked her in the face somehow missing her arms. James walked in carefully, his hair long and damp from the shower. He hated the silence that always greeted him when he first walked into a place, but Rosemary didn't hear it, she just heard little barks and scraping, looking outside to see if maybe a stray dog had wandered through the yard. She didn't see anything but sunlight.

"What're we all doing in here?" James asked, taking a seat away from his brother, but somehow still within Wolfgang's aura. Everyone had noticed their new sense of connectedness, but something about it felt stressed, like gravity competing between two forces almost the same size.

"Just hanging out," Rosemary replied.

"Speak for yourself, I've been waiting to get in that bathroom," Wolfgang replied, bolting up as if there weren't a single other bathroom to use in the entire house. Nothing felt as right as their own though, on the third floor that nobody used but them. Security was comforting.

When he left, calmness fell over the other three. James looked out the window quietly, seeming content enough. Lucy finally got out of bed, finishing up a routine of stretches and looking around for a certain pair of shorts to change into. Rosemary didn't move from bed, instead taking the time to look out the window as well, and watch James while he did so. Something dark had happened to him, the story of the cliff no longer holding up in her mind. She rarely dared to think about it, because when she did, she began to feel trapped in a whirlwind of dark fog and prickly lightning. She'd never asked, and he had never told. Even now, taking in the small cuts on his face that were nearly healed, a well-bandaged arm that she would never realize was a burn and not rough skin; she didn't think to ask. When he looked at her, realizing he was being watched, she noticed his eyes held almost nothing but survival in them, and perhaps a little bit of hope sparked by a destiny she had never heard him speak of. Rosemary thought about her sister's dream when she saw his eyes.

"We're going to eat breakfast on the porch together in a bit if you want to join," Rosemary said to break the tension. James nodded, accepting the invite.

"What did you want to do today?" she asked. He shrugged. He didn't really know how to make decisions for himself; it had rarely ever been an option. When he didn't say anything, leaving himself open to everyone else's will, Rosemary decided to push.

"Are you okay?"

Lucy froze in the corner of the room, having already changed her clothes without anyone noticing. She'd gotten very good at the skill, able to do it almost anywhere and at any time. She looked from her sister who was shakily earnest over to her youngest cousin. Something dark seemed to emanate from him with the question, a visceral defense. Some of it seemed like a taste of his brother, and some of it felt entirely new and unknowable.

"I'm fine," he replied, voice curt. Rosemary had hoped he would open, and he might have a month ago. But not now. There had been an edge, and he had been pushed off into the other side. They had all noticed too late because they had never wanted to notice at all. He was stuck wandering a fog-covered place, all his fears grown and free. There was no dreamland for him, simply a nightmare, always.

"Sorry, you just seem...far away," Rosemary mumbled, feeling small in a space she rarely ever did. When she looked at James, she saw the darkness Lucy felt, a piece of it Wolfgang's energy but the rest unfamiliar. She hoped a warm meal would fix it, but it never had before. Too simplistic a solution. The bedroom door opened again.

"Ready for that cereal?" Wolfgang asked, showered and dressed for the day in front of them. He said it to defuse the situation, to take away the focus from his brother. James didn't take it that way, because although he didn't want to be seen anymore, he still hated the feeling of being swept under the rug because whatever the dark energy was, it was too much for everyone else in the room. They didn't want it. James never knew why they didn't see it was too much for him, too.

"Hopefully we have milk," Lucy mumbled, trying to be funny as she walked past everyone and out of the room, ready to go downstairs and move around. The others followed her silently. No one seemed to be in the house when they made it to the kitchen, a note on the fridge stating most everyone had decided to go down to the lake for the day, something their parents rarely did anymore when visiting home.

Once in the kitchen, they each fell into a comfortable routine of making separate meals for themselves and getting ready to go outside and eat in the sun. James handed Rosemary the butter for her toast without being asked, wanting her to know that he appreciated each kindness she gave out, even though he was too far away to receive them anymore. With food in hand, they wandered out onto the porch at their own pace, Lucy perching herself up on the railing while Wolfgang sat next to Rosemary on the porch swing and James sat alone on the floorboards, wanting to stretch out his legs and be held by nothing. At first they were quiet, silently eating their simple meals and just relishing in the comfort that only family can give sometimes. No matter how volatile it could be, it was familiar. And no matter how volatile, it wasn't always.

"Summer is waning," Lucy said, looking up at the sky after her last bite of fruit. Rosemary studied her sister before she had anything to say about cooler days ahead. With the declaration, she started to imagine her sister out in the world. What was she like, when she wasn't surrounded by family and large trees? Rosemary knew she was social, people begged her to be their friend, followed her around hoping she would never leave them behind. Rosemary always wondered how a relationship like that felt, what it was like to be so seemingly wanted. She didn't know her sister had her own hazy filter.

"Are you excited for your trip?" Rosemary asked. Lucy took a moment to reply.

"Yes. But I'm not wishing the summer away," she said. James knew how that answer felt. He thought about the impending fall, and his chest seized up.

"Europe, is it?" Wolfgang asked, using his leg to rock the

bench back and forth. He sounded bored the way he asked, his way of always keeping things at a tolerable emotional distance.

"Yes, we're backpacking through a few countries," Lucy replied. No matter how long they were at this, it always stung talking about their lives outside of their summertime together. In the world, they were more or less strangers. Thanksgiving, Christmas, were all holidays that lasted just one day and not everyone always made it to the party. It was a breeding ground for small talk, boisterous conversations of accomplishments and activities. Nothing was as sweet at the hot days spent on Sara's land, with nothing but never-ending time and sweat to bring them all together, taking away everything they had but themselves.

"Don't get lost," Wolfgang replied, yawning. Lucy wanted to snip back, but she knew it was a dangerous road bringing up his time outside of the three months she spent with him. While the details always seemed faded, she knew about the trouble he got into, the activities he fell back into, and the joblessness that followed him from one short-term employment to the next. He had the same qualities Lucy did, an energy that brought people in, needing him to want them the same way they wanted him. But unlike Lucy, he could be directly unkind, painfully cruel. It was a game that had been played so many times on himself, he had finally succeeded at throwing it back at those around him.

"I'll try not to," she replied, voice pointed but fair. Wolfgang almost felt bad about being dismissive, but that negative feeling in his chest pleaded for him to say something worse. It was the cruelty, ever-present, a battle to not lash out, to not make others feel small. The sound of a truck rolling up the driveway stopped him from saying anything more, as the four of them looked to see who was visiting. When Silas jumped out of the driver's side, no one was surprised. Rosemary felt a pounding in her chest.

"Hey," Lucy greeted from her perch as he walked up the side of the yard and up the new steps where they all sat. He nodded hello to everyone, smiling.

"Everyone's all here, together, what a sight," he said, leaning comfortably against the railing with his hands deep in his jean pockets.

"Happens every so often," Wolfgang replied.

"How've you been?" Rosemary asked, looking at his face and the healing marks across his brow. He nodded, a warm smile on his face.

"I'm doing good, I know it's been a while since I've been around last," he replied. She liked his honesty, liked the way he saw the good when all that seemed to shadow them were secrets and curiosities.

"Yeah, a little while," Rosemary replied quietly.

"I'm honestly kind of busy today, I'm just here dropping some things off for your grandma that she had me order a while back. Trying to get everything done before the storm comes through," Silas replied as everyone looked out at the sky, seeing nothing but unabashed blue.

"I don't think it's going to rain," Lucy laughed, taking in the warm sun on such a perfect day. Silas shook his head, looking out past the trees towards the horizon.

"It's gonna storm pretty bad. It's not something you can see just yet, but you can definitely feel it in the air," Silas replied, closing his eyes and breathing in deeply. It was something that if anyone else had done would have been silly. But when Silas did so up on their porch, it felt calming and they found themselves closing their own eyes and listening for water in the air. Still, all they felt was sun, but they believed him.

"How've you all been? Enjoying your summer?" Silas asked. They felt the smallest of intrusions, but something about breathing in and wishing for rain kept their bodies calm and no one felt too guarded when answering the question.

"Just sitting here realizing it's almost over," James said, looking up at Silas. They shared a look for a moment. Silas had that way about him, he was comforting. He'd always been someone who felt safe. And James knew him from the hunting season, times when no one else seemed to be around but him. He was someone who never left the land, and also wandered the woods, looking for something.

"Almost over is still not the end," Silas replied, his words cryptic. Everyone let that sit in the air for a moment, wondering how it fit in with everything else.

"Is Sara inside? I'm just going to bring this box in for her," Silas asked, already taking a few steps back towards the truck. Rosemary jumped up, setting her empty plate down on the side table and walking over to the steps.

"I can help you," she replied, walking over to his truck beside him. He seemed different somehow, lighter than the last time. He was more in charge of himself in that space, if that was the difference. She caught him looking at her seriously, but he didn't seem to have the words to explain why. She wanted to know, though.

"I kept meaning to call, but I haven't," he said as he grabbed a box out of the bed of his truck, letting it rest on the tailgate for a moment. She nodded as if that was all she needed to know. But it wasn't even close.

"I appreciate what you did for me last week," he continued. She nodded, then shrugged, as if it was nothing. It hadn't been, but something else seemed more encompassing. He didn't avert his eyes, wanting her to know she didn't need to brush anything off. His appreciation was true.

"Things seem good around here?" he asked her, looking around and then back up at her family. She knew what he was starting to get at, but what she could never figure out was how he seemed to know about all of it without her ever sharing a word, and mostly only because she didn't know how to make the intangible tangible for him. The ground was beginning to roll, the sky so blue it hurt her eyes because it felt like she should be expecting rain. Her bones were beginning to feel the anticipation of a storm.

"Different, I guess," she said.

"For a lot of reasons," she added. It was the truth.

"Another day we'll have to hang out again, do something fun for once. If you want," Silas said, finally picking up the box and starting to walk back to the house. Rosemary nodded, perhaps too earnestly, so she tried to cut back and keep her energy steady.

"I have nothing but time," she replied. She opened the front door for him and told him to set the box on the bench in the entryway and she'd let Sara know he had brought something by.

"What is it?" she asked, looking at the box, curious what her grandmother had needed help ordering.

"You'll have to ask her," Silas replied, already heading out the door. The moment he stepped back outside, a breeze blew through the porch, cooling everyone's tingling skin. The sky still seemed bright; the sun still warm but there was something brewing farther out. Silas seemed rushed.

"It was good to see you guys," Silas said, waving as he jumped down the steps and headed back over to his truck. Lucy waved at him, shouting for him to come back and spend some time whenever he was free. Just as quickly as he came, he was backing out of the driveway. As he passed them, he honked the horn for one final goodbye before disappearing down the hill. Rosemary climbed up the wooden steps slowly and sat back down next to Wolfgang, still swinging on the bench.

"I've never seen him in such a hurry," James said, looking out at the vacant yard.

"Yeah, me either," Lucy replied, feeling ready to do something else. Their group quickly fell apart as they went inside to clean up their dishes. Lucy wandered outside to a lawn chair, shirt off, and with a good book in hand. Wolfgang found his way into the big tree that shaded his grandfather's grave and lit up something to take the edge off. Rosemary and James were left alone for a moment in the kitchen, Rosemary wanting to ask what was making her cousin so nervous but worried about his reaction. When the last dish was dried and put away, she turned to look at him sitting at the counter, looking out the window and nervously picking at the edge of the bandage on his arm. It was the first time she had really noticed it for more than a moment, and she wondered why that was on her part. James turned to her for a moment, sensing her wanting to ask, but knowing she wouldn't. He felt like none of his choices were ever right.

"I told my mom I'd do some things around the house for her, so she could take a break. Wanna help? It shouldn't take too long," James offered, his eyes cast down at the countertop; his rough hands filled with calluses and bent bones. Rosemary thought it was the best offer she'd been given all week.

"Yes. Where do we start?"

Together, with Beth in mind, they started first on the laundry, then cleaned both downstairs bathrooms top to bottom. Rosemary scrubbed the showers down while James wiped the sink, counters, and toilets. When the dryer buzzed, they folded all the towels and linens and dropped them off to the respective rooms and closets they belonged. When that was all finished, they dusted and vacuumed the living room, taking their time and enjoying each other's silent company. Neither knew what to say to the other, but their presence alone said more than they ever could have, and it was articulated so perfectly. While Wolfgang and Lucy seemed like family, James and Rosemary always had as well. Both quiet, cautious, and deeply sensitive to the smallest changes. It wasn't something they bonded over.

"Busy bees," Sara commented, coming down the steps slowly from her room. She'd been keeping to herself more so than usual that summer, whether it be out of grief or that Ramone wasn't there to encourage her to try any harder. She wandered into the kitchen, grabbing an apple out of the basket and pouring herself a glass of iced tea before heading out to the porch to sit in her favorite shaded spot come the afternoon. Both her grandchildren watched her move, always feeling her strong presence as a force to be reckoned. They knew their grandmother well, and her ability to switch from docile to viper in seconds was both frightening and mesmerizing.

"When will your parents be back?" she asked as she was on

her way out the door.

"Soon, I think," Rosemary replied. The door almost slammed shut before Rosemary could get out her next words, "Silas dropped a package off for you!"

Sara came back into the house, looking around until she saw the box.

"Thank you," she replied, grabbing the box and taking it outside with her. When she stood out on the covered porch, she could feel the storm in the air. She wondered what it would be like, how hard it would hit. Her package had almost come too late, though she knew the damage had mostly already been done. She'd let Ramone down, again. He was shaking his head from his grave, she knew it.

"Do you want a drink?" Rosemary asked as she headed into the kitchen to pour herself some of her grandmother's iced tea. James agreed, and she came back with two glasses. They sat together on the couch, sipping their drinks and feeling good about all the work they'd been able to accomplish. Rosemary didn't spend much time with her Aunt Beth, but she knew she worked hard and tried to please as many people as she could. She wondered why none of them talked to her more, knew more about her. Her whole family seemed that way, the more she thought about it. The quiet was mostly new, Ramone had always asked everyone about everything, and it had seemed easy to talk about then. Now, the air was different. She missed him.

They heard the sound of a car up the road, their parents returning from the lake. While the sky didn't seem quite as bright, it still remained cloudless, no visible sign of a storm drawing near. That's how it went sometimes, clear skies until they weren't – smooth going until it wasn't. They heard the voices of everyone as they got out of the car, all six of them fitting into one vehicle. Lucy could be heard talking to them, asking how the beach was, joking around with everyone easily. She was so personable; it killed Rosemary to witness sometimes.

"Come outside, they want to have a barbeque," Lucy said

through an open window, looking in to find out where her sister was hiding. Rosemary didn't seem like she wanted to move from the couch, and neither did James.

"Come on, at least sit with me out here while our dads cook," Lucy pleaded.

"Aren't you burnt yet?" Rosemary asked.

"I don't burn," Lucy laughed, waving her arm to insist they come out. Both of them knew she wouldn't give up easily, so slowly they stood up from the couch and the quiet and the shade and wandered back outside, sitting in the slew of lawn chairs that were always set up.

"We could play bocce ball?" Lucy suggested, after a few moments of sitting around and hearing about how crowded the lake had been that day but how refreshing the water was in contrast. Heidi went on and on about how a huge fish had swum past her, touching her leg. She swore it was a piranha even though there was no chance. Rosemary agreed to the possibility.

And just like that, it was a party. Henry, Lewis, and Seth started grilling, already a few beers in. Heidi and Beth started tossing a salad together and getting corn on the cob husked and ready to grill. Delphine was emptying their cooler of melted water so she could refill it with fresh ice and all new drinks from the garage fridge. Sara sat back, giving directions, but they weren't unkind. Wolfgang was missing, nowhere to be seen. His spot in the large oak was empty when Rosemary covered her eyes to see better. They wondered where he could be.

The girls started their game, while James somehow became roped into helping his father and uncles grill. Rosemary watched as he tensely fell into their jokes, standing as far away from the grill as he could, as if it might move and bite. He didn't fit in with them, Rosemary wasn't sure if he ever had.

"Hey girl, your throw," Lucy directed. She was standing ready, ball in hand. She looked effortless and sun-kissed in her jean cutoffs, bathing suit top, and long blonde hair flowing over her shoulders and down her back. She was always ready for a party, every event perfectly situated for her and almost always her alone. It was something about being a creator. She had the energy.

"Girls, you want something to drink?" Delphine asked, dragging the cooler out of the garage.

"Took you long enough!" Lewis shouted out to his sister, waving an empty bottle in hand. She waved him off but smiled anyway. She signaled to him that he'd have to wait; it was ladies first around there.

"I found some different types of beers, those seltzers you and Heidi like so much, and these weird cocktails in a can. I'm not sure how good that can be, but I think I'll try one," Delphine said, rummaging around in the ice. She handed Lucy a mixed cocktail and Rosemary a seltzer in the flavor she asked for. There was something about the carbonation she craved.

"Did you girls have a good morning? You look so dark," Delphine said, hugging Lucy into her as Rosemary finally took her turn and tossed the red ball towards the small white one out in the field before turning around.

"Rose did chores all day, but I've been reading this great book I think you should borrow when I'm done, hopefully before summer is over," Lucy replied, easily talking to her mother about the trials and tribulations of the characters in the novel her lit professor had privately given to her during office hours before the summer holiday. Their conversation was easy, it always had been. They understood one another, so it made it easy, allowed it to be. Rosemary looked out at the crowd, missing the person who made her feel understood.

"That does sound really good, please try to finish before we leave. I'd love to read it and talk about it when I'm done," Delphine agreed.

"Hey! Where's the cooler?" Lewis yelled out, still waiting on his drink. Delphine laughed, waving at him as she went up to the cooler and dragged it over to the grill, setting it in its final resting place as she joined their conversation, falling into it much easier than James ever could. The girls continued their game.

"Where's Wolfgang, do you think?" Rosemary asked as their game took them farther out from the group. They all seemed to be united that day, more or less, comfortable with one another in the rare moments of a fading summer.

"Exactly where he wants to be," Lucy said with utter focus as she tossed her ball, getting dangerously close to the goal. She smiled excitedly, taking a sip of her mixed drink in a can. She tilted her head from side to side as the liquid rolled over her tongue.

"Not bad," she finally declared. She watched as her sister took a large gulp of her own drink, recognizing immediately that she was in a mood. Lucy couldn't entertain it, she wanted to stay happy, blissfully ignorant to the world as a whole and exist only in the moment, a good time spent barefoot in the grass with her sister. She went out and saw the world just so she could come back home and tell Rose all about it.

The girls continued their game, playing a few more rounds before dinner was finished cooking and it was time to head back. Both felt the buzz of alcohol on an empty stomach, and nothing felt sweeter on a summer evening. Lucy's laugh was contagious, and it had gotten Rosemary to open up to its possibility and be in the moment with her where worries were almost always cast aside. Usually, an entire world was occupying the inside of her mind and to leave it unattended felt almost impossible, but somehow her sister dragged her out, showed her the big world around her and how amazing it could be, even with so little control. Rosemary laughed as Lucy danced childishly around where the ball had landed for her winning throw, feeling the smile on her face as something honest. She relished in the moment. It was a perfect evening, before a storm.

Wolfgang came trudging up from over the hill at a far point of the property. Lucy saw him first, watching as he ambled up to them. She looked back at Rosemary setting up another game before dinner, taking in every easy movement she made, the happiness and ease still painted across her face. When she looked up at Lucy, she smiled. And Lucy saw the exact moment she caught sight of Wolfgang walking up to them, and felt her own heart flutter as the anxiety of the world crept back in.

"Sick invite," Wolfgang said, standing with his cousins as they looked over at the adults cooking and drinking. James hadn't seen his brother yet.

"We didn't know where you were," Rosemary replied, looking him over for any clues as to where he had disappeared. His eyes were glassy, but it could mean a variety of things. When she got close to him, he smelled like flowers.

"Don't lie, they were hoping I didn't show up," Wolfgang replied, watching his father with some kind of malice neither Rosemary or Lucy recognized.

"I wasn't," Rosemary said. Wolfgang grinned, but it wasn't kind.

"Let's get the party started then," he said, walking over to the crowd just as dinner was being plated and passed around. The girls followed him. Everyone welcomed him back, handing him food without him needing to ask. It was one of those rare occasions where everyone was having a good time, so they weren't looking for a reason not to. Wolfgang grabbed a beer out of the cooler and took a seat across from his father, just because he liked watching him talk. He found it interesting, how impassioned he could become and command space, which sometimes didn't initially intimidate. Every time Wolfgang went to speak, he saw people wince, almost cower, not sure what he'd do. The irony only furthered Wolfgang's own internal swirling of storm clouds, fascinated by how people perceived danger so incorrectly. He watched his brother, too. The way he moved like a ghost, his eyes always focusing on something far away, yet able to snap back so easily to any moment or conversation as if he hadn't been drifting. There were six years between them, but it had never felt like it. Wolfgang was young; James was old. If there was some middle ground to meet on, they were standing on it now.

James found himself unable to move away from his father and

uncles, even after the food had been passed around. Someone had given him a beer, at least. He knew to only take one, anything after that would make him falter and he never let down his guard or his ability to please in front of family. As they talked about hunting and traveling, apparently two very relatable things, James's mind did begin to wander. He couldn't help it. A cloud passed over the sun, appearing from nowhere, and for a moment the whole land was cast in shadow. From it, out far in the fields, he noticed grass moving about as if something was crawling between the blades. He tried to focus. The cloud passed, the sun returned, and the grass moved only in the slightest breeze, though it was cold. The food on his plate no longer seemed appetizing. There hadn't been much sleep for him the night before; he'd been stuck in an awful loop of thinking. It was why he couldn't face Rosemary. She had been looking for him; he'd seen her from the darkest corner where he had been hiding. He hadn't wanted her to find him, didn't want her to see what he'd become, what had happened to him. He didn't want anyone to lead him back to bed just to have to wake up again and again in the same place.

Always the same place.

A cloud passed again, grass closer to the house started moving. Something was crawling. If it howled, would everyone else hear? If it jumped out, could anyone else see it? James looked up at his father. Lewis was rambling; talking wildly with big arm motions about the absolute respect he had for the animals he tracked down, while only bringing back their carcasses. James wondered if he would ever tell anyone about what he did with their souls, always only bringing back carcasses. The shadows were moving in the barn now, he could see them race past the door. Elusive sections of the darkness moving so quickly, no matter how fast his eyes darted or he moved his head, there was no finite object to see. There was just stillness, stillness and maybe time would slow down enough to see something. A soul, a need to breathe. The sky was building with clouds.

Lucy looked up at the vast towers of clouds, amazed that they were forming in the first place. She hadn't really believed Silas when he had threatened a storm, but he had always been able to feel things deeper than she could. She looked around at her family, a perfect picture of a good time. That's how she wanted to see it. She walked up to her mother and aunts, entering their conversation easily and laughing about a past story. No matter how deep she got, she continued to scan the crowd. Because even though it may have taken her longer, she did feel the storm coming, she just didn't know the source yet.

Look!

It was her sister's voice, only her ears could hear. Rosemary was staring off at something, frozen in her chair alone at the edge of the group. Lucy raked her head from her sister to where her sister's eyes were focused, watching as their Uncle Lewis checked to make sure the grill was turned off, then moved forward and lit a cigar he pulled from his pocket, something he did when he was drinking with family, unlike his usual. Wolfgang hated him comfortable. The cigar lit, warm light at the front, and he continued talking. James's face looked strained at the conversation, a few pieces of ash floating off the end of the cigar and falling into his face. It was slight, harmless. But someone wasn't.

Somehow, a motion was repeated. Lucy blinked and watched as he reached for the grill again; making sure the gas was off. Nobody knew he had a cigar to pull out and light just yet. He turned away from the group, tapping his lighter for a single flame. Except the gas wasn't off, the knob on the grill turning back to ignite; he wasn't far enough away from it. A wave of heat flew up in his face as he roared in surprise and pain, falling back away from its intensity. Delphine and Beth shot up from their chairs, running to him lying on the ground. Heidi stood motionless, hand over her mouth. Henry rushed over, turning the gas off on the grill and helping Lewis sit up. Seth held a hand to James's back for a moment before he shrugged it off, taking his own few steps back and away. Sara stared at Wolfgang, though he could not feel it amongst the rest.

"You're okay, you're okay!" Beth kept shouting, running her hands over her husband's face, checking for any real damage. Other than burnt eyebrows and a painful rash across his face, he was fine, having taken just enough steps away from the cloud of invisible gas before lighting his cigar. Fury filled him, standing up quickly on his own and yelling at everyone to settle down, yelling about the damn grill, yelling about nothing, yelling about it all.

Did you see it again?

Beth walked Lewis into the house, insisting to look at his face in the lighting of the bathroom and for him to at least put some cold water on it. And just like that, everyone started scattering, finding tasks to do, things to put away. The wind picked up as soon as they started walking into the house, and when James looked up at the sky, it was filled with clouds, the sun completely blocked out. Some were darker than others, a sense of lightning building in the biggest, heaviest clouds. He looked back down, across the lawn at his brother. His face was neutral, with perhaps the faintest light in his eyes.

"Bring in the chairs, I don't want them to get wet," Sara shouted at her four grandchildren, who were simply standing exactly where they had been since it started. Perfectly across from one another, though she doubted they even knew why they chose those places to begin with. She looked at them with her bright eyes, then wandered inside. She thought of offering them something of a gift, but wasn't sure they'd take it. They'd been left alone too long. They wouldn't listen to her. Her husband would have been disappointed, but he often saw the good he wanted to see in people when there perhaps wasn't any to begin with. For better or worse, she was staying out of it this time. She was just going to watch.

The four of them brought in the chairs, threw out used plates, and dragged the cooler back into the garage next to the refrigerator. The wind picked up, the trees singing a warning song as their leaves moved back and forth with each great gust.

"We have to bring the grill in," Rosemary said, looking out at it standing alone in the back lawn, the party around it having completely evaporated. Together, they ran out and started dragging it in, just as thick drops of rain fell from the sky, pelting them heavily. The grill felt stuck, the wheels refusing to turn. All of them threw their backs into dragging and pushing, making it to the barn rather than the garage because it was the closest form of shelter. When they finally had it inside, they stood looking out at the sheets of rain falling heavily with no sign of stopping. It was so dark that the house, garage, even the woods seemed absent from the landscape. They were alone in a leaky barn, water dripping from their bodies. It was finally just them, and them alone.

"Why did you do it?" Lucy yelled, breaking their silence as she turned to look up at Wolfgang. He stared at her with absolute stillness. Her voice didn't seem that loud, competing with thunder.

"Do what?"

"You turned the knob! You...you saw it. And you changed what was supposed to happen..." Lucy rambled, looking down at the ground as she pushed wet hair back away from her face. She didn't understand it, didn't really want to. Understanding it was opening a door and losing all control. That's how she viewed it.

"No, he didn't check the grill. He should have if he was going to light up a cigar," Wolfgang replied, his voice so even that it sent chills down everyone's spines, though for the moment, they preferred to assume it was just the rainwater. They didn't realize he'd done it more than once, better at each go.

"You knew he had one!" she yelled.

"I didn't know until I saw it," he replied.

"You saw it *twice*!"

A hush fell over them when she said it, finally acknowledging. The storm howled outside the barn's walls, covering up anything else other than their argument. James looked at the two of them, barely recognizing his brother. He saw pieces of him everywhere, but all melded together it seemed too much to take on.

"Lucy," Wolfgang started, after a long break of silence between them. She took a step back away from him, holding up her hands so he would come no further.

"How could you do that? Why would you do that?" she asked, her voice breaking. She felt danger creeping up her back, hugging her shoulders. What was to stop a similar voice from whispering in her ear to turn the knob back, leave the water on, lock a door?

"He's not a good person..." Wolfgang said, stunned that was her worry in all this.

"It doesn't matter. You can't just..." Lucy looked around, exasperated. Rosemary and James stood quiet as she begged them with her eyes for help, for reason, for anything that would help explain that this was wrong and that perhaps all that had happened and felt *good*, wasn't. She was fighting for the place she wanted to live in, but it had only ever served her.

"We can't ever look for it again," Lucy said stronger.

"Lu."

"And... And we might have to close it."

No one was ready for Wolfgang's reaction. The storm cracked a thick string of lightning just as Wolfgang's eyes bulged, jumping out at Lucy. She screamed, falling backward. He stood over her as she crawled back away from him, Rosemary jumping at him to push him away from her sister. She yelled too, begged him to stop. He was shouting threatening things, telling them there was no way they were going to look for a way to close the rift. He more than demanded it as he stood over Lucy huddled on the floor, shielding her face from him, crying. Rosemary pushed him again, and he turned to her.

"You showed us! Why would you just to take it away?"

She didn't know. The messages had gotten muddled in translation, all she had meant to do was look for greater possibility, find some kind of meaning. But this hadn't been the ideal she was searching for; this wasn't what was meant to happen. Thunder cracked again, she backed up, but Wolfgang followed her.

"Don't you dare even try, because I will..." he yelled, eyes wild in his face, energy so dark and looming it was strangling everything alive in that barn, amidst a curtain of dark grey pounding rain. James finally moved, trying to go against injustice.

"Stop it! You're acting just like him."

Wolfgang rolled his head over to his brother. There was an unsteadiness there: anger. Perhaps a hatred, but he had worked so hard for it to not be. No matter what he knew or thought he did, the pain of not being the chosen one would always hurt. It had shackled him for his entire life. The relationship was twisted and broken, all toxic, but it didn't matter. To survive, he had needed it. And James would always have it. Lightning lit up both of their scared faces, mirroring one another.

"Don't act surprised," Wolfgang said, spitting on the floor as he said it. James's eyes widened at the statement, excepting something else from his brother. They all looked at him, taken aback by the creature before them. Wolfgang looked back at all of them, standing before the rain in the doorway, lit up by great streaks of lightning. He was the storm, the possibility of both life and death. He was the monster they expected to see, so he became just that. Lucy couldn't stop her tears, looking up at the cruelty she'd always heard about but never met so intimately. Rosemary felt trapped in her own actions, unsure of how something that had seemed so good and pure had brought them to that moment. And James, he had to go to another place.

Wolfgang turned, walking out into the storm, his back fading into the grey thickness. Strong gusts of wind continued to throw the rain through the open barn door into the room, coating everyone in water but it didn't matter. They couldn't move. Thunder boomed, lightning crackled, and they sat alone together in the barn, watching it storm, unable to do anything about it.

"We have to close it, we have to close it," Lucy sobbed, hugging her knees, feeling blood drip from a slice on her arm when she'd fallen. Rosemary crouched next to her, whispering that it would be okay, somehow. James sat down where he had stood the entire time, eyes uncomfortably focused on the downpour outside, watching as little shadowy beings weaved in between raindrops, howling.

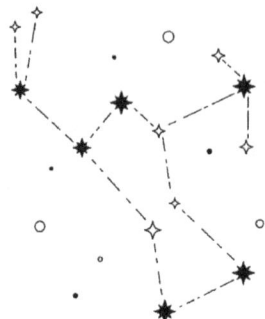

Twenty-One.

There was a lot of damage left in the midst of the storm. Trees had fallen, shingles had been ripped off the house, and pieces of the porch had been torn apart and destroyed. When Rosemary woke up the next morning, she found herself alone in her room after a very quiet and restful sleep. There were no dreams to be had; she'd already lived them. When she glanced over to the other twin bed, she wondered where her sister was.

Carefully she climbed out of bed and walked into the hallway, the bathroom empty. She peeked into her cousins' room; James curled up and asleep, his brother's bed empty like it had been all night. She grabbed a pair of tennis shoes and walked down the staircase and went outside to stand on the porch. From there, she saw Lucy struggling with some fallen branches at the far end of the property before the grass got tall and the woods opened up. She watched her work for a few minutes, throwing her whole weight into moving each branch before she made the trek over to her. It was a soggy walk, grass flattened everywhere by the amount of water still holding at the surface.

"Hey," Rosemary said, standing away from her sister's immediate space. It took her a moment before Lucy looked back at her, still working on yanking the branches out and dragging them to the side of the barn to be cut up and turned to firewood.

"Hey," Lucy replied, breathing heavy. She didn't stop her work.

"When'd you start doing all this?" Rosemary asked, surveying the amount of wood already moved. It was strange, to see Lucy working so hard when her entire aura all summer had always been relaxation. The rest of the year, her sister didn't even so much as visit a gym, instead doing morning salutations with the sun on her apartment's deck.

"When it stopped raining," Lucy huffed, heaving another branch onto her pile before walking back over to the fallen ones still lying around the few sparse trees in the field surrounding the lawn and house. Rosemary followed her, leaving ample space between them.

"When was that?"

"When the sun rose."

She stopped following her sister, still continuing to watch her work, dragging another set of branches to the pile by the barn. She was muddy, dirt stretching up her legs and arms. Her hair was tied back in a messy bun, sweat pouring down the back of her neck and brow as she moved. It was incredibly humid. There was no stopping her.

"Do you want help?" Rosemary finally asked. Lucy didn't reply, her only response a huff, holding her arms out at the mess around them before continuing to drag in the fallen branches. Rosemary double-knotted her tennis shoes, pulled up her own short hair off her neck, and got to work clearing up the yard. It was silent between them as they worked, moving branches around for a couple of hours. The humidity worsened as the sun rose, but after they were each coated in a certain amount of sweat that didn't really matter anymore. They hardly felt it unless the sweat dripped into their mouths as they breathed, a salty aftertaste on their lips. There was no thought about water, though. Stopping wasn't an option; all that mattered was clearing those branches, bringing in every last one. And they did, together. It took hours. Rosemary thought for a moment that once the last branch was in Lucy was going to start cutting and stacking the wood, and Lucy did consider it, but her body betrayed her, begging her to stop.

"Are we done?" Rosemary asked.

"I don't know," Lucy replied, her voice cracking, standing still and looking at their work for a long time. Rosemary didn't mind standing there with her, looking at the pile of wood for as long as it needed to take.

"I want to jump in the lake, but I don't want to walk through the woods," Lucy admitted, her voice small in comparison to their vast stack of labor. Rosemary understood that, especially at the moment. And she knew she didn't want to go to the beach either, and see any of her friends. There needed to be solitude of some kind.

"I know a place. I'll drive," Rosemary offered, and without another word, they walked through the water-filled field over to the old beater car, keys in the visor, and started it up and took off. Rarely when they were together did Rosemary drive, but she did then, flying over the country roads that led out of the collection of farmland and into the more occupied town. However, she made a sharp right turn before the town's horizon and followed a dirt road around the lake to a much more secluded spot, one Lucy had never known existed. When they parked, Rosemary waved her down the hilly bank to a small sandy shoreline. It was exactly what they needed. The sisters jumped into the lake, cooling off in the fresh water, wiping mud and sweat away. Small pieces of dried blood flaked off Lucy's arm, leaving nothing but a soft pink mark. They took their time swimming small laps, floating on their backs then sinking to the bottom, holding their breath for as long as possible. Nothing felt magical that day.

"This is a good place," Lucy finally said, when they were resting in the sand after finally exhausting their bodies of all physicality and emotion. Rosemary nodded, looking out at the lake, trees all around them besides the small shoreline, the car too far up to see, resting on the side of the narrow dirt roadway.

"Yeah, I found it a few summers ago. It's quiet, and beautiful," her twin replied. Lucy looked at her, wondering what summer she was referring to. She thought she might know, but it was often hard to think about.

"A few years ago, when you didn't really talk that much?" Lucy asked. It was the only way she knew how to phrase the question. Rosemary didn't move at first, then nodded, giving in to her sister's inquiry. They weren't identical, had almost nothing in common, and spent very little time out of the year together. And still, somehow, their souls were always fighting to be one entity.

"It was, yeah. I just needed someplace quiet. I couldn't hear my own thoughts anymore," Rosemary replied, thinking about that period of time. It had been a dark six months, a long week of silence, her eyes unable to focus or unfocus. Heidi had called it a season, moods come and go all the time, she'd said. She'd made sure her niece got up, walked around, ate some food and took time to watch a television show, or read a little from a book. It couldn't all be sleep, unfortunately.

The summer had happened at the tail end of her six-month stint of depression, of utter loneliness and apathy, and perhaps a little bit of an iron deficiency. Rosemary remembered hearing Heidi tell everyone, *she's doing better, just give her a chance, some time to keep growing.* Her parents hadn't even realized they hadn't spoken to their daughter in six months, and not because signal was spotty in Sudan's deserts.

"I was worried about you, that year. You didn't even answer when I called," Lucy teased lightly, knowing that her sister was immediately thinking about her parents' lack of communication. Lucy was sometimes hard to reach too, when she was out in the world. But she always called back, every single time.

"Yeah, I appreciated that. We all slip sometimes, I guess. It's hard for me, I don't know why. That's just the way it seems to be," Rosemary commented, playing with the sand around her, letting it cover her toes and flow through her fingers. It was dirty, filled with small twigs and old fallen leaves.

"I understand that," Lucy replied. The silence lasted too long, sitting uncomfortably between them. Rosemary wondered if she did understand, but wouldn't have been upset if she didn't. There was something nice about people not understanding the void, never having visited it themselves. Then again, it only made the abyss of nothingness all the more lonely. Lucy let her mind drift, stopping herself from fighting it to fit in a neat little box. She thought about a time waking up in a much different bed than her own, makeup smeared so thick around her eyes she'd had to fight to open them.

"I had to get my stomach pumped last year," Lucy said, her voice breaking a mirror. She was hardly able to meet Rosemary's eyes. She felt her sister's energy surround her, but it was warm and calm, exactly the kind of embrace she needed to feel. The judgment, the pity, it was all too much sometimes. Everyone thought Lucy was an open book, but she only read some chapters aloud, always disappearing before the ending could occur.

"What happened?" Rosemary asked.

"Ah, you know. Just partied a little too hard. I passed out in the snow, too drunk and too high. Someone called an ambulance for me. The nurses were really nice about it," Lucy replied, scratching her legs absent-mindedly as she thought about gathering her clothes out of a plastic bag and walking herself back to her apartment with no shoes, sleeping for three days straight. There were times in her life that the world seemed too accessible, that there were no boundaries to push up against, so she threw herself around at every opportunity. She always wanted to be on top, feel everything and nothing all in the same twirl of time and space. What was there to protect?

"I'm thankful someone called for you," Rosemary said, looking over at her sister as she rested the side of her head on her raised knees. Lucy smiled at her, her eyes sparkling a little as she did. No matter how the world saw it, they were sisters.

"I wish you'd come visit me sometime. We could stay in my apartment the whole time if you wanted and eat pizza and watch terrible movies," Lucy said. Rosemary laughed, thinking about the proposition. She wanted to, sometimes, more often than not.

"I will make a conscious effort this year," Rosemary replied, sticking out her pinky finger to signify her promise. Lucy linked hers with her sister's and they shook. By the water, the humidity seemed less intense and the temperature had gone down significantly since the day before. There was no hope it would stay so cool, but without knowing it, each girl was thankful for the small amount of respite.

"It's strange how Silas knew it was going to storm..." Lucy started to say, dancing around the edges of what they were both truly thinking. Rosemary had wondered when they would talk about it, and she wanted to. Fear of something had made them both feel it was a moot conversation but now alone together on neutral land, they wanted to.

"He's really in tune with that kind of thing," Rosemary replied.

"I think it's more than that," Lucy replied with a shrug, looking over at her sister without imposing too much. Rosemary felt it though, she wanted the truth and she wanted it freely. Things wouldn't be the same if Rosemary couldn't give her that, and sitting there alone with her on the banks of the lake, she thought there was no reason she should keep it all to herself anymore. Not all of it, anyway.

"He knows about...the rift. I think he may have seen it too, at some point. I don't know much, I just know that he knows how to cross over, sometimes," Rosemary replied, choosing to look up from the sand around her toes. To her surprise, Lucy was already looking directly at her.

"I have questions, and I don't know why you always make me feel like I can't ask them," her sister said, voice hoarse as it was honest. Rosemary nodded, understanding what she meant. There wasn't much power Rosemary held within the world, and privacy of herself and her ideas seemed the only thing she could hold onto that nobody else could reach for and take away.

"I know. I'm sorry for doing that to you. But I'm honest right now, I will be about all of it," Rosemary said, shifting her entire body to face her sister, instead of the lake. Lucy took the opportunity readily, wanting to use it wisely.

"How'd you know about the rift? I know we all *felt* it. I have, for a long time now. It makes sense, in a way that also doesn't. And James might have heard some wild shit about it from his father, but you *knew* so much about it. How?"

"Same way Uncle Lewis thinks he knows exactly what it is and how to find it," Rosemary said.

"How?"

"Ramone," Rosemary replied. Lucy's eyes widened, then softly closed as they began to water, thinking of all the gifts he had given her, and how in light of everything it was appreciated that particular summer of such loss and gain.

"Do you see him in your dreams?" she asked, more for herself than to follow the path of understanding what had happened with Wolfgang the night before. She had never felt so powerless or exposed. The feeling haunted her.

"Sometimes, yes. He's the same in all of them, how he always has been. You know, kind," Rosemary replied, her own voice low as she thought about him, wishing for more than fanciful maybes, short little encounters inside of her imagination, if nothing else.

"That sounds nice," Lucy replied softly, wiping at her face before asking another question. The girls gave it some time, thinking about their grandfather, the loss barely comprehensible at the funeral. They'd lost their guide.

"So it's real? I mean, I know it's real. God, I know it's real. But what even is it, and how can we just...it seems dangerous, now," Lucy said, her hands somehow reaching their way up to clutch her chest, the beating sun still radiating light from within her, an entirely new source of energy. She knew it was different, but she liked it. Whatever Wolfgang felt, he liked it too. But there was also a sense of reserve, something she had never felt a day in her life, especially at the next party she went to on night four after her three-day slumber. Lucy knew it was important to listen, at least hear it out.

"It is what any rift is, I guess. A crack across the surface of something. I guess a crack within the universe, or reality, or whatever this all is. A conscious choice to dream, perhaps? I don't really know," Rosemary replied, feeling less sure of herself the more she had to talk about it out loud. Lucy was trying, though. She was remaining open to these far-fetched ideas.

"That seems insane,"

"Isn't everything we do?" Rosemary laughed. Lucy cracked a small smile, but it faded. She thought maybe that was true, and was no longer convinced it was good.

"It's like I don't remember that night at all and still, I can't forget it," Lucy said, struggling with the words and grappling with her own mind and how well it understood something so vast she felt no bigger than a speck, barely even a pinpoint of light on a clear night sky.

"I feel that way too. It was just, dreamlike. And nobody can remember their dreams perfectly," Rosemary replied, trying to be optimistic. Lucy looked at her strongly.

"You do. You always remember your dreams, every detail," Lucy replied.

"No, not everything. Maybe more than you, but not everything," Rosemary said. She didn't know how it worked either, if maybe she was pitied by great universal forces so much so that her mind gifted her with brilliant explorations of her own, ones that saved her body the trouble of formulating enough anxiety to paralyze a horse.

"Do you still remember that dream you had, when we first got here?"

"Yeah, I do," Rosemary replied.

"That one felt different," Lucy said, acknowledging that somewhere, somehow, she had felt the edges of her sister's dream and hadn't been able to lose sight of it since.

"It was the rift, I think. We were so close to it and we didn't even know, until we did," Rosemary said, not sure what she was saying or if it was making any sense. There wasn't a lot of logic to be had surrounding something so entirely supernatural and futuristic. There was no good way to describe an energy so deeply embedded in the woods that it affected their bodies, called out to their minds, and tapped into their subconscious so that their consciousness might one day join a collective.

"Do you think we're better for knowing?" Lucy asked, wanting to throw herself down on her back in the sand and stare up into the sun until she was blinded. She was beginning to feel her legs tingle, ready to do something else, her exhaustion never lasting long enough to really give her the chance to change. She knew her problems, but was caught in a forever moving body, unable to pause.

"That's an age-old question."

"But do you? Think we're better for knowing?"

Rosemary thought about it. In a way, she thought there was never a time she hadn't know about it, or at least hoped for it. The world that surrounded her had always felt too intense, too hard to manage or assimilate into. Wasn't there always hope, that the universe was far greater, far vaster than the systems humanity had constructed?

"I'm happy I know," Rosemary said. Lucy accepted it.

"What happened with Wolfgang last night...that wasn't okay. I don't know what to do about it, but there has to be something," Lucy said, finally bringing them to the place that she had been dwelling upon all along. She couldn't get his eyes out of her mind, backlit by the lightning; desperate to preserve whatever he thought she wanted to take away from him.

"I know. It's him though, he's just..." Rosemary started to say, but her sister cut her off before she could finish the thought.

"No, it's all of us. We could all fall into that. We probably all will," Lucy said with conviction. The way she looked at Rosemary forced her to come to terms with that fact, and it was something Rosemary had always known. It was hard, to change the feeling of such greatness into something more self-appointed. In a dream, Ramone had whispered that to her, hoping she could hear him.

"I know," Rose agreed.

"Whatever it is, we have to close it," Lucy said, strong with authority.

"Probably," Rosemary said, looking out across the water one more time as if she might see it again, and she could. Pieces of it were everywhere, scattered around, waiting to illuminate some new truth, alternate feeling.

"I think it's how Ramone died, trying to do that," Rosemary finally said, surprised when Lucy nodded readily, accepting her words so easily.

"I think I've come to realize that," Lucy said. It was true, she had. When nothing made sense, everything started to. And she'd had her own feelings, wandering around the house, walking through the woods, bearing witness to the corners of her sister's dreams, and watching the way the rest of her family interacted with one another. They all held gifts, things they wanted to understand. Only some of them could, she realized.

"Do you think everyone is the way they are...because of it?" Lucy whispered, not wanting to really accept that kind of understanding. It made the world large, the universe a possibility of more than just the plastic stars stuck to the ceiling of her childhood summer bedroom that lit up when the sun went down. Rosemary sat with the question, finally deciding what she'd say.

"Lucy, I think you are everything you've ever wanted to be. And you can always be more because that's what you want, not as some sign of fate."

It was what Lucy needed to hear, to know that no matter before or after, for now she was an accumulation of life with its own self-guided purpose. It made her smile.

"It has to be closed," Lucy said again, softer this time. Rosemary nodded.

"You're right, it does," she replied.

"We can't tell anyone we're going to close it. No one,

understand? This has to be you and me," Lucy urged, and Rosemary realized that truth. There was no one else to be impartial, no one else who could have seen and known lifetimes worth about the rift. It was constantly trying to open up farther and deeper, it always would. But for now, it needed to be closed, to be inaccessible to the people around them driven so deeply in their search for it. The rift would answer no questions, simply provide unasked for possibilities. It was a dangerous game.

"Okay. But I do know someone who could help, without us necessarily committing to anything," Rosemary said, finally starting to feel the heat of the sun again across her brow, on the bases of her shoulders. The trees around them glistened with golden light on bright green leaves, moving about in a gentle breeze that made all the birds sing happily just to be there.

"Silas?" Lucy asked, guessing immediately. Her twin nodded.

"There's some history there. You know, his grandfather died a long time ago and they were friends with our grandparents. I bet it's all connected, somehow," Rosemary said, giving up almost everything she knew for her sister to consume. Lucy contemplated, then nodded, accepting his involvement. He had known it was going to storm, after all.

"Okay."

The sun had grown too hot for their skin, so again they plunged their bodies into the cool lake water, the mud at the bottom not bothering their bare feet. They spent some time in silence, cooling off and basking in the sunlight, trying to appreciate the day for what it was and not what it could be. There was comfort in that silence, a lack of voices or boats, just the wind and the sounds of creatures humming with life. Eventually, they talked again, about small things that added up to little stitches in their own rifts, binding them closer without very much effort or acknowledgment. They needed it; it was what they had wanted for a very long time.

Finally, when the day had been long enough, they dried off in the sun, gathering up their clothes as they walked back to the car, long-abandoned at the top of the hill. It sat there, waiting for them patiently. Lucy took a few moments before getting in to finish wringing out her long hair, while Rosemary slid into the driver's seat. For a moment, she looked at herself in the visor mirror, an astonishing amount of freckles dancing across her nose. Her eyes seemed bright in her face, some pieces of her dark hair lightening after a long time out in sunlight. Were there some blonde streaks to be found in there? Before Lucy could climb in, she opened up the glove box to search for the keys; never worried they wouldn't be there after a day spent on the lake's shore. Right before her fingers touched the cold metal of keys, they slid over the feeling of fresh and upright wildflowers, a pairing of two, orange and purple, tucked away and waiting just for her.

Twenty-Two.

Silas had spent a lot of time in the woods; especially since almost all of his life that he remembered had been spent at his grandmother's house. There weren't many memories alive in his head before he moved in with her, mostly just the smell of clean soap and a flash of black hair falling around his own shoulders when he was given a hug. His mother had left before he had time to memorize her face.

His father had struggled for a long time, moving back in with his mother almost immediately after the breakup, his young son in tow. Things didn't get better with that support, and soon enough the time in-between visits with his father were so infrequent; he forgot to hope for them entirely. He still saw him sometimes, struggling for the most part. Silas understood the hardships he'd gone through, losing his own father young and growing up with a single grief-stricken parent. The body had never been found. Loneliness was en masse in the Reid household, until someone from the outside chose to break the cycle.

Ramone had started coming over again when he heard Marigold's grandchild was living with her. At first, it was just to bring over a few cooked dishes, perhaps even rooted in selfishness to get a glimpse of the house once again or a smell of the air. Things changed when Silas developed a fever that lasted for days, his fever dreams wild and grand, but eventually leaving his body and taking most of his hearing with it. Ramone came by every day during that stint of time, trying to be helpful in all the ways a wife generally relies on a husband. When Silas went in for his cochlear implant surgery, Ramone drove them to the fancy hospital in the city hours away. He paid for their hotel room. From there, the tasks began with a leaky pipe under the sink, then a place on the roof where the shingles needed to be mended. Eventually, he started helping Marigold with all the small jobs that she needed fixed around her house, not just in times of turmoil, but because he felt it was part of his debt to pay. The tension between them was palatable, but with Silas around, they kept it contained. It had been a long time ago, at the very least.

Silas grew up knowing Ramone very well. He would teach him how to fix things and how to use all the tools in his own grandfather's work shed. He was also the first person in his life to show him sign language, learning different signs and sentence structures together. Silas looked forward to his time with Ramone, because in addition to all of the skills and company he was giving the young boy, he was also a fantastic storyteller.

They never worked in silence. Whatever Ramone was fixing with his hands, he was also telling vivid stories about Nicholas Reid, keeping him very much alive with his words. Silas learned all about his grandfather growing up, how he loved to swim and be outside in the woods. He had been so happy when he'd saved up the money to buy the land he owned, building the house on the far end of the property in exactly his vision. Silas heard all the stories of him as a young man, and the trouble he'd get in when he was in his twenties, though Ramone always phrased it as fun. He talked about him all the way up until that night he went missing. Few things Ramone kept from Silas, especially at the end of his life, but the night his grandfather died was one of them. It was a secret that needed to remain because it was too entangled with his own life for him to allow it to break open. Ramone knew it was his burden to carry. He told Silas about that night in other ways, always being sure to mention how kindhearted Nicholas was, a loyal friend, and an optimist until the end. There were few other moments Ramone kept to himself, and not because he was afraid for Silas to know, but because there were some memories meant just for them as they were the only two people who occupied them.

As Silas grew older, he started to do more of the work, while Ramone sat back and watched, giving him pointers and allowing him to learn at times by trial and error. Their time together became less about the work that needed to get done and more about companionship. The things Ramone had to teach Silas were less about what his hands were capable of and more about what his mind and heart were capable of. Ramone was a good man, and he tried his best with everyone he met. Silas would always feel that way about him as he carried his voice inside his head, the vibrations echoing in his chest.

There had been a point, and it had been recently, that things with Ramone had changed. Some might have called it aging, but Silas knew it was greater than that. He knew it deep inside of his soul and Ramone recognized that in him, hoping he would always have the ability to hear it calling. If anything, Silas's deafness made him stronger, able to acknowledge the feeling in his chest before many others even noticed it enough to give it a name. In the last few months of Ramone's life, he talked candidly with Silas. He told him about the rift, something that Silas had already sensed while out in the woods. Ramone warned him about it, how humanity would always be on a search for more and there was indeed so much more, but it was too great a mass of energy to take on, or even pretend to be able to control. He showed him out in the woods about the balance of nature and how even the slightest disruption could have dire consequences. He didn't tell Silas about how closely death loomed, how easy it was to return to dust. That was for him to deal with, not the young man before him.

The last time he saw Silas, he talked to him about family. Silas knew a lot about Ramone's family, he talked of them often, his own children even creeping into some of the stories Ramone had told him about his own grandfather. And Silas had met them on occasion, when they came to visit. Silas had felt stirrings of jealousy towards them sometimes, in the peak of summer heat. He missed Ramone's constant company, instead looking onward at him enjoying his own abundant family. But this time, Ramone talked about what you do for family. He talked about the challenges of opposition, how sometimes giving up or staying silent was easier to fall into than fighting to make it work. He told him how you always showed up, no matter what was being asked, what the sacrifice, or the danger. It didn't matter how many times.

"Some people will need you to show up more than others. That says nothing about them, but everything about you if you don't," Ramone had said, really looking into his eyes, using his hands along with his words to relay the message. Silas took all of it in, nodding, giving the old man the respect he well deserved. At the time, he hadn't known what had prompted Ramone to give such a heavy speech, but when he heard of his death, he thought he might have an inkling.

From his words, Silas could sense how deeply his love for his family went. He could see how painstakingly he had become involved with each and every member trying to do right and good as much as he knew how. His impact was felt, even if it was not seen. There was talk of forgiveness, too. Silas knew he meant his wife. He wasn't sure what she had done, but the stories had all become overlapped, so he felt he might know if he reached out far enough. Silas also knew he meant his son. He could see that harshness sometimes in the fall, his own son wandering through the woods behind him. They didn't speak of it, but again Silas felt if he reached out far enough, he'd know. Forgiveness flowed evenly into Ramone's strong words about showing up because when someone didn't, everything falls apart and everyone is left standing with nothing. He stressed there was always something to gain, always something worth saving. He signed it all, as he spoke.

And when he left, he put his hand on the top of Silas's head, gave him a strong look, and told him he loved him just as much.

His grief had nearly strangled him when Sara came and told them the news. She stood outside, only talking to Silas. Marigold had stayed in the house, eyeing her from behind a curtain covering a window.

"I thought you should hear it from me," Sara had said to him, always having appreciated the boy Ramone had taken under his wing. His hard work around her own house as Ramone grew older hadn't gone unnoticed.

"Thank you. If you ever need anything, let me know," Silas had managed to choke out. For Ramone, she had reached out and given Silas a short, icy hug before walking back into the woods. She knew he was worth the price. When he came into the house, Marigold had asked what had happened. She cried with him, because even though it had taken so many years, she could forgive Ramone. Her grandson was a product of his love, and she would always be grateful for that support. Because he knew, that even when it was hard or easier to stay silent, showing up was always worth it, because there was always something to save.

As Silas was cleaning up debris from a storm that had happened days ago, he found himself thinking about Ramone. And when he looked up, he was hardly surprised to see his two granddaughters walking down the road, waving hello. He watched them walk down the drive for a minute, then raised his hand into the air and gave them a welcoming wave back.

"Hey! I hope we're not bothering you by just stopping by. Are you in the middle of anything?" Rosemary asked once they reached him. Silas looked down at the wood he was moving but shrugged anyway, looking back up at the two girls.

"Nothing that can't wait 'til later," he replied. The breeze blew by them, a knowing sign. Silas felt it across his skin, a small and cool whisper that autumn was coming, eventually, if not soon. The sun beating down on them overhead kept the sound to a mere whisper, but they all felt it, knowing.

"We were just on a walk and thought we'd come down and say hello. See if you were busy with anything. Is your grandma home?" Lucy asked, already peering over to the house. Frankly, the girls had never been to Silas's house, and had almost no idea of how to get there. All they had ever been told was that it was just over the hill. In truth, it was over several hills and winding roads, a variety of small houses clustered together in small wooded areas, a subset of the town that rested more predominantly by the lake, untouched by consumerism. This was the old town, their grandfather would have told them. The original place where people settled and started to grow, and from there had grown a town beside a lake that drew in people with money. But everyone else stayed up in the hills where the land remained mystic.

When Lucy asked if his grandmother was home, they all looked back at the house, the girls taking it in for the first time. It wasn't nearly as large as the house they'd walked from, but it was a pleasant two-story home with the same style wrap-around porch. It was colorful, the siding a different color than the yellow paint on the porch railings and green shingled roof. There were all sorts of things littered around the yard, amongst a chicken coop and shed in the back. It seemed to be a real working place. Silas's whole property and where it was situated felt very far away from the rest of the world. This was not to say it felt small, because truly it felt larger and more real than any place they'd been before. It felt like its own world, an entirely new way of life to explore and understand and take in. Rosemary felt ready for that exploration.

"Yeah, she's inside. Have you met her before?" Silas asked, curious. Lucy shrugged, but that hardly answered his question.

"I've heard a lot about her, the old stories, you know," Lucy replied, wishing his grandmother would come out on the porch, invite them in, talk with them about anything. Maybe she would, but it wouldn't be for Lucy's silent begging.

"There's a lot of them," Silas replied with a short laugh, wiping his hands with a small rag he had in his back pocket, one of the many bandanas he owned at one point of its life but now nothing more than a greasy ripped piece of fabric. Still, it served its duty.

There was silence between them for a moment; no one knew what to say. The girls didn't know how to ask him their questions, and Silas had yet to determine exactly why they'd come. Silence had never bothered him though, he felt comfortable standing in it for a while, reading their faces better than they could themselves. He decided to play along, to see what it was they were after. If not for his own curiosities, or his leniency for Rosemary, then he'd do it for Ramone. Autumn was now a thought in the air, after all.

"Do you want to join us for a late lunch? My grandma was making sandwiches and a tomato salad earlier. She'll like the company," Silas said, using sign for some of his words as he talked out of habit and love. Rosemary nodded, smiling at him. Lucy was grateful for a way in, the longer she stood in the backyard, the more she wanted to get inside the house and see everything. It felt like the vastness wouldn't stop once they were inside the walls of the house.

"Oh, that would be really nice," Rosemary said, as Lucy already took a few steps towards the house. She kept her hands on her hips, brows furrowed, feeling like she could hear something coming from somewhere, but couldn't place just what. Silas caught up to her, leading both of them up his porch steps and opening the door into his house. Immediately, they were hit with the smell of many different herbs all mixed together. Plants hung from the ceiling by the kitchen window, others rested in pots all around the counter and table space. The pantry was open, large glass jars containing things that seemed less for food and more perhaps for tea, medicine, or added spice. The house felt different than their own, in that it felt lived in, every corner and space used for something that had meaning and value, ultimately purposeful. They heard his grandmother coming down the stairs, one step at a time.

Marigold looked different than either sister had imagined in their minds. Mostly, she looked so much like Silas it was stunning, though her eyes were brighter and more piercing, and when she stared at them, they both had to look away. Her hair was just as dark as his, long and swooped back in a low ponytail. She walked with a small limp and even though they knew she was Sara's age, there was an air of age to her that Sara had not embraced, but rather rejected.

"Oh, hello. I didn't know we had guests," she said, looking over at her grandson. Her words were light, unabashed by the intruders. She seemed just as curious about them as they were about her, because immediately she knew who they were. Pennyfather girls, it was unmistakable. One looked like Ramone, and one looked like his daughter, someone Marigold had always regarded highly and had decided was ultimately worth sacrifice. What a parent will do for a child, it had taken her a lifetime to know. It was by that thought she opened up more, welcoming them in.

"This is Rosemary and Lucy, Ramone's granddaughters," Silas said, seeing the change in her demeanor and breathing a soft sigh of relief. People said her grief had gotten the best of her, that it had destroyed what was once there. Silas had grown up watching her, and he knew that wasn't true, there was more than that. Amongst the good things about her, it needed to never be forgotten there was insanity that also stirred in her mind when the feeling was close or too open. He had paid the price for it many times. He was worried what the girls' presence would set off and so far, was happy to see inherently nothing other than curiosity. He knew Marigold would always be yearning for it, the cost of getting a small taste and then nothing more.

"Of course! Come in, please sit. Are you girls hungry? I was just getting ready to set out some lunch," Marigold greeted, ushering them in with her hands to come and sit around the big wooden table in the middle of the room. Both girls sat down together on one side of the table on a long wooden bench. It was surprisingly comfortable.

"You know, your grandfather made this table," Marigold said, looking at the glistening oak planks, running her hand across the surface. Lucy and Rosemary looked at it, wondering why they didn't recognize it as his handiwork. There was something more elegant about it than any of the other furniture he had made, having decorated his own home with his creations. Marigold caught their surprise quickly.

"I guess it was a team effort. He didn't build it alone. My late husband helped him, it was their project," she continued, this time watching the girls' faces carefully. She could tell easily they did not know. It was all right, she hadn't known for a long time. Silas shuffled in the background, getting the food together and setting small things on the table as preparation. He nervously watched as they talked.

"Were they close?" Rosemary asked and Marigold laughed, nodding as she sipped at her mug, something dark brewed inside.

"Very," she replied. It was an uncomfortable answer, and Lucy dove straight into the reply, awkwardness never causing her to shy away. It was protection others tried that never warded her off.

"How so?" It was pointed.

"Very close. Always together, always doing everything as a joint effort," Marigold started off saying, but became increasingly aware of her grandson in the background. She wanted to lay out all the traps, catch the girls at every corner of the twisted story they obviously had no knowledge of but wanted to hold in their hands. That seemed very typical of Sara, her old friend. But Ramone…he felt untouchable, in a way. Even at fault, he was precious. And she knew how much he meant to Silas, how much he had done for the both of them in the wake of everything. The girls' eyes were hungry for Ramone's story, but she thought it better to give them one they weren't aware to ask for.

"Your grandmother never told you about the old days?" Marigold asked, a small up-click on the last few syllables of her words. A silence fell, and she kept back a smile. It shouldn't have made her happy, but it did, seeing the faults in her friend she'd found seemingly faultless, until she could pretend no more.

"She doesn't talk about the past, never really has," Rosemary replied, taking a sip of her water that Silas had just set in front of her, along with plates and silverware for everyone. The food was almost ready.

"That's a pity, we all used to be so close. But then I guess when Nicholas went missing..." Marigold said, Lucy interjecting just like her mother.

"Your husband?"

"Yes, my late husband. It was a night that really changed all of us," Marigold said, looking at both the girls, wanting to put her hands on each of theirs. They were magnetic, in a way, especially together. Two opposites yet two halves of the same whole. Next to each other, they became identical in the ways their eyes moved, their tongues licked their lips, their hair fell into their face and then tucked back quickly with the same ring finger.

"What happened?" Lucy asked, her tone low, the only indication of her ability to tread lightly and with some kind of moral compass. Marigold's vision went static, both in sight and in mind. It always did. Silas felt the shift.

"No one really knows," she replied. The temperature in the room felt almost like it dropped, summer evaporating from their space as if cast out viciously by a curse. Marigold felt it too, and knew it was her responsibility to manage. But she was grieving, eternally, and there wasn't always the want to rein it back. It was the power she had left, the pieces of the rift that had stuck to her body, holding onto that grief. It was immense, and it was infinite.

"Who's alive, anyway."

The skin on the back of Rosemary's neck prickled, and even though the room had not changed, she felt that the air had. There was a deeper meaning to Marigold's words, and Rosemary was able to look past the simple blame. That was superficial, the real action went deeper, and Rosemary felt herself wondering what it meant to be alive, anyway. Lucy remained still, her spine stiff. She wasn't deterred, or revenant.

"You don't remember the night he went missing?" Lucy asked. It was stunning, the way she was able to be so direct at an unannounced lunch visit and still somehow come off as both strong and sincere. Perhaps though, it was because it was all true.

Marigold thought about it. Everything was hazy at that point. It had never been easy to see, or sort through. A large catalog of dreams, often ending before she even had the chance to wake up. She saw her husband's face sometimes, distorted into a million fractals. Sometimes she heard someone crying. Often, she felt the air change when she reached out for hope, almost like she wasn't worthy. There had been no one to ask, no one to talk to. All she'd seen was Sara become stiff around her, no longer coming over with her children, her three healthy children. Marigold had been left alone only with a tenacious boy to raise on her own.

The food was set on the table, Silas sliding onto the bench beside his grandmother. The women didn't notice the movement, the intensity between them palatable.

"Not in any kind of real way. It's all just...a collage of sadness, really. My mind is old now. It's given up making sense of it. There wasn't much I could offer my son, so I've tried to do better this time around," Marigold said, speaking honestly from her heart as she glanced over quickly at Silas, his face focused on his untouched full plate of food.

"That must have been incredibly hard, I can't imagine. I'm sorry you felt so stranded," Rosemary offered, a few notes of sympathy. Marigold looked up at her, searching her eyes intently until it was too uncomfortable. Stranded was exactly what she'd been, but most everyone else had called it *being alone*.

"You remind me of Sara, a little," Marigold said. It was Rosemary's turn to feel seen in usually unnoticed ways. Most everyone called her Ramone's. She had his dark features, but his light undertones. She was inquisitive like him, deeply kind in the form of small acts of service, often indirectly seen. But Marigold's words echoed a small little expression she'd only heard every so often, and only from her grandmother, and one time a customer at a small shop downtown when she'd been grocery shopping alone with her grandmother. It was a word she'd heard loudly with an eternal echo, but her sister and cousins had only heard whispers. Some thought it was an insult flung, but the real power came when the realization hit that it wasn't a dirty word at all, simply a dark word to cover a pool of possibility. The word was used by people who didn't understand the feeling that passed when she walked by. None of them knew what it meant, not really, not when Sara said it. Yet it always came at uncomfortable times, a feeling that maybe there was something peculiar to be seen, to be commented on. Reined in, perhaps. It was well hidden, a piece of her that didn't see the light of day willingly, unless she used that kindness to let it unravel. It was power, mostly unnoticed.

"witch!"

"You remind me of almost all of them, really. The Pennyfathers," Marigold said simply, recanting just enough so that the air remained a comfortable temperature, one that invoked talking and didn't shutter it away. Everyone finally took a bite of their sandwich, a taste of the tomato salad. There were cheese and crackers, mixed fruit on a plate, and a bowl of olives to pick from.

"Heavy stuff, for your little visit. I'm sorry for that, I don't know where my head goes sometimes. How has your summer been?" Marigold asked, her face changing shape so quickly it was almost like a different person sat before them. Rosemary could sense the quick changes, glancing over at Silas and seeing only the faintest impression of glass cut skin. She wondered how he could be so good; work so hard for everyone and for always. He reached over for more crackers and cheese, Rosemary watching the way he assembled each one perfectly with his calloused hands as Lucy chatted easily about long lake days, drunken family dinners, and all the vegetables their own garden was producing even though she'd never tended to it a day in her life. There was a way she spoke where everything seemed to belong to her, and even though Rosemary knew it couldn't, she also felt it still somehow did.

"We've had a bit of a mite problem though, too many are

eating away at the leaves of our plants," Rosemary heard Lucy say, wondering how she even knew that. Marigold had hung on to every word, caring quite a bit about gardening. It had been one of the things to help her carry on, and feel like she could.

"Oh, there's a simple remedy for that. A little pepper in some water. Or get yourself some ladybugs. They always do the trick," Marigold replied eagerly, and Lucy in turn hung onto her words. There was something about the woman she found fascinating, if not possibly her own sense of slight superiority. Lucy imagined this was perhaps the way her mother felt, growing up with Heidi. Or perhaps how Sara felt, around almost everyone. There was a dark side to the feeling. But Lucy was lucky enough to have a twin, an extension of herself more or less that continually grounded her. So while Lucy talked with Marigold about the garden, being polite but also seeking out information that could be useful to her plight, she was always at least mildly aware of her sister beside her, speaking silently to Silas every so often with a shared smile, an extra serving of tomato salad, or a quickly flashed sign. Lucy regretted never learning any. There had been many opportunities.

Rosemary was thankful Lucy could be so cutthroat in her investigation, and also have the decency to mask it behind genuine interest. She knew her sister was kinder than that though, she wasn't anyone other than herself. Lucy's magnetic personality worked on everyone, and only because everyone was searching for that striking authenticity she seemed to possess so easily, almost candidly. She looked back at Silas, who she couldn't read his thoughts but knew he'd give them up if she asked nicely enough, or asked the right questions in the right order. For a long time, she had known he was guarding something. It all felt familiar, as if a familiar hand had orchestrated the entire thing and Silas had simply been put in charge of the key. He smiled at her with his dark eyes, and hers flashed right back with that same light. It reminded her of walking a sandy shore with him, pink skies and pink water all around them, lapping at their skin. A place where it was warm and calm, always.

"You know, there are lots of special tricks for all kinds of things…"

"Really? What ones do you know?"

Lucy was committed, that was for sure. She was determined to know what she needed for the world to become normal again for her. Rosemary's determination was fading; she could feel that as she sat next to her. No matter, she hadn't brought her sister along for encouragement, but rather to remind her of the reason. Rosemary rather liked the feeling, forgetting the dangers quickly when the feeling came over her, reminding her of that vivid and painful fever dream she'd had her very first night back home.

More? Silas signed, pointing towards the fruit bowl. Rosemary nodded, agreeing that a few more strawberries wouldn't be a bad thing. Vaguely, she heard Lucy and Marigold's conversation as she watched him cut up a few more strawberries by the sink, washing them free of bugs and dirt from outside. Some of the things Marigold said echoed her own grandmother's words. Looking around, the jars of herbs seemed similar to the ones Sara kept in her own pantry, neater if nothing else. Rosemary wondered where Marigold had learned about all of this, and what she'd been inspired by. Was it her loneliness, or was it someone preying upon it? A knot grew in her stomach, her attention suddenly forced over to the two other women, and away from Silas and the strawberries.

"You know, a lot of it is about a feeling. If you can hone into it, almost anything is possible," Marigold said, her voice hushed. Silas struggled to follow along with her words, but by watching both Lucy and Rosemary's faces, he could tell where the conversation had drifted. He watched carefully, hoping to know their responses.

"I think I know what you mean," Lucy breathed, feeling like finally she'd seen the first sight of gold, her façade momentarily dismantled. Marigold nodded, continuing.

"I bet you have, both of you. I can see it on your bodies; I could the moment you stopped by my yard. But you don't know much about it, do you?" Marigold asked, her eyes pointed at both of them. There were a few skills one gained from loneliness after decades, and it was simply knowing when someone was there for you, and when someone wanted something from you. Marigold had seen Lucy's play all along, however, she wasn't sure what side of the line either of them stood. Just then, she didn't happen to care much. She found it exhilarating to play the role a long ago friend had filled.

"Is it that obvious?" Rosemary asked, her first words in a long while.

"No, it's not obvious at all in a place like this," Marigold replied.

"I'm always looking. Aren't you?" she continued, looking pointedly at Rosemary. She assumed maybe she was, even when she was stationary. She was always looking up at the sky, not moving, letting the world rotate around her. Lucy watched her sister think about that, wondering why she hadn't been looking.

"I hadn't realized," Rosemary said, nearly a whisper.

"We don't really, until we stumble upon it. Then we know, and it's hard to let go," Marigold replied, resonating with the sadness she felt from Rosemary, something that was embedded in her body and would be until the end. That was okay. Marigold turned her attention back to Lucy, the one foraging for the answers.

Marigold felt a shift inside of her, and then a small nudge from her grandson. Her eyes changed, as she thought about asking them for details about what they knew, because she could see it on their faces that they were different. They'd seen the chasm, even touched it perhaps, and had gone on to remember the feeling. Marigold cried for her lack of memory, her inability to know what had truly happened that day. She had been abandoned, deemed unworthy by all involved. The rejection had nearly killed her, but instead left her thirsty for the smallest taste of retribution. But Silas nudged her, waking her up from the dark pieces of a nightmare. Sometimes he couldn't get her to leave it, other times it was an invitation she accepted. That afternoon, she accepted it.

"You asked me about that day, you're curious about my husband's disappearance," Marigold started, only scraping the surface of the Pennyfather girls' curiosity. She couldn't give them everything, but maybe she could give them something.

"Everything is connected, all of the time. The most minute details can have the biggest consequences, because everything grows into something. Everything," Marigold said, looking around at the three young adults she had for an audience. Was this her purpose all along, to call out a warning? She wondered if anyone would heed, if she would have in similar circumstances. Marigold chanced it.

"You know, there's a mirror image of everything, like a tree's roots beneath it. A copy completely, but an entirely different existence, wouldn't you say? Both real, both true. Both necessary. To keep the tree alive, there can't be any holes in the dirt to expose the roots for any long period of time, or the roots will die and then so will the tree. If there's an upheaval, you fill it in so that both can continue living, and nothing changes. Because even if the change is great, eventually the disorder turns rotten, and things can die."

Their visit continued for hours longer. It eased into lighter topics of conversation, eventually moving out onto the porch with lemonade in their hands. Silas had work he wanted to do, but had already given up the idea of finishing before the sun began to set. Besides the pressing issue, both girls were beginning to realize there was more to learn from Marigold than what they had originally set out for. Rosemary saw pieces of her in Silas, as she told a story about the chickens battling together to ward off a snake. It was comical and silly, the way she told it, rallying behind the hens as if they were more than just a possibility for dinner. Lucy enjoyed the story for different reasons, but it comforted her all the same, to know that mistakes didn't mean the end of anything, rather the continuation of something.

Silas walked them to the end of the road, just up the hill when Marigold had finally excused herself, saying she was tired and needed to spend some time lying down. She had thanked the girls for their impromptu visit, wishing them both the best and giving out an open invitation. They'd accepted it graciously.

"It was nice of you to spend so much of your day talking with her, she gets lonely sometimes," Silas said, when they all stopped walking for a moment. The spot they stood on felt so high up, vast rolling hills around them spotted with trees that grew in density the farther out they reached. Along the horizon, small pockets of deer could be spotted grazing in the evening light.

"She knows a lot, it was nice to hear her talk," Lucy said, giving Silas a short hug before kicking some rocks up the road with her feet, drifting away from her sister and him for a short while. Evening sun felt warm on their skin, kind.

There was a silence between them, neither knowing exactly where to start or what to release into the open air. One day, the uncertainty would have to fade away. For now, they were more used to the silent passing of meaning between one another, or meeting in a dream.

"Are you going to keep the tree alive?" Silas finally asked, his eyes keen on hers.

"Is it in trouble of dying?" Rosemary replied, looking up at him. He moved his eyes to look out at the land surrounding them, the immensity of the trees he called the woods, a place that always felt like home.

"Your grandfather thought so," Silas said, looking back at Rosemary. Her eyes widened out of surprise. He hadn't known how to tell her, when to bring it up.

"He did?"

"Ramone was a really great man, but you already know that. And he worked really hard to keep everyone safe, but you know that already too. He spent a lot of time with me while I was growing up, especially at the end. Like my grandma said... I think he was trying to keep the upheaval leveled, but it always takes so much," Silas said, his voice coarse and sad as he spoke. Neither knew the sacrifice the missing man-made, but they had always been able to feel it in the air, regardless of recognition.

"I thought as much," Rosemary replied quietly. She tucked a piece of her short hair behind her ear, feeling so small all of a sudden. It wasn't a new feeling.

"Whatever you want to do will be the right thing," Silas said with such certainty, she wanted to believe it.

"I don't think that's how it works," Rosemary replied, laughing slightly, shaking her head.

"He'll tell you what to do," Silas said. She thought about it. There had been a lot of messages to understand, imagery to process and put into practice. Silas had so much hope for her, and for Lucy, but there was another feeling growing deep inside of Rosemary that they didn't share. She tried to ignore it, hoped that she could do what Lucy wanted, close the rift, and then the feeling would have to relinquish itself. There was a whisper though, her own voice, telling her something no one else knew. A possibility, perhaps. She wondered if it would be true.

"We all do what we can," Rosemary replied. She gave Silas a hug before walking up the hill further to meet her sister. They almost left, but Rosemary turned back around, seeing Silas still looking up at her. She hoped her possibility wasn't a certainty.

She waved, saying goodbye.

Twenty-Three.

The chill in the air didn't cease, instead sticking around both mornings and evenings, bringing back a bitter bite after each long hot day. It was the first sign of change, sweeping through the Pennyfather house like a breath of air after a long time underwater. Things changed within the family, how they related to one another, their level of ease throughout the natural rhythm of the day, and of course, their conversations.

All it took was one day.

"Pass the salt, would you honey?" Delphine asked, looking up from her newspaper at her husband across the table. She needed a little salt with her eggs, even if it wasn't good for her. He slid the small container past everyone else over to his wife, who nodded her thanks as she sprinkled it over her two eggs with a heavy hand.

"Morning Lucy," Delphine greeted as her daughter came down the steps, her hair a mess from sleep. She wore socks and a sweater over her usual shorts and tank top. The mornings were now a little cold, just enough with the dew to warrant a warmer layer before the sun found its place up high in the sky.

"Morning mom," she mumbled heading straight for the coffee. She was the last to wake up, besides Wolfgang. He'd been nothing other than scarce over the last few days, showing up to sleep and eat every so often simply to avoid being labeled as missing, and because it turned out he'd discovered his body was human after all. He didn't look at anyone, and they found themselves purposefully avoiding his eyes as well. At first, Lucy had wanted to talk to him, get angry and insistent with him a second time but she decided it didn't matter. She had already made up her mind about what she was going to do.

Lucy got herself some toast after her coffee was poured and slid into a seat next to James, ripping the bread apart more than eating it. Henry looked up from his phone, smiled at his daughter, then turned his attention to his wife.

"Del, did you make sure to use the vouchers when you booked the plane tickets?"

"Yes, I remembered them. And the company will reimburse us when we land for our layover flight," Delphine replied, thinking back over all the details and making sure there wasn't anything she'd forgotten. Travel required a certain amount of finesse. Rosemary swallowed hard; Lucy heard it from across the table.

"Work?" Lucy asked.

"Yes, it's almost that time to get going on another assignment," Delphine replied with a warm smile, setting her reading down and getting up to refill her mug. She said it absently, like it was normal and mundane. And it was, it always had been. Rosemary couldn't believe she was about to be the only one of her family left on that particular continent and no one seemed to notice. Why would they though? It didn't matter. They were all adults now; there was nothing more to do.

"How long will you be gone?" Lucy asked.

"Mmm, tough to say. So far this is a four-month stint, but it could stretch out longer if we find something worthwhile to follow up on. And we hope we do," Henry replied, his voice even and candid while his excitement for the trip grew. He loved the travel, loved carrying around his camera equipment and capturing all the moments his wife so eloquently wrote about in her pieces.

"Quite the life," Lewis interrupted, his breakfast plate almost empty from the corner where he sat, having been awake since before the sun rose. James didn't look at him as he talked.

"Well, you do something similar, months of tracking in the woods," Henry replied, and the two were off chatting about the differences in their passions, and how travel was always a necessity to understanding. Rosemary turned her hand into a gun and held it up to her forehead so James could see, and he smiled a little as she pretended to play dead. When she looked up, post-resurrection, her mother was shaking her head.

"You know Rose, maybe you wouldn't have such a narrow view if you tried to venture out. Go to college, make some new friends, travel with your sister on just short trips here or there. You might really like spending your time that way," Delphine offered, trying to be kind and helpful but instead coming off the way her mother most often did, condescending and out of touch. It didn't bother Rosemary the way it once used to.

"Yeah, maybe I should," she replied, thinking about her life in Heidi's guest house, still among the trees, still among a small town that could be biked around in its entirety. All that vastness never seemed to register to her as a small outlook.

"I'm being serious," Delphine said, exasperated. Rosemary nodded, taking a bite of her own toast and jam.

"I know you are," she replied.

"So why aren't you taking the suggestion seriously?"

"Probably the same reason you don't take me seriously."

The table stopped with its side chatter, looking at the two women as they stared at one another. Delphine had never been challenged so directly by the younger of the twins. She didn't know the next word to use, had never considered an alternative viewpoint outside of idleness. Lucy interrupted, saying something inconsequential and only partly funny to ease the tension away, and slowly everyone started talking again except Delphine and Rosemary, who suddenly felt a strong need to finish their breakfast. Heidi eyed both of them from her perch at the other end of the kitchen, Seth beside her looking up as she watched them. She seemed younger than almost anyone there, her features still girl-like, her stature the opposite of imposing. He rubbed her leg to comfort her, and get her attention.

"You're worried?" he asked, already seeing the signs of her tension in her face, her tight shoulders, and the overall protective stance she took whenever the conflict seemed real.

"I just wish they understood each other," she murmured, looking at her sister and wondering where she was sometimes. Though it hardly seemed the right question, because Heidi knew that Delphine was the same as she always had been, and if not for Rosemary, it would be her being questioned about life choices when any conversation needed a scapegoat. Heidi found it amusing how she'd never been asked when she was housing her daughters in their childhood, however. Then, of course, everything was fine.

"Mothers and daughters fight," Seth replied, trying to be reassuring. And he was, to a point. Heidi nodded, still watching, still sipping her coffee.

"Yeah, everyone does," she replied. There was a tension between everyone she could not name, but absolutely felt echoing through her entire body. It was almost reaching for her soul. It was different than the usual end of summer tension, where leaving started to sound so sweet. This time, it was growing differently.

"We're going out one last time before summer's done. I want to be ready before fall hits with all our bases covered. And last time we found some really exciting areas, didn't we?" Lewis said, looking over at James who was finally forced to look up. He nodded, though could hardly remember what excellent land they had discovered together. But he was mistaken, it hadn't been together. In reality, Lewis didn't know much, but he had sensed the change in his son when he finally stumbled back upon him. He didn't care about the burns or his scraped up face, he was blinded by the glow from his own, a rolling deep ember, a sign that he had seen it. The other side, the extension, the rift. He had felt the feeling, and Lewis had rejoiced. There was no way to ask about it, he knew. Their walk home had been silent, Lewis carefully plotting out how and when he could convince his son to show him the promised land. James knew he would always need more; there were no allowances for a breaking point.

"So you're going out again? When do you have that planned?" Henry continued; interested in the way Lewis hunted. He had a plethora of trophies to show for his sportsmanship, his tracking skills always impressive when out on day hikes with Henry, his favorite brother-in-law. Of course, he kept his darker nature hidden, somehow it seemed easy. Only James had ever seen it, alive in the woods at night, his own shadow ten times the size of his body.

"Tonight," Lewis replied.

"Tonight?" James choked. He looked at his son as if they had already spoken.

"Yes, tonight. Did you forget?" It didn't sound like a threat to anyone else in the room, but James knew it was. He'd heard the tone before, in a much different setting. He shook his head, falling silent. It was always taken as agreement.

"The first turn of the season is in the air, it's good to get out there and feel that difference as soon as it hits," Lewis said, continuing his conversation with Henry. They talked a little longer, Lucy watching them chat more than she watched her cousin push his food around nervously, almost a pro in the same way she was. Her mind was preoccupied with taking a little more of her uncle's stash, her thoughts never getting close enough to realize what it was like for James while his father swallowed the same ones. She thought she might take one, during the day, a peaceful entrance that might give her some clarity, some idea of how to move next. Mostly, she wanted to relax. Her days on high alert had been far too many, and her body begged for rest in a way it probably wouldn't if she would eat her toast. Looking around the kitchen, she wondered where Wolfgang was hiding.

"Mom, good morning. How are you feeling today?" Heidi asked as Sara entered the kitchen, already showered and dressed for the day. She'd been slowing down the last few months, quieter than usual, part of less controversy than usual. No one was certain what it really was, be it old age, hosting an entire household for a season, or the mourning of her dead husband. Everyone tried to help her when they could, little favors here and there so she still felt independent and in charge. Mostly, she did. Sara always would. Her mind would never go; it would always be her sharpest tool and her way into any situation or intention she had. She nodded back at her youngest daughter, wondering vaguely what life without her would have looked like. Heidi had brought about a lot of happiness to them all, even if she was the weak one.

"Good, I slept well," Sara replied, making herself a cup of tea. She sat with her family for the rest of breakfast, making her way to the porch for a little bit of reading in the rising sun, her daughter joining her and keeping her company. Delphine and Henry went off to continue their talk about logistics for their upcoming journalistic deployment, while Lewis sharply told his son to finish packing, suggesting that he had even started. Beth jumped up from her silent place at the counter to start washing the dishes everyone had set by the sink, never bothering to question the routine or take notice of it. No one thought to ask Beth what she would do with her time if she weren't washing dishes.

While everyone dispersed, James slowly trudged up the stairs to his room to pack a bag he had dared hope he was done with. Wolfgang was nowhere in sight when James began packing for that night's trip. He wasn't sure if he was wishing for his brother's presence, or cursing his absence. There seemed no way of escape, either way. As James began rolling his clothes and tucking the fabric deep inside his pack, a mounting feeling was growing in his chest. It had started out small, a little whisper at first, then a more harmonious drum line of sound, pushing his anger forward above all other feelings. *You've been timid too long*, the voices said, *look where that's gotten you.* James thought about it, his arm aching even though it looked nearly healed. The skin was still a soft pink, tender to the touch as a reminder of how deeply the wounds went, but to everyone else it looked cured. *How long are you going to do this?* they asked. James shook his head, continuing to pack. It wasn't as if he'd never gone down that line of thinking before, but it had never made much of a difference. Any protest he'd had was always easily and mercilessly struck down. The price to pay for a small moment of clarity was too steep.

He heard his cousins talking from outside on the lawn, their voices drifting up to his open bedroom window. He couldn't quite catch the phrases, but he imagined their voices to be carefree and easy. Lucy, always bubbling with enough confidence to conquer any mountain, and Rosemary, simply falling off the map every year to live freely in the woods with their aunt, locking herself out of society with mastered ease. The feeling in James's chest grew, perhaps making room for newfound jealousy. It was like a disease spreading through his body with each pump of his heart. His own fever dreams taking focus, although it was poisoned from the beginning. He'd never had a chance.

Where was Wolfgang? He'd been elusive since the fight in the pole barn. James didn't blame him for steering clear of everyone but still, he'd held out hope that something between them had really changed. His brother's kindness that summer had given him hope to continue, that maybe there was someone who would understand and listen to all the stories and have empathy to give not just pity and disgust. But when he'd seen his brother's eyes flash just as bright as the lightning from the storm, his hope had been dashed and once again he'd been reminded that there was no way out. This was forever. *You can do it, you can be your own change*, the voice hissed, now seemingly coming from under the bed rather than from his own head. James didn't move, didn't dare to be anything other than still in the room trying to eliminate the ideas forming, trying to battle the anger and keep it at bay. He didn't think it would work, didn't want that to be the only way to leave the horrible situation where he found himself. His breathing quickened as a cold sweat broke out across his face. His view of his packed bag went blurry as the room swirled around him. He reached out for one of the bedposts to help steady himself against his thoughts.

The season is just beginning; you know that, don't you?

He knows you've seen it. He knows you've been there.

You think it's been bad, having to help look for it all this time?

What happens when he decides to look inside you?

James gripped the sides of his face, trying to hold it all together. He'd known for a long time that he would start to go mad from it all. He'd heard about it growing up, researched it even when the curiosity of his own demise was too tempting to not know. Somehow, he'd made peace with it, when he'd decided it was okay to let go, just be used, work this hard for this little reward. But now, facing the actual moment, he didn't want to lose himself. He didn't want to go back in the woods only to be stuck there forever, all fall, all year, all of his life.

They make you take all of it, the voice kept whispering, and with it, James's anger mounted. He wanted to lash out, but was tired of begging people for help who didn't listen, and didn't care to notice. It had to be him, he had to save himself. He wasn't sure if it was going to be worth it because he hated himself; god, had he been made to hate himself. But with that little voice coming from under the bed, out of the darkness of the closet, whispering from behind the pushed back curtains, he thought maybe there could be a time when he didn't. Maybe there was a chance he could be whoever he wanted to be, whoever that was. A long time ago he'd lacked the energy, the ability to crawl out of the dark hole he'd been thrown into, but a new rage was awake inside of him. If Wolfgang had been there, maybe he could have seen the extra glint in his brother's eyes, given him a real voice to follow. Because Wolfgang had meant his promise to his brother, but it was hard to save someone from drowning when already under as well.

Where was he?

The girls had wandered out to the yard, a tension in the air that kept them from making plans, instead causing them to gravitate around the house and stay prepared for something, though they didn't know what it was. The chill in the air had vanished, a nice warm sun above in a cloudless sky. It was the driest part of the year, right before fall hit. All the grass was stiff and yellow, having bathed in that warm light and dry air all summer long. Rosemary dragged a lawn chair out to where her sister's chair was, sitting down to keep her company. Lucy wasn't laying down though, she was sitting up, holding her face in her hands and looking at the fields around the house, her eyes trying to peek into the woods that boarded them on all sides.

"Is this because we're leaving soon? I can't decide how I feel," Lucy mumbled. Rosemary didn't feel the same tension as her sister. If anything, she wanted to simply let the summer play out and end the way it always did, with everyone scattering in a very unceremonious way. They were lucky to hear a goodbye.

"I'm not sure. Have you seen Wolfgang?" Rosemary asked, lying back on her chair to try and create an air of normalcy. Lucy wouldn't relax. She just shook her head.

"What do you think he's out there doing?"

"Whatever he wants, I guess," Rosemary murmured.

"We're going to close it. No one is leaving before we do," Lucy reminded her sister, tapping her leg with her hand to make her eyes open and stare into her own, conveying her absolute resolve. Her sister didn't fight her.

"I know," Rosemary replied, laying back once again and closing her eyes. She wondered what big mound of dirt Lucy was going to find to cover the exposed hole. It was the only thing halting Lucy, holding her back from doing the one thing she was so committed to. Lucy huffed, sitting cross-legged on her lawn chair, continuing to look around at the woods and think about the rift. A small piece of her begged to see it again, but she didn't want to admit she didn't know the first thing about tracking down that glorious chasm, the slash in their reality that seemed to move and simultaneously be completely unmovable. It felt like a dream, one big fantasy taking up space only in her mind. If her body hadn't continued to be so visibly shaken from the experience, she would have chalked it up to no more than a dream, or a drug-induced delirium. But the way her human heart beat in her chest, both pumping blood throughout her body and also spreading that shining star's light, she knew it had been real. As she looked out, watching everyone come and go around the house, she knew it was affecting them too. She didn't want it to anymore, because the longer she lived with it, the more it seemed poisonous, insidious. There was some dark hidden nature to that pulsating energy – perhaps a black hole, and as Lucy looked up to the window of her cousins' bedroom, she knew there were consequences. She just didn't know how many there would be.

With the sun beating on her skin, Rosemary found herself drifting in the chair next to her sister. At first, she'd tried to stay in tune with her twin's own nervous energy, but after closing her eyes and laying back, her mind began to wander out farther, abandoning the limits of her body. It was like flying, in a way. Moving through walls, hearing and seeing things that her body could never allow. Carefully, she eased into that feeling and it took her to faraway places, even though they were all right there.

She felt water on her fingers, her eyes straining to see against all that harsh sunlight. It didn't feel warm anymore, everything was cold. The waves kept lapping at her body, sitting on the shoreline, foaming water passing by in even strokes. It was cold, but her body didn't shiver. Something was in the water, she knew not to go out any farther. Dark shadows swirled around, she could see them so easily yet had no idea at all what they were. The water kept lapping at her body as she sat. Far out in the distance, there was the figure of a person walking along the shoreline. It was too far out to see a face, and the image felt oddly like a mirage. Rosemary strained her eyes, holding her hands around them to see better. The person was pacing, trying to decide something.

A shadow passed over her body, and when she spun her head back there was someone standing behind her, but it was friendly. *Silas*, she breathed, having a hard time making any sound at all. She didn't know why that was. He just waved at her, signing hello and sitting next to her on the shoreline, the water never quite reaching up high enough to touch his body. Together, they looked out at the person pacing, back and forth continually, trying to decide what to do. Rosemary wished she knew their problem; she'd try and help solve it. But something about the dark figure made her understand that this was not a question that warranted advice. It was deeply personal. Silas turned to Rosemary and smiled at her, but it didn't touch his eyes. It was sad.

What's wrong? She signed, unable to speak. At first, he said *nothing*, then held his hands up to his ears and moved them to his heart. He did it a few times, Rosemary watching intently. His cochlear implants were missing, but it didn't seem to matter.

I don't know what that means, Rosemary signed, looking into his eyes. He stopped moving his hands, instead hoping to communicate by holding hers and staring back into her eyes. She was searching for some kind of meaning, but there didn't seem any to find. Instead, she just found herself thinking about him, feeling the callouses on his hands, and wondering what it had been like for him spending all that time with Ramone.

Suddenly, a scream erupted from out in the water, the dark shadows swimming quickly towards it. Silas didn't react, but Rosemary stood up and watched fitfully for some kind of glimpse at what was happening. The shrill cries continued, and after a few moments Rosemary realized they were not cries of fear, they were sounds of mourning. Out in the distance, she could see waves and splashes against the painted sky, but couldn't tell what was happening. The dark figure on the other side of the lake suddenly wasn't alone anymore, and when she looked next to her, Silas was gone. The coldness grew, and Rosemary huddled into herself, crying silently as the screams continued and the shattering of the water's surface far out didn't end. There was a feeling of absolute solitude, like nothing Rosemary had felt before. She'd thought over the course of her life she knew what it felt like to be alone. But she hadn't. Standing there on that beach, her own arms wrapped around her body, the sound of grief radiating throughout the air she thought she occupied, but was merely a guest, was torturous. Her heart was dead in her chest, her own body failing to make her feel like there was anything alive out there on that shoreline. The water kept grabbing at her feet.

Looking around, she silently begged for someone to come out. It felt like Ramone should, she wanted to see him again, wanted him to guide her out of that awful place. But he didn't, instead, the sound of crying changed to bargaining, and very faintly, like small wisps of breezy air, Rosemary thought she heard, *you didn't listen.*

The feeling of solitude grew. She began to wonder if she was always going to be alone, if there had ever been a time that she hadn't been alone. She stepped up closer to the water, looking into its reflective surface. Her face didn't look back at her; instead, it was someone with lighter features, long blonde hair, bright blue eyes. Was that person inside of her? Who was she? She wanted to scream out, too.

Listen to what?

A cat howled.

"Rose!" Lucy yelled, grabbing her sister's arm and yanking her through the water back to the prairie, to the sun, the warmth of summer. Rosemary sat up, awake and alert, looking out to where Lucy was pointing, already tucked up onto her sister's chair. A cat wandered out from the thick brush, swaying back and forth, skinny and full of mange, a wild look in its eyes. When it saw them, it hissed, growling and becoming stiff. Neither girl moved, knowing fully that if they did, it would bite. With no action to take, they watched as the cat came closer, its body showing signs of having been in several fights and winning all of them. The way it howled was revolting, a deeply instinctual sense of aversion growing in both girls' stomachs. The hair on the back of their necks prickled all the way down their spines. This was danger, this was disease. The body of the cat crouched lower, ears back, a sickening sound coming from the back of its throat.

"Please, please," Lucy whispered, to no one.

The cat jumped, a shot rattling through the air. Lucy yelled;

the body fell to the ground, dead. Rosemary whipped her head back to see their Uncle Lewis coming up the yard towards them, his hunting rifle over his shoulder. Lucy couldn't tear away her eyes from the mangled cat, blood seeping out of a wound almost the size of its entire body.

"I had to do it, that thing was going to tear you girls apart," Lewis said, standing next to his nieces still sitting on one lawn chair huddled up together. Neither of them had words to say as they looked out at the dead animal, its small body ripped open.

"You should know, Rose. That's probably the same cat that tore you up the first time, isn't it? Can't have animals like that wandering around," Lewis continued, still not moving towards the animal, or away from them.

"Isn't it?" Lewis repeated. Rosemary looked at it; she couldn't tear away her eyes.

"I can't tell," she replied quietly.

"Well, it probably is. Wonder where it came from, what it's been doing all this time," Lewis said, finally taking a step forward towards the dead animal, flies already landing on its body and drinking the blood. The smell wafted over, nauseating Lucy's already sensitive stomach. All he did was move it slightly with his shoe.

"Something's out there, letting this happen," Lewis murmured, more to himself than his nieces, as he looked down at the animal he'd shot. There was a glint to the cat's eyes, one of the only things left intact about the animal. A small light, fading much slower than the rest of the body had. Lewis recognized it, had suspected it, wanted it. He didn't see anything else, other than that slow-burning light.

Lucy watched her uncle's face as he looked down at the animal. She saw the glint in his own eyes, caused by nothing more than desperation. Her own face changed, realizing something. The way he clutched the gun, the way he moved around the cat as if there was something else to learn from it. He didn't see the ugliness, the death. All he saw was possibility, and that made Lucy breathe in deeply and quickly, a realization hitting her so hard she almost fell over. Rosemary felt Lucy's hand clutch down, her sister's fingernails digging into her own skin.

"Don't worry, I'll bury it. Why don't you girls go inside? You're looking a little burnt out here in the sun," Lewis said, hardly looking back at the girls to notice anything about the way they were looking. Lucy took one last long look at the scene before her, burning it into memory, then clutched up her sister and dragged her back to the house without so much as a word to their uncle. He didn't notice. Rosemary struggled to keep up with her stride.

"Lucy, it's okay, it's dead. It didn't get to us...Lu!" Rosemary said, trying to hold her sister back from her near sprint. Lucy stopped suddenly, spinning around and sticking her face into Rosemary's so quickly they knocked heads. Lucy didn't react.

"Did you see that?" Lucy asked, her voice cold.

"See what?" Rosemary asked, confused.

"Don't act like that right now. God, do not act like that *right now*," Lucy replied, leaning away from her and shaking her head. Her blood was boiling, all her nervousness and fears rising from the pits of her stomach to the highest point in her chest.

"Lucy. What is it?"

"Don't you see? He's going to find it. He knows about it, and that's what he's out there hunting for all the time. It's not about the animals; it's about the *rift*. He's so close to it. Tonight, he's going to find it tonight. We can't let them, we can't," Lucy said, her voice frantic as she spoke but with much sought after directness. Rosemary turned around, looking back at her uncle still standing and studying the carcass. He was completely in his own world, having forgotten anyone else could see him. They watched as he bent down and touched the side of the cat gently, as if studying a rare treasure, looking for some hint. Rosemary had lied, the howl had been unmistakable.

She watched, and she knew. Her uncle was a brute, a man driven by his ego and his desire. He had grown up there, feeling all kinds of things, and this is what he had channeled it into. And somehow, still, when Rosemary looked at him and knew how dangerous he was, saw how steadfast he was in hunting down the very thing she now knew they had to close and could no longer avoid or protect, she still only saw one man instead of two.

"We'll close it tonight. We'll find it again, first. And we'll close it," Rosemary said, a promise to her sister, a move of steadiness that calmed the storm between them if not just for a moment. Lucy didn't ask how, convinced the only requirement was to be dedicated to doing it, and the rest would hopefully come to light.

They didn't talk anymore about it, instead walking inside together and finding someplace cool and shaded to sit, ready and watching. Never had the two of them been more aligned. If someone had seen them, it would be strange to watch the way they moved exactly in unison. They sat, watched, and waited. The day passed by, the sun eventually finding its way across the sky. When it began to suggest falling, James came down from his bedroom. He didn't even see his cousins. His mother gave him a kiss on the top of his head and a packed meal, as if that would make up for it. He said goodbye to his aunts as he passed them in the living room, Delphine hardly looking up from her laptop, Heidi giving him a small wave and a tight smile as if to suggest she knew, but she didn't. If she did, she wouldn't have smiled. But Heidi had been blind for a long time; it was a price she paid for a sacrifice she hadn't realized she'd made. When she turned back to the book she was reading, she clutched her necklace, a small pendant her father had given her on her thirteenth birthday. It burned.

"Good luck out there," Sara said from her rocker on the front porch as James came out to meet his father in the yard. He simply nodded, already moving towards the steps, spotting his father out by the truck with his uncles.

"I hope it's you, who gets the deer," Sara said. James stopped, slowly turning to look back at her. She was just sitting, rocking. More stoic than anyone he'd ever known. She always seemed to know the most, yet have no desire to share any of it. There was something odd about the way she spoke, always seemingly last minute, even though there was never a rush to her words.

"We're not going out for deer this time," he said, perhaps meaning more than it simply wasn't the season, but perhaps not. Sara nodded, a soft smile on her face.

"All the same," she said, leaving it at that. James continued walking to meet his father. They talked for a few moments, then waved as they started their hike out, Lewis feeling like this time he knew exactly the path to follow. This time, he had a real idea.

Wolfgang watched his brother follow his father out towards the woods. Everyone wondered where he was, but no one had bothered to look. He'd been sitting up in the hayloft of the old pole barn for quite some time, wanting to leave that place but finding himself unable to. In his solitude, he'd been given plenty of time to think. He thought about what a disappointment he was. There seemed no expectation he wasn't capable of shattering. As his brother marched back out into the woods, Wolfgang couldn't even feel anger build inside his body, simply a hollowness that had consumed him a long time ago, for no real reason at all. There was no way to forget how Lucy had looked up at him from the ground he had pushed her down onto. She had been afraid of him, and for him. He knew that some people thought there was something in him worth saving, but he couldn't find it. He would always let everyone down around him; it was just how it was. From that acknowledgment, came a hatred. He thought he hated himself. Spending time alone with himself was its own personal torture, but he was unable to escape. It was why he wanted the rift to continue to exist, because in that warm energetic light, the accumulation of all creation he had not been alone. He had been golden. He realized he didn't deserve it, especially at the cost of everyone else. If he could have just one more taste…

When he saw Rosemary and Lucy run out of the house, headed towards the woods, he climbed down the ladder and followed them into the trees.

Twenty-Four.

It shimmered.

Anyone else would have thought they had something in their eye, raising a fist to rub out the foreign entity. But Lewis focused on that shine; he thought he could see it finally. His own mind was giving in to his sick delusions, but perhaps they weren't so wrong, even if his methods of both procurement and comfort were cruel. His whole life, he'd reached out for this deeply embedded force, something that he felt had become a part of him after so many years spent roaming those lands. In that moment, however, he wasn't focused at all on his feelings or his own body's sense of direction. For once, he was tuned into his son's every flutter, feeling sure that he knew exactly where it was. Somehow, he had raised a guide to take him to that sweet place of clarity and magnitude. He thought, anyway.

"Now, why don't you chart our course," he had said to his son, the moment they were a mile or so into their hike. James didn't know how to say no, so he just started walking. As time passed, he grew more anxious because there was no place to go, no hidden nirvana waiting out there behind the brush. While they walked, Lewis beginning to drink as he always did, James found himself fighting to remember how Rosemary had brought them all to the shores of the rift. How had she done it? Had she been out there, listening for some voice to lead her to it? Did she just simply know, a feeling in her bones signaling the way? The sun was fading away quickly, but James assumed there would be no camp to make. Lewis was intent that this was the time they would find it, the thing he had always been looking for. So many words attempted to encapsulate what that was exactly in his mind, but he didn't know. Any ideas he had, any feelings that had passed through his body had only been manipulated further by the drugs and the drinking. It was like that, for successful men. They kept their poor habits to only be performed out in the wilderness, where they felt it was fitting to be barbaric, an outlet of some kind. James had never been a part of the wilderness, but he'd been forced to exist there. He could feel his father's desperation, and it was turning into impatience.

"Wherever you think is best, just keep on walking," Lewis said, calling up from behind his son. James didn't know what to do with his false encouragement. Truly, there was nowhere to go. He wanted to suggest they stop, but he didn't really want to stop either. All James wanted was to go home. He wanted the hunt to be over.

Neither man knew they were being followed. Somehow, Rosemary and Lucy were able to track their family through the dark woods, hardly outfitted to do so, yet achieving it with somewhat talented ease. Every once in a while, they could hear their uncle talking, but they were far enough behind that they couldn't see them directly.

"Do you think they know how to find it?" Lucy whispered. Her sister shrugged.

"Do you?" Lucy asked. They stopped walking, Lucy looking at her sister with strained eyes in the darkness of an evening forest.

"You found it last time. You can do it again, before they can. I know you can," Lucy said, her voice remaining low and soft, trying to encourage her sister without pressuring her. Inside, she was anxious. But they had been following James's circling for a long time, and it was obvious to them he didn't know where anything was, either. It was evident he was lost. All Lucy knew was that they couldn't stumble upon it before she and Rosemary arrived there first, and if they never stumbled upon it, all the better.

"I don't know. It just felt right, last time. It was calling and all I did was answer," Rosemary replied, looking around her for any kind of clue. Her fists were balled up on either side of her body, her own anxiety rising. Lucy set her hands on her sister's shoulders, breathing in and out slowly.

"That's okay. If it's not calling, then you call for it."

"I don't know how," Rosemary replied without much forethought, hardly meeting her sister's complementary eyes.

"Yes, you do," Lucy replied, giving her shoulders a squeeze and then letting go. She took a step back from her sister, allowing her some space, allowing her to feel the darkness trickle over her, the cold air rise from the ground and wrap itself around her bones. Lewis and James were getting farther away, and they did not know a wolf was watching them. Rosemary stood still and thought deeply, calling upon every part of her being. She knew it was a part of them, and also wasn't at all just yet. She knew her grandfather was a part of it, and so was everyone else who had ever passed, and would ever be. She knew it was just as much a part of the universe as the dirt she stood on, the trees that towered over her, or her sister standing right in front of her. How amazing, her single cell refusing to grow alone, demanding two. Rosemary took a deep breath in, closed her eyes, and thought about the shoreline, the pink skies, Silas's eyes, her grandmother's herbs, Heidi's laughter, and her sister's golden hair. She breathed out and started walking.

James felt the shift in the air the moment it happened. He thought he could hear it, a rippling effect from the center of something cataclysmic. Carefully, he edged a glance back at his father, whose eyes were dilated, obsessed with everything that passed by, hoping it might be a clue towards the rift. He felt his son steady himself against a disturbance only he had felt.

"What is it?"

James didn't know how to answer. He knew the pain wouldn't stop if he led him to the rift, it would only continue on a much larger scale. He hoped for some kind of sweet release, but found himself alone with the hunter. The only solution would be the one he came up with.

"Nothing, I don't see anything," James replied quickly.

"But did you *feel* something?" his father asked, almost snarling his words. James shrugged, thinking it would defuse things, take away attention, direct his mind elsewhere. It did none of those things. His father grabbed his shoulder, pulling him back harshly. He placed his head next to James's ear, murmuring his words with authority.

"Don't think you can keep anything from me out here," he hissed. Something flashed over James's eyes with the threat. He knew his father meant it; he had experienced it his entire life. His body wanted to turn over, melt away from his touch, and go to some other place so that he could just get through it. But that night, things were different. He had felt something out there and he decided maybe it was time to call back. Shadows whizzed past them periodically, darting throughout low-growing ferns. James decided not to go to some other place, he decided not to simply crawl through the mud and hope he could make it home one more time. He decided to hunt.

They kept on. James's pace was different now, hurried almost. It made his father excited, feeling like they really might find it that night. After years of solely trying to figure out what it was, how it worked, what it could do, he felt like perhaps that night he would finally see the thing he had been after all this time. And James would lead him there. Along the way, it was easy for him to forget everything he'd put James through because he'd never really thought about it before. Lewis only acted out of his own self-interest, his own desires and wants. Never did it cross his mind out there in the woods that James had consented to none of it. He didn't want to hunt but regardless of that now, it was embedded in James, and he was good at it. His father had coerced him into being very good at the chase.

Wolfgang was wandering alone mostly, out in those woods. He had felt the ripple too; the moment the rift first pulsed, opening up. He'd followed the girls for a good while, but had turned inward at some point. More time alone with himself, and his mind grew muddled with the reasons he was out there. He hated himself, feeling more alone in the woods than any other place. Everyone was working towards something, and he was just wandering alone, hoping to catch a glimpse of some fantasy he had built up in his mind. He was angry, too. It rolled throughout his entire body, his lungs panting as the anger worked through him and out into his hands. He wanted to do so much good, but it was always so far away, and his approach was always wrong. He failed a lot, he knew that. James was wandering around those woods again because he had failed. His cousins were trying to stitch together something meaningful because they thought it was too dangerous for him to handle. They were probably right. He hated himself. All he felt was the utter lack of feeling; he tried to make choices on how others felt, and he still couldn't get it right. He never would. He knew that.

The woods around him were dark, with very little light streaming in from a crescent moon to indicate where he was walking. Another person might have been afraid, wandering the woods alone. But he knew he was the worst thing out there, a hollow man, an angry one. He had absolutely nothing to lose or gain, he simply was. He thought he heard a whisper.

It's the breeze, he thought. He heard it again.

It's rabbits or squirrels, he reasoned.

Maybe it's someone, he finally decided. That didn't stop him from walking forward. And he was right, it was someone. Someone who loved him.

The girls were closer to him than he thought. Rosemary was walking carefully forward; around a ridgeline she had no business of knowing existed. Lucy held her sister's hand tightly, not wanting to get separated or stop her from her mission. She had felt it, the moment her sister opened her eyes. She wondered if anyone else had. There was no light, but Rosemary could see just fine as she guided her sister carefully through the woods, much like she had that first and only time they'd seen the rift. As they walked, Lucy began to feel light-headed, and she knew they were close. The trees around them began to shimmer with a dark blue and green glow. The ground felt different the farther out they traveled. It moved to meet their feet; it moved to push them forward. Leaves of brush shook like there was a window, but the air was motionless. It was still so dark, but the farther in, the less it mattered. There was always more she could see, even in that darkness. Lucy never let go of her sister's hand, pulling her through. Somehow, Rosemary knew the way. Somehow, Rosemary was a part of all this. Excitement started to gloss over Lucy's nervousness. She couldn't believe it was real, that it was coming. The land around them continued to shift, the plants and trees shaking with colors that glaringly resembled optical illusions. Except this wasn't an illusion at all.

Lewis knew it was real too, though he couldn't see it yet. James continued walking; having no idea where they were going, but knowing he would never show his father the rift. It was out of mere spite over anything more. At some point, Lewis could tell they had drifted farther, not closer. He grew angry.

"Where are you going?" Lewis called out, his son stopping ahead.

"I don't know, I'm just trying to find it," James replied, head titled downward.

"No. You're walking away from it. What's the matter with you?" Lewis yelled out, approaching his son. He grabbed his face, forcing him to look up at him. He liked the fear he saw cross his son's eyes, he always had. There wasn't a reason, he just did.

"After everything, you would just walk away from this? Why?" Lewis asked, his fingers tightening around his son's face.

James reached up to pull away at his arm, but it only made his father's grip tighten. He was beginning to see smoke, he didn't know where from.

"There's something out here. I have always known that! We're not going to walk away. We are hunters; we must hunt it down," Lewis demanded, throwing force into his hand as he pushed James back away from him. He stumbled, falling. Lewis rolled his eyes, waving for him to stand up. They had to continue.

Lewis didn't understand the rift. He thought it was an entity, someone that he could take something from. That was why he hunted. He thought there would be a fight, and that if he could kill something, he could take its power. It's what he had trained his son to do all this time. Tracking the beast, becoming the hunter of the monster in the dark. That was their purpose. When James looked up at his father, he thought he was the monster. Maybe he was, or maybe that energy was rolling around the woods, slipping in between trees and laughing at him all these years he suffered. The shadows were out, running around in the underbrush, laughing the way raccoons do over a pile of trash. James did feel something, perhaps someone standing over him. Was it that shadow, shaped almost like a person? He looked around but saw nothing. He felt it though, maybe gently against his cheek. It was a kind touch, love. It evaporated as his father stormed towards him, still sitting on the ground. Quickly, he was yanked up.

Wolfgang thought he was being followed. His own mind began to finally wander away from focusing on himself. Out there didn't seem to comfort him, as the whispering grew, the soft howls from animals he couldn't see, the drumbeat of trees lined up along a hidden rift. There were voices that told him he wasn't good enough. There were voices promising him that he was kind. Some muttered about every time he'd hurt someone, others reminded him about every favor he'd extended. He didn't like feeling on trial, alone in the woods, the trees oddly beginning to shift around him. He rubbed his eyes with his hands, focusing on them instead of the voices. They were moving, swaying, pulsing. He followed them, a glowing tree here, another over there. Slowly, the whole woods came to life before him, a secret show he thought he was alone in seeing. He didn't hear any footsteps, didn't think to listen for them. Somehow along the way, he had forgotten anyone else was in the woods. He had been trapped with himself for too long and he thought maybe just ahead there was a way to rid himself of that company. He felt it coming. Maybe the way to be better was almost within reach, if he could only push to keep going a little further. His skin was sticky from sweat, shining in the glow of the plants around him. The ground began to move underneath his feet, all around him, swirling. It didn't startle him, he enjoyed the perspective.

Someone encouraged them to all come together, though if asked, they wouldn't have known about it at all. As Wolfgang continued walking, someone else came out of the dark bushes beside him. When he faced his cousins, he wasn't surprised and neither were they. They all took a moment to look at one another, their faces calm, almost blank. Everything from before simply melted away as if it didn't matter. Looking into each other's faces, they felt the love for one another, tied together forever as family. The bond was unbreakable, even in the face of this enormous energy, a rift through the universe. The trees hummed with that energy, lighting up, begging them to continue. Or maybe it was their own selves begging to continue. The feeling was magnetic; it pushed them together only to continue pushing them forward. Lucy looked at her cousin, and held out her hand to him. Wolfgang studied it, watching it shake like everything else around them. He reached for her hand to steady it. Rosemary nodded at them both, unable to speak, pulling them forward. They kept walking.

There were no ways to quantify what it was. Rosemary pulled them through the last bit of thick dark trees and suddenly, it was all light. Bright, rolling, full of dark shadows and glowing embers. The magnificence of this crack across the universe, this collection of dead stars and new life was nearly indiscernible. None of them knew how they felt, because their feelings were all happening outside of their bodies. Never had they felt so small as they did amongst the immense possibility before them. It was a center, and it was also just an edge. Their eyes became transfixed on the glory above, so close they could reach for it, but their bodies remained paralyzed as their minds attempted to understand what the rift was. It was everything, coating them with radiance, healing their bodies, minds, and souls and bringing forth the absolute best combinations of their matter. The three of them stood on the edge of that chasm, begging to be submerged. Lucy had no thoughts of closing it. Wolfgang had no thoughts of himself. Rosemary had forgotten there was ever a sinister whisper telling her to listen to its secrets. In awe of the break in their reality, in the possibility of anything, they remained still.

When they stepped into the rift's light, James felt it. A deep ripple flew through the woods. He didn't know who, or what, but he knew that something was accepting energy from that rift. And then, he felt Lewis's anger, because it seemed the two would always be connected.

"Why are you keeping it from me?" Lewis roared, pushing James forward so that he fell into the darkness, nothing to brace his fall. His backpack was ripped from his body as his father flipped him over to stare him in the face, a nasty snarl mixed with evil eyes.

"I'm not keeping anything from you!" James shouted. It was met with a harsh hit before he even finished getting the words out. He didn't understand why this was his reality, of all possibilities, he had to endure his father's insanity and cruelty. There was anger left in James yet, and as his father continued to beat into him, demanding answers for questions he hardly even knew how to form, James felt fire in his chest, the smoke filling up all around them. The world was hazy, transforming around them. Lewis hardly noticed it, his own rage blocking out everything else.

"It's not my fault you can't find it!" James yelled out, pushing his father back away from him as he tried to stand up. Lewis was bigger than him, he always would be, and he came back at his son full force. With the liquor on his breath, his mind high on power and opioids, there was seemingly no way for James to stop him. He didn't care though; he would die fighting him off that night. For once, there was nowhere else to go. There was nowhere else to be but right there. James was hit again and again, continuing to try to push his father off of him, get away, crawl and hide. It felt almost impossible, a mountain he could not climb. But the woods around him felt another ripple, a new growing energy around them. The trees shimmered; he recognized the signs. Then, the shadows emerged. They bounded out of all directions, circling the two men as they fought, howling and barking in ghost-like ways. Blood trickled down James's face, his body already feeling sore from the battery. Something about the proximity of the open rift was strengthening Lewis's fanatical perceptions, intensifying his violence. James took the beating, like he always did. He thought about the fire he'd been tossed into, the threats and agony. He internalized all of it, allowing the fire in his own chest to build and grow, propping him up so that he could stand up again after each blow.

James took his father into his own mind. The world around them shifted, hazy and full of smoke. He began to see his father less than human, a demon of the woods. The shadows bounded around them, their edges wisps in the air, their mouths wide open gasps of darkness, eyes glowing like planets in the night sky. Maybe Lewis began to see these things, or perhaps he had always imagined them. For a moment, he became blindsided by the mounting supernatural, and James was able to push forward. He stood up and took a shot at the man before him, pushing him back, making his own face bleed. Lewis roared, his vision blurred. In his mind, he thought maybe James wasn't the key at all; perhaps he was the one thing in his way.

Smoke continued to grow around them, a dense fog that clouded their minds, fed into their own internal infernos. It was all anger, all pain. James wanted so badly for it to be over, to rest and never have to fight another day in his life. His life had only been about survival, and about seeing the absolute darkest corners the world had to offer. He hoped to be done with it. Lewis hoped to be done too, so he lunged again as James. They fought, shadows growling and biting at their feet. And then, a third pulse of energy radiated through the woods, and James took it all into his body, the light blinding his father for a moment as he stood up. The shadows accumulated, always wanting to bite into the demon of the woods, but James had never allowed it before. He had never known he could incite it. Again, energy rippled out of the rift and into the surrounding woods. The fog was heavy, and all it allowed James to see when he looked down was his father unable to get back up, having fallen too hard.

Bellows from the monster echoed through the woods. James turned his head to look out into the hazy darkness as he stepped away from his father. Anxiety raced through his body, followed by large throbs of adrenaline. It was real, the beast. James felt in his heart that he had to find the rift first, defend it from those who would take it away. He was determined to find it and kill it, to be done with all of this once and for all. He began running blindly through the woods, wiping blood from his face away from his mouth, the metallic taste a bitter reminder of what was at stake. It strained his eyes. He was convinced the beast was out, roaming. He knew he had to find it, continuing to run, getting deeper and deeper into the woods until silence was all that he heard, and foggy darkness was all that he could see. He stopped, breathing heavily for a moment, spinning around hoping to see anything, to not be alone anymore.

What he thought had been calling him hadn't, so when he heard the sweet notes of energy, the enticing need to belong and exist and be harmonious, he followed the sound. Small little whistles from birds, soft moss under his feet, the singing of leaves waving in the breeze. It was calling to him, wanting to connect so deeply with his soul. But James had been through perhaps too much. His arm where his father had burned him ached, and he mistook the pain for a feeling that equated to what he was searching for. He had long ago gotten lost running away, and confused the path for escape as something much more sinister. As he traveled deeper into the woods, nature around him began to shift. He felt hot, sweat gathering above his brow, running in long lines down his back. The trees began to shimmer, sway with their whole beings in the wind, echoing some kind of ancient song from the future. Woodland animals hid deep underneath small plants as James wandered by, feeling chaos before it was to show up. The rift waivered, feeling his energy as he approached, but was forced to welcome it. It welcomed all energy, because all energy demanded a place. It was never creation or destruction, it always just *was*. Tragedy was only for humanity. Rosemary and Lucy were lost in their own daze of power, feeling such extraordinary things so deeply they hardly noticed the shift, had never felt the need to be aware a day in their lives, if life was even measured by sunrises and sunsets anymore. Wolfgang felt the shift. It hurt deeply, pain shuddering in his body, but he turned away from the glory he couldn't believe to exist, a stunning display of cosmos, and turned to look out into darkness. It was a choice he made.

And James saw it.

Finally, what he was always looking for, both hoping and dreading its discovery. A monster so vicious it justified his years of hunting, all that time spent alone with his father in the darkness. The beast stretched up on its hind legs, roaring with pent-up fury. It stood tall, enormous in the sky; a face filled with brimstone. Didn't it? James felt fire in his face, the burn deep in his heart. *This*. This was what he'd been forced to hunt all this time. His father's sick delusions were alive and real right before him. There was a true monster that roamed the woods, tapping on glass windows, begging for prey. He pulled up his rifle. This had to end, all the pain and work, so interchangeable. He saw his opportunity, a dark haze clouding his eyes. The beast wanted him, yearned for him, but James couldn't surrender into it. He couldn't understand, it was too late. His mind chanted what he thought he knew, thought he believed. This was his life's purpose, after all. Wasn't it? It would stop his father. It would save himself. Wouldn't it?

"Steady…" he whispered, closing one eye. He heard the screams as his finger pulled back.

The beast fell, dead.

Wolfgang's body lay still on the ground, amongst dirt. The smoke cleared from James's eyes. The rift swirled up and closed; the sisters behind his vacant body cried.

James had killed his brother, his father's beast.

Twenty-Five.

Early mornings on the lake were becoming frigid, especially with a summer's tan still peaking out of the collar of a sweatshirt. It didn't matter though; there was always work to be done at the docks. Beau was up early, the sunrise greeting him as he washed his face, then sat down for breakfast and coffee before heading out. He took his time eating, sipping the coffee from his favorite mug as he looked out the window of his family's large sunroom at the water lapping the beach just below. There was a morning fog over the lake's surface, and although it didn't look particularly inviting, Beau had always found himself appreciating those small bits of gloominess. He didn't need summertime to enjoy the lake, the water, and wind in his face. Genuinely, he was good, and he held an appreciation for most things in his heart. He'd always felt good in that place.

The first thing he did in the mornings was greet the old man at the dock house, giving him a coffee he'd always pick up on his way. The man would hold up the coffee silently, then take a sip and smile before returning to his solitude posting. Beau would then stop and say hello to the fishermen in their little boats, getting ready to go out and catch another load before the heat sweltered back up. He'd continue down the dock towards the more expensive boats, boats with upper and lower decks, boats with bathrooms and kitchens and outdoor seating. His was among those.

There was always some maintenance to do, something to clean or fix or improve. He spent a while working, putting things away from the last long night and getting ready for another, should the opportunity present itself. As he worked, the sun beginning to rise properly overhead, he stripped off the sweatshirt, continuing to work. And like a ghost who knocks, he felt the need to look up from his work and down at the shoreline, a mirage-like figure standing there, watching him. He waved, and she waved back, slowly walking down the dock towards him.

"Hey," Beau greeted, hopping down from the upper deck to the lower one, walking down the small ramp onto the wooden boards of the dock to greet her. Lucy smiled shyly up at him; her eyes squinted in the sunlight.

"How are you?"

"Okay." It was hollow.

"What're you working on?" she asked, shifting the conversation with one firm push. Beau looked up at the boat. It shined, because he cared. He shrugged.

"Just cleaning up in there, fixing a cupboard hinge. The usual putzing around, old man bullshit," he replied, cracking a smile that had always melted Lucy's heart. It was because it was so pure, a rare find in lake water.

"Well, it really shows," she replied, her voice soft. They stood there for a minute, basking in sunlight, the only sound between them the water beneath, slowly rolling over itself and hitting the posts of the docks, the boats swaying softly beside them.

"I wanted to come say goodbye," Lucy said finally, looking up at him from where her eyes had been focused on the water. Her eyes were still squinted, one hand held up over her brow to help shield them from the rising sun. It was bright.

"That's nice of you to come say goodbye," Beau said, looking over at the girl he dreamed about all year long. He found himself often looking for her, at crowded bars or parties, in supermarkets and on beaches. Sometimes, he found someone close. But they were never her. She nodded her head slowly, eyes focused on the waves of the lake before them, lapping at the dock right below their feet.

"Yeah, I thought I should," she said gently. He looked again at her, studying her face, a wave of clarity rushing over him. She never said goodbye, usually just floated away for the rest of the year, always announcing her return by standing on the dock by his boat the next year, beers in hand. But it was different, now. He didn't know how to feel, so he stayed numb for as long as he could in the moment.

"You're not coming back, are you?"

Lucy finally looked over at him, her eyes wide and sad, a small smile on her lips as she nodded her head at what he'd said. Beau looked back out at the water.

"Is there anything I can say..." he trailed off as she shook her head. He wanted to beg her to return again next summer, or perhaps not even leave. It was a selfish request, because he knew she did have to go. He hadn't known much about what was going on that summer, but he had felt it whenever he was with her.

"I just have to go," she replied, her voice cracked whispers. She said it with certainty, but not without sadness.

"I understand," he mumbled, thinking about the last week of summer. He'd been there, when they put him in the ground next to his grandfather. A hunting accident, so the story went. People talked, of course, but no one could even begin to understand the complexities of the Pennnyfathers. Lucy thought an accident was a fine way to phrase it. Any more responsibility, and she wouldn't be able to bear it. Family land was a strange thing. Lucy didn't say anything; she hoped he did understand. And looking at her face, the grief so evident, he really did. The fun had come at too great a cost, and there was a shine she always had to her that was no longer coming from her body.

"I'll always appreciate everything," she said, her words tight.

She didn't know how else to phrase it, but she hoped that would be enough, that somehow that would encapsulate things for him. She would forever appreciate his kindness, his generosity, and his ability to care and not have it come at any sort of price. Lucy found herself in the company of many, and yet none lit up her face the same way Beau did on the first day of summer. He nodded, shaking it off like it was nothing. Still, humble.

She leaned over and held his face for a moment, kissing his cheek gently and with an immense amount of love and appreciation. When she pulled back, her eyes were glassy. Carefully, she stood up, giving him a small little wave, her throat too hard to speak, and walked back down the dock. Beau swung his head around to watch her go, holding on to every single moment he had left of her. The moment her body was gone, he felt the loss like a drop, a sudden lurch throughout his entire body. He didn't know what to do, but he knew she had to go.

Wolfgang's death was the only way Lucy was able to go. She had no idea what awaited her, what her possibilities were. But with him gone, a sheep in wolf's skin, someone who had enjoyed her antics and not needed them, she had to go. She couldn't hold anyone up anymore. It just wasn't possible. She didn't want to go into that fog at all, she wanted to walk far away from it and never see it, never feel its possibility or promise. She carried Wolfgang in her heart of gold, locked away deeply to keep him safe, to shelter him from any more pain. When she made it back to the house, she finished packing up her belongings in the simplest way and headed out to see her sister one last time before getting a car to the airport, a whole world waiting for her so that she could escape this small corner of it.

Rosemary was sitting under the big oak tree, looking at the family graveyard, knowing only two names, the dirt above them fresh. She didn't cry, or feel too particularly sad. There was a numbness throughout her body, an inability to comprehend what she was looking at. With time, she was sure she'd be able to understand it all, but for now she could only rip apart small blades of grass by her feet, looking at the holes in the ground as if they should be something more than just two mounds of dirt.

There had been a lot of silence in the house for the past couple of days, and also a lot of wailing. Even some shouting, in the parlor at the front of the big old house, when Silas had looked at Sara in the face and accused her of watching death again and again with not so much as a whisper of mercy. Sara had said nothing in return, simply looked at him with sad eyes and nodded. She was not the best at anything, she had discovered. Rosemary had watched Silas storm out of their house and leave, walking furiously back to his own house and finding no real comfort there, either.

She hadn't told anyone yet that she was staying. There hadn't seemed like a good time, and no one seemed to care or wonder, anyway. Rosemary didn't know what the rest of her family was doing. Sure, she had seen some things. Lewis's battered body, his inability to explain what had happened. Lucy's silence, her tear-stained cheeks. Her parents' hushed whispers, nervous glances as if there was some kind of infectious disease spreading through the household like wildfire, as if insanity was contagious. Beth wailed and didn't stop, until they sedated her. Lewis left after the funeral, alone. It was one of the last times any of them would see him again. As much as James couldn't believe it, that was only the top of the spiral Lewis would find himself on. In years to come, he would be a weathered beggar, standing in crowded parks and preaching about the coming of end times. No one would listen; they would catch a glimpse of his cloudy eyes and continue walking. Heidi would end up taking Beth home with her, to grieve and be released from her role in the world. She would spend a lot of time in the guesthouse, looking out the window, crying for souls she missed and souls she had wanted but never tried hard enough to reach. Each morning, the two women would take a long walk, and they would talk about those deep insecurities and share about every moment of vulnerability they had encountered. It would be the only thing to keep them going.

Delphine and Henry would continue to travel, their

communication outside of the professionals in their field shrinking to less and less. It had always been destined for that, the deaths in their family too great and too peculiar to become a part of. They were runners, they always had been. It was what they were best at. Rosemary and Lucy would read about them in the papers often, watching them in online interviews and during award shows. Sometimes, they'd get a phone call. Sometimes, they would gather at a restaurant for Thanksgiving, Christmas being simply too far away to plan out just yet.

Lucy would be successful. No one would be sure quite how to define her career, quite how to put into words what she actually did that generated the money she had at her disposal. It was simply her, at the end of the day. She was someone everyone wanted around, and she continued to be that person no matter her greatest personal tragedies. There would be a few times Rosemary would travel to see her sister, loose on some kind of bender that needed a twin's touch to come out of. They would talk about the old days, when they were young. It would always seem like no time had ever passed.

In just a few short years, the Pennyfather house and all the land it stood on would go to Rosemary, the only family left to claim its possession. Sara would pass away on a cold winter's morning, suddenly and with absolute finality. It would be against her will, but she would still go voluntarily, knowing it was her time. There would never be an end to the race for her, a place to finally stop and smile and understand that she had made it. For her, there was always a search to be more than, to be better. She would look everywhere except within herself, and only know the answer to that question when she no longer had a body to occupy. Rosemary would be kind to her, those last two years. They would talk in short sentences, pieces of hidden knowledge being secretly passed under the dinner table where they sat. Sara never called her that word again, but they both knew in some sense it was true. It meant more than either of them felt the need to understand.

While Rosemary sat looking at those dirt piles, she somehow

knew exactly how it would go for everyone. She just did. It was how she knew she had to stay.

She knew that Wolfgang had always wanted to walk into the chasm. And that moment had been the only moment in his life to give him a will to live. And with his will, he'd jumped in front of destruction. It was both the most selfless choice in his life, and the most selfish. He'd never wanted anything more than what experiencing the rift had given him, true acknowledgment of talent, uniqueness, and wholeness. Finding it had unleashed in him true euphoria for the first time in his entire existence. Nothing had ever tasted so sweet. And the thought of closing the rift, banishing it from their home had cut into his soul much too deep. He knew it was selfish to leave them behind, because facing evil or not, he'd have gone anyway. He was forever after more, always roaming around like the lone wolf he was. He had nothing to lose, he had never been able to find himself anywhere else. He hadn't realized it before, but his spirit had been taken from him the moment he was born. Always, Wolfgang was a dark shell, a being that wanted to be something, but felt nothing. Until he had the energy and beauty of the entire realm at his actual fingertips, he had never felt warm inside. He'd never had such a spectacular fever before. He had never known internal power and connection like he had those weeks with the energy and magnitude of the world calling to him, working its way deep inside his body. He hadn't realized he had no will until he was given one.

And then, to see it spread, to have those around him question that, and to eventually choose to expel that force back into hiding, broke him. The moment he saw his brother's clouded eyes, full of a force turned dark, he understood the warnings. So he took care of it, for everyone, perhaps his purpose all along. When the shot rang out, he stepped forward. When that lead hit his body, his spirit splintered into a million shards of energy that fell away from one another, spreading into the earth and sky. Wolfgang's body broke. It was less of a choice, and more of just passing through. He heard the screams, as he did it. There were pleas. Chopped up words of *please fight* and *don't go*. And, right before it all faded away, he heard *please, I am sorry*. That let him rest. It was strange, as his mind drifted away; he had a hard time remembering the people the words belonged to. He felt he should remember, the voices strung out beside him as they floated away with him. But maybe this was just another reason to keep going into the fog, the nothingness. He was already there, why maintain the body? The dust was needed for other things now, his mind free to roam, truly its own unique creation. The voice of ghosts beckoned him. Strung him along, wanting the man to follow him into that good night, that valiant end. *I can comfort you*, it had been saying all along. For better or worse, he believed that voice. He had never had a voice of his own in his head; this one was the only one he could remember. And he followed it, the fog surrounding him, until the voice was his voice, and he was left wandering. There were no needs, no wants, nothing to desire. He just walked, on and on, and sometimes, he'd catch a hint of rose, a small sound of a wild laugh, feel the breeze of someone who wanted to be close, but couldn't be touched. They made the fog better, but he was still okay with closing his eyes.

Wolfgang's death was a catalyst. His final act was for the first time able to not abandon his brother, and to pay the price for having done so his entire life. Because in the end, Wolfgang realized something, just as his soul splintered into a million pieces, spreading himself across the galaxy. He did not hate himself; he knew he was worthy of love, and worthy to give it. He hoped they would know that, but even if they didn't, he finally did.

"Hey," Lucy greeted, standing over Rosemary's shoulder. She took a moment before looking up at her sister, a halo of sunlight around her head. She gave her a small smile, happiness always spreading through her body when she saw her other half.

"I'm getting ready to go. Are you okay?"

"Yeah, I'm okay," Rosemary replied, holding a hand up for her sister to grab so she could stand and look at her eye level. They stared into each other's faces for a few moments, recognizing small pieces of themselves in one another. It was a comfort.

"I love you, Rose. It's you and I, okay?" Lucy said, holding onto her sister's shoulders and staring her directly in the eye as she said it. When Rosemary nodded, she pulled her in for an embrace. They swayed together for several minutes, not wanting to let go of one another. The air felt calm, the buzz finally silenced.

"Call me when you land, okay?" Rosemary asked, when they finally separated. Lucy nodded, knowing she might not, but it would be all the same.

"You'll always have me, you know?" Lucy said.

"I know."

"You sure you're okay?" her sister asked one more time. She nodded.

"I will be. Go catch your flight, don't be late," Rosemary insisted, pushing her off, her car already waiting for her at the end of the driveway. Lucy kissed three of her fingers, then pushed her hand gently onto Rosemary's forehead before wiping away a few tears and stepping back. Lucy stopped at the side of the oak, looking down at her only cousin. She bent down, placed her hand firmly on his shoulder, whispered something in his ear, and then walked off. She knew Rosemary would take care of him.

James couldn't say anything as Lucy went, walking down the road, only a canvas bag to her name. He just watched her, eyes blank. As time would go on, he would be the one to wander the woods, screaming out, hoping to draw something out. He would think he was looking for a monster, but would always be hoping for a wolf to howl back. He'd stop remembering why he wanted that. Rosemary would try to make him remember that he wasn't a monster, and there was none to look for. All the monsters were gone, but he'd stop talking. It would be years before James would begin to try to get better. Rosemary finally would see all the scars he was carrying around, all the deep wounds that had been inflicted upon him that he'd hid well for so long. At first, they would just need to be seen. Then eventually, they worked on healing them, one by one. He'd talk again, and she would listen. He'd stay in the house, in his parents' old room. Rosemary herself would move down a floor too, the upstairs once again becoming boarded up. James would carry around the smell of his brother, rose petals in his pockets. He'd forget they were for him, because he would press them in his pockets from far away, hoping for something softer.

Rosemary looked at James, knowing the hardness wasn't over. Somehow, he knew but also didn't, that he'd been the one to pull the trigger. The energy of the rift did interesting things to their minds, and when James thought about it, he didn't see his brother as the monster, but rather already in its mouth. The mounds of dirt stood still before her. She reached out; touching the wet earth with her fingertips, then leaning back again against the bark. She hardly noticed James was there anymore. Her dreams had changed, since the rift closed. Everything was calmer, simpler. She didn't mind, in fact, she welcomed the chance to focus on the things before her, instead of the possibility of things over her.

Rosemary had thought it was to be her, lying in the ground. She had heard the whispers, and when they stopped she thought it was because there was no sound in the ground. But when that light had folded up into itself, closing together in a seamless way, she had been stunned to see not herself on the ground, but her cousin. The world had found him cruel, but she had always known he wasn't. She had always known he was kind, his roughness only an eagerness to shield others and jump in front of cruelty.

Rosemary watched as Lucy walked off, stepping into the foreign car that wasn't the only one loaded and rattling to go in the gravel driveway. She would cry later that night about it, but knew Lucy had to do it to be whole. It was okay, because Rosemary would stay. She wouldn't wander off, or wander at all. She would stay and be present. She would work on fixing things, anything at all, just as Ramone always had. She would enjoy the sunsets, swim in the lake, build a garden, and sing songs she knew with friends at the bar down the road with ripped barstools, and go home and hum them just the same.

Rosemary would stay. She would stay.

As she looked out across the grassy fields around her home,

she pulled a singular wildflower from her coat's pocket, pulling away at its petals and letting them drift in the wind as she watched the parade of cars leave the grounds under a bright and cool sun. She looked up into its bright beams, temporarily blinded. Far out on the horizon, Rosemary could see the shadow of a full moon watching over them and she wondered vaguely – if you whistle in a dream, do you hear it the next day?

Allison Astorino

ABOUT THE AUTHOR

Allison Astorino is the author of *A Place to Stand* and *Blue Bird*. She currently resides in the Great Lakes state of Michigan with her sprawling Italian family and an exceptionally clever one-eyed sheep named Sox, who keeps great company. She studied English Literature and Psychology at the University of Michigan and was a part of several writing workshops and staff at the on-campus literary journal. Allison has been filling notebooks with vivid stories since she was a young girl, and her passions for the creative have always remained steady throughout her life.

Made in the USA
Monee, IL
07 June 2021

70555781R00208